The Lobo Outback Funeral Home

Other Titles by the Author

Confessions of an Eco-Warrior

The Big Outside (with Howie Wolke)

THE LOBO OUTBACK
FUNERAL HOME

DAVE FOREMAN

WITH A FOREWORD BY DOUG PEACOCK

Johnson Books

BOULDER

Published by Johnson Books, a division of Johnson Publishing Company, 1880 South 57th Court, Boulder, Colorado 80301. Visit our website at www.JohnsonBooks.com. E-mail: books@jpcolorado.com.

9 8 7 6 5 4 3 2 1

Cover design: Tangram Design

Library of Congress Cataloging-in-Publication Data
Foreman, Dave, 1946–
    The Lobo Outback Funeral Home/Dave Foreman.
        p.   cm.
    ISBN 1-55566-339-7
    1. Wolves—Reintroduction—Fiction. 2. Burn out (Psychology)—Fiction. 3. Environmentalists—Fiction. 4. Women biologists—Fiction. 5. Wilderness areas—Fiction. 6. New Mexico—Fiction. I. Title.
    PS3556.07223L6 2004
    813'.54—dc22   2004000395

Printed in the United States by
Johnson Printing
1880 South 57th Court
Boulder, Colorado 80301

Printed on ECF paper with soy ink

ACKNOWLEDGMENTS

This is a work of fiction. The characters in it are figments of my imagination. However, this novel is inspired by the heroism and commitment of my many friends in the wilderness and wildlife conservation movement.

My wife, Nancy Morton, and great friends, John Davis and Michael Soulé, read an early version of the manuscript. Their wise suggestions made *The Lobo Outback Funeral Home* a much better book than it would have been otherwise. However, they should not be blamed for anything other than keeping me from embarrassing myself.

My agent, Joanna Hurley, doggedly pursued publication of this novel. She has my boundless thanks for her good work in shepherding it into print.

I must also thank Jody Bolz, Marcy Willow, Marc Brown, and that legend of the West, Spurs Jackson, for their long-ago literary advice to me. It helped a lot. Thanks, friends.

This one's for Nancy. With love.
And thanks.

FOREWORD

Doug Peacock

"The strength of the warrior lies in his joy of loving the earth," quipped Ed Abbey, taking another puff of his cheap cigar. "You're cribbing from Kazantzakis," snorted Bill Eastlake, looking out the dusty window towards Mexico.

At least, that's what I remember. The time was the mid-seventies, in Bisbee, Arizona, and a number of drinks were involved. The only clear recollection is that a few months later I met the man whom Abbey, Eastlake, and I would in time come to associate most with this sappy quote.

That man was of course Dave Foreman, now a legendary warrior of the modern conservation movement. I first ran into Foreman at a strategy meeting in Santa Fe, New Mexico, during the days of the battle for the Kaparowitz Plateau, a coal-rich region southwest of the nasty little town of Escalante, Utah. The Black Mesa Defense Fund people were there, along with Brandt Caulkin, Jack Loeffler, and others. I'd heard about Foreman from Loeffler, at whose pad I was crashing. Dave was a fit-looking man with a pretty wife, an easy manner and a twinkle in his eye.

In 1975, Dave Foreman still worked as the Southwest regional representative for the Wilderness Society, a job he started in 1973 and continued, as Director of Wilderness Affairs, in Washington, D.C., until 1980. This latter assignment, I might point out, is very high powered, suit-wearing, stressful lobbying—about as mainstream and tough as conservation gets.

It's necessary as hell but very hard on those who labor within the grim political realities — stripped clean of any possibility of dreaming, receiving the daily congressional ass-kicking, enduring heartbreaking defeats and endless compromise in defense of the earth.

During the same decade, the rumble of change was rolling over the land and through the so-called environmental movement. Spawned in the great landscapes of the Southwest, you could almost feel the energy crackling in air. The origins (built on the foundation of Thoreau, Muir, and Leopold) of our western modern conservation movement and Ed Abbey's *Desert Solitaire*, were, I believe, at least synchronous. In 1975, Ed Abbey had just published *The Monkeywrench Gang*, planting the seeds of the more militant branch of wilderness preservation. The events that followed would have much to do with Dave Foreman.

But Dave's own life was also in transition, I would later learn, disillusioned with mainstream conservation, his marriage unraveling; he left his job and wife in D.C. and moved back home to New Mexico.

Flash forward a couple of decades (forgetting about Foreman's own role in the founding of Earth First!, the Wildlands Project and emerging as the most visible spokesman for the American wilderness movement), and we meet Jack Hunter, the hero of Dave's strongly autobiographical novel, *The Lobo Outback Funeral Home*.

Unlike the author, Jack has returned from his conservation-lobbyist job in D.C. as a total burnout. Cynical as hell, he has given up on saving the wild, believing it to be a lost cause. Like Foreman, Jack makes a living shoeing horses; he likes gin, wolves, cigars, birds, beer, women, poetry, and wilderness — not necessarily in that order. Like a damaged veteran, home from a distant, unpopular war, Jack cannot endure the horror of the modern world: the death of biodiversity everywhere, too many people endlessly consuming the earth's limited resources. His disease is occupational Post Traumatic Stress Disorder. Hunter can smell between the lines of a stuffy Environmental Impact Statement, sensing the stench of dying wolves and dead bears. Accordingly, he is not always a pleasant animal to hang with. Self-diagnosing himself as "hypersensitive," he avoids relationships, entanglements, action (except for the usual machismo type), and broad engagement. In short, Jack suffers from a massive case of "commitophobia."

Foreman's own life provides the texture and context of the *Lobo Outback* story. The Diablo National Forest is the Gila National Forest, country Dave knows as well as Jack does the Diablo. The section of the novel dealing with the addition to the Wilderness Area is part of southwestern conservation history in which Foreman has played a significant role. The descriptive passages of landscape and natural history are especially comfortable reading, as the man knows whereof he speaks.

The lobo herself is a fictional, albeit essential, part of the battle for wildness in the lower 48. In real life, we never found one, not a reproducing female wolf at least. I had a glimpse of a Mexican wolf in 1972 when Ed Abbey and I worked at Arivaipa Canyon. Known locally as an expert ham stringer of beef calves, this lobo disappeared shortly thereafter. The sighting, I was later told by knowledgeable friends, was possibly the last in Arizona. Wolves persisted in the Sierra Madres of northern Mexico until recently but, to my knowledge, none were seen in New Mexico until they were reintroduced in the '90s. Hunter's lobo is both a symbol of wild potential and a living political instrument, in that the presence of a previously extirpated species can kick in full protection for the animals and their habitat under the Endangered Species Act. As the history of Mexican Wolf reintroduction has murderously demonstrated, it's no wonder the local rednecks want to kill such an inconvenient predator.

What Foreman also brings to this juicy sprawl of a novel is an abundance of raw autobiographical musing, testosterone and detailed accounting of the daily workings of the conservation movement. Some may be overwhelmed. On the other hand, I can't imagine a better way of getting to know the real man: *Lobo* is an intimate, revealing family portrait, better than any biography of Dave Foreman yet written, bold and free the way few such autobiographies are (as Abbey often pointed out: you don't need to let a lot of unimportant facts get in the way of a good story). For better or worse, masculinity ran unfettered during those early days of Earth First! and the shop-talk in *Lobo* is, among other things, an historical contribution, a valuable menu of what it was like to plan and strategize, of how went the mundane work of the preservation world. Where else is this sort of daily detail recorded? Dave Foreman no doubt considered this material carefully; after all, as I once heard him respond to a question about what happened to the ecology movement: "It died of boredom."

One of Jack Hunter's (and certainly Dave Foreman's) favorite passages in conservation literature is a brief, beautiful narrative by Aldo Leopold in *Sand County Almanac* describing a wolf he killed in 1909, not far from the fictional Rio Diablo of Foreman's novel. Leopold and his Forest Service companions blasted away at the female wolf. A pup crawled off dragging a shattered leg. They rode down to finish the job:

> We reached the old wolf in time to watch a fierce green fire dying in her eyes. I realized then, and have known ever since, that there was something new to me in those eyes—something known only to her and the mountain. I was young then, and full of trigger-itch; I thought that because fewer wolves meant more deer, that no wolves would mean hunter's paradise. But after seeing the green fire die, I sensed that neither the wolf nor the mountain agreed with such a view.

Green fire haunts *The Lobo Outback*. It lives in the female lobo's eyes, in his lover's eyes; it is the light of the true wilderness. But the fire can die. In the end, all that Jack loves is violated. Violation is the consequence of his lack of commitment, of his stationary inertia and slackness of purpose. Hunter recalls Blake:

> But he who kisses the Joy as it flies
> Lives in Eternity's sunrise.

Instead of his sunset shithole born of inaction. As long as Jack hesitates, the violation of life, of the good and pure, continues. The metaphor of violation here might provide material for several American Literature theses or a study within the Environmental Studies Department. My own favorite passage, however, comes near the end, announcing Jack Hunter's reentry to the world.

Dave Foreman has left us a legacy, a body of work and several books, including a delightful novel. Unlike Jack, Dave never took a sabbatical from activism; indeed, he's spent the past three decades walking point at the forefront of the conservation movement, co-founding Earth First! during the '80s, the Wildlands Project in the '90s, writing and lecturing all the time. He paid his dues: Foreman was busted by the FBI for exercising his First Amendment rights. Recalling Ed Abbey's words, "I would never betray a friend to serve a cause …," Dave stood loyally by his co-defendants even when he could have rolled over and saved himself another five years of federal abuse.

It has been a pleasure to have squatted at the edge of the light of the campfire these past twenty-some years, witnessing the voyage of my friend Dave Foreman. In part, I owe that privilege to William Eastlake who introduced me to Edward Abbey. Among the primary purposes of Earth First!, Dave said, was, "To inspire others to carry out activities straight from the pages of *The Monkeywrench Gang*." As one of the novel's characters was loosely based on a younger Peacock, we had that connection in common. I remained decidedly on the sidelines while Dave and others led the charge. But I got to watch. Besides, I had begun my own work with grizzly bears. After all, the only thing worse than reading your own press is becoming someone else's fiction.

The co-founders of Earth First! considered themselves a warrior society, "committed to maintaining a sense of humor and a joy in living." In loving the earth, their purpose was to give something back: "To return," wrote Dave, "vigor, joy, and enthusiasm to the tired, unimaginative environmental movement."

May our own hearts be emboldened by the success of his journey.

1

June is the hot, dry month in New Mexico. In July and August thunderheads crowd the afternoon sky like bison once filled the Great Plains, but in June the skywater has not yet flowed north from the seas off Mexico. The sky is cloudless, unable or unwilling to break the sun's siege of fire.

Jack Hunter had finished shoeing Buck Clayton's three cow ponies in what had passed for the cool of the morning. Now that the sun had topped out, only Mrs. Clayton's favorite barrel racer was left to shoe. But this gelding was the worst of the lot—high-strung, ornery, and wont to rest its weight on Hunter's back while he had one of its feet in his lap. There was no breeze, and the horse had maneuvered him out of the shade of the line of Lombardy poplars into the full force of the sun. The horse's hide hung over him like the walls of a river runner's sauna. A bandanna knotted around the horseshoer's head was soaked and dripping; his eyes burned from the salt. Like Messerschmitts and Spitfires over London, flies buzzed them both.

Mrs. Clayton's horse was also a farter. Hunter heard the rumbling begin deep in its guts, and, by listening to the pops, gurgles, and squeaks, traced the path of each gas bubble to its eventual liberation. Horseshoers thrive on stink, though. Even rotting, cheesy hooves don't bother them.

With his ear pressed close to the horse while trimming the front hooves, Hunter had been in the best position to listen to the alimentary symphony. Now, nailing shoes on the hind feet, he was in the best place to sniff the bouquet. But he quit paying the farts any mind; he tuned out the rumbling. The heat blocked all else. Sweat dripped in a steady stream from the tip of his nose, and a damp circle of earth spread below.

Jack Hunter put down the horse's leg and straightened up—stiffly.

"Hell's bells." *That* wasn't a fart. Hunter barely had time to step away from the cascade of turds from the horse's winking anus. He wondered if it was possible for a horse to shit on your back while you were working on its hind feet.

Mrs. Clayton's toy white poodle left the hoof parings on which it had been gnawing all morning and trotted up to the horseshoer's feet. Gingerly, but all aquiver, it sniffed at the fresh road apples. It chowed one down.

"Stupid shit-eating dog. Jesuschrist, you don't want to do that. It'll make you sick. Make you puke your guts out."

The poodle ignored the warning. Steaming road apples were a rare delicacy, as the dog was usually confined to the house. Visiting the horse corrals was an uncommon privilege.

Freedom. Sunshine that burns the soul right out of your body. Physical labor that leaves you stiff, crippled, and torn. Low pay. Cantankerous, shitting horses. Shit-eating poodle dogs for company. Freedom. Yeah, freedom. He drove in the last nail.

There was weight to the sunlight, to the heat. There was a force to the sun-blows that drove a man to his knees, that pushed him into the baked, burned Earth. Like a blacksmith over his anvil, the sun hammered down.

Hunter filled a tumbler with water from the round orange cooler on the tailgate of his truck and slugged down a quart. The plastic glass had a Blake's Lotaburger design on it. He stood in the shade of the poplars and let his stomach suck up the water.

The poodle dog chewed on shit, and Hunter chewed on the sight of the dog chewing on shit. Some archaeologists think that the Mexican hairless dog—the Chihuahua—was bred by the Aztecs to eat human feces. These dogs were the sewers of Tenochtitlán and kept the streets of that magnificent city clean of human offal. Bernal Díaz, the chronicler of Cortés's conquest of the Aztecs, commented on how the streets of Tenochtitlán were cleaner than those of any of the great cities of Europe.

Maybe . . . maybe French royalty bred the toy poodle to do the same thing. Hunter imagined a scene one morning at Versailles: Marie Antoinette cries hysterically for her chambermaid to help her poodle pry his head out of her 14-carat gold chamber pot.

He refilled the plastic glass and sipped at it, while he watched the poodle gag and upchuck.

He looked up from the dog, to the distance, to the blue mountains walking the horizon. The Diablos reared up like a whale breaching the bedrock of the Earth. The next day Hunter would be up there—in the Diablo Wilderness Area. After too long gone. He planned only a week-long backpacking trip, but that would be time enough to visit old haunts, to walk again in the heart and soul of southwestern New Mexico. Only after that trip would he feel at home again.

All business, Buck Clayton came putting down from the big house on a motorized tricycle. The rancher looked like a rockabilly singer of the 1950s. Sleepy LaBeef, say, or one of the other early stars of Sun Records, Hunter thought, hearkening back to his mother's old records. Or maybe Li'l Abner gone to jowls and paunch. There was a mean glint to his eyes, a cruel curl to his lip. But he wore his black handlebar mustache as a Dallas businesswoman wears big hair.

Giving the horses a glance, Clayton said, "Looks like you're doing a good enough job here. I've got to go up to Albuquerque on business, but Jodi's finally up. Just go on up to the house when you're done, and she'll write you a check."

"That'll be fine," Hunter said. He watched Clayton ride back up past the house to the airstrip and airplane garage. *Poor, starving rancher,* Hunter thought, *that plane has to be at least a year or two old.* Clayton zipped down the strip and off into the wild blue yonder.

Hunter shaped the last shoe on the anvil, checked it against the hoof for proper fit, and returned it to the anvil to make tiny changes. When working on hind feet (of a horse, that is), a farrier lays the horse's leg across his thigh so that the hoof is in his lap. For front feet, he brings the horse's leg up between his thighs to grip the hoof in a steady working position. Hunter carefully lined up the shoe on the right front hoof and drove in the first nail, angling it so that its point would exit the hoof wall up about an inch and a half where he would bend it back and clinch it off. Just as the inch of sharp horseshoe nail pierced the wall, a horsefly bit the horse's rump. The horse flinched and jerked its foot back.

"Hold on, goddamnit!"

The yank drove the nail through Hunter's leather shoeing apron and into his Levi's where it pricked the flesh of his inner thigh.

"Shit fire, a little higher and I could be a gelding, too," he muttered. Forearms straining like a python around a pig, he held onto the hoof and pulled against the horse's thrashing.

"You goddamn miserable nag, calm the hell down and I'll let you go!"

If the nail stayed caught in his apron and Levi's, and the horse broke his grip, he would be attached to its flailing leg. Broken bones? Concussion? Or worse yet, no balls?

"Yii!" The nail dug in.

He sensed the calming of the horse's fit and wrenched the nail out of his apron. He clinched it off and quickly drove in the other five nails.

"Jesuschrist," he puffed as he put down the leg. He stood back and blew. What a day. He wiped the sweat from his eyes with a damp forearm.

A retching noise caught his ear, and he found the poodle behind the truck praying for death with its guts.

"I guess that'll teach you, boy." Hunter grinned in a wry feeling of brotherhood.

The misery in his back called the horseshoer away from the dog. He squatted on his heels. In half a minute he stood, reached for the sky, and touched his toes. After four horses, he felt like he had been driving horseshoe nails into his own backbone instead of into horses' hooves. He shouldn't have jumped back into horseshoeing so fast. Should've worked into it more slowly. Dear holy god, it was hot. Sweat burned his eyes. He pulled the leather gloves off his hands, tossed them onto the tailgate, and sat wearily beside them. They were soaked through with sweat. Using the sodden bandanna from around his head, he cleaned his face with its own sweat.

Mrs. Clayton was watching him from the house a hundred yards away. Standing in the kitchen door of her ducal manor, she didn't try to hide when he noticed her watching. For forty-five or whatever—a handful of years older than Hunter—she was one hell of a semigood-looker. What did she see in Buck Clayton? Money? No doubt. Status? That, too. The richest man in Fall County should have a trophy wife. The State Fair Rodeo Queen from a quarter century ago *was* a trophy. Hunter plucked his hat from a corral post.

Whatever. It was still nice to be stared at by a pretty woman. Hunter knew that women deemed him good-looking, even if in a cross-grained sort of way, as the first ex-wife had been fond of reminding him. In his thoughts, Hunter always called Suzanne "the first ex-wife," even though she was his only ex-wife, indeed his only wife, and Hunter was bound and determined that she would be the only such mistake he would ever make. She had once told him that his face looked like something one of those northern California Highway 101 tourist trap artists—those fellows who hack out life-sized sculptures of a bigfoot or grizzly bear with a chain saw—might carve from a redwood burl. He would block out a cube for Jack's head, slice a mouth parallel to the square jawline, crudely fashion a flat nose only slightly out from the cheeks, and rip another straight gash with the chain saw for the line of his narrow eyes and horizontal brow.

Hunter led the newly shod horse to the nearest pasture and let it out of its halter to rejoin the others. Ten acres were divided into six horse pastures by white metal fences. Fancy stables were attached. A barrel-racing arena was nearby. Next to it was a more formal exercise track. Around it all, a couple hundred acres of prime bottomland had been turned into irrigated permanent pasture and alfalfa fields.

Mrs. Clayton was into her horses. Buck Clayton may ranch cows, but she bred quarter horses. A couple of wetbacks—real *vaqueros*—were forever busy doing her bidding. Hunter thought it odd that they didn't do the shoeing. Hey, don't look a gift horse in the mouth, hoss. He reckoned there were close to thirty horses. Keeping them trimmed and shod would be a tidy part of his income—if she liked his work today.

He gathered up his tools, fitted them in the toolbox, and put the box into the big, locking truck box against the cab in the pickup bed. Even though he was a grungy horseshoer, he was tidy. You take care of your tools, and they take care of you, he believed. A place for everything, and everything in its place. He cradled the horns of the hundred-pound anvil with his forearms, lifted it off the stump on which it sat, and slid it into the back of the truck. No need to lock it up. There wasn't anybody dumb enough to try to heist it and run. He wiped his forehead again with his arm. She was still in the door.

A mist glistened on the hair of his chest and arms; sweat glazed his back. Drops nosed out of his armpits as if from seeps in the sandstone below Glen Canyon Dam on the Colorado River. The drops joined and slid down his sides in salty chutes. Through squinted eyes under the brim of his worn straw cowboy hat, he looked up at the sun and shook his head. He loved it. Nothing like New Mexico sun to burn the poison out of a man.

Hunter shook out his short-sleeved, red-checked western shirt and slipped it on while he strolled up to the house. It was too hot to snap it; he left the front open and the tail in the breeze—except there was still no breeze to suck away the claustrophobic sweat. Mrs. Clayton stood in the kitchen door, barefoot, long tanned legs, short shorts, a western shirt also unsnapped, but with the tail tied in front, Jack Daniel's in one hand, Marlboro in the other, no makeup except for yesterday's eyeliner and mascara. Framing her face was bouffant red-brown hair—the dark red-brown hair of a woman in conspiracy with her hairdresser against gray. Behind her an air conditioner worked against the sun.

The house was a big, architect-designed—what?—Italian villa surrounded by a white brick wall, a green manor lawn, and tall Lombardy poplars. It had a tile roof, but the tiles were light pink and pastel blue instead of the traditional Spanish red. The house was out of place for Rio Diablo, New Mexico, but perfect for Lord Clayton and his Lady.

"It looked like Sonny gave you a little trouble there," she said.

"Nothing much. A horsefly got him excited is all."

Hunter knocked most of the manure off his boots and followed her inside to the kitchen. The shock of the temperature change sent a shiver through his body. She put her empty glass down on the table and stubbed out her cigarette in a full ashtray.

"Would you like a beer? You look hot."

"Sure. A beer would be wonderful. Thanks."

She fetched a Coors Light from the refrigerator and opened it for him. Coors. The white bread of beers. Silver bullet, my ass. At least it was cold.

"How much do I owe you?"

"Four horses—that'll be one hundred and forty dollars," Hunter said, pressing the cold beer can to his forehead.

She sat down to write the check. "What happened to your arm?"

Hunter looked at his right forearm—a three-inch-long rip ran down it. Blood had mixed with sweat and horse dirt and had hardened in rivulets down the back of his hand and out onto each finger. The nail had left a souvenir.

"Aw, it's nothin'."

"Let me fix it for you."

"It's okay."

She took him by the arm and led him through her bedroom to its bathroom. "Jack, my horse hurt you, I'll take care of you." She cradled his forearm like a rock in her hand and gently sponged it off in the sink.

Hunter was impressed. Real marble for the counter top. A fancy ceramic basin. Were the fixtures really gold plated? And, good god, there was a bidet. It had to be the only bidet in Fall County.

"You have beautiful arms," she mused. "I like a man with muscle." She found hydrogen peroxide, tape, and gauze in a drawer and bandaged Hunter's arm.

"Thank you. I generally don't get this kind of treatment."

"You should," she smiled, and set the adhesive tape down on the marble counter. "You have an awfully nice chest, too." She ran a long, pink fingernail between his pectoral muscles down to his flat belly. Her nail stopped at his navel and stayed there, leaving goose bumps in its wake. "I was watching you work while you had your shirt off. You have a very attractive body." With her free hand she removed his hat. "And a pretty face."

Whoa, Hunter thought. *Is this really happening? Is this actually going to happen to me today?*

She tugged at the slipknot holding her shirttails together. The shirt fell open to a teeny-weeny black bikini top across a freckled, deeply tanned chest.

What the hell. Go for it. It had been awhile. "You have a lovely body, too, Mrs. Clayton. And a very pretty face." He touched the exposed curve of a breast with a callused finger.

"Jack, please call me Jodi."

Jodi Clayton slid into his arms. The kiss came as hard as a thunderclap. She was as thirsty as he was. He stroked her back under the loose shirt and then moved his hand around to her front. Lady Luck works in mysterious ways, Hunter thought. Maybe this was her way of making up for that gelding. Her knee slid up between his legs. It felt a lot better there than the horse's hoof had.

"Buck is long gone. My wetback maid is shopping in Platoro today. We're alone." Her tongue followed the moist words into his ear.

Lord love a duck.

"There's a lovely view from my bedroom window," she said when she came up for air.

"I reckon we'll have to go take a look at it," he said.

She took his hand.

No one looked at the view from the bedroom window.

An hour later, after the bedroom, a dip in the pool, and a new bandage on his arm, she wrote out the check at the kitchen table. "How soon can you come back to do more of the horses, Jack?" She wore her shirt, open at the front, and the black bikini.

Hunter was drinking another cold Coors. It tasted good now. "How about next week? If I spread out the whole remuda to a few each week, I could keep them all in good shape."

"Don't be late," she smiled, leaning toward him with the check. "I wouldn't want my horses neglected."

He took the check and caressed her cheek with a scabbed-over knuckle. "Don't worry about that, Jodi. If one throws a shoe or something, just give me a call, and I'll be right over."

"That'll probably happen. I ride my horses hard."

Jack Hunter sauntered out to his truck. He waved to Jodi Clayton as he drove across the cattle guard that separated the house compound from the fields. She stood in the kitchen door with Jack Daniel's and a Marlboro, the black bikini beckoning through the open shirt.

The frolic with Jodi Clayton was an out-of-the-blue but more than welcome lagniappe. Perfect sex. No commitment, no promises. Just good, clean fun. Recreational animal rutting. Nothing to mess it up.

Hunter switched on the radio to Platoro's country music station. The deejay announced the time as 1:43 P.M.

"Pretty good," Hunter said aloud to himself. "Four horses and one filly done, and it's barely afternoon. I should have time to get into Platoro and pick up some grub for the trip and get back in time to soak my poor ol' stiff body in the hot springs tonight." He meditated on his good fortune and whooped. "Goddamn! *God*damn."

2

The Clayton Ranch held sway over the widest part of the Diablo Valley. Jack Hunter guessed at the irrigated acreage as he drove through, did a quick seat-of-the-pants calculation, and figured that it took in half of all the irrigated land in the valley. After one mile of gravel road, he and the dust plume behind his truck reached a narrow, paved state highway. The village of Rio Diablo was five miles to the east. He turned west. Five minutes later he hit U.S. 666—the highway leading southeast to Platoro, which was a little less than an hour away.

Hunter had a thermos of iced tea in the cab of the truck—at least it had been iced tea in the morning when he had filled it. Now it was somewhere on the road to lukewarm. He filled the Lotaburger tumbler, took a long pull, dribbled tea down his chin and chest, and headed the truck down the blacktop to Platoro. He kept a bottle of ibuprofen in the glove box, and he gobbled three now for his back. He shifted the wing window to blow the road wind onto his wet chest: a poor boy's air conditioner.

The deejay talking through the truck radio announced a "gold nugget." The whiskey voice of Hank Williams curled up out of a grave of four decades like smoke out of an overflowing juke joint ashtray.

"Maybe, Hank, maybe," said Hunter, "but I'd rather be lonesome with the whippoorwill than in my wife's bedroom."

After Hank came the sappy lament of a lovesick urban cowboy: Nashville sound. Even country music's gotten duded up and headed to the city, Hunter scoffed. He punched at the radio with his right forefinger and got Platoro's other station, this one top forty. He cussed as he was mugged by the musical jabberwocky of something that sounded like a 500 kV power line shorting out. Driving with his left hand, he leaned across the cab and fumbled in the glove box. He grabbed a cassette—"San Antonio Rose" by Willie Nelson and Ray Price—and stuffed it into the cassette deck, ending the misery of the androgen now performing over the radio.

U.S. 666 cut through a high savanna of juniper, mesquite, and yucca. This was cattle country, though; so the high, healthy turf found refuge only in the fenced right of way. On the other side of the barbed wire, where cattle lowed and chewed, were eroding gullies, steep-walled arroyos, snakeweed, cholla cactus, and prickly poppy. The grass was chewed down to roots and bare dirt. Cow-burnt range. The Real West. Marlboro Country.

Just before Platoro, he pulled up behind a dawdling RV. The bumper sticker read, "We're spending our kids' inheritance."

"You bet, folks. You just don't know how much," Hunter said as he passed. "Soil, oil, water, air, wildlife, forests—we're spending their inheritance. Posterity? Hell, what's posterity ever done for me?"

Hunter cashed Jodi Clayton's check at the Platoro First State Bank. His stiff back talked him into walking the five blocks to Lotaburger. Passing the Cobre Christian Supply Store, he was seized by the thought of entering and eagerly asking, "Do you supply Christians? Great! Can you deliver a couple of dozen? We've got a stadium and lions arranged, but no Christians yet." Hunter did not act on the thought. It was part of the unending jabber in his skull box; outside of it, he didn't get involved. The world was spiraling down into chaos. Hunter couldn't do anything about it, except try to stay out of the way of the coming anarchy.

Platoro was a fading mining town located at the 6,000-foot-high break of land where the Chihuahuan Desert washed up from Mexico against the foothills of the Diablo Mountains. Soaptree yucca and alligator juniper merged in the intertidal zone. Shopping malls and upscale national franchises had not yet found the 15,000 residents of the Platoro metroplex.

Big Macs and Kentucky Fried Chicken had only recently invaded. Another hour south, Interstate 10 cut across southern New Mexico on its way to California. The nearest shopping mall was in Las Cruces, 120 miles down the pike. Tucson, Arizona, was 220 miles to the west.

Platoro had been named by prospectors who had braved Victorio's warriors for dreams of silver. Those who hadn't found a morning Apache lance in their last night's beans and tortillas had found copper—not silver. The Virgin of Guadalupe mine—a mile wide and 1,500 feet deep—was touted as "the world's most beautiful open pit" by the chamber of commerce. Like its faraway coal cousins in Appalachia, Platoro was tied to the modern age by a frayed thread. Downtown, with its cracked sidewalks and cramped stores, hadn't changed much since Ozzie and Harriet had beamed in to the first black and white TVs in Copper Country. Pickup trucks shared the main drag with lowrider Chevies. The rigs throbbed at the bottom of the bass range like constipated elephants in musth. The lowriders sported carpeted dashboards and tiny steering wheels of welded chain loosely gripped by sleepy young men. Sharks on 'ludes. Horny, hungry, but cool, man, cool.

A pack of middle-school boys on skateboards zipped past. They wore up-to-date uniforms of baggy shorts, T-shirts their overweight fathers couldn't fill, expensive black sneakers, and ball caps with the bills in the back. "Wonder how much it cost to retool all the cap factories to stitch the bills on the backs?" Hunter asked the universe. The kids reminded him of a school of young barracuda cruising a bonefish reef in the Caribbean.

Crossing a side street, Hunter glanced at the mining town Madonna behind the wheel of her shot rod at the stop sign. The car was a beat-to-shit Oldsmobile farting blue smoke. The vinyl roof was cracked and peeling. The bumper sticker on the front bumper roared, "It's a CHILD, NOT a choice." She was a dishwater-blond young woman with a cornmeal mush body. A cigarette with a long ash dangled from her lips. Four towheaded little boys, in stair steps from the infant in an unbuckled car seat to one of kindergarten age, filled the car. She walloped a whining middle one, cussed, and wiped the snot from the back of her hand onto the fraying seat cover.

Hunter judged that she had another in the oven and mentally responded to her bumper sticker *weltanschauung*, "You bet, mom, how about a future mass murderer?"

He imagined her husband—a fierce little runt with a ponytail and scraggly black beard came to mind. He probably worked at the smelter. Drove a pickup. Smoked dope, drank Coors, watched TV sports, had voted for Perot. . . .

Hunter was so busy with his sociological musing that he was nearly run down when a four-wheel-drive contraption jacked up into the stratosphere made a right turn. It had a roll bar and a bank of halogens on top that could light up Monday night football. The pilot was one of those broad little guys inflated like an overstuffed sausage in a Botero painting. Tiny eyes, nose, mouth, and mustache were lost in the wide moonface without a chin. Hunter recalled his theory that the size of a man's dick and his wheels had an inverse relationship. The sticker on the rear bumper—"Hungry and out of work? Eat an Environmentalist!"—confirmed it.

Lotaburgers were a sentimental tradition with Jack Hunter. He could remember them from over thirty years earlier when he had been a little kid in Albuquerque. The monstrous burgers had been only thirty-nine cents then. The price had gone up, but Lotaburger was still genuine New Mexico funk. McDonald's was America; Carl's, Jr. was Southern California. Lotaburger was New Mexico.

Hunter took his double-meat, green chile cheeseburger, fries, and extra-large iced tea outside. He sat down at a round concrete table with a red and white metal umbrella. He hoped the food would hush the Coors and warm tea in his otherwise empty stomach. The ibuprofen was playing water polo in the soup. He grinned at the Blazer in the parking lot: a low-rider Blazer. It had about half an inch of clearance. *Now, that's the kind of four-wheeler I can dig,* he thought. The paint job was as red as a slinky lady's fingernails.

"Hey, turkey-butt." The sun was blotted out by the shadow of a very large mammal.

Hunter turned around. It was his buddy Bill Crawford. Hunter said, *"Hola, amigo. Que paso?"*

The big man plopped down at the table—after first picking a spot in the shade—and pulled off his hat. His black hair, hanging to the bottom of his ears, was full of sweat curls. He took off his sunglasses and mopped his furry face with a wrinkled, damp handkerchief.

After grooming himself, Bill scowled and said, "Man, let me tell you, Jack, things have really heated up on the wilderness front this week. Know how I was telling you that we've goosed up our campaign to add Mondt Park and some other country to the Diablo Wilderness? How we're trying to get a bill introduced in Congress?"

"Yep. Over twenty years we've been working on it and still no cigar."

Bill nodded his head up and down and bugged out his eyes. "You're telling me. But as if we didn't have enough work, now the assholes are trying to declassify the whole Diablo Wilderness Area!"

Bill was in his uniform for the summer: Teva river sandals, Patagonia boatman's shorts, a short-sleeved cotton shirt with tropical fish on it also from Patagonia, sunglasses, and a black felt cowboy hat. The shirt was unbuttoned halfway to his navel. Drops of sweat decorated the black mat of chest hair like ornaments on a Christmas tree. Bill Crawford was not a naked ape. The rank pelt of his chest grew up his throat and over his face to the top of his head and down his neck to his back, leaving only his cheekbones, eyes, and low forehead bare.

"I can't believe anyone's serious about that," Hunter said. "Sure there's always been opposition to enlarging the Wilderness Area, but to do away with the Wilderness entirely? C'mon, you gotta be kidding."

"Don't you read the papers?"

"Nope."

"Well, you listen to the radio?"

"Hardly ever." Hunter snorted. "The music's all garbage these days. I can't stand the 'ain't-I-cute?' chatter of disc jockeys. Even worse are the banal ads. . . ."

"You're just trying to resign from the human race, aren't ya?"

"Yep."

Bill nodded his head. "Not a bad idea. I thought I had. But this antiwilderness crap, they've really been trumpeting it the last couple of weeks. The chamber of commerce has a petition in favor of declassifying the Wilderness. The bastards even asked Audrey to have one at the Shady Lady! We resigned from the chamber for that."

"They had actually let the Shady Lady join the Platoro Chamber of Commerce?" Hunter raised his eyebrows.

"Hell, they'll take anybody," Bill grinned. "Audrey told me that when she worked at Mrs. Johnson's cathouse back in the mid-60s they were even in the chamber of commerce."

"Terrific."

"Anyhow, Barf Puke . . ."

Hunter laughed. "Our honorable congressman."

Bill Crawford shook his head slowly back and forth. He narrowed his eyes. "That sonofabitch. He's all balls out for this. He just introduced a bill to declassify the Diablo Wilderness Area, and he's on the Natural Resources Committee this session. . . ."

"Might have known he'd be riding this new hooray."

"You oughta know. He's an old buddy of yours, ain't he?"

"Right, Bill, right. About like the clap."

Bill Crawford laughed. "God, it's hot today. Must be a hundred. You don't mind if I have a sip of your tea, do you? Good." He wrapped his paw around it and swilled it down.

"Not at all, go ahead."

"Hey, listen, Jack, since you're back living in these parts now, you gotta start coming to our Diablo Wilderness Committee meetings. We need your help."

"Sorry, buddy, like I told you when I moved back, I fought my share of the fight—eleven years in Washington, D.C., while you were having a good time here in the wilderness. Excuse me while I go get another tea. Mine seems to have evaporated in this heat."

"C'mon," Bill called after him. "We could use you to talk to Senator Reed. He's going to be the key to this whole thing. He'll listen to you."

"Karl will listen to you all as well as he'll listen to me," Hunter said when he returned with two iced teas. He set one down in front of Bill. "Show him there's lots of public support for the Diablo Wilderness Area. He needs to hear from the grass roots, not from a burned-out lobbyist."

"Yeah, but you and Reed are old drinking buddies."

"That doesn't mean he always voted right. Besides, I'm retired now. I'm just gonna be a horseshoer. You can do it without me. I don't think Pugh's declassification bill will be hard to stop. Ranting and raving against Wilderness is part of the catechism down here. Ever since I first came here with my parents, some locals have been talking about how 'opening up' the Wilderness would make the area boom."

"That's bullshit," said Bill.

"Of course it's bullshit, but politics is bullshit. Don't worry too much, though. The big mining and timber boys are trying to piggyback anti-conservation stuff onto the antifederal government feeling. Even if the right-wingers took over Congress, they wouldn't be able to declassify existing Wilderness Areas. And if they tried, that would be political suicide.

The best way for you all to fight Pugh's bill is to push all the harder to enlarge the Diablo Wilderness."

Bill set his jaw and folded his arms across his chest. "Don't worry. We'll protect the Wilderness—one way or another."

"I hope so, but I'm not counting on anything anymore, old buddy. Whatever we protect is only temporary. Until famine and disease pare us back, we're going to tear up a lot of ground. You might save a little bit here, a little bit there, but . . . none of our sweat's going to do much good. The only thing that'll help is for the industrial bubble to pop. It's going to happen, but I'm afraid it won't happen soon enough. Get me drunk some night and I'll really tell you about my little trip around the world. It's bad, Bill."

"Thanks for the pep talk."

Hunter continued, "Hey, it's hopeless, amigo. What do you want me to say? I'm not going to sugarcoat it. There are nearly six billion people in the world. When we were born there were half that. And we're not old men. What's worse is that it's not slowing down. World population grew in absolute numbers more last year than any year before. This year will be even more. . . ."

"Hey," Bill held up his hand to stop the rant. "I know all that stuff. I've got so many statistics about resource depletion, extinction, erosion, overpopulation, and all crammed in my head I feel like a fucking State of the World book. So what if it's tough? We still gotta try. We gotta fight. What are you going to do if they do declassify the Diablo?"

Hunter twisted his mouth and shrugged his shoulders. "It'll kick me in the nuts. I'll feel it just like you will. But what can you do?" Hunter sipped his tea. Ever since first grade he had been baiting his best friend.

Bill's eyes bugged out; his voice cracked. "Well, I'm not gonna roll over and play dead for 'em! They'll rip up my Wilderness over my dead body!" He pounded the concrete table with his fist. He stood up. "Jesus, man! You can't keep running forever! You gotta stop and fight somewhere. Sometime. This is my home! They won't take it from me. This is where I've stuck my spear in the ground and this is where I'll fucking die if necessary!"

"Good rhetoric, Bill, but I'm telling you, in twenty years there's not going to be anything worth fighting or dying for."

"Sure, sure, with that kind of attitude." Bill Crawford sat back down and sucked on his iced tea. He glowered at Hunter. "Hell's bells, Jack, I never thought I'd hear you talk like this. You were the pro. You were the guy who had dedicated his life to saving wilderness. Shit! What the hell; I'm still glad you're back in these parts."

"Good a home as I know. I do appreciate you selling your horseshoeing business to me."

"Don't mention it. I'm glad to be rid of it. The doctor told me my back would be ruined if I kept it up. Besides, I was sick and tired of the welfare ranchers I had to work for. Oh, speaking of welfare ranchers, did you ever get over to shoe the Clayton horses?"

"Yep, finished up there about an hour and a half ago." Hunter smiled. And it still tasted good.

"Uh-huh. Was Buck there?"

"Nope. He flew up to Albuquerque," Hunter said.

"That's good. He's a total asshole, but Jodi's a fine person and one hell of a woman."

"I'll testify to that."

"You don't say, now." Bill grinned like a teenager coming up from the back seat at a drive-in movie. "There are certain advantages to being a horseshoer."

"Yep," Hunter said and nodded.

Bill Crawford slapped him on the back and laughed. "Well, I reckon I better move it on. I've got some errands, then I've got to get over to the Shady Lady. We've got a new dancer who's hotter than that black asphalt out there."

"I'll have to come over and see her dance sometime." Hunter smiled inwardly. Bill Crawford could still shift moods as fast as a New Mexico spring could shift weather.

"You do that. Name's Wendy Storm. Built like a sack full of wildcats in heat. Hot damn!"

"That's a terrific name for a stripper—Wendy Storm," Hunter said.

"Huh? Oh, yeah. *Yeah*, it is. I hadn't caught the pun on it yet. That's really good."

"How do you like being a businessman?" Hunter asked. "You sorry you spent most of your inheritance buying into a topless bar?"

"Hell no. Fulfilled my lifelong ambition. Some of it's a lot of hassle, sure, but getting to supervise the employees makes up for it! Heh, heh. Actually I don't have that much to do, other than bartending and bouncing now and then. Audrey runs the place—I just came up with the bucks to keep her open when she needed it. Like you know, I spend most of my time on conservation and on my half-assed guide service. Why don't you come on over to the Shady Lady now? I just got Guinness Stout on tap. I'll buy you a pint."

"That's a deal. Next time I'm in town, though. I gotta hit the feed and tack store for horseshoes, the grocery store, and thought I'd check out the new backpacking equipment store. I'm so stiff today, I just want to kill all my rats and head back to Rio Diablo and soak in the hot springs. I'm going to head up into the Wilderness tomorrow for a week. Say 'hello' after all these years."

"Good. You need to do that. Maybe seeing that country again will put some sand back in your craw." Bill Crawford pushed his ugly black-bearded bulk up from the table. With a thigh-sized arm, he shoved his black cowboy hat down on his head. "See ya, hoss. Don't neglect them Clayton horses. By god, they had the best cared-for hooves in the whole damn state when I was shoeing them."

"I'll do it. Don't worry."

Hunter watched Bill Crawford amble away on his businessman's rounds. When Bill had started his guide service in the late 1970s, Hunter had never thought he'd pull it off. There must have been a couple hundred other hippie backpackers who thought they could make a living guiding city folks through the wilderness. Maybe four or five in the whole western United States had lasted longer than a year. Hunter hadn't thought his buddy would stick to it and make it work. But he'd done well. Float trips when the river was high enough in spring, a little hunting in the fall, and backpacking in the summer, combined with his horseshoeing until his back went out—the man had made it. And now he was part owner of the only topless bar in southwestern New Mexico.

It was always good to see his oldest buddy, though Hunter was a little miffed that the previous horseshoer had gotten the same kind of care from Jodi Clayton he had gotten. It wasn't jealousy. It was just that Hunter had been pretending it had been his irresistible animal magnetism that had swept her off her feet and into bed.

Hunter thought. She *had* asked him to keep working on her horses without checking the job he did this morning. What did that make him?

3

The sun was winding down its sluggard trek across the long June sky when Jack Hunter got back to Rio Diablo. Not a cloud had crossed the sky all day. Soon the sun would settle into the pink horizon like a hog into its wallow.

Underwood's Beer Joint was up on the right. Hunter pulled into the parking lot; the truck sent a long, lazy shadow across the gravel. Only one other vehicle—a well-traveled Jeep CJ5—was outside the bar, but the neon sign was lit, and an "Open/*Abierto*" sign hung in the window. Hunter had forgotten to get a bottle of gin in Platoro; he figured Underwood's would have some. The saloon was housed in a seventy-year-old, false-fronted board and batten building. Stepping from the oven of the truck into the swamp-coolered darkness of the tavern was like plunging into a cave. A lonely pool table, empty booths, and bare tables filled the room. Stuffed dead critters, heads and whole bodies, were on the walls. A snarling mountain lion perched above the mirror behind the bar. Lighted signs for this and that beer clashed with the Wild West bar counter and mirror. No customers. A slow night in nowhere.

The young woman tending bar looked up from her book. When she saw him, she smiled. She was pretty—very pretty, thought Hunter. But there was something else: something known, something from the past. He knew the smile, the eyes—the wild green eyes.

She flashed a spring snowmelt smile and said, "It's nice to see you again, Jack. What'll you have?" Her voice was low and husky; she could have taught Bogie how to whistle. Dusty as a fine old cabernet.

He hadn't planned to have anything, just pick up a bottle of gin and go, but the woman was lovely, she seemed to know him, and she was friendly. What the hell. Today was going very well. He looked at the line of beer bottles on the shelf above the mirror and below the lion.

"Oh, I reckon I'll have a Pacifico." He smiled in phony recollection.

She put the bottle in front of him and opened it. "Glass?"

"Naw. Bottle's fine." Hunter's mind was racing through corridors, up and down stairwells, madly rummaging through cobwebby old photo files stashed away in the library stacks of his cerebral cortex.

"Don't you remember me?" Her eyes laughed; they teased him. Her smile belonged to a cat: a cat playing with a ball of yarn, a mouse, a dying bird—whatever she held in the claws of her green eyes.

Jack Hunter settled in on the stool, hooked his boot heels in the braces, took a sip of the Mexican lager from Mazatlan. Hell's bells. Who is she? Where do I know her from?

Keats lent a hand:

> . . . a faery's child,
> Her hair was long, her foot was light,
> And her eyes were wild.

Ah, yes. MaryAnne McClellan. Phil McClellan's daughter from up in Albuquerque. She *did* grow up. It was his turn to grin, to tease.

"Now how could I forget someone as pretty as you, even if the last time I saw you, you were a scrawny prepubescent teenager? What are you doing down here in the Diablo, MaryAnne?"

"You do remember me!"

"Didn't you go off to college at Colorado State?"

She said, "Yes, I did, and then I went to the University of Alaska in Fairbanks for grad school."

"Lordy, that makes me feel old. You were still in high school when I was working for the Sierra Club in Albuquerque before they hauled me off to Washington. What are you doing here?"

"I'm living at the old Delaney place. I finished my dissertation in wildlife ecology spring a year ago, and now I have a grant developing a Mexican wolf reintroduction proposal for Arizona and New Mexico. I just fill in here at the bar now and then for Red Underwood."

"Yeah, I remember now that you planned to be a wildlifer. I got a minor in biology from UNM, but wasn't enough of a scientist, so I got my degree in literature. Quit at a master's, though. Wrote my thesis on the very nonscientific topic of wilderness attitudes in English poetry." He glanced at her left hand. No ring.

"I know." She opened a bottle of Pacifico for herself. "I read it."

"What? You read that thing?"

"Of course. You gave a copy to my daddy, remember? One wintry weekend when I was left home alone in high school—he had a girlfriend then who liked to ski, but whom I didn't like—I found it and read it. I thought it was awfully romantic. It made me want to read poetry. I was terribly in love with you and heartbroken that you had gotten married."

"Ohmigod!" Hunter laughed, and hopped to another subject. "Remember when we went on that field trip to the Rio Grande Zoo's Mexican wolf captive breeding project? We had a nice talk about wolf reintroduction there. I told you it was a great idea, but that it was politically unrealistic."

"Sure, I remember. How could I forget? I was shattered that you were such a wimp. But I still had a crush on you."

"I hope you developed better taste with your higher education."

"Oh, I don't know. I think I had pretty good taste back then."

Hunter laughed and drained his beer. "I might as well have another one if I'm going to get compliments like that."

MaryAnne fished another Pacifico out of the ice bin. "I'm really glad you came in, Jack. Bill Crawford said you were back in the area and were going to take over his horseshoeing business. My horse hasn't gotten trimmed or shod since Bill threw out his back. Could you take care of him sometime soon?"

"Sure. I'm taking off tomorrow for a few days to go backpacking in the Diablo, but I'll be able to do it next week."

"Good."

"But, gee, I thought you were happy to see me, not just that I could service your horse."

"I'm glad you came in so I could ask you about shoeing my horse, Jack. I'm *ecstatic* to see you again otherwise, though."

"That's better." They looked at each other over their beers. The pause in talk was almost as unsettling for Hunter as meeting a grizzly on the trail. "So, what was your dissertation on?"

"The long-term cyclical relationship between wolves, moose, and willows in the southern Brooks Range of Alaska."

"Sounds fascinating."

"Well, it is! It's a . . ."

"No, no. I'm serious," Hunter said. "I wasn't joking. I've hiked in the Brooks Range. Spent two months there a couple of summers ago. Been up a couple of other times, too. Tell me about your research."

"Good. I'm a little defensive. The Alaska Fish and Game Department just wants to produce a maximum moose population to keep the hunters happy, and kill off the wolves so they don't prey on moose. And my research shows that you need wolf predation on moose—even regional extirpation of moose by wolves—to prevent excessive predation by moose on willows. You can imagine that the game farmers in the department don't like the direction my . . ." MaryAnne grimaced at the squeak of the screen door. "Oh gawd," she moaned. "Circle K."

Hunter twisted on his stool. A TV-bellied, middle-aged man was moving to a stool at the far end of the bar. Hunter would have described his gait as a "waddle" except that it was too single-minded to be a waddle.

MaryAnne said, "Hello, Kenneth. Coors Light?"

Circle K spread his cheeks on the bar stool and nodded his assent. MaryAnne drew a glass, took it down to his end of the bar, and tried to make her getaway.

"I've got something for you." His little pig eyes tried to hold her there.

Hunter took the opportunity to glance at the book MaryAnne had been reading when he came in. It was a fat, academic tome entitled *Quaternary Extinctions*. The dust jacket blurb said it was about the die-off of large mammals like short-faced bear, mastodon, and saber-toothed cat ten thousand years ago—probably caused by overhunting by the first Indians. It looked interesting, but more interesting to Hunter were the looks of the bartender. He gazed down the length of the wooden bar, well-oiled by a century of dirty elbows and spilled beers, to get a full view of her.

Jack Hunter had his fancies in women, the traits he doted on, and MaryAnne had them all. Big eyes. Dark brown hair. High cheekbones. Wide mouth. Thin lips. Trim, compact, athletic figure—or so it seemed under the loose "Save the Diablo" T-shirt. The striking green eyes earned her bonus points. So did her clean, arching eyebrows—Hunter didn't go for the woolly bear caterpillar look.

Circle K's voice rose. "MaryAnne. I really think you should read this. Your immortal soul is at stake."

"I appreciate your concern, Kenneth, but I'm really not concerned about my soul. I don't think it's your concern either."

"It is my concern. I wouldn't want a fine young girl like you to burn forever."

"I'm just not interested in your religion, Kenneth. Thanks, but no thanks."

"MaryAnne. Let me ask you a question. Don't you believe in God?"

She looked quietly at him for a moment, then said, "Of course. And I am her!"

The squirrel in Circle K's skull crawled onto its little wire tread-wheel and began to move. At first it spun the wheel slowly, then it picked up speed. Finally the answer popped out: Blasphemy. Circle K's eyes widened like he had looked into the belly of hell and had seen MaryAnne smiling and happy and serving up cold beers. He left his beer, twisted off the stool, and lurched for the door. Hunter thought back to his recent months in Africa. Circle K looked like a hippopotamus moving for water at daybreak.

MaryAnne tossed the religious tract into the trash. She smiled as she returned to her stool across from Hunter. "Oh, me, I hate to lose customers for Red Underwood, but maybe Circle K will quit trying to convert me now."

Hunter chuckled. He remembered her as a feisty little fart when he had been in college and had first met her and her dad on a wilderness study trip. She had been about nine years old. "Yep. I think you may have gotten rid of him."

"Good. I should have done that a month ago."

"Who is he?"

"Kenneth Sanders. A maintenance man for the local ranger district. Jack Mormon newly converted to the local holy roller church." She rolled her eyes.

After Circle K, a few people came in for package goods, but none stayed to drink. Hunter and MaryAnne talked about old times, wilderness, wildlife, and whatever came to mind. He remembered her tagging along with her daddy to every field trip or conservation event in Albuquerque in the 1970s. Her mom had died in a car wreck or something when MaryAnne was young, but her dad, who had been New Mexico's leading conservationist, had done a good job of raising her.

She, too, told Hunter about Bart Pugh's bill to declassify the Diablo Wilderness. There were other, more immediate threats to the wilderness, as well. She was worried about possible timber sales in an area she was fighting to add to the Diablo Wilderness Area. The Forest Service wanted to build a high-standard logging road into it. Hunter knew the area well: Mondt Park. He was planning to hike through it during the next week. The thought of it in danger dragged him down. But he pushed the crisis out of his mind and fixed back on the bartender. The talk came easy as it does when two people are chatting with more than their tongues.

"Nice trogons."

She touched one of her terra-cotta earrings. "Amazing. You recognized them as trogons. You wouldn't be a birder, would you?"

"Of course."

"Well, that's great. I need a birding companion."

"That's me. Have binoculars, will travel."

"My local hiking partner, Ralph Wittfogel, doesn't bird," she said. "Just walks. And walks and walks and walks."

Hunter was wondering about the friendship with Wittfogel, when she asked him about the bandage on his arm. He told her about the gelding and the nail.

"Well, I hope mine is better mannered!" MaryAnne said.

"So do I. I may start charging double when that happens." He slid off his stool. "Guess I need to make room for some more beer."

Jack Hunter ambled off to the men's room, after getting directions. It was located to the side of the front door. Standing in front of the urinal, rocked back on his heels, letting the beer flow out, he felt an immense peace. Since divorcing Suzanne, he had been with a fair number of women, always just for casual affairs or one-night stands like the one with Jodi Clayton. A couple of gals—that river runner in Tasmania and the rhino researcher in Botswana—had wanted something more serious, but Hunter had skedaddled when it started getting sticky. Sitting in Underwood's Beer Joint tonight, talking with MaryAnne McClellan, though, was something else. Something he had dutifully avoided since Suzanne. He'd drunk enough beer to shut up the little man in his skull, so this knowledge didn't fully crop up behind his blurring eyes; if it had, he would have pulled his hat low over them and let the night wind blow him away.

He buttoned his jeans and left the john. A man was leaning over the bar talking to MaryAnne. His back faced Hunter. There was no laughter in MaryAnne's eyes. Nor was there fear. Hunter held back and stood quietly in the shadows.

"You goddamned environmeddlers. Save the Diablo Wilderness! What about saving people? This town? Jobs! Somebody ought to teach you a lesson." He grabbed her arm. "Maybe I ought to just rip that shirt off of you. You probably'd like to go around like that anyway, you fucking e-cologist slut!"

Before Hunter could move, MaryAnne took the man's hand—now reaching for the front of her shirt—with both of her hands and twisted it over and around so that she had his thumb at the point of dislocation.

"Don't ever touch me again, or I'll hurt you real bad." Her words were as cold as a buzzworm's rattle.

Thrown off balance by her unforeseen move, he danced back and forth trying to lessen the pain of the hold she had on him. He only made it worse.

"Are you ready to leave?" MaryAnne asked.

"Okay, okay." He sounded like he was running uphill.

"The door's behind you."

Hunter walked forward as the man, rubbing this thumb, headed for the door. He was about forty, average-sized but wiry, a greasy mechanic-looking kind of guy, with a dirty, billed cap pulled down to his ears. Stringy black sideburns ran down from the cap. He was a tough little mongrel dog.

"How do, pardner," Hunter grinned with a redneck's comradeship. "Barkeep a little tough for you?"

The man hissed the smell of stale tobacco through clenched teeth as he brushed past.

Hunter gave his best good ol' boy smile as his boot caught the other's. The man did a face plant in the chipped linoleum.

"Sorry about that, amigo! Here, let me help you up." Hunter grabbed his collar and belt and rushed him out the screen door and into the gravel of the parking lot where he went head over heels.

Hunter, brushing off his hands, returned smiling to the bar. MaryAnne wasn't smiling.

"Who was that asshole?" he asked.

"You know, Jack, I had taken care of him. You really didn't need to add anything."

Oops. This was not your standard damsel in distress needing a white knight. Rough times, these. Hard to know how to be a gentleman, much less when to be gallant.

"Uh, sorry about that. I guess I shouldn't have butted in. But he pissed me off."

"No, you shouldn't have butted in."

There was a silence. Hunter felt about seven years old.

"That's okay." MaryAnne put her hand on his. "I appreciate your concern, it's just that I can take care of myself."

"Okay."

"He's also a weird guy. Not very big, but he is potentially dangerous. Wife beater. Real nice guy. You may have just given him something that will fester."

"Uh-huh. Who is he?" Hunter asked.

"Oh, his name is Harry Jukes. Does some trapping. Runs a bulldozer for Clayton Construction now and then. Used to be a stock car mechanic in Alabama or someplace."

"Has he ever given you any trouble before?"

"The regular low-key anticonservation stuff his kind gives all the conservationists around here. He must have been drunk tonight. I really don't think he'll bother me again."

"Well, I won't butt in again, and I don't think you need any help, but, if you do, let me know. You can count on me, MaryAnne."

"Thanks, Jack. I'm sorry I grumped at you." She set out another beer. "This one's on the house. Friends?" She put out her hand.

"Friends," Hunter said, taking her hand. The calluses and muscle behind the squeeze were surprising. This was one hell of a woman. He took a drink. "I'll have to get Jukes to come in more often."

"Please don't!"

"Where'd you learn that little trick with his thumb?"

She smiled. "The winter nights in Fairbanks are long. And the drunks can be insistent. I took a couple of martial arts classes for both reasons. Besides, I was a gymnast in high school, and I still work out, so I probably can beat most men at arm wrestling."

"I'm not sure I'd want to try."

"Oh, you never know. I *might* let *you* beat me."

Hunter laughed.

She reached over and felt his upper arm. "Actually, you could probably win if I played fair, if I didn't cheat. Of course, I know lots of ways to cheat. That's necessary when you're as small as I am." She flexed her arm. "Wanna feel mine?"

Hunter wrapped his hand around her arm—the fingers failed to close the gap by several inches. It was carved out of marble by a long-dead Greek. "Hooee! You are a strong little fart."

"Don't you forget it." Her sweet smile either belied or underscored the words. Hunter wasn't sure which.

Outside, Venus followed the sun across the Pacific. Inside, MaryAnne and Hunter continued to talk, laugh, drink beer, and flirt. Jukes was forgotten. Hunter's plans for soaking out his stiffness in the hot springs were laid aside. He was soaking out plenty of stiffness on the bar stool in Underwood's this night.

A couple of hours after the dance with Jukes, Hunter looked at the bar clock and said, "Well, I guess I could stay up all night talking to you, MaryAnne, but I better head home while I can still drive."

She looked at the clock behind the bar. "On slow nights I close at midnight, so I'll let you be my last customer."

"Let me get rid of the last of my beer." He headed for the john.

MaryAnne turned off the outside lights. Hunter came back to the bar.

"How about next Friday to shoe my horse?" she asked.

Hunter peeled his Day-Timer out of a back pocket and looked at the date. He jotted down a note. "Yeah, that's fine. Where do you live?"

"You don't know where the old Delaney place is?"

"Roughly."

"I'll draw you a map." She took his Day-Timer. "Pretty organized for a horseshoer."

"A constipated habit I picked up in Washington."

She handed back the Day-Timer newly inscribed with a map to her house—and her phone number.

He looked at it. "Yeah, I can find it. No sweat. Oh," he said as he slid off the bar stool to go, "I came in here originally to buy a bottle of gin, and I guess I got sidetracked talking to a pretty bartender. I s'pose I best get that gin now. Tanqueray."

She fetched him the bottle and took his money. "Don't forget next Friday now."

"Don't worry, I'll be there."

"I know how notoriously undependable you horseshoers are."

"I'll make a special effort." Hunter was in a state of beery indecision. What would Miss Manners say? Do you tip the bartender when she is first an old friend and is second the bartender? When you're not quite sure where things might head in the future . . . ?

"G'night, MaryAnne. It was great to run into you again." He left the couple of bucks change from the gin on the bar.

"It was nice to see you again, Jack. I hope I don't have to wait so long to see you the next time."

"The pleasure was all mine, my dear." He made an exaggerated bow and swept off his hat. "And you won't have to wait long until I come calling."

"Get out of here," she laughed, and turned to lock up the night's take in the cracker-box safe.

Hunter's hackles rose as he pushed open the screen door. Outside, the night was clear and moonless. An ocean spray of stars washed overhead. The air was still warm. He pushed the heebie-jeebies out of the way. Just the change in temperature from the coolness of the bar, he reckoned. Almost—but not quite—relaxed, Hunter sauntered to his truck. Rolling with the looseness of a beer drinker, he hummed a Marty Robbins tune with questionable accuracy and twirled his keys.

Then—there it was. In the farthest corner of his field of vision, he caught the motion in the shadows to the left. He spun—something grazed his straw hat and knocked it to the ground—and the Tanqueray bottle in his left hand shattered into another galaxy of stars. A man went down. Hunter's spin took him two-thirds of the way around to his starting place.

A large shape moved on what had been his right, but was now his left. Hunter folded his keys into his right fist and waded into it. He felt a glancing punch on his face. Hunter buried his fist halfway to the elbow in Big Boy's tummy. Big Boy sagged to his knees like a poleaxed steer. Hunter swung both hands together from on high to chop him behind the ears. Big Boy melted into the parking lot.

Hunter dimly saw a third form hurtling at him. The man looked small. It was too dark for anything fancy, so Hunter just ran into him. He flattened the man. Before this one could get up, Hunter wheeled around in the parking lot gravel, lost his balance, but caved in the little guy's ribs with a boot before he sat down hard. There was a "whoof" as the air left the other man's lungs.

The outside light blazed on. Hunter clambered to his feet. The third man—Jukes—was on his hands and knees. Hunter grabbed for his greasy hair, but he scurried away like a stray dog. Hunter was left with the picture of Jukes's cur face.

The melee was over. It had taken fewer than thirty seconds. MaryAnne was beside him, a snub-nosed .38 in her hand.

"Are you okay?"

Hunter was breathing heavily. Beer and adrenaline rampaged through his arteries like elephants drunk on village hooch in Assam. He checked the bodies. "Looks like Jukes and some friends tried to jump me." He toed the first man with his boot. "I seem to have wasted my gin on this poor bastard."

MaryAnne, still covering the scene with her revolver, looked at the poor bastard. "Wow. Charley Rath."

Hunter looked at him again. He was a good-sized young man—nearly as big as Hunter—but his pimples said he was barely out of high school. He was out cold. "I'll bet that Tanq's going to sting in all those little cuts on his face when he comes to."

MaryAnne took Hunter's hand and stood by his side. "You're going to be a legend in your own time after taking out these lugs. Charley is the local brawler. And Jukes and the other guy, Onis Luebner," she gestured with the gun toward Big Boy, "aren't practicing Quakers either."

Hunter realized for the first time what a short little shit she was—a foot under his six-foot-two.

She turned to look at the champ. "Jack, you're hurt." She put the gun back in her fringed leather purse, took out a handkerchief, and dabbed at his lip. She showed him the blood. "And look at the back of your head. There's blood there, too."

"That must be what's causing the ringing in my ears. I thought it was 'cause you were standing so close to me."

"You're hopeless."

"Luebner managed to get in one punch, I guess." Hunter rubbed his chin and looked at the big man on the ground. He picked up a two-by-four among the shards of bottle glass. "Charley tried to get me first, nearly did." He tossed the stick, picked up his crunched hat, and tried to reshape the crown. "Hell's bells and little bitty pissants. Looks like I might have to get a new hat."

"Oh, it just gives it more character," MaryAnne said.

"If you say so." He shrugged and put the hat on. "Guess we better get out of here before these bullyboys come to. I'm no barroom brawler like Bill Crawford. Heck, this is about the only fight I've been in since high school. I must've been lucky. I don't know if I could do a repeat performance. You might have to shoot 'em."

"Are you sure you're okay? Maybe you should come home with me and let me doctor up your wounds?"

"Naw, I'm all right. It's no worse than what I'll probably get every day shoeing horses." He kicked himself for not taking MaryAnne up on her offer. He would have with any other reasonably attractive woman. He didn't quite understand things tonight.

"Are you sure?" she asked.

"Yeah, I'll wait till you get things locked up and are in your Jeep, though. I don't think we'll have any more trouble, but there's no use taking chances."

MaryAnne turned off the outside light, locked the front door, and allowed Hunter to walk her to her Jeep. She quickly kissed him on the cheek before getting into it. "I'm sorry to have caused you all this trouble."

"Don't be sorry. I had a wonderful time. Heck, I kicked the daylights out of three jerks. It was terrific. Besides I even got a kiss from a pretty girl." He kissed her cheek just as quick, turned, and walked a less-than-straight line back to his truck.

"Don't forget our horseshoeing date," she called.

4

Mormon settlers had named Hellsgate. It was the gash the Rio Diablo cut through the western face of the Diablo Mountains. To the latter-day saints, the towering pink and gray pillars of rock had marked a portal into another world—a passage from civilization to wilderness, a frontier between Man and Nature, between will-of-the-land and human will.

After leaping free of the mountains, the Rio Diablo meandered to the southwest, creating a mellow valley that had welcomed settlers. Northwest of the valley lay Cat's Paw Mesa—a sweep of grama grass, mesquite, and juniper running up to the toe of the mountains. Southeast of the valley were ridges and canyons spilling off the Apache Peaks—Nana, Victorio, Cochise, and Geronimo. The Apache Peaks rose a mile above the 4,500-foot elevation of the valley. Like Hellsgate, they blocked human ambitions. Behind them, the never-glaciated, rounded summits of the Diablo high country stretched up another 1,500 feet to top out at 11,000 feet.

The mountains, the river valley, and the surrounding benches and mesas were all part of the Diablo National Forest. In the river valley and nearby benchlands, fewer than a dozen square miles were privately owned. The rest was National Forest land, owned by all Americans, yet nearly all of it was under lease to eleven local ranchers, the biggest chunk to Buck Clayton.

Alfalfa fields, trailers, old homesteads, and the village of Rio Diablo (all on the scattered tracts of private land) elbowed their way into a lush deciduous forest along the river. In this river *bosque*, Fremont cottonwood, Arizona sycamore, Arizona walnut, netleaf hackberry, and Goodding willow grew rank. Actually, the trees only seemed to flourish; along much of the stream ever-present cattle nipped off the tender new shoots of cottonwood, willow, and sycamore as favored delicacies—"ice cream" species in the formal lingo of range science. Few new trees grew to replace the hoary sages nearing bosky senescence. Big live oaks— specifically Arizona white oak—grew back from the river at the base of the bordering mesas and benches. Mesquite and juniper drifted down into the lowlands on the flanks of the hills and terraces.

Along the escarpment of Cat's Paw Mesa, deep erosion channels cut the conglomerate, a mixture of ancient river cobbles not quite munched into rock but not loose gravel either. Red and white cliffs rain-sculpted into Spanish ruins sprouted helter-skelter in the foothills of the Apache Peaks.

A highway ran west through the valley from road's end at Hellsgate. Downstream and west of town, a small concrete irrigation ditch paralleled the road. Water trickled from it down rows in bright green alfalfa fields between the ditch and the river. Big gray clumps of chamisa and spiky stalks of yellow-flowered flannel mullein grew along the roads. Heavy equipment had been at work in the bed of the Rio Diablo, like biker elephants rampaging on methamphetamines, leaving dikes of cobble and bulldozed earth.

A band of Mormon pioneers had founded the village of Rio Diablo. They spent five years fending off the Apaches. They outlasted Victorio, the last Apache war chief except for Geronimo. But when the United States had established a gentile government, they packed up their families of many wives and many times as many children and trailed south to Chihuahua and a new Zion. Thus they left Rio Diablo to the Texans and their cows.

Through the mid-twentieth century Rio Diablo plodded along as a ranching center and a bucolic resort. An airstrip on Cat's Paw Mesa brought in well-heeled vacationers from the East Coast and California—including a few movie stars and the owner of a major league baseball team—to the

Rio Diablo Lodge at the upstream end of the valley beside Hellsgate. They came for refined rusticating—pack trips, fishing, hunting, barbecues, and soaking in the hot springs.

The lodge had closed by the late 1960s. Retirees trickled into the valley. They bought acre and half-acre lots in the bosque, built little houses, or set up mobile homes. Carved bleach bottles twirled on their fences. Pink flamingos staked down their lawns. Fruit trees, flower beds, gardens, and a few horses further civilized their ranchettes. In the 1970s, a couple dozen back-to-the-landers moved to the valley. "Hippies," the locals called them.

Three hundred people lived in the fifteen-mile-long Rio Diablo Valley. The 1900 census had tallied five hundred.

Five miles downstream from Hellsgate, where the narrow state highway crossed Calkin Creek over an even narrower bridge, was downtown. The Rio Diablo store, motel, cafe, and trailer park were on the downstream side of the bridge. A quarter mile up the river and highway was the Underwood establishment of trading post, motel, and bar. The village's second bar, the Hereford, was across the street from the Rio Diablo Cafe. It was seedier than Underwood's Beer Joint and drew the rowdies. The Rio Diablo Cafe was the only restaurant in town, although an elderly couple ran a "Snack Shack" in one of the outlying suburbs down the valley. Underwood's Beer Joint had kitchen facilities, but, other than burgers and sandwiches for lunch, hadn't served regular meals in five years.

Jack Hunter's place was north of the highway and across the river on a bench hard against the cliffs of Cat's Paw Mesa. He was a couple of miles west of the village of Rio Diablo. He got up early the morning after meeting MaryAnne McClellan. He had some packing to do—packing he should have done the night before.

The experts who write books on wilderness travel warn against going alone. They tout pricey tents, high-tech internal-frame packs, and gas stoves that roar like Navy jets taking off to smart-bomb Baghdad.

Jack Hunter shucked such advice. This morning, he went down a typed list and checked off each item as it went into its comfy spot in his old, reliable, external-frame Kelty backpack. For food, Hunter took jerky, raisins, nuts, sunflower seeds, whole wheat crackers, and dried fruit. The pack weighed fifty pounds—25 percent of Hunter's weight.

Thus outfitted, he drove eight miles east, where the state highway dead-ended at U.S. Highway 666. Down the river from the 666 bridge into Arizona, the Rio Diablo boxed itself off from civilization once again.

Forty-five miles southeast of the junction was Platoro, the county seat of Cobre County—the county south of Fall, but here Hunter turned north. Thirty miles north of the junction was the Fall County seat, Homestead. With three times the population of Rio Diablo, Homestead was the big town for sprawling, lightly populated Fall County. A sawmill in Homestead was the largest employer in the county, except for the Forest Service.

Ten miles up 666, Hunter took a Forest Service road to the east that switchbacked up the mountains. After following it for twenty-five miles, he came to the little-used Kezar Creek trailhead on the north side of the Diablo Wilderness Area (elevation: 9,128 feet).

One hundred yards down the trail from the parking area stood a wooden sign reading "Diablo Wilderness Area." Beside it was a small metal sign declaring the area beyond closed to motorized vehicles. Hunter put his hand on the wooden sign, breathed in the must of old-growth spruce-fir forest, and whispered, "God, it's good to be home." After three years of roaming the world, of seeking adventure in rainforest, tundra, steppe, and high peaks, he was back home to the mountains that claimed his heart.

He was free for a week. Alone and with nothing to cook, he had no need to build a fire. A ground cloth and tarp would do if it rained, and that was unlikely in June. The remote spring where he planned to camp tonight was twelve miles away—not a tough walk for Hunter.

He turned onto the well-trodden Diablo Crest Trail after five miles. The topographic map said the elevation was now 10,560 feet. He needed to backtrack on the crest trail for two miles to find a minor trail that led east and downhill to Mondt Park, twenty-seven trail miles away. A hundred yards down the crest trail, he heard a party of other backpackers. Hunter slipped off-trail and hid behind the trunk of a fat fir. After they passed, he hustled on, hoping he could steer clear of other hikers until he got to the overgrown route away from the crest trail. Humans were not what he was seeking on this trip.

At the beginning of the trek, worries settled down on Hunter's head like vultures on a giant cardón cactus outside a Sonoran chicken farm. They rolled in rhythm with his steps and ate the miles beneath his feet. There was much to chew on. Home, for one. Had he come home? How long would it last?

But hungrier vultures waylaid him in the dusty backways of his mind. They were the vultures he had met as he had tramped through the wild places of the world.

In his mind, they played rat-a-tat-tat like a film by Godfrey Reggio, music by Philip Glass. The Virunga volcanoes in Rwanda, home of the mountain gorilla: Peasants swarm like machete-stingered bees up the slopes. The great Amazon rainforest of Rondônia in Brazil: Ranchers burn thousands of hectares like suburbanites torching fall leaves. The stinking back alleys of Kuala Lumpur in Malaysia: Rotten-toothed hustlers hawk rare birds, cats, monkeys, and snakes like dope peddlers outside an inner city high school. Bustling ports in Sarawak, British Columbia, and Australia: Japanese freighters load up wood chips and thousand-year-old logs like Valley Girls with credit cards at a shopping mall. The killing fields of Kenya and Zaire: Tuskless elephants are strewn about like victims of a shooting spree at an Oklahoma post office. The high polar sea turned blood red: Degenerate sons of the Vikings hack whales into tatsuta-age. School lunches in Japan. The sea blood red . . . *the blood-dimmed tide*. The world was falling apart.

Everywhere people, people, people. Twice as many today as the day Hunter was born. Most now under twenty years of age. Girls and women with swollen bellies bringing death to the planet. Boys and men chalking up their rank by the number of women they pump up with their pricks.

Behind it all, the grow, grow, grow economies of industrialized nations, mainlining oil, soybeans, beef, pulp, and aluminum like junkies in Zurich's Platzspritz.

Global industrial civilization is a culture of teenaged boys, for teenaged boys, and by teenaged boys. It *is* a teenaged boy. Horny. Hungry. Heedless. Today and only today.

Hunter stopped. He stood in a blue-green-gold meadow of Rocky Mountain iris and goldenpea. Aspen, spruce, and fir fringed it; the sky formed a dome of bright blue overhead.

Somewhere Hunter had read of the psychological numbing that happens when one stands before an immense evil—like the Holocaust. Hunter had so diagnosed himself. The pillaging of the diversity of life was an evil that dwarfed even Hitler's.

Hunter had misdiagnosed himself, however. He was not numbed. Instead he was hypersensitive. He could not read an article or look at photographs about ancient forest logging in Oregon, rhino slaughter in Kenya, or drift netting in the North Pacific. . . .

He chewed on the horror. The horror. The heart of darkness he had found was not the swallowing jungle seen from a steamer on the river

Congo, but the baked, stripped hell brought by Komatsu, Stihl, and semen. The heart of darkness was not held by wilderness, but lurked in the breasts of men and women.

Finally after two days, the routine of the trail seeped into his bones, the wildwood grabbed his heed, and the cares of the world slipped away. He busied himself with birds—Williamson's sapsucker, western pewee, red-faced warbler, sharp-shinned hawk, and flowers—rattlesnake orchid, orange sneezeweed, and columbine. The track of a mountain lion.

But for one, the haunts in his head were gone.

This phantom of delight came in the evenings after dinner.

Hunter sat on his sleeping pad and used his sleeping bag in its stuff sack against a tree as a backrest. It was the time for judging the tonality of owl hoots, counting the stars, and smoking a cigar. In the chilly mountain air, he wore all the clothes he had with him.

Five foot two and eyes of green. Doesn't rhyme. But sure does dance.

According to psychologist Julian Jaynes, one's consciousness can be thought of as a homunculus analog of oneself who dwells in the bony penthouse in the head, who peers out at the world from that room with a view. Hunter bought this individualistic model (he may have been alienated from Western Civilization, but he was *of* it). The cranky little man in his skull was used to being alone. Memories of other people were played as if on a movie projector.

But this person—this MaryAnne McClellan—had boldly waltzed into the manikin's quarters, into Hunter's braincase, and had claimed it as her dance studio. When Hunter's homunculus wanted to sit back in smoking jacket and overstuffed chair and enjoy his solitude while carping at Hunter's moral failures, this creature, this invader, this diva, came pirouetting through. Disturbing. Damned rude. But enthralling.

Most folks from Rio Diablo motored down 666 every week or two to shop at Safeway, K-Mart, Yellow Front, and the local stores in Platoro. A couple of years earlier, an article in one of the Albuquerque dailies had called Platoro a "K-Mart Kind of Town."

The scene of downtown Platoro skated across MaryAnne McClellan's irises as she drove through. Platoro was no longer a K-Mart kind of town, she thought. The new Wal-Mart and Albertson's blob on the eastern outskirts had not killed downtown. Something in fading mining towns called to artsy folks. Maybe it was because such towns are quaint and have cheap Victorian houses, she thought, or maybe it was because mines happened where minerals happened, which was pretty country.

Some of MaryAnne's conservation colleagues mourned the recent gentrification of Platoro. It had brought more people—Californians and other yuppies. But, MaryAnne thought, these new folks were drawn by the quality of life afforded partly by the nearby Diablo Wilderness Area. They were not in search of jobs at the smelter, in the mines, on ranches, or at the lumber mill seventy-five miles away in Homestead. They had brought tony subdivisions to the outskirts of town. Downtown now hosted art galleries, Indian craft stores, a bed and breakfast, and a bistro serving cappuccino—yes, cappuccino in Platoro, she smiled. Even a New Age crystal shop. But, more important to MaryAnne, they had also brought a recycling center, a backpacking shop, a natural foods store . . . and a budding change in the political and social climate. MaryAnne knew that many of the new residents and business owners supported the Wilderness Area, and did not kowtow—or should it be *cow*tow?—to the ranching, logging, and mining gentry. Platoro was eons behind Telluride—thank goodness!— and it would never be a Moab, but it was becoming part of the New West.

She wondered if the change would be enough to save the wilderness. Or would the newcomers destroy what had brought them to Platoro?

Her thoughts skipped like a stone on a pond when she saw the Diablo National Forest headquarters—a modern version of a Quonset hut. Surrounded by asphalt, it sat on the northern edge of Platoro, where tentacles of blacktop reached out to new subdivisions and trailer parks. A new hospital sprawled on the other side of the boulevard.

He was waiting in the parking lot, leaning against his motorcycle, when MaryAnne drove up.

We tend to disparage the Neanderthal, she thought as she parked, use them as the butt of our jokes—an example of dull-wittedness; but *Homo sapiens neanderthalensis* was of our species, their blood still flows in our veins, their heritage is in our hearts, many of us carry their bones in our faces. Neanderthals were artists, had religion, loved those close to them; indeed, their brains were larger than ours today. Physical anthropologists tell us that if we could take a family of these old ones, shoe their feet, enclose their frames in modern synthetics, brush their hair, and set them loose on our busy sidewalks, they would go unnoticed, would blend comfortably into the herd.

Bill Crawford was a Neanderthal, thought MaryAnne. The forces that had shaped him had reached darkly out of the repressed memory of the past along thin strands of DNA and had touched him in his mother's womb. The large head, heavy brow, generous molars, strong jaw, and robust frame marked him as a descendant of those who were no more—of those who as a race preceded the cave bear into the darkness. This stubby, callused finger from the last ice age had touched more than his physique alone, for his pulsing eye watched the passage of night stars, his watchful ear heard the distant call of goose music, his listening heart felt the deep tug of the full moon. Like a sixteen-and-a-half-inch shirt on his nineteen-inch neck, civilization fit him too tightly.

"Bill!" MaryAnne took the big guy's arm in hers. "You are so *de-boner* and *swa-vay!*"

Bill Crawford looked down on her from his considerable height. "Now what did I do?"

"You are just so cool in your nerd glasses!" She flipped the clip-on sunglasses up onto his forehead.

"Nerd glasses, huh? My damn prescription sunglasses have a stupid red tint that screws up all the natural colors, so I'm just using these clip-ons on my regular glasses now." He turned them back down. "Anyway, when you look through a camera with a polarizing filter on it and you have on sunglasses, it's really weird, so I can just flip these guys up and look through the camera and still get things in focus. . . ."

"Bill! You don't have to justify your nerd glasses to me. I think you're cute in them, buckaroo. Really! Especially when they're flipped up." She flicked them up again. "Then you look like some really monstrous insect. Something out of an old Japanese horror movie—or that one where the man turned into a fly. . . ."

Bill Crawford had been putting up with this crap from Phil McClellan's daughter for twenty years. He loved it.

"Shall we?" MaryAnne asked. She took his arm in hers, and steered him into the National Forest office.

Bill clomped along. "I hate having to see that asshole Cooter."

MaryAnne smiled up at him. "Believe me, Bill, Bob Cooter hates seeing us more than you hate seeing him." She thought back to an earlier meeting with the supervisor of the Diablo National Forest when Bill had said, "Bob, it's time to bury the hatchet. In your head." MaryAnne grinned at the memory. Bob Cooter had only been able to respond with nervous laughter. As she thought about the forest supervisor, she realized that she could never remember what he looked like until she saw him again. Cooter was a person of no color, she thought, his eyebrows and eyelashes were invisible. The thin hair on his head was the hue of sun-bleached straw.

As supervisor of the 3.5 million acre Diablo National Forest, Bob Cooter had a private office at the forest headquarters. His secretary was a standard issue matron that all forest supervisors seemed to have. She announced Dr. MaryAnne McClellan and Bill Crawford at Cooter's door and ushered them inside.

"Hello, Bob," MaryAnne said and offered her hand.

He jumped to his feet from behind his desk to take her hand. "Well, it's nice to see you, MaryAnne. You always make my day." A look of disappointment crossed his face. "And you brought Bill along, too. How are you doing, Bill?"

Without a word, Bill Crawford crushed the proffered hand in his paw.

Cooter quickly turned back to MaryAnne McClellan and indicated a seat for her. "Well, what can I do for you today? I suppose you're in to try to convince me to sell more timber?" He laughed.

Bill Crawford glared at Cooter. He flipped up his clip-on sunglasses and leaned back in the chair he had taken.

MaryAnne smiled and said, "No, Bob, I'm afraid not. We'll leave that to the logging companies. Or have they been in asking for more Wilderness?" She made sure that the loose skirt of her summer dress covered her crossed knees.

Cooter forced a laugh. "Very good, MaryAnne."

MaryAnne regretted wearing a summer dress. It wasn't low-cut by any stretch of the imagination (except Cooter's?), but it left her collarbones bare. She could feel Cooter trying to look down it. That made her skin crawl.

She switched to her professorial voice. "Actually we're here to check with you on two issues. First, how is the reconsultation with the U.S. Fish and Wildlife Service going to be handled? Are you going to declare a moratorium on road construction and logging in the Mondt Park area while the northern goshawk, southwestern willow flycatcher, and Goodding's onion are considered for Endangered Species listing, and while you consider the impact of roading and logging on the now-listed Mexican spotted owl and Diablo trout? Second, we're interested in how your study of additions to the Diablo Wilderness Area is going."

The last got Cooter's attention off her chest. His eyes popped up to her face. "The what?" His voice squeaked in surprise.

MaryAnne said matter-of-factly, "Your review of roadless areas that could be added to the Diablo Wilderness Area. Surely you've received the directive from the assistant secretary of agriculture—Dennis Wilson? We're hoping you will use this opportunity to recommend the addition of the entire Mondt Park–Davis Prairie area to the Wilderness." She pinned him with her eyes.

The forest supervisor nodded his head a little too rapidly. "Oh, I understand what you're talking about now. But you're making it a much bigger deal than it really is. We *are* taking a look at possible additions. It's been nearly twenty years since Congress established the Diablo Wilderness, and we thought we might want to make some minor boundary adjustments—based on current needs and data, including Mexican spotted owl habitat requirements. But, no, it certainly isn't any major review. I don't foresee any large changes. I really think you're reading more into it than you should."

MaryAnne pursed her lips and waited five seconds before responding. "Hmm. That's interesting. That's a different interpretation than we received from the assistant secretary's office last week."

Cooter tried to affect a breezy manner. "Actually, this whole review came out of this office. Yes. I suggested it to the regional forester, as a matter of fact. But it really is nothing significant. We're simply trying to respond to new concerns and information. I don't think it will involve more than five thousand acres, if that."

MaryAnne looked up from her notebook—she was trying to get Cooter's words down verbatim. Tiny beads of sweat had broken out on his pate. "Hmm. Who's in charge of the study?" she asked.

"Huh? Oh, Donita Pacheco, our recreation and lands staff gir—uh, person . . . officer. You know Donita, don't you?"

"Yes."

"Good. You should drop in and see her about it today. She'll be happy to have your input. Though, again, I warn you, don't build this review up any more than . . ."

MaryAnne broke in and said, "To be perfectly honest with you, Bob, we're worried that the Forest Service is trying to obfuscate efforts to enlarge the Diablo Wilderness. From a biological diversity standpoint, it's vital for the Wilderness Area to include the prime wildlife habitat of the old-growth ponderosa pine forest in Mondt Park and the high-elevation grasslands of the Davis Prairie country. Stowe Creek, in that area, has documented southwestern willow flycatcher nesting and supports the healthiest population of Diablo trout. Mondt Park is the best habitat in the Southwest for the endangered southern population of the northern goshawk. . . ."

"The goshawk has not been designated as an Endangered Species yet," Cooter interjected. "Although it may be in a decline, the Forest Service does not believe it merits listing under the Endangered Species Act. None-theless, we are currently modifying timber harvest practices to protect the bird, even though our biologists believe that logging improves hunting conditions for the goshawk."

MaryAnne didn't lose her beat. "Most biologists disagree with the Forest Service position on the goshawk. Breeding pairs in New Mexico and Arizona have declined to only 122 at the government's last count. The Diablo Wilderness Committee is joining with Forest Guardians, the Platoro Audubon Society, the Southwest Center for Biological Diver-sity, and other groups to sue the Fish and Wildlife Service to force listing and to halt all Forest Service timber sales in old-growth ponderosa pine. The regional forester's guidelines for goshawk management are bio-logically unsound. They disregard the concerns of the U.S. Fish and Wildlife Service, the New Mexico Department of Game and Fish, and the Arizona Game and Fish Department. Independent scientists have blasted them."

At least Cooter isn't trying to look down my dress anymore, she thought. She glanced at Bill Crawford. She could almost hear him pop his jaws at Cooter. She was sure Bill had noticed Cooter trying to cop a glance. Bill was an expert in such things. And when he was playing mean as he was now, he looked like the villain in those old Popeye cartoons. Bluto— had that been his name? Or was it Brutus?

That chain of thoughts took only a second. MaryAnne continued, "We are very concerned about the road building and logging planned for Mondt Park and Davis Prairie, and we are determined to stop it. With its high populations of elk, pronghorn, and mule deer, it's the best potential wolf habitat on the Diablo National Forest, and is absolutely critical for successful reintroduction of the Mexican wolf in the Southwest. We think that this review called by the assistant secretary of agriculture is a perfect opportunity to expand the Wilderness to better protect . . ."

Cooter broke in. "Excuse me, MaryAnne. You—and Bill—know that I am a strong supporter of the Wilderness idea and of the Diablo Wilderness in particular. To be perfectly honest with you, I think that Congressman Pugh would not be trying to declassify the Diablo Wilderness Area at this point in time if it hadn't been for your extreme proposal to add additional productive forest to the Wilderness. Now, you know what the current attitude is about Wilderness. After this spring's flood on the Rio Diablo. With concern for sawmill jobs. And—the fact is—the timber in the area you propose to add to the Wilderness is needed to keep the mill in Homestead running. I am very worried that support for Wilderness is evaporating. People are tired of insignificant species like the goshawk standing in the . . ."

"Bob! The goshawk is not insignificant."

"Of course it isn't, MaryAnne. At least I don't think it is. I meant that the people of this area who depend on the National Forest for their livelihood—loggers, ranchers, miners, trappers—believe that it and other species no one even knew the name of a decade ago are standing in the way of their efforts to make a living. This goshawk thing—and the Mexican spotted owl—could explode into something like the northern spotted owl controversy in Oregon and Washington. I'm afraid that we might not be able to retain protection for the current Diablo Wilderness Area, that we could end up with—not additions—but deletions. My best advice to you, MaryAnne and Bill, is to be happy with what you already have. Spend your energy fighting declassification. Don't push for more Wilderness."

Bob Cooter cleared his throat. He was on a roll. "Moreover, this talk about Mexican wolf reintroduction has the local ranchers and hunters concerned. Even parents here in Platoro are worried about their children being snatched out of their front yards. . . ."

"Bob! There has never been a documented account of a healthy wild wolf in North America killing a person. You know that. Or at least you should."

"That may be, MaryAnne. But you'll never convince the people of New Mexico of it. Face reality. The wolf is not going to be reintroduced into the Diablo. The more you talk it up, the more opposition you will build to Wilderness." Cooter reached out and touched MaryAnne's hand. "Tempers are running high. When proud men can't buy a new pickup truck because of a bird, there is no telling what might happen, who might become a scapegoat."

MaryAnne didn't wait for the forest supervisor to finish his speech. She pinned him down like a goshawk on a vole. She asked him for specifics on her two points: reconsultation with the U.S. Fish and Wildlife Service on logging of Mondt Park, and facts on the revision of the Forest Service study of Wilderness additions. Cooter squirmed out as much as he could from under her grasp. He said that Donita Pacheco would have the specifics.

MaryAnne thanked Cooter for his help. She and Bill took their leave and trooped off down a bureaucratic tunnel to the recreation and lands office.

Donita Pacheco was a slender, dark-haired young woman. She was shy, but had an air of efficiency. MaryAnne and Bill spent an hour with her going over details of the boundary revision study. They collected an armload of documents, and left her with a copy of the Diablo Wilderness Committee's latest map and a write-up of their proposal. MaryAnne pointed out to her that their new additions would enlarge the Diablo Wilderness Area from 803,000 acres to 1,118,000 acres and would close some minor dirt roads and jeep trails on the periphery.

Donita said, "It's a good proposal. But you may never get a chance to add it to the Wilderness." She lowered her voice. "Follow me," she said, and led MaryAnne and Bill back into a filing cul-de-sac. "No one can hear us here, if we keep our voices down. Listen," she whispered with intensity, "Cooter is doing everything he can to speed up road building and timber sales in Mondt Park to prevent its addition to the Wilderness Area. Road alignments have already been surveyed and internal timber sale analyses are being fast-tracked. I've been told, and the hydrologists and wildlife biologists on the Diablo National Forest have been told in no-uncertain terms, that our reports will show no significant impacts. One biologist who balked was transferred to shuffle papers in the Albuquerque Regional Office. Hey," she said, "it gets worse. Dr. George Tolisano was ordered off the Forest yesterday by armed law enforcement rangers on the technicality of not having a permit."

"Hardly any independent researchers have to get permits!" MaryAnne said. "Tolisano has the longest running goshawk research project in the Southwest. . . ."

"You're right," said Donita Pacheco. "The permit requirement is in the regulations. It's just usually ignored. In this case, he had an informal verbal agreement with the Forest. But when Cooter heard what Tolisano was going to recommend, he shut him down. Tolisano applied for a permit this morning, but Cooter denied it because of his previous 'violation' and the supposed threats he made. If Tolisano tries to do any more research on the Diablo National Forest, he'll be arrested."

"Good lord, Cooter's running a police state here." MaryAnne shook her head.

Donita nodded. "Try working for the Forest Service in the Southwest Region if you want to know what a police state is. Anyone who resists getting the cut out has their career ruined. Since we got our new regional forester—Donald Carlton—it's been unbelievable. We're essentially ordered to break the law—the National Environmental Policy Act, the Endangered Species Act, the National Forest Management Act, the Administrative Procedures Act, you name it. And—get this—Carlton is going to refuse to adopt the U.S. Fish and Wildlife Service management plan for the Mexican spotted owl, because it would restrict logging in New Mexico and Arizona. He just released to the timber industry a predecisional document from Fish and Wildlife. No one else got a copy, and the release was not authorized by Fish and Wildlife or by the Washington office of the Forest Service."

"Fuckers," Bill growled. "Uh, excuse me."

"That's okay," Donita said. "I feel the same way sometimes. I'm a professional. I take pride in my job. I want to be proud of the Forest Service. But this . . . I don't know what to do."

MaryAnne said, "I just received a copy of the letter Donald Carlton sent to the New Mexico and Arizona congressional delegations opposing Endangered Species listing for the owl, and encouraging them to work against it to save the timber industry in the Southwest."

Donita shook her head from side to side. "A lot of us are just lying low and waiting for the day when Carlton is gone as regional forester. Conservation groups and independent biologists like you have to throw every roadblock you can in his way. And, believe me, Cooter is his willing lieutenant." She sighed. "Just don't let anyone know you heard this stuff from me." She looked around to make sure they were still alone. Then she handed MaryAnne a stack of photocopied pages. "Here. This is the environmental analysis for the Bearwallow Timber Sale. This EA won't be released until next week, so don't let anyone know you have it yet."

MaryAnne and Bill quickly paged through it.

"*Goddamnit*," said Bill, "it's right up next to the Wilderness Area boundary!"

"That's the idea," Donita Pacheco said. "Punch a high standard log haul road in and do a major cut in the heart of Mondt Park, and any chance of adding it to the Wilderness evaporates. Cooter is going to run this EA through as fast as he can. Even if the road can't be completed by fall, trees will start falling."

"Oh, boy," MaryAnne said, "this is worse than I thought."

"Yeah, but, believe me," Donita said, "this EA is worthless. It can't stand up to an appeal. I think even a timber beast like Donald Carlton would have to stay the sale and order a full environmental impact statement if it's appealed."

MaryAnne set her jaw. "Don't worry; we'll appeal it. If necessary, all the way to the secretary of agriculture. And, if that doesn't work, we'll file suit."

"Good." Donita Pacheco handed her another binder-clipped stack of paper. "This might help. Burn it after you extract the information for your appeal. Some of us who wrote the Bearwallow EA have some ideas where its weak points are. Your appeal will stop any activity this year. A final EIS couldn't possibly be done until next year."

Outside in the parking lot after they had left Donita Pacheco, Bill flipped down his shades and snarled. "Jesus, I hate that Cooter. What a slimy asshole. He reminds me of a goddamn suppository. That's it—a suppository. He just sat there and lied to us. He's planning to cut the heart out of Mondt Park. What horseshit! We oughta get in there and rip out those survey stakes. We can't let them get a road in. . . ."

"I know that, Bill." MaryAnne cautioned him with her hand. "But hold off awhile. We can stop it this year with an appeal." She shook her head. "Whew! I wasn't thinking that the situation was as bad as Donita told us. Remember that we do have some influence with the new administration. . . ."

"Sure, sure," Bill snorted. "I even voted for the turkey-butt. An environmental president. Ha! And then he shafts us on grazing fees, mining royalties, and deficit timber sales. And now he's about to screw the ancient forests in the Northwest. Do you really think they'll pay any attention to something as remote as the Diablo? Do you really think this wimp administration is going to go to bat for Davis Prairie and Mondt Park?"

"We do have a hole card, Bill."

"Is it time to tell Fish and Wildlife about it?" he asked.

"Not yet, buckaroo. It's not safe to tell anyone else yet."

"You're the boss."

MaryAnne smiled. "That's how I like my men—obedient. Speaking of men, guess who came into Underwood's Beer Joint a couple of nights ago."

"Robert Redford."

"Somebody even cuter."

"Oh god, you aren't talking about Jack Hunter!"

"The same."

"He's not so cute. I'm cuter than he is."

MaryAnne stepped back, held her thumbs and forefingers in a square as if composing a photograph, and shook her head. "Bill, I have really bad news for you." She took his hand and looked glumly into his eyes. "You're sweet as a chocolate eclair. You have a good personality. But you aren't pretty."

5

Hunter plotted a route off-trail. It would take him across an area of the Diablo National Forest that few people—even serious hikers—knew. Hunter knew it. He and Bill Crawford had found it over twenty years ago when their college wilderness group had surveyed roadless areas on the Diablo National Forest. It was not a spectacular landscape in terms of scenery. Many hikers would have even found it dull: flat to rolling forest and high prairie. Jack Hunter knew better.

During the last two days, he had crossed the Diablo Mountains and dropped two thousand feet down their eastern slope. Now he was on the edge of a sprawling old-growth forest of ponderosa pine and Gambel oak: Mondt Park. This was where he'd been headed.

Hunter sat on a rock outcrop studying his map. He was in the middle of a roadless area more than a million acres in size. This wild fastness sprawled nearly seventy miles east-west and over thirty miles north-south; it was the biggest highland wilderness in the Southwest. The Diablo Mountains, to Hunter's back and right, made up the western and south-central part of the roadless area. Hunter looked east. Thirty miles away another mountain range—the Sierra Prieta—ran north-south and formed the eastern part of the roadless area. Mondt Park and Davis Prairie were the north-central section of the Diablo roadless area. The forks of the Diablo River gathered rain and snow from all directions of the high country; together as the Diablo River they cut a mighty canyon west through the Diablo Mountains.

While the entire roadless area was undeveloped and wild, part of it was wilderness with a small "w"—*de facto wilderness,* or wilderness in fact but not in law. Two-thirds of the roadless area, 803,000 acres, was designated as the Diablo Wilderness Area. Though the Wilderness Area was protected from roads and logging by Congress, the rest of the roadless area—including the northern two-thirds of Mondt Park and Davis Prairie—was run-of-the-mill National Forest land potentially open to "multiple-use"—roads, bulldozers, vehicles, and chain saws—and, according to MaryAnne McClellan, the bulldozers and chain saws were poised to invade. This galled Hunter. He had begun his conservation career fighting to include Mondt Park in the Diablo Wilderness Area, and the job still was not done. He counted it as a personal failure that the 1980 New Mexico Wilderness Act had not added the rest of Mondt Park to the Diablo Wilderness. That bill had protected seven new Wilderness Areas and had added land to four existing Wilderness Areas in New Mexico. But the New Mexico congressional delegation had shied away from making additions to the Diablo Wilderness Area. Now the local yahoos were scheming to take away protection for all of it and open it to roads, logging, and god-knows-what.

Despite its lack of full legal protection, Hunter knew that Mondt Park was the wildest part of the Diablo country, which made it the wildest mountain area in the Southwest. It was the center of Hunter's universe. And now it faced destruction.

Hiking through the park-like forest, Hunter came upon a herd of elk loafing in the tall grass and chewing their cuds. He recalled his first visit to Alaska, how, on a backpacking trip through Denali National Park, he had marveled at the bounty of large mammals—moose, caribou, Dall sheep, grizzly bears, gray wolves. Alaska had indeed been the Great Land. Then he had realized that wildlife wasn't that rife in Alaska, that Alaska actually was slim pickings for most critters, that it seemed to be teeming with wildlife only because animal numbers had dropped so sharply in the rest of the United States. Tell a tourist from Kansas—or Ohio, for crissakes!—that it hadn't been long ago that her state had more big game than Alaska, and she would laugh at you. But it was true.

Elk, for instance, thought Hunter. He knew that, once upon a time, there had been five subspecies of elk in North America. One, the Eastern elk, had ranged from Georgia to New York and west to the Mississippi. Despite its wide range and abundance, overhunting and destruction of its habitat by homesteaders and loggers had caused its extinction by the mid-1800s. Three of the elk subspecies survived, although the native tule elk of California was down to a scant sixteen hundred or so (but up from a paltry two hundred). The subspecies native to New Mexico and Arizona, Merriam's elk, had vanished forever as the nineteenth century became the twentieth—not because its habitat had been taken by homesteaders, but because professional hunters had shot it into nothingness to feed mining camps.

Hunter knew that the elk he watched were descendants of a small herd of Rocky Mountain elk from Yellowstone National Park introduced into the Diablo by the New Mexico Department of Game and Fish in the 1950s. He thanked nameless wildlife managers for bringing back the elk after the absence of half a century. But they had done something else, too, thought Hunter. The return of elk had a hidden boon that made Mondt Park the most pristine, healthy ponderosa pine forest in the Southwest. Yes, Mondt Park had never been logged. And, because of its remoteness, Smokey the Bear hadn't been able to keep all the natural, lightning-caused fires from burning. But the third factor in this equation was Mondt Park's healthy bunchgrasses—there had been no cattle here for nearly forty years because of elk.

He knew that about the time he was born, in 1953, the New Mexico Department of Game and Fish had bought the Mondt Ranch. Through negotiations with the Forest Service, the "animal unit months" allocated to cattle had been switched to elk. The state wildlife biologists had believed the survival of the transplanted elk depended on getting the cattle out in order to improve the forage.

Hunter left the elk, following his nose and his compass. Around him, the plate-barked yellow pines reached up 130 feet; some of the gnarled Gambel oaks touched fifty. Skeleton snags of the big trees—dead from age or lightning—were high-rise apartments for birds, insects, squirrels, and bats. When the snags finally found their angle of repose in the duff, the decomposers—fungi, bacteria, invertebrates, what-have-you—melted the carcasses back into the soil to make other trees and bloom the flowers. The journey took centuries.

In this natural forest it was easy to walk without a trail. The big trees grew wide apart. Fire thinned new sprouts. Bunchgrass and bracken fern brushed Hunter's thighs. A flock of wild turkeys scurried away; the tall grass hid all but their heads. Blooming lupine washed a blue tide through the forest. Hunter spooked a great horned owl from a branch. He stood in the silence of its flight.

The elevation dropped from 8,500 feet, the ponderosa pines became smaller, and the scattered Douglas-firs melted away. Smaller trees like alligator juniper—so-named for its rough, checkered bark—and Emory oak sifted up into the forest from lower elevations. Over a span of six miles the mesa ran down a thousand feet. Suddenly, a canyon broke the woodland. Its walls dropped five hundred feet to a fork of a fork of the Diablo River called Turkey Creek. Douglas-fir once again grew on the cool, north-facing side of the canyon. Hunter stood on a point of rock above where the canyon widened. A side stream—Stowe Creek—ran into it from the other side.

Hunter worked his way down the buttress of rock to the creek. He and Bill Crawford had camped in this spot in 1972. There was enough daylight left to hike two more hours, but this open streamside park of ponderosa pine and narrowleaf cottonwood was where he wanted to be. After sloughing his backpack, he found a huge cottonwood whose trunk and roots made a wilderness La-Z-Boy. He kicked back against the tree and inspected his home for the night.

Arizona alder and willow crowded the edge of the stream. Poison ivy girded it. Green gentian, larkspur, skyrocket, and tall green grass grew back from the stream in Stowe Creek Meadow. Dark piles of rich earth showed the soil-turning toil of pocket gophers. Like Mondt Park, this riparian meadow had been free of cows for Hunter's lifetime. There was no clover, thistle, or prickly poppy—the plants of cowed meadows. Acorn woodpeckers played flycatcher from a pine snag. Like tiny, feathered baleen whales, violet-green swallows scooped up aerial plankton. Hours later, owl hoots and the bounce of water over cobbles made a little night music. Hunter thought it the perfect campsite.

The next morning, he wandered a mile down Turkey Creek before he found a slope on the opposite wall that promised a route for a man laden with a backpack. The south-facing slope was dry—too dry for ponderosa, but ideal for brushy chaparral. The thick mountain mahogany and ceanothus were a bitch, even for a bushwhacker like Hunter. Though he had been out long enough to be moving like a resident cat, he was glad when he topped out and was back in the ponderosas.

At a little past noon, Hunter came out onto a rimrock. It was a high, windy place overlooking a vast and broken landscape. Twenty miles to the east, the Sierra Prieta walled the horizon. The pines along the ridge lulled him into laziness. Below was the cut of a dry drainage, and beyond was a rolling, grassy plain freckled with junipers and a few stubby ponderosas. Davis Prairie.

He worked along the ridge until a spot said lunch. He dropped his pack and peeled out of his sweat-drenched camouflage shirt. After hanging it and his equally damp boonie hat in the sun, Hunter nestled down into the carpet of needles shed by a wind-ripped Colorado piñon. He pulled off his boots, hung his socks to dry on piñon twigs, and propped up his feet. He leaned against his backpack, which leaned against the piñon trunk. An ancient world stretched out before him. It ran to the horizon and beyond. There was no spoor of Man. It was a landscape with a will of its own. Wil-der-ness: will-of-the-land.

Jack Hunter crunched his mixed nuts; MaryAnne McClellan danced through his skull. He tried to ignore her. A movement outside his head caught his eye. It was up a side canyon, across the dry stream, halfway up the slope leading to the tongue of the mesa. A deer? Hunter focused his binoculars on the place where the movement had occurred. No, it was a coyote . . . a coyote at her den! There were pups, too. Hunter had seen hundreds of coyotes, but never before had he been treated to watch their home life.

In the shadow beneath the piñon, he was screened so long as he was quiet and made no sudden moves. He unstrapped a lightweight tripod from the outside of his backpack and attached one of his cameras. Hunter was a serious photographer, though far from a Muench or Dykinga. He carried two 35-mm Olympus cameras—Olys because they were the lightest good cameras, and two so he could load one with slow 25 ASA Kodachrome for color-saturated scenics and one with fast 400 ASA Ektachrome for use with a telephoto. Hunter unscrewed the 70–210-mm zoom lens from the camera that had the faster film and screwed on a 500-mm telephoto lens. With the coyotes in the sunlight and with 400 ASA slide film in the camera, he figured he could get the shots he wanted. The coyotes wouldn't hear the shutter release thanks to distance and wind noise.

Hunter clicked off a few shots before he picked up his binoculars for a more leisurely view. He hadn't looked closely at them earlier. Now as he watched them, he realized something was amiss. This was the biggest coyote he had ever seen. There was a ruff of fur around her neck. Coyotes didn't have that. She had shorter, more rounded ears than the high, pointed ears a coyote had. He had first thought it a deer because this critter had much longer legs than a . . .

Ohmigod. These weren't coyotes. This was a lobo. A lobo and her den of pups.

Hunter lowered his glasses and stared, gape-jawed, where the wolves played. He didn't take a breath for at least a minute. He had never before been so stunned. Wolves.

Wolves hadn't lived in the Diablo for sixty years.

The chatter in his brain shut down. Nothing was abstract. Nothing was intellectualized. Hunter was no longer a Rational Man. He was an animal. His being was being. Not analyzing, not abstracting. Once again, he was truly alive, thoroughly in place. Being. Letting being be.

Hunter's homunculus did not stay quiet long, though. *What's going on here?* he asked. Not just a stray, solitary lobo wandering up from Mexico, this was a female with a den of pups. Four pups, he counted through the binoculars. That meant there was a male somewhere—probably out hunting. Sometime back in the early 1970s, a Mexican wolf had supposedly denned near San Luis Pass this side of the Mexican border in the Bootheel of New Mexico. But these wolves were one hundred and fifty miles north of there. There hadn't been a for-sure wolf sighting in the Diablo highlands since the mid-1930s. The federal government's Predatory Animal and Rodent Control pogrom had cleaned them out like Stalin had cleaned out the kulaks those same years. Species cleansing. Making the West safe for Herefords.

Hunter picked up the binoculars again. They had to be wolves. They weren't coyotes. Hunter called up the memories of all the gray wolves he'd seen—in Siberia; in the Boundary Waters of Minnesota; a fleeting glimpse in Slovakia; the unworried pack in Alaska's Arctic National Wildlife Refuge; the fleeing ghosts in India; the bored, neurotic ones in zoos; the photos in books; the diorama at the Smithsonian.

Wolf! *Canis lupus!*

The photos took on new weight. Hunter shot three rolls of thirty-six exposures, using both the zoom and the longer telephoto, bracketing exposures to ensure some perfectly exposed slides. The photo frenzy finished his 400, but there would be no wildlife sightings to compare with this on the rest of the trip. He also shot a series with his other camera using a normal 50 mm lens. The lobos would be mere specks in these slides, but the country they were in would be shown. He carefully marked his location and that of the wolves on the 1:24,000 scale U.S. Geological Survey topographic map covering this part of the Diablo. He saw from the map that the dry stream course was one of the headwaters of Stowe Creek.

When mama and pups went back into the den for an afternoon siesta, the little man in Hunter's head barked his order. *Okay, asshole, get out of here now before they come back out and see you.*

Hunter threw his gear into his pack and skedaddled over the ridge away from them. It would have been unforgivable to spook them by being there. If they saw or heard him, the mother wolf would possibly abandon the den and try to move her pups. He knew the stress could cause the loss of a pup or even of the whole litter. This litter of wolves had to be protected so it could form a pack and then grow large enough to break into two packs, then four, then . . .

The evidence from Glacier National Park in Montana in the late 1980s had shown that when gray wolves moved into unoccupied territory and were left alone, births soared, and the new wolves spread out to fill the habitat. Grizzly bears, on the other hand, were slow breeders and could not lift their cub production to take advantage of such a situation. Give wolves a chance, though, and their numbers and range would rebound with startling swiftness.

Hunter realized that this sighting, these slides, this marked map could well be the padlock to shut down the planned logging and road building for Mondt Park that Bill Crawford and MaryAnne McClellan were fighting. Wait until I show these slides to MaryAnne! he thought. She'll have a conniption fit.

Wolves.

Wolves. Hunter's head was awash with the thrill of his sighting as he headed through the huge, ancient trees of Mondt Park into the afternoon sun. With each step through the duff of the forest floor, through the tall grass and ferns and lupine, he spun webs of political strategy: how to use the presence of the wolves to halt all development in the area; how to get Senator Karl Reed to push for adding the wolf-occupied territory in the Diablo Wilderness and to kill Representative Pugh's declassification bill; how to keep the wolves alive and spreading. For the first time since leaving Washington, his conservation heart was pumping blood.

Certain happenings crystallize life and being. The senses climb from the dull plain of mere existence to a howling peak. The wolves had taken Jack Hunter to such a pinnacle. If there was a heaven, this was it. Like Blake's Maiden, the wolves had caught Hunter in the Wild.

The wolf sighting left Hunter soaring and wheeling and *quorking* like a raven in love. It came on the heels of a whole slew of uplifting tidbits: the out-of-the-blue roll in the hay with Jodi Clayton, the flirty evening with MaryAnne McClellan at Underwood's, the primeval jolt of the fight with the Jukes gang, a solitary week in the Wilderness, and further dreams of MaryAnne. Hunter picked at his thoughts and emotions like a scab. The wolves had left him in such a rare state, however, that he didn't try to tease out why he was flying. He was merely feeling good and rolling in it.

The return to his vehicle, to that token of the sights, sounds, smells of the everywhereness of civilized Humankind on the planet, was more painful than usual. After first sighting the truck at the trailhead, he turned around to look at the uncut, unroaded, undammed, untrammeled, unpeopled wilderness—the lobo's wilderness.

A few puffy little white cumulus clouds scouted the high country when Hunter came out to his truck. But later, down in the Diablo Valley, there was only blue, blue and lazy pink as the sun drifted low. The horizon puckered its lips and sucked the sun down into it.

Despite the dusk, Hunter had enough light to see the arrow in the old plank door of his adobe. What the hell? Geronimo had been taken into shackles more than a hundred years ago. The arrow pinned a note to the door. It wasn't from Geronimo, but it was from another tough customer.

Hi, Horseshoer:

Hope you got back safely from the mountains. City slickers like you should be careful about traipsing off into the wilderness alone. If you do make it back alive, though, why don't you come over after lunch on Tuesday to shoe my hoss and then we can run together (I know you run—I've been investigating you) and have a swim before I fix you one of my world-famous gourmet dinners?

MaryAnne

Jack Hunter read the note three times.

He fixed tacos for dinner. After a week of dried food, he needed a grease fix and his tacos—hamburger, onion, garlic, and lots of green chile, fried together, folded up with grated sharp cheddar cheese and sour cream in a soft-fried corn tortilla—were greasy. They were also *picante*. He drank a couple of Dos Equis with the tacos—nothing like good, dark Mexican beer to cut the grease off your teeth and quench the fire. Hunter had a four-star rating for New Mexican food: one, if his forehead sweated; two, if his eyes watered; three, if his nose ran; four, if he burned in the morning.

After dinner, he filled a tall glass with ice, squeezed in a quarter of a lime, splashed in two inches of gin, and topped it off with tonic water. He pulled out a good cigar—a Royal Jamaican Maduro, licked it down, and clipped the end. He pulled the dog-eared copy of Aldo Leopold's *A Sand County Almanac* from the bookshelf and went out onto the porch. There was no moon—the new moon was two days away by his reckoning. A host of stars floated over the dark bulk of the mountains. A great horned owl hoot tumbled down the rocky ridge behind the house. Its mate answered. Rodents surrounded. Hunter moved the rocking chair into the window light, leaned back, propped his feet on the porch railing, fired the cigar with a wooden kitchen match, and opened the book to "Thinking Like a Mountain."

In that short narrative, Leopold told about the wolf he had killed in Arizona's Apache National Forest in 1909. That killing ground was only fifty miles northwest of Rio Diablo, thought Hunter. It took no time to find the passage—he had marked it with a hi-liter when he had first read *A Sand County Almanac* twenty-one years ago as a freshman at the University of New Mexico. The print should have been fading from a thousand readings, but the words still stunned like the sudden strike of a snake.

> We reached the old wolf in time to watch a fierce green fire dying in her eyes. I realized then, and have known ever since, that there was something new to me in those eyes—something known only to her and to the mountain. I was young then, and full of trigger-itch; I thought that because fewer wolves meant more deer, that no wolves would mean hunters' paradise. But after seeing the green fire die, I sensed that neither the wolf nor the mountain agreed with such a view.

Those words brought the smell of the wolves back to Hunter's nostrils. He saw them frisking around the entrance to their den on the dry, grassy slope. He sent smoke rings up to the stars. He reveled in the sighting for long, nighttime minutes, sloshing it around in his mouth with the gin.

Wolves. I never thought I'd see them in the Diablo, he thought. *Good god. What to do?* If the ranchers found out about them, or the loggers, or the trappers, they would clean them out before the pups ever grew up to mate and produce pups of their own. The good ol' boys of Fall County sure as hell wouldn't worry about the Endangered Species Act.

The road into Mondt Park and Davis Prairie, and the logging to follow had to be stopped.

But this wasn't a fight for Hunter. He'd done his part. He'd tell MaryAnne and Bill about the wolves. They could handle it.

Jack Hunter threw the dead butt of his cigar into the night.

6

The sun came up, and Jack Hunter rolled out of bed. He puttered at putting away his backpacking gear. He cleaned house. Then he sat down at his desk and figured up the horses scheduled for the coming week.

He was due forty-five minutes of water from the irrigation ditch at 9:30 A.M. After a week of neglect and no rain, the garden looked like Ethiopia. He soaked the garden and then ran the water into a hidden ditch feeding back to the Rio Diablo. Two hundred yards of the stream flowed through his property. Hunter the farmer was growing willows, cottonwoods, loachminnows, leopard frogs, and willow flycatchers in addition to his salad. During the summer dry season before the monsoons, irrigation diversion dried up stretches of the river. By sending back most of his acre-feet, Hunter was keeping his part of the Rio Diablo alive. In New Mexico, this was illegal. Allowing water to run down a stream was not considered a "beneficial use" for one's water rights.

He champed at the bit the rest of the morning, feeling like a racehorse forced to pull a little old lady in her buggy to church. He threw his running shoes and shorts into the cab of the pickup, ate leftover tacos for lunch, scrubbed his teeth, and looked at the clock.

The sun had curled the leaves on the careless weed by the time he arrived at the old Delaney place. Nonetheless, it was cooler than a week ago. The deep heat of early June had broken while he had been in the high country; the temperature was down to a run-of-the-mill ninety-two or ninety-three for a high.

MaryAnne McClellan bounded down the porch steps of the old farmhouse when he parked his truck next to her Jeep. "Well, I thought you might not be coming, that you got lost in the mountains, or eaten by wolves or something," she said.

"Let me tell you something, darlin', about wolves." He put a foot up on the rear bumper of his truck and pushed back his hat with a haughty air. "I saw one . . ."

"What?" MaryAnne was slapped into momentary silence. She bounced back. "You saw a wolf? Where?"

"Not just a wolf. I saw a lobo at her den with four pups. Watched 'em for an hour or . . ."

"Are you sure they were wolves? It's easy to mistake coyotes for wolves at a distance."

Hunter smiled and shook his head. "No, they were wolves. I've seen wolves before. I've seen lots of coyotes. These weren't coyotes; they were lobos. I'd stake anything on it."

"Did they see you?"

"No. I was hidden in the shade of a piñon across the canyon. After they went back in their den, I left so I wouldn't disturb them."

"That's good. Where did you see them?"

"Up around Stowe Creek, off Turkey Creek, on Davis Prairie. Here, I marked it on the topo. I brought it along for you to see where they are."

She studied the map and chewed her lip.

"I tell you, MaryAnne, it was great! I've seen wolves pretty close in Alaska, and I had a short look at a couple in the Boundary Waters; I've seen 'em in Slovakia in Eastern Europe and had a really good look at a pack in Siberia, but here in the Diablo! And I had a great view of them. I shot four rolls of slides. . . ."

"You photographed them?"

"Yeah. I sent the film off today in mailers to Kodak."

"Oh, boy. Jack, please don't tell anyone else about this, and please don't show anyone but me your slides for now."

"Sure . . ."

"There have been some unconfirmed sightings of Mexican wolves in that area," she said. "We've been trying to investigate, but we've got to figure out how to use this in the best way to stop the logging in Mondt Park. Until then, we have to keep it absolutely quiet."

"That seems wise. As soon as I get the slides, I'll show them to you so you can confirm that they are wolves. But I'm sure they are. You're right, though. This kind of thing is a real wild card. We have to figure out how to play it right."

MaryAnne heard the "we" and smiled. Jack's newfound interest was a card to play wisely, too, she schemed. Bill Crawford had told her it would be like pulling hen's teeth to get Jack Hunter involved again. She had told him that they'd see about that. The wolves were obviously a hook.

Hunter continued, "It was the most surprising wildlife sighting of my life. Topped anything I saw in Africa for sheer shock. Even the jaguar I saw in Belize. I can hardly believe it—wolves in the Diablo."

Hunter's jaguar sighting galled MaryAnne. She'd give her eyeteeth to see a jaguar. "That's wonderful, Jack. You're really lucky. Well! Shall we get to work? The corral is this way."

Hunter followed MaryAnne to the corral. This woman was very good at running talk. She did not want to talk any more about the wolves, that was plain to see. This lured Hunter further.

There was other wildlife to ponder, though. In the sunlight she was even prettier than she had been behind the bar. Green ribbon tied her thick dark hair into twin ponytails. She wore running shoes, shorts, and a black jog bra. The outfit showed that she had a hellaciously fit body. Hunter noted that she shaved her legs and underarms. Another bonus point on his checklist.

"Well, how do you like him?" she asked.

Hunter looked at the animal. "Hell's bells. I thought you said you had a horse. This is a goddamned mule."

"Oh, did I say it was a horse?"

"You know damn good and well you did."

"It's all generic."

He lowered his eyebrows at her. She looked innocently at him from under hers.

"I ought to charge you extra," he huffed.

"Bill warned me that you were afraid of mules. Said they were too smart for you. Told me about Jumbo. . . ."

"I don't want to hear about Jumbo."

MaryAnne lifted her nose imperiously and continued. "Told me that this giant mule where he and you worked at a wilderness pack station in Wyoming took a dislike to you and constantly outsmarted you and went out of his way to get you."

"Humph."

"Said he ate your entire rain slicker once to get a Hershey bar you had rolled up in it. It rained the whole week you were out and you never were dry."

"I don't want to hear about Jumbo. I don't like mules."

"Zeke's a perfectly nice mule! Aren't you, sweetie?" MaryAnne hugged him. Zeke took a look at Hunter. "Watch. He's gentle as a kitten." She lifted a foot. "See?"

The mule glared at Hunter as if to say, "Wait until *you* try it."

MaryAnne fed Zeke a carrot from the pocket of her shorts.

Hunter looked the mule over as it munched the carrot. It was good-looking—dark brown, solid. Big, too. Probably a hell of an animal. "He looks like Francis the Talking Mule. And he's probably as smart-assed." Hunter looked low at him. "Goddamn! He's not even gelded!"

"How would you like to be gelded?" MaryAnne asked.

"Well, it makes mules and horses a little more docile and easy to work with."

"It would probably make you more docile and easy to work with, too."

Hunter snorted in defeat. He stepped up to the mule. "How ya doin', Zeke?" He handed MaryAnne the tether and slapped the mule softly on the chest. He rubbed his neck and reached up to scratch his ears. "What do you use these things for, stud?" Hunter turned to MaryAnne. "You sure this isn't just some big ol' jackrabbit some fast horse trader swindled you with?"

"He's the best mule you'll ever work on."

"No doubt. He's probably the only one." Hunter bent over and ran his hand down the left foreleg. Grasping the pastern, he leaned against the mule and lifted its foot. With a hoof pick from his back pocket he scraped away the dirt from the sole. "The sole is nice and clean."

"I try to clean them out every day."

"Good." Hunter put down the hoof, moved under the mule's head to the other foreleg, and repeated his perusal. Finishing there, he stroked the mule's back, made small talk with him, and moved to the right hind leg.

He rested his arm on the animal's rump, ran his hand down the leg, and hoisted it up. He slipped under the leg and laid it across his hip. After finishing with the other hind leg, he patted Zeke's back and scratched between his ears again.

"Good hard hooves," he said. "They look good. You been running him barefoot long?"

"Bill and I were using him to pack river gear into Diablo Forks for float trips this spring. After the season, Bill pulled the shoes off and trimmed him. Then he threw his back out the next week. We wanted to use him this summer to drop supplies for backpacking trips, and Bill figured he ought to be shod again since we'll be using rocky trails."

"Well, Bill knows hooves better than I do. I'll tack some shoes on." Hunter walked away a few paces and squatted. "So you're working with Bill on his trips?"

"Whenever he needs help. Not too often, though. I'm a Jill of all trades: bartender, river guide, mule packer, conservation biologist. What are you doing now?"

"Checking the angle of the hooves. The front surface of the hoof should be on the same line as the pastern. They look pretty good—maybe a little long in the toes. Walk him away from me and then towards me."

"What's this for?"

"To see if the leg is straight up and to see if the hoof swings in or out in the stride. Zeke, old buddy, you look damn good. Which is not surprising considering that Bill Crawford was taking care of you." Hunter stood up. "Why don't you take him under that cottonwood on the other side of the corral, and I'll bring the truck around?" He put his hat on a corral post and reached into his rear pocket for his bandanna to make a sweat band. "That's funny, I thought the . . ."

MaryAnne laughed.

"What's so funny?"

"You shouldn't have talked about cutting off Zeke's *huevos* at first."

Hunter looked at the mule. A few scraps of red cloth trailed from its mouth.

MaryAnne smirked. "He took it out of your pocket while you were looking at his feet. You're even now. He'll be good. I'll go get you one of my bandannas. I'll even make sure I haven't blown my nose on it."

Hunter drove the truck over to the corral and backed it in near the cottonwood. MaryAnne handed him a red-checked bandanna already tied into a headband. He slid his wooden toolbox under the corral fence and climbed over. A zephyr rustled the leaves of the tree. He buckled on his shoeing apron and clinched the straps around each thigh.

The mule had already littered the ground; Hunter kicked the crumbly dung away with the side of his rough-out boot. The legs of his Levi's dragged the ground at the heels where they were worn ragged.

"I'm sorry," MaryAnne said, referring to the road apples.

"That's okay. Better on the ground than on me."

"Will you tell me what you're doing as you do it?" she asked.

"Sure. Will he be all right if you tie his tether to the fence so you can stand back here and see what I'm doing?"

"You bet."

"I'll give you an anatomy lesson first," he said. *Yeah, you'd really like to do that, wouldn't you, asshole?* the voice upstairs butted in.

She hunkered down where she could watch the hoof as he lifted a foreleg and brought it between his thighs. Her arms clasped her knees and crowded some cleavage out of the jog bra. She sure as hell didn't need a Wonderbra. Hunter tried to keep his eye on the hoof.

"This outside part of the hoof is called the hoof wall. The part on the bottom is called the sole. Right in here," he said as he traced a semicircle around the outer part of the sole, "is the white line. It's the dividing point between the sole and the wall. This triangular-shaped, spongy thing back here on the sole is the frog. The hoof wall, which runs up the outside of the hoof all the way to the hair line here on the leg, is the weight-supporting part of the hoof. The outer part is dead just like the ends of your fingernails. This horny, flaky stuff on the bottom of the sole is also dead tissue with the live sole deeper in. The frog is very important because it's an auxiliary blood pump for the animal. Even after being shod, the bottom of the frog should still touch the ground since the pressure of stepping on it when the horse—or mule—is moving helps pump blood through the leg. The heart alone just isn't adequate to force enough pressure way down here."

He looked up at her. She was pretty beyond words, he thought. He would have to toss out all his previous standards of feminine beauty. "You got that?"

"Yes, sir."

"All right. I've already told you that the important thing is hoof angle. You also need to be sure that the front hooves are the same length and that the back ones are, too, in order to get a proper gait and no interference between the hooves when the horse is moving." She smiled at him when he looked up. Thoughts of swimming with her flooded his mind. What would come after dinner? He plotted a seduction. *C'mon, Percy, help me out here. How does it go?*

> Good night? ah! no; the hour is ill
> Which severs those it should unite;
> Let us remain together still,
> Then it will be *good* night.
>
> How can I call the lone night good,
> Though thy sweet wishes wing its flight?
> Be it not said, thought, understood—
> Then it will be—*good* night.

Hunter took a thin, hooked knife out of the toolbox. "This is a hoof knife. It's used to whittle down around the white line to get to nearly live tissue. You can tell you're getting there when tiny blood specks show. Then you use the knife to relieve the dead sole almost down to where you took the white line so that the sole is cupped. Then we trim up the frog a bit. Normally, I'd use these big nippers to chop off the hoof wall down to where it should be, but since I'm not taking that much off, I'll just rasp it down. I keep checking as I rasp for hoof angle, and to make sure that the hoof is being rasped evenly and level, and that I'm not making any low spots in the hoof wall or dropping the heels too low. There're a couple of places along the sides here where the wall is thinner and if you rasp with the same pressure there, you'll make a low spot."

Hunter sighted along the hoof and put it down. He stepped back to study it. "There. One trimmed hoof."

"That's all there is to it?" She knew very well that was all there was to it. Jack knew what he was doing, she decided.

"Yep. Of course, Zeke's hooves are in good shape so it took less time. But the important thing is to know what needs to be done and to get it even and at the right angle. If you don't, the hoof might look trimmed, but the horse could go lame. There's lots of limping cowboy ponies in Fall County."

Hunter finished trimming the other hooves and then nailed on the shoes. Flirting with MaryAnne sure made shoeing go smoothly, he decided. He brought up the wolf sighting and she changed the subject to the jaguar in Belize. He wasn't surprised.

After having her walk Zeke around for his inspection, he nodded and said, "Okay. That'll do 'er to 'er."

MaryAnne turned the mule loose in the half-acre pasture. He galloped off, full of snorts and ground-pawing.

"I think he's glad that's over with," she said.

Hunter put away his tools in the back of the truck. "Him and me both."

"How much do I owe you? I'm sure that you will want to charge extra since it was such a difficult animal to work on—being a mule, particularly one that wasn't gelded."

"How about if I trade the shoeing for this world-famous gourmet dinner you're going to fix me. Okay?"

"That's a deal." She eyed him and arched one eyebrow. "You sure do get all hot and sweaty shoeing a mule."

"Hey, it's warm out and having to snuggle up to half a ton of hot mule meat doesn't help any."

She laughed. "We can take a nice dip down in the pond after we run. That'll rinse the sweat off and cool you down."

"Sounds good," Hunter said. He doubted that it would cool him down much if she was planning on skinny-dipping. "Let me go get my shorts and running shoes."

He dug them out of the truck cab, pulled off his jeans and boots, and slipped into them. He kept the truck between him and MaryAnne. He walked back to her while swinging his arms side to side. "Gawd, I'm stiff." He bent and barely touched his toes.

"Does horseshoeing make you *that* stiff?"

"Yeah, I'm about a foot too tall to be a horseshoer. It ain't natural to be bent over like that all the time. It kills your back. A horseshoer ought to be about your height with shoulders about five feet wide. No wonder Bill's back started giving him problems. I'm amazed it didn't happen to him sooner. He's a couple inches taller than I am."

"Would you like a back rub? I'm pretty good at it."

"It's okay. Maybe later. Why don't we stretch? Then the run ought to loosen me up."

"Okay. Just offering." She walked toward the house and beckoned him to follow. "I have a little grassy spot up here in the shade where I stretch."

While they stretched, Hunter said, "Franklin Delaney's a fine old gentleman, but he's hell on wheels against wilderness and predators. He once told me that he'd killed forty mountain lions in his life, and he claims to have killed the last wolf in the Diablo country back in the thirties. How does he let a radical preservationist like you live here?" He admired the snaky way she stretched.

MaryAnne smiled. "It's because this isn't the old Delaney place anymore. It's the new McClellan place now. My daddy and I bought it from Delaney over a year ago."

"Ahh, so you're another landed citizen of Fall County."

"You bet."

After ten minutes of stretching, MaryAnne asked, "Well, you ready to burn up the road?" She shook out her twin ponytails and knitted them into one. That ponytail went above the back strap of a billed net cap she put on.

Hunter stood. "I'm ready. Lead on."

She put on sunglasses and Croakies. "You don't wear sunglasses when you run?" she asked.

"Naw, I don't like sunglasses. The only time I ever use them is when I'm driving, and it's really glaring."

"You should. I met a scientist with the EPA at a conference a few years ago. He said that ozone depletion was much worse than was being admitted—political pressure from DuPont—and that increased ultraviolet radiation was going to cause a rash of cataracts. He recommended wearing sunglasses or regular glasses coated with UV screening whenever you're outside."

"Giardia, ultraviolet radiation—we're taking the fun out of being outside anymore," he grumbled. "I'll take my chances."

"You have awfully nice legs," she said.

He stretched one out and flexed it. "As good as Betty Grable's, huh?"

"Well, they're a little hairy. But if we shaved them and put them in panty hose, you could get 'Best Legs' at a drag queen ball." She led him down the dirt road at a vigorous walk.

"I think I'll pass on that. I'll keep them as they are."

"That's okay. I like them fine."

Hunter looked at MaryAnne's legs. They weren't long-stemmed beauties like his and Betty Grable's, but they were *curved*—and without a ripple of softness anywhere in them from her ankles all the way up to the swell of her butt under the edge of her running shorts. A fine net of thin white scars and red scratches broke the tan like a crazy pair of fishnet stockings. The scratches marked her as a Southwestern hiker—legs courtesy of shindagger, cat claw, and chaparral.

"You've got pretty damn nice gams, too," he said.

She wiggled her rump at him.

"Pretty nice butt, too."

"Thank you. Yours has caught my eye, too," she said.

"I'll need to start fairly slow to warm up. Shake off the stiffness." That was always a good alibi, though Hunter didn't think he really needed one. MaryAnne looked fit as a lobo, but he figured he could outrun her. He would dawdle today and take a nice, slow run at an easy pace for her. No reason to run her into exhaustion. He had other plans for that. He was smug because he'd been running five or six miles a day.

She pursed her lips and gave him a sideways smile from her eyes. "Okay. That's always a good strategy. Especially for middle-aged men like you. Don't want to injure yourself. My usual course is down the dirt road through the bosque, up a jeep trail onto Cat's Paw Mesa, and then loop around on a couple of dirt roads up there and back."

Hunter quickly figured that going to the top of Cat's Paw Mesa was a climb of about five hundred feet. If she did that without stopping, she was in good shape.

They started out slow, bouncing down the valley road in the mottled shade of cottonwood and sycamore. By the time they reached the jeep trail, Hunter was warmed up, breathing deeply, and lathered with sweat like a pack mule. MaryAnne breathed easily. She chatted as if they were on a bird-watching ramble.

The jeep trail climbed an open draw. The scattered junipers, mesquites, and yuccas were useless for shading the south-facing track. He leaned into the slope and thanked the sweat band guarding his eyes. He felt like a steak being barbecued.

MaryAnne glided along with him, speaking in sentences and paragraphs while Hunter responded with one-word grunts. He glanced at her. Above the jog bra, her freckled chest was dappled with drops; a tiny stream coursed from the sweat-logged bottom of the spandex down her flat belly. Hunter smiled about the shape of the jog bra. He liked the way it moved. Sweating, running women. His weakness. He remembered Washington. He was running along the C & O Canal Towpath in late spring. Women runners passed in the opposite direction. The strain of exercise was on their faces; their bodies gleamed with sweat; their breasts bounced beneath damp T-shirts. It was enough to make a man throw himself in the canal. . . .

"What are you thinking about?"

"Huh?"

"You looked lost in thought," MaryAnne said.

"Oh," he puffed. "I was just concentrating on getting up this damn hill."

"It's really a good slog, isn't it?"

"Yeah." He pushed along. "It doesn't seem to be giving you any problem. You might as well be on the flat." The words came out as puffs.

"Well, I'm just used to it, I guess."

The hill steepened, and she pulled ahead fifteen feet. Hard muscles bunched into balls at the tops of her calves. Somewhere—probably the "Bodywork" column in *Outside*—he had read that climbing hills was the best exercise for a great butt. The proof was in the view ahead of him.

They reached the top, and the broad mesa swept out before them. The weight soared away from Hunter's shoulders like the mother of all vultures. To the southeast, the Diablo Valley sliced across the foreground; the foothills and great west wall of the Diablo Mountains—the Apache Peaks—lifted beyond, dwarfing the runners. No clouds; just a hot blue sky.

Even with the headband, sweat ran down and burned Hunter's eyes; it dripped from the end of his nose. He knew, god, he knew now that MaryAnne was a runner. The little man in his skull mocked him. *Right, asshole. You were going to go slow to let her keep up. Ha!* He brushed away the voice like a bothersome fly. The sun felt good on his back. He rotated his shoulders.

"Isn't it beautiful up here?" she asked. "I love this view of the Wilderness."

"Terrific view."

"I love running up here. Wonderful view, clean air, solitude. Once I took off all my clothes. It made me feel so alive, so free. But women aren't meant to run without some support, so I only did it once. Talk about sore. Arghh."

Sweet Jesus in a candy store. The vision overwhelmed him. He had thought the wolf had been something. "Yeah. It's nice to run without your laundry." The effort of those few words put the vulture back on his shoulders.

They topped a slight rise and a long, level course unfolded. Scattered cholla cactus and yucca rose above the snakeweed and grama grass.

MaryAnne wiped her forehead with the terry cloth band on her wrist, and said, "I usually like to speed up here and really stretch it out for a couple of miles. If we don't keep together, we can meet up at that windmill. Okay?"

The windmill was a speck in the distance.

"Okay." Hell's bells, Hunter thought, haven't we been stretching it out already?

Her strides lengthened and quickened. She rolled out ahead of him, loping with the same ghostly grace the wolf had had. Her ponytail swished from side to side like the sassy tail of a healthy animal. Hunter trudged ever farther behind like a dying buffalo. Sweat burned his eyes. The headband was worthless. He pulled it off and squeezed a pint of brine out of it. Lactic acid coiled in his legs. The little man in his skull sneered.

She vanished into the immensity of the continent. He followed her tracks left in the dust of the road. They were unending. He understood infinity. Beneath its thumb, he was ground into the bones of the Earth by the sun.

Hours later, or so it seemed, she was back by his side. Like a bluebird. Chatting! Dear god, chatting. They came to a fork on the dirt trace.

"Just up here we can go either way," she chirped. "If we go to the left, we circle around over . . ."

"Which is longest?" he panted.

"The left."

"Maybe we better go the other way. The heat's pretty intense today."

"You're probably right."

They loped along together, working their way back to the edge of the mesa, and took another trail down it. The sun had boiled his brain in its own juices. He hallucinated that she had taken off her laundry. He was a zombie. He couldn't look. She was stunning. High, wild, and free, her breasts coasted along like the figurehead on a ship, the tiny nipples cutting the wind for her—that was it: She was more aerodynamically sound. *Don't think about it, asshole. It's too much. You'll get confused. Fall in the dirt. Twist an ankle. She'll have to throw you over her shoulder and carry you back. . . . Oh, god.*

The trail cut into a shady canyon. It was cooler. It was downhill. Hunter regained his sanity. She had her jog bra on. She had never taken it off. They hit the flat of the valley and ran down the dirt road at his limit. He was pushing it; it was clear that she was holding back. It was a death march for him, a Sunday stroll for her.

Suddenly, she slowed and said, "It's only a quarter mile or so to the house. I usually stop running at this sycamore and walk the rest of the way to cool down."

It was like being awakened from a nightmare, Hunter thought. They walked together; MaryAnne looked at birds and flowers; Hunter coughed, sneezed, and spit out great globs of nasty crud the consistency of cold Karo syrup. His chest rose and fell in huge heaves as he tried to catch his breath. Her chest rose and fell, too, more gently, but splendiferously. It was as hypnotic as watching a waterfall. He tried not to watch. He knew he would walk into a tree if he watched the flow of her breathing.

"Oh, nice Scott's oriole," she said as the yellow and black bird flew in front of them. "Such a gaudy fellow."

He could talk again. "Good lord, MaryAnne, you're a hell of a runner. What are you—Tarahumara?"

"Nope. Nothing that exotic. Just a regular all-American girl from Albuquerque, New Mexico. Scottish, mostly. A little bit Cherokee."

"How far was that?"

"That's my medium course. Twelve miles."

Yeah, and one bitch of a hill to get to it.

"My long course is fifteen, but I can add more to it for a full twenty-six."

Aha. Twenty-six. The magic number. "Are you training for a marathon or something?" Hunter asked.

"Not really. I used to run two or three a year. I ran my first one when I was fourteen. When I was an undergrad at Colorado State, I got into ultramarathons. I've done half-a-dozen fifty-milers and once ran the Western States One Hundred. Those are killers. But I really don't have time to train for such things anymore—not with all my conservation work. I'm scaling back on running. No more competition, at least for awhile. Aren't you a marathon runner?"

"Lord, no. That twelve miles was the farthest I've ever run."

"That's funny. Bill Crawford said you were a marathon runner."

"That sonofabitch. That sonofabitch."

"What?" she asked.

"That rotten Crawford did that on purpose. He told you I was a marathon runner knowing full well I'm not just so you would run me to death. He's probably laughing about it right now."

She laughed. "I'm sorry," she said, touching his arm. "I really thought you would enjoy this. If I had known . . ."

"It's not your fault. That jackass Bill Crawford. I guess I'll have to take up marathoning now just to defend my honor." Hunter grinned. "I'd like to see you take Crawford's two hundred and fifty pounds lumbering over that course. He'd keel over like a damn elephant."

"He did make it up the hill once."

"Really? I'm surprised he didn't cave in the side of the road. Well, you tell him that I made it up it, too."

"You were a lot faster." She squeezed his hand briefly to add to the compliment.

"Good. You tell him that." Hunter wanted her hand back.

"I will. You know, though, Bill is in remarkable shape for his size. I've seen him tote a hundred-pound pack twenty miles a day in rough country."

"Yeah, I know. The guy's a damn grizzly bear." Hunter decided this wasn't the conversation to try to hold hands.

"I was thinking about that," MaryAnne mused. "Bill is built like a griz, while I'm built more like a lobo. But what are you?" She turned to inspect him as they walked. "A big cat, I think. Maybe a mountain lion? No, you're a little too heavy for that. I know. A jaguar. That's what you are. A jaguar." She touched his shoulder with her forefinger as if she were dubbing him.

"It's interesting that you've picked three animals native to New Mexico, but that were exterminated—except I guess the wolves have moved back in from Mexico."

"My job is to understand wild carnivores," she said and turned her head to look at him again. "*Our* job is to protect the habitat for lobos, grizzlies, and jaguars so they can all come back some day. Then New Mexico will really be New Mexico again and we will have earned the right to live here."

They were back to MaryAnne's house.

"I don't know about you, but I'm ready for that swim," she said. She sprang up the steps of the porch and reappeared from the kitchen with a couple of icy beers. "Here, cowboy, catch." She tossed Hunter a bottle. He was sucking water out of the flower bed hose.

Clumsy as a guy with feet for hands, he dropped the hose and grabbed the slick bottle out of the air. He did a better job shagging the bottle opener trailing behind it. He popped the top and took a welcome drink, ignoring the spray from the toss. He smiled with a mustache of beer foam.

"You're cute," she said. "The pond is down there by the river. See the big cottonwood? There's a rope on it you can swing from."

The pond. Swimming. Skinny-dipping for sure. Hunter wondered if he could remember his multiplication tables. It wasn't as if he had never seen a naked lady before. But MaryAnne—now, she wasn't outlandishly built like the silver lady on an Arkansas trucker's mud flaps, but what she had was so *alive*.

"Look!" MaryAnne pointed. A black hawk was cruising the bosque.

"Wonderful," he agreed. Their hands came together like those of two fifth graders on the way home from school. Finally, he thought.

"There's a vermilion flycatcher down here, too," she said. "He's got the pond staked out as his turf."

They were startled by a flock of Gambel's quail exploding beneath their feet. After watching the birds' flight, their eyes came together, and Hunter felt himself being swept down a rapid. In *Of Wolves and Men*, Barry Lopez had written about the communication between a pack of gray wolves and a moose, of the understanding that passed between their eyes when the moose was ready to die. To surrender. Hunter wondered if such a communication was happening now. What was it like to be a moose? But who was the moose and who was the wolf?

But before the kiss, she broke away and ran to the pond. She stood on the bank, looking back to him. He jogged to her. The seduction was going to be easier than the run, he was sure. He checked his head to make sure he still had the words there:

> To hearts which near each other move
> From evening close to morning light,
> The night is good; because, my love,
> They never *say* good-night.

The pond was an oval, probably one hundred by sixty feet, Hunter figured. Half of it was in sunlight, the other half was in the shade of the cottonwoods around it. The bright flash of red was the flycatcher hawking bugs over the water. A rope dangled from the biggest cottonwood. It was a Norman Rockwell painting, though ol' Norm had never painted skinny-dippers like the one inhabiting this swimming hole. Or maybe he had, maybe he had in the privacy behind puffs of pipe smoke.

MaryAnne shed her running togs, drained her beer, and dove in. The glimpse of her naked told Hunter he was a dead man. He pulled off his running shoes and socks and stepped out of his damp, sweat-stinking shorts. He walked into the lukewarm water to mid-thigh and fell face-forward with outstretched arms. The water wrapped around him; it washed away the sweat and the steam and the stink. It floated him afar to a temperatureless, gravityless, careless nirvana, to a far land where you didn't have to run up steep hills in a blast furnace, eating the dust of a girl. When his lungs finally begged for oxygen, he lifted his head out of the water.

She was already across the pond to the cottonwood and the rope. Hunter paddled his hands and feet only enough to keep his eyes and nose out of the water. He pretended he was a crocodile. He watched her. He drank her in. He hoped he wouldn't be struck blind. How could Mark Twain's damned human race have produced that? With the rope in tow, she walked far up on the levee bank and swung out high over the water. She flowed into a flip from the end of the rope and entered the water with no more splash than a kingfisher would have made.

Hunter tried to fathom what he saw, tried to weave it into his world experience. When Socrates told Phaedrus, "I'm a lover of learning, and trees and open country won't teach me anything, whereas men in town do," the pedantic old pederast had charted the course Western Civilization has sailed ever since, a ship of fools on a journey of madness that has ripped the vitality and meaning out of everything other than Lord Man. One of the questions he and his buddies had knocked back and forth like a shuttlecock—"What is Beauty?"—had been impossible to answer with that attitude, thought Hunter.

Beauty was here. This creature—so alive, so wild—was Beauty. The meaning of Beauty could not be found in the marble courtyards of Athens, in the mousetrap dialogues of Socrates, in the abstraction of the Greek language, but in the opposite of that: in wilderness. In wolves.

Socrates and his boys had constructed their highfalutin' theories like delicate Greek vases. And Henry Thoreau had smashed them to smithereens with one simple Huck Finn rock: "In wildness is the preservation of the world."

Jack Hunter sculled in the warm, green, primal water, and spit a stream of it from his mouth. He watched MaryAnne McClellan, pond-slick and naked, swing out on the rope again and explode like Krakatoa. *You're right, Henry,* he thought. *Wildness is the preservation of the world. And in Wildness is Beauty. That's what Beauty is, Socrates. But you were blind to it. And you've blinded twenty-five hundred years to it.*

She swam up to him. Wild green fire flashed in her eyes. "Are we having fun yet?" Her body brushed his as she treaded water beside him. It seared him like a burning brand.

He found words. "This is a terrific pond. I might actually recover from the torture you put me through on Cat's Paw Mesa. If I could always come down here for a swim after shoeing horses, I might survive."

"You're more than welcome. It's my own little private slice of paradise."

And you're certainly the naiad to dwell in it, Hunter thought. "I guess I'll have to try the rope. Although my barefoot-boy-with-cheeks-of-tan days are a long time gone. I'm no gymnast like you. Promise you won't laugh?"

"I promise," she laughed.

They swam together to the shore, and she left the water with him. He tried to behave and not ogle her. Right, and Odysseus hadn't listened to the sirens. Hunter grabbed the rope, whooped like Alley Oop, and made a mighty swing out over the pond. He tried a flip and crashed down on his back. *Thank god, it was the back,* he thought as he sank to the bottom. *If it had been the belly that hit, big guy, you'd have split open like a ripe watermelon.* He floated back to the surface to see MaryAnne arching into the sky from the end of the rope. For a second he felt like an about-to-be-harpooned whale. But she easily missed him. He turned to look for her to pop up. She didn't reappear. He looked behind himself. No. To the sides. No. Suddenly he was grabbed by the heels and jerked under the surface. He clawed, choking, to the air to see her back-stroking away, laughs dancing back like water striders.

"You need some more practice from the rope! I'll swim around out here and supervise you. Go on, give it another shot," she called.

Lamely, he took the rope up the bank, gripped it, and readied himself for another disaster.

"This time, just swing out easy. Let your feet go up at the completion of the arc of the rope and come down head first!"

It worked. After a fashion. Hunter worked on his form. She pulled herself out on a wooden deck that sloped into the water from the shore across from the rope.

Hunter watched her from the cottonwood. She stood up and shook out her hair in the sun. He swung out on the rope and cut his best dive of the day. Best to quit while you're ahead, he decided, and breast-stroked over to where she lazed. He took his time and now allowed himself to drink in her body. He was as entranced with her as he had been with the lobos. In Wildness is Beauty. Indeed.

She sat back down and patted the dock beside herself. He climbed out on the deck. She hadn't left him much room; his hip touched hers where he sat. Her foot reached toward his. Her toes parted and she pinched his instep.

"Ow!"

"Did I tell you I have prehensile feet?" she asked.

"I guess I wasn't watching your foot. It snuck up on me."

"Look! There he is again!"

Hunter looked up. The black hawk, on deep, wide wings, soared past looking for crawdads. A white band broke the black wedge of its tail. Its shadow crossed their bodies. Her shoulder nuzzled his arm as they watched the hawk. He slipped his arm around her back; she squeezed closer. The hawk disappeared over the canopy of the gallery forest. She turned her face toward his. His eyes were caught in the green fire. Will drained from him like blood from a moose. He fell into a kiss.

Somewhere far away, there was goose music. No, it was too dissonant to be geese.

MaryAnne pulled away and stood up.

"Oh, no," she wailed. "It's my daddy honking the horn. I thought he wasn't coming down until tomorrow to go fly-fishing."

She rose on her tiptoes, her fists on her hips, and her head craned up to look over the bank. Her rump was at the level of his eyes. MaryAnne sat back down beside Hunter. She ran her fingers through his short hair and stroked his cheek.

"Darlin', I'm really sorry. I was looking forward to this so much. But we're going to have to break it off here or we're going to be caught in a very embarrassing situation since my father is walking down to the pond right now." She looked into his eyes. "We better get dressed."

"Uh, yeah." Hunter snapped out of it and leapt up for his shorts. He pulled them on and stumbled into the pond.

MaryAnne ran to her father after she slipped into her shorts and jog bra. She jumped into his outstretched arms. "Hi, Daddy! Guess who's visiting me? You remember Jack Hunter. . . ."

7

Jack Hunter clambered out of the pond to greet Phil McClellan. The cool water had made him presentable—he hoped.

Under other circumstances, he would have been glad to see Phil. MaryAnne's father had been Hunter's first mentor in the conservation game. In 1961, when he had been beginning his career as a nuclear physicist at Sandia Laboratory in Albuquerque, Phillip T. McClellan, Ph.D., had testified at a congressional field hearing on the Wilderness Act. Six years later he had founded the New Mexico Wilderness Association. When Jack Hunter and Bill Crawford had honchoed the Wilderness Committee of Students for Environmental Action at the University of New Mexico in the early 1970s, Dr. McClellan had taken them under his wing.

Phil McClellan spread his arms wide and wrapped them around Hunter. "How long has it been, Jack?" he asked. "Five, six years?"

Hunter leaned back after the *abrazo*, still gripping Phil's arms. "God, it must be, Phil. You're looking good, though." Hunter couldn't tell if Phil knew what he had broken up, not with the permanent twinkle in his eye and the smile—the always joyful smile—planted in his jack-o'-lantern big face.

Phil's smile grew even broader in response to the compliment and said, "Well, I retired from Sandia last year. Early retirement when I turned sixty. Guess I lost any interest in playing with atoms. I'd rather spend my time playing with trout. But I'm running regularly and getting back into serious backpacking shape. I decided last Christmas when a little girl came up to me in Winrock Mall and starting telling me what she wanted for Christmas that I either had to shave off my white beard or lose weight." Phil laughed. "So, I decided to lose weight."

Hunter remembered boundary study hikes with Phil McClellan to proposed Wilderness Areas. Phil had always been in serious backpacking shape. The little man in Hunter's head dropped a slide into the projector—Phil spooning some awful freeze-dried glop into his mouth while his face was crusted with mosquitoes. And Phil loving it. Hunter also remembered the foxy, feisty little girl with him. They still doted on each other, it was plain to see.

Hunter rolled his eyes at himself. *How plain is it that you now dote on the foxy, feisty little girl?* Hunter chanced a glance at MaryAnne, and she threw back a wry but sexy smile. He couldn't believe how green her eyes were. He couldn't believe how much he wanted her. He couldn't believe her father had walked in when he had.

Phil slipped his right arm around MaryAnne's shoulder and his left arm around Hunter's. Together, the three walked up to the house. Hunter tried to dog-paddle his thoughts away from MaryAnne's naked embrace. He might be forty, and she thirty—but he felt like a gawky, geeky, horny sixteen almost caught by her dad.

At the house, MaryAnne brought out beers and directed her father and Hunter to lawn chairs under a big cottonwood. Hunter excused himself to his truck to change out of his running shorts to jeans, boots, and shirt. He rejoined the McClellans and took the empty chair.

Planted like a patriarch in his chair, Phil leaned back and inspected Hunter. Hunter felt as if he was strapped into a chair with a bright light shining in his face. His heightened awareness of MaryAnne was like a bobcat who'd climbed straight up his back and now gripped the sides of his head with eighteen claws.

"This is a wonderful opportunity, Jack, my boy. I've missed our old strategy discussions. I always thought you were my finest protégé—except, of course, for my lovely daughter here." Phil McClellan looked at her fondly.

He turned his attention back to Hunter. "Yes, Jack. You know I spent thirty years in a rather collegial atmosphere at Sandia Lab, ten before that at the University of California, and I've always found that the best way to develop new ideas, find breakthroughs or fresh approaches, is to review a problem and discuss it in a relaxed manner. I'm afraid you're a captive here for an exercise of mine, and you will have to humor me."

Hunter leaned back in his chair, took a swallow of beer, and said, "Shoot. I'm all ears." MaryAnne, however, had positioned her chair alongside his, and her bare foot brushed his boot. His ears were far from his reigning body part.

If Phil smelled the pheromones, he ignored them. "Well, Jack, I'm sure my daughter has told you about our current battle for the Diablo. It seems to be the culmination of all my conservation work to date. I am the president of MaryAnne's Diablo Wilderness Committee and I am spending much of my retirement at the task."

Phil leaned forward with his beer in his two hands between his knees. "As I said, I've always thought you had one of the best strategic minds in the business, Jack. So, let me take this opportunity to recapitulate the history of the Diablo Wilderness Area, and then have you respond with your take—things we should be on guard against, any clever ideas you might have for how we should proceed."

"Sure, I'll be happy to, Phil, though I'm not very involved these days."

Phil grunted. "We'll see about that later. Now, let's quickly review how we arrived at the current situation. In 1928 the Forest Service established the Diablo Primitive Area. As such, it was one of the first areas given that protection. The primary motivation for designating the Diablo and other Primitive Areas in the Western states was to prevent roads from being constructed into backcountry areas popular for long pack trips with Forest Service officers."

Hunter tried to look attentive, but the littlest smile crossed his face. He knew Phil McClellan's careful, plodding approach. Two decades ago, Hunter had often been on the receiving end of it. Phil had hammered the details of the Wilderness Act into his head so well and so often, Jack Hunter could have almost recited the entire legislation word for word. It had been Phil who had pushed the books—Leopold, Nash, Abbey, Shepard—on him and had made sure he read them. Hunter knew the history of the Diablo backward and forward, up and down. He didn't need to hear it from Phil again. But—Phil was right: Hunter was a captive. He looked at Phil, but his brain was down in the boot being touched by MaryAnne's bare foot.

Phil interrupted himself. "Oh! Is that the black hawk?" He stood, pulled his compact binoculars out of a shirt pocket, and focused over the pond.

Hunter kissed at MaryAnne from two feet away. She kissed back at him. *Good night? ah! no? yes? yes! But when? Not tonight.*

Phil sat back down and asked Hunter, "I assume MaryAnne has told you that we now own this marvelous bird habitat? As fine as a Nature Conservancy preserve—and even better protected. Now, where was I? Oh, yes." Phil continued with the history of wilderness preservation: the Forest Service protecting Primitive Areas in the 1920s and 1930s through administrative action, conservation groups pushing for the Wilderness Act in the 1950s, and the signing of the Wilderness Act in 1964, which gave congressional protection to Wilderness Areas and called for public hearings to consider additional areas.

The bobcat suddenly climbed back up Hunter's neck. MaryAnne had casually draped her foot over his boot.

If Phil noticed, he didn't show it. He rattled on with his history lesson. "The public hearing for the Diablo was in 1972. I believe you and Bill Crawford testified there, Jack, on behalf of the University of New Mexico wilderness group."

"That's right, Phil. You bought the gas to get our carload down to Platoro."

"And MaryAnne, not yet ten years old, also testified. You were the youngest person to speak at the hearing, darling."

She smiled. "Yes, Daddy. And it was one of the thrills of my life."

Phil McClellan continued with an explanation of the conservationists' one-million-acre Diablo Wilderness proposal, and the Forest Service's 750,000-acre recommendation. "Congress passed an 800,000-acre compromise Diablo Wilderness bill in 1976, a bill which left out most of Mondt Park and Davis Prairie. In 1980, we almost got them added to the Diablo Wilderness as part of the New Mexico Wilderness Act, but Mondt Park was dropped in last-minute bargaining—we decided the members of Congress from New Mexico would not support an adequate boundary. You, of course, Jack, know all about this since you were handling the Washington end of things on that bill. Now that I recall, you and Bill Crawford were the young turks back in 1972 who did the field work on the Davis Prairie–Mondt Park region and agitated for its inclusion in our Wilderness proposal."

"I didn't know that," said MaryAnne. "My hero," she smiled, and touched his shoulder. She left her hand there.

Hunter tipped an imaginary hat. He wished she would behave in front of her father.

But Phil only smiled and said, "Yes, indeed, dear daughter, our friend Jack here is the original defender of our special place. So, here we are today. Southern New Mexico's congressman, Bart Pugh, has introduced a bill to declassify the entire Diablo Wilderness Area. I will let you contemplate all that, my boy, while I go to relieve an old man's bladder. I shall return with replacement beverages and to hear any words of wisdom you may have."

"Same old Phil," Hunter said after he left.

"That's my daddy. Best in the world." MaryAnne plopped herself in Hunter's lap.

The chair fell over. They paid it no mind.

The screen door squeaked. Hunter straightened out his chair before Phil rejoined them.

Phil handed out cold Pacificos. "So, what comes to mind, Jack?"

"Well, several points," he said, glad MaryAnne hadn't been wearing lipstick. "As a preliminary, remember that Pugh is not a powerful, respected, or even well-liked member of Congress. He's lazy and not terribly bright. Mean, yes, and a hard-line right-winger, but mediocre through and through."

Phil smiled. "Ah, yes. Mediocrity. There was some Republican senator back in the Nixon days who defended a very lightweight nominee for the Supreme Court by saying the mediocre needed to be represented, too. I can't remember the names of the principals. . . ."

"Hruska and Carswell," said Hunter.

"Yes, that's them. And the honorable Pugh in his shining, stinking mediocrity does indeed represent some residents of New Mexico's southern district. But, continue, Jack."

"Okay. Basically, Pugh's declassification bill is a ploy to kill any additions to the Diablo. It's also a dog biscuit he's throwing to the wise use/ militia yahoos. I've heard that other right-wing Republican congressmen from the West are talking about similar legislation. Some jackass from Utah wants to declassify a bunch of National Parks, others want to give the National Forests to the states or private industry, still others want to repeal the Endangered Species Act, and the Alaska pea-brains want to drill for oil in the Arctic National Wildlife Refuge. It's part of the whole antifederal, down-with-regulations, no-taxes populist revolt from strip-mall businessmen and resource extraction industries."

MaryAnne shook her head. "It gets even weirder down here, honey. Some of the right-wing populists in southwestern New Mexico make Bart Pugh look like Ted Kennedy's drinking buddy."

Hunter asked, "Didn't Fall County pass some crackpot 'custom and culture' ordinance recently that declares that county ordinances take precedence over federal and state law?" Had MaryAnne really called him "honey"? In front of her father?

Phil laughed, "County supremacy ordinances are appearing in rural counties throughout the West. Fall County's was the first. It's the latest expression of the sagebrush rebels."

MaryAnne turned to her father and said, "No, Daddy, it's worse than the sagebrush rebellion. They're threatening to arrest any forest rangers who try to carry out management contrary to Fall County ordinances—as though the Forest Service isn't doing everything possible to skin the Diablo National Forest for the benefit of loggers, miners, and ranchers already!"

"Well, yes," nodded Phil. "But the solicitor for the Forest Service recently wrote Fall County to warn them that if they try to enforce their idiotic law it will be in violation of higher federal laws. The head of New Mexico State Game and Fish also wrote saying the ordinance violates state laws, and that if the county sheriff tries to interfere with state game management, he'll be arrested."

"Oh, what a jewel our new sheriff is," MaryAnne sighed. "Frank Mayer. I couldn't believe he beat dear old Chuy Baca in last fall's election. He's really bad, Daddy. The sagebrush rebellion back in 1980 was just the old rape and scrape crowd, but this wise use/militia bunch is crazy. They're taking over the county rights movement and forming county militias. Fall County just passed an ordinance requiring every home to have a gun. They're convinced the United Nations is going to send in foreign troops to enforce what they call 'environmental tyranny' and 'homosexual rule' here in the United States. According to some of their material, Yellowstone National Park is already being run by foreign troops, and Russians are training in northern Michigan. That's why they're so agitated about gun laws."

"Do you really think they're that bad?" Hunter asked, wrinkling his brow.

MaryAnne smiled. "Oh, I'm probably exaggerating. Guys like your friend Harry Jukes are gullible but paranoid lunatics. I don't know if they're dangerous or not."

"Do you feel threatened here, MaryAnne?" Phil asked.

"Me?" She laughed. "Oh, no! They won't bother me. They're scared of me already—but they're terrified of Jack."

"How so?" Phil asked and looked at Hunter.

Hunter rolled his eyes in an embarrassed way.

"Oh, Daddy, you should have seen it!" She poked Hunter in the ribs. "Jack came by the bar last week, and this Harry Jukes character was trying to give me a hard time about Wilderness. I'd run him off, but Jack butted in and roughed him up. Later, when Jack left, Jukes and two friends jumped him in the parking lot. Jack beat the living daylights out of them. It was awesome."

Phil laughed and clapped Hunter on the shoulder. "Well done, my boy! That may have been the end of the Fall County militia. But, we've strayed from the main trail. I wanted to talk strategy with you. How should we proceed against Pugh's bill and to add Mondt Park?"

Hunter looked at Phil. He couldn't decide whether MaryAnne's father was convinced there was nothing to worry about, or whether he was trying to disguise his concern for his daughter. And what of MaryAnne? The hundred-pound toughie? She wasn't the type to be afraid, but something in the tone of her voice gave Hunter pause. Now it was Hunter's turn to act nonchalant.

"Well," he said, after knocking back a swig from his beer, "as you all well know, the key is local support. The bottom line is people at hearings, letters to Congress, local business support, letters to the local newspapers. You know this as well as I do. So, what do you think? Can you turn folks out? I imagine that the popular impression is that people down here are in revolt against any more Wilderness. You have to turn that impression around. At the very least, you have to show that there is considerable support for Wilderness here, that the locals are not united in a revolt against the federal government."

Hunter looked up to the skyline of the Apache Peaks. "It'll take work, sure, but I don't think it will be difficult to kill Pugh's declassification bill. But that doesn't protect Mondt Park and Davis Prairie. I was just in there. We all know it's the best country in the Southwest. We also know how easy it would be to punch in roads and log it. And we know that it doesn't have much of a constituency. It's a classic example of the 'place no one knows.'"

Hunter chewed on his lip, wondering if he should discuss the wolves. MaryAnne had said not to mention them to anyone. Did that include her father? Surely, she had told him. But she had said no one. Her eyes were underscoring that now. And her fingernail was digging into the top of his shoulder.

Hunter probed a little. "That country has some very special values as we all know."

Phil looked as if he was about to say something. Hunter saw MaryAnne look at her father. Phil cleared his throat.

MaryAnne looked back to Hunter and smiled; she removed her fingernail. Phil knew about the wolves, Hunter was sure. MaryAnne didn't want him to say anything about them to Jack. MaryAnne knew that Jack knew about the wolves, but didn't want him to say anything to her father. Moreover—Hunter now remembered—when he had told MaryAnne about seeing the wolves, she had not let on that she knew they were there, only that there had been "unconfirmed reports." But the behavior of the Doctors McClellan fairly shouted that they knew about the lobos. Of course, if he couldn't talk about the lobos, there wasn't much more he could say about strategy. Which was fine with Hunter.

The sunset was dusty orange at the horizon. A lustrous pearl gray spread over a quarter of heaven's dome. Hunter, the lobbying pro, leaned back in his lawn chair.

Phil leaned over and slapped Hunter on the shoulder. "Well, this was very good, Jack. It helped clarify my thinking on the issue."

A bottle of cabernet was pulled out, and Phil wheedled Hunter into talking about his adventures in Africa and elsewhere on his overseas trip.

Hunter begged out of dinner. His hormones were bubbling like a crab boil from the interruption at the pond, and he was tired from the intrigue of having to skip around the wolf issue. MaryAnne walked him to his truck. There were promises in her lips—long promises which at once lured and frightened him. Bob Wills and the Texas Playboys echoed from the jukebox in Hunter's brain: *Lips so sweet and tender, like petals falling apart.* . . .

"I'm really sorry, Jack. I hope we can take up where we left off."

He touched the tip of her nose. "Thinking about that, cupcake, will probably keep me from getting to sleep tonight. That and the fact that

I'm stiff as a board from running twelve goddamn miles at pronghorn speed." He got in his truck.

"Come by late tomorrow afternoon," she said, leaning into the open window of the cab. "Daddy will be off fishing." Very sweet petals fell apart.

Hunter was awakened the next morning by the telephone; it was his sister in Albuquerque. Their mother was in the hospital. He called his two customers for the day and put off their shoeing dates. He tried MaryAnne's number next, but it was busy. He threw a couple of changes of clothes and his shaving kit into a duffel and headed the truck to Albuquerque.

MaryAnne's phone was busy because she was on it, first to Ralph Wittfogel and then to Bill Crawford. "Bill, we've got to talk. Something's come up. Can you get up here today to talk to me and Daddy and Ralph?"

Hunter reached MaryAnne three hours later when he stopped for lunch at Frank and Lupe's El Sombrero Cafe in Socorro. He told her about his trip to Albuquerque and said he wasn't sure when he would be back. MaryAnne told him to come over as soon as he got back. She wished his mother good luck. Hunter hung up the phone and waded into the plate of *carne adovada* brought to his table on the patio.

MaryAnne hung up with Hunter just as Crawford and Wittfogel pulled in. Her father was walking up from the bosque where he had been birding. She had told him about Hunter's wolf sighting last night over dinner.

The man who parked beside Bill was lean—lean and long and ropy like a strip of beef jerky. But Ralph Wittfogel was not cut from cheap flank steak. He looked to have been sliced out of an aristocratic filet mignon. His fingers were particularly long and lean, like those of a concert pianist. His clean-shaven dark face was that of a once-great brain surgeon gone to drink or of a small-time intellectual hoodlum.

"What's up, darlin'?" Bill asked as she came out on the porch to greet them.

"Our wolves have been discovered, guys." She paused. "Why don't we sit out at the picnic table in the shade? I've got some sun tea made. Let me get it and some glasses with ice."

When everyone was settled and served, she told them about Hunter's sighting of the wolves. And the slides.

"Can we trust him?" Ralph Wittfogel demanded.

"We might not be able to count on ol' Jack to do much for us in this fight," said Bill, "but he can be trusted. You told him why we don't want any word to get out yet?"

"Not in detail," MaryAnne said. "But I did extract an unconditional promise that he wouldn't talk about it. And he passed a test last night—he didn't mention the wolves in talking to Daddy, even though I'm pretty sure he figured out that Daddy knew about them."

"I wouldn't worry about Jack, gentlemen," Phil said. "I believe that my daughter has a certain influence over him."

She kicked him in the shin.

Her father laughed.

Bill asked the trees, "I wonder if the poor bastard knows what he's getting himself into?"

"More than he can handle, sweetie," she grinned. "And he's also going to end up helping on the Diablo—whether he knows it or not right now."

Wittfogel was tired of the small talk. "I'll accept your judgments on him."

MaryAnne turned to her father. "Daddy, why don't you tell Ralph and Bill about our discussion last night?"

Phil recounted Hunter's thoughts on strategy. Bill nodded his head. Ralph had a few questions.

When Ralph had been answered to his satisfaction, MaryAnne said, "Now, on to other matters. I telephoned Monica Montoya's legislative aide this morning, and she confirmed that Pugh plans a field hearing on the Diablo in Platoro toward the middle of August—tentatively Saturday the fourteenth. Montoya is planning to attend." She looked at her father. "Thanks, Daddy. Your organizing in Santa Fe and northern New Mexico is paying off."

Phil said, "Many people have helped. I've only done part of it. Considering that this is only her second term in Congress, Montoya's becoming a real friend for conservation. We need to organize more in her district. She could become our champion in the House. Jack was correct last night. Protection for Mondt Park is going to be decided by how much support we can build for it in New Mexico."

"Speaking of which," said MaryAnne, "how's the slide show coming, Bill?"

"Pretty good. I got some great Mondt Park and Davis Prairie slides from Jack Dykinga. They really help give it some class."

"You have some very nice shots, too, Bill. Don't deny it. You're a fine photographer. I think the slide show will win Mondt Park strong supporters. Are you still willing to take it on the road in July to organize attendance at Pugh's hearing?"

He shifted his bulk. He didn't like public speaking. But he loved the Diablo. "Yeah, I guess so."

She touched his knee. "Thanks, Bill. I wish I could do it with you, but I'm afraid I'm just going to be too busy on my wolf reintroduction proposal to spend two weeks on a road show then."

"You sure it's your wolf report and not something else keeping you from going?"

"That's for me to know and you to wonder about."

He scowled behind his black beard. "Okay. I'll do it. I think I've got one backpack trip with five clients during that period, but I can get someone else to guide it."

"Thank you, Bill," she said. "I really appreciate it." MaryAnne looked around. "Well, we should take advantage of being together to work on more concrete plans for our campaign. Have you heard that Senator Reed is coming to Platoro in two weeks.? Looks like it'll be the fifth of July."

After Bill Crawford and Ralph Wittfogel left, MaryAnne asked her father for a small favor before he headed up into the Wilderness to fish.

"Of course," he said. "What is it?"

"I was going to go down to Underwood's to get my paycheck, and I thought if you went with me, it would be an opportunity to try to get Red to say where he stands on protecting Mondt Park. If we could get his support—and he is county chair of the GOP, plus on the county commission—that would significantly undercut Pugh, and it would help us a lot with Senator Reed."

Underwood's Beer Joint was empty of customers when they walked in.

The man behind the bar looked up from his Tony Hillerman mystery. A friendly grin broke out across his all-American, airline-pilot-handsome face. "Why, howdy, MaryAnne. Bartender's holiday?"

"You don't expect me to have a beer down at the Hereford, do you?"

"Guess not," he said with a twinkle in his eye.

"Red, do you remember my daddy, Phil McClellan? He's been in here before, swilling beers with me."

"Sure I do. How you doin', Phil?"

"Fine, fine. Good to see you again, Red," Phil said as he took the offered hand.

Red grinned. "Or should it be Dr. McClellan? As I recollect, you're a Ph.D. like your daughter here."

"Phil it is. And, yes, but my doctorate is in physics, not wildlife ecology like MaryAnne's."

Red folded his arms and leaned back, the grin still on his face. "Yes, sir, I never dreamed that one day I'd have a Ph.D. tending bar for me. Though as good as she is, I thought she was a Doctor of Mixology."

"I did have some chemistry, you know."

"That must be it. But I suppose you came by for your check, MaryAnne."

"That and a couple of beers. Pacificos if you have any."

"I bet if I fish around, I can find a couple."

Underwood set the two bottles out, drew himself a Coors, and shook a little salt in it. He asked, "What are you doing down in this neck of the woods, Phil? Anything besides visiting your pretty daughter?"

"Well, there's a stream I know up in Mondt Park that has some fighting little rainbows. I think they might be hungry for some new flies I tied."

Red nodded. "Not many folks know that country, but if you do, there's some great fishing. Good country. The best elk hunting in southwestern New Mexico, too."

Phil said, "Indeed. MaryAnne, Bill Crawford, and I all filled out our tags up there last fall."

"It's where I always hunt," Red said.

MaryAnne didn't need any more encouragement than that. "Red, what do you think of the Forest Service's plans to cut the big pines in Mondt Park? Did you know they're planning to offer the Bearwallow Timber Sale? There'll be over forty miles of new roads built."

Underwood was silent for a long while as he stared into his glass of beer, as though plumbing its depths for an answer. Finally he spoke. "Not much, MaryAnne. You know that I like that country. Not just for the elk. I like going up in Mondt Park with my hounds to chase lions, too." He noticed MaryAnne's glance at the snarling stuffed mountain lion displayed above the bar. "Now, MaryAnne, I know you don't approve of that—of shooting cats. I don't shoot 'em anymore. Hardly ever. I just like the chase. And I been hunting elk up there ever since that herd got big enough to hunt. Cutting those big yellow pines could ruin it. And I like keeping roads out of the wilderness."

MaryAnne realized she was nodding her head. She was happy with his answer. She even believed it was honest. But there was no reason to telegraph her approval. She stopped nodding.

Underwood divined the Coors again. "But a lot of folks around here see the Diablo Wilderness Area as good land going to waste. I hunt it because I have horses. Most folks around here hunt by pickup or ATV these days. Because they can't drive in the Wilderness, they feel they're locked out. They figure all the timber in the Wilderness Area and in Mondt Park would keep the mill in Homestead going forever. We are a depressed economy here in Fall County. We got really high unemployment. Maybe the county could do a better job of managing the Diablo National Forest than the Forest Service."

Phil said, "But don't you think those economic claims are exaggerated?"

"Oh, sure. But folks in this county are hurting."

They mulled over their beers. Red was riding the fence. Much as he liked wilderness, he was a rural politician who wanted to please. She had nodded her head too soon, MaryAnne thought.

She could also tell that Underwood was ill at ease with the conversation. This concerned her. Fall County Commissioner Underwood was a key to her strategy on saving Mondt Park. It was clear that he couldn't be pushed too fast.

Phil, too, sensed they had gone as far as they could with Underwood. He finished his beer. "Those little trout are calling, MaryAnne. I better get up there."

Red said, "Good fishing, Phil. Let me get you your check, MaryAnne."

Outside, she whispered, "Oh, Daddy! You're in luck."

"How so?"

"You know how you were asking about my term 'luebner' for an ass crack that rides above a redneck's jeans when he squats or bends over?"

"Yes," he said.

"Well, right over there is the eponymous Mr. Luebner." She pointed surreptitiously.

One hundred feet away in the parking lot of Underwood's Motel, Onis Luebner worked. His two-and-a-half ton Chevy, with a metal flatbed and side-mounted toolboxes, was parked next to a Winnebago. The Winnie had its hood up, and Luebner was bent over into it. His dirty white T-shirt rode up his back, and his dirty white underwear and blue jeans rode down his hams. Half a moon winked at Phil and MaryAnne from the gap.

Luebner pushed himself out of the engine compartment of the RV. He had a thick neck, short legs, and dull look. Rheumy hound-dog eyes, droopy mustache, jowls, and not much of a chin made his face. He was a mouth-breather; his thick lower lip rode a slack lower jaw. He clomped over to his truck and rummaged through a toolbox. He walked bowlegged and slightly stooped forward as if he was trying hard not to shit in his drawers. He bent back under the hood.

"That is a 'luebner,'" she said.

"And what a magnificent specimen," said Phil.

"All brought to you courtesy of Rio Diablo's very own shade tree, fly-by-night mechanic and contribution to the enrichment of American slang. Oh, by the way, Luebner was one of Jukes's friends who tried to jump Jack in the parking lot last week."

"Really? Luebner's a large man. Jack really took on all three of them?"

"Cleaned their clocks." She grinned.

"Impressive." Phil McClellan nodded his head and stroked his beard. "I wouldn't be surprised with that from Bill Crawford, but Jack never seemed like the fighting type. He's big enough. And he gives the impression of being the kind of man who can handle any situation. But, in my experience, he's always been the type of man who tries to avoid confrontations."

"He didn't have much choice. I sure was glad he *was* the fighting type."

8

Hunter visited his mother in Lovelace Hospital that afternoon, and spent the night in Albuquerque at his sister's. He left for Rio Diablo at noon the next day after visiting his mother in the hospital again, and after stopping by the cigar store in Coronado Center. The twinge of guilt for not staying longer was washed away by thoughts of MaryAnne McClellan. Driving back, his head was full of her. Pond-slick body. Gymnast muscle. Runner muscle. Girl-curves. Sashaying ponytail. Piss and vinegar. Green eyes. Spicy kisses.

Shelley's "Good-night" poem played again in his head. Had ol' Percy used it the first time with Mary Godwin? Hunter practiced his lines.

> The night is good; because, my love,
> They never *say* good-night.

Just south of Homestead on 666, he spied the Diablo Mountains riding the southern horizon. The land took on a whole new sense of wilderness. Lobo country. Again. Wolves, running wild in New Mexico. Once more whittling the legs of deer and elk into fleet-footedness. New Mexico without wolves had been like enchiladas without chiles. Now the *picante* was back in the land. And it tasted good to Hunter. It tasted better than anything had ever tasted to him.

Late in the afternoon, he rolled down the state highway along the Diablo Valley. He passed the road to his place and drove through town. Two miles east of downtown, he pulled off the pavement and looked through his binoculars at the old Delaney place—*pardon me, the new McClellan place.* Hunter was a bird junkie; binoculars and the National Geographic Society's *Birds of North America* were always in the truck. Through a gap in the trees, he saw her Jeep; her father's pickup camper was nowhere in sight.

He shook caution out of his mind like dust out of a throw rug, and found the turnoff to her house. He parked next to her Jeep and knocked at the kitchen's screen door.

"MaryAnne?"

Her voice came from inside. "Just a second. Who is it?" She appeared in the kitchen. "Jack! You're back already." She opened the screen door and quickly kissed his cheek. "How nice! I wasn't expecting you . . . oh, I'm sorry. How's your mother?"

"Fine. False alarm. A drive to Albuquerque for nothing." The kiss on the cheek reassured Hunter that shaking out caution had been a good call.

"Well, I'm certainly happy she's okay," MaryAnne said. She gave Hunter a fetching smile. "I'm also happy you're back—and that you came to see me."

Hunter grinned. "I've been . . ."

"You didn't perchance come by to collect on that dinner I owe you, did you?"

"Well, the thought did pass through my mind."

"You're in luck, cowboy. The fixin's have been waiting in my refrigerator for whenever you decided to show up. By the way, my daddy's up in Mondt Park fly-fishing, so it's just you and me." Her smile became even more fetching.

"I guess you've twisted my arm." He started to touch her hand, but she turned away.

Over her shoulder, she said, "You look hot. Help yourself to a cold one. I've been working on my wolf reintroduction report—bogged down somewhere on the information superhighway trying to track down some data. Let me go find an off ramp, and I'll join you on the porch. It's cooler outside, I think."

Hunter sat down on the edge of the porch to drink his beer and watch the long shadows of day's end. In the front yard cottonwood, an acorn woodpecker and a western kingbird faced off like a couple of guys on

Muscle Beach. The woodpecker left. Kingbirds weren't called kingbirds for nothing. The buzz of the highway began to fade. *Take it easy, buster. Don't rush it. Don't blow this chance.*

MaryAnne came out on the porch with her own beer. "Let's see now, where were we? Ah, yes, down at the pond." She lifted Hunter's hat and emptied her bottle of icy beer on his head.

He whooped and jumped up.

MaryAnne dashed away toward the pond, bounding through the tall Johnson grass. She looked like an African antelope, all grace and bounce and speed, Hunter thought. He thundered behind, feeling like a lion. She flung her T-shirt and bra aside. At the pond's edge, she ripped off her sneakers and shorts, and dove in. Hunter closed the gap. He dove in behind her and grabbed her foot. She wriggled free and stroked away.

"Arghh!" he spluttered.

"Do you always swim in your boots and blue jeans, cowboy?" she taunted from her refuge in the middle of the pond.

He pulled himself out of the water. "Just wait, just wait." He poured water out of his boots and hung his wet Levi's on a branch.

"I like you, Jack. You're big and slow and easy to handle."

Hunter dove in the water after her. She swam away. He chased her for a few laps around the pond. She scrambled out at the rope; he was close behind. MaryAnne grabbed the rope and swung past him. Hunter slipped on the mud and crashed to the ground.

She called from the center of the pond, "I can't understand why I'm attracted to someone as dumb and clumsy as you are."

He threw himself out of the mud and into the water. She back-stroked away, just out of reach. He gave up and lurked in the middle of the pond. Only his eyes and top of his head were out of the water. She climbed out on the wooden dock and stretched in the long rays of the sun.

"I guess the only way you'll catch me is for me to give up."

He paddled up to the dock. He caught his breath while hanging on it with his forearms and chin.

"I promise not to run again if you'll come up here with me." She reached out with her leg and gently pinched his nose with her toes.

Hunter kissed her toes. And then her foot. He dragged himself up on the deck.

MaryAnne smiled. "Now where were we a couple of days ago? Oh, yes." She drew him into a bottomless kiss.

Frogs croaked on the edge of the pond. Dragonflies patrolled their jungle like American helicopters on search-and-destroy missions in Vietnam. A garter snake slithered in the tall grass beside the deck, and the black hawk cruised above. The vermilion flycatcher ignored the humans. There were far more important things—like bugs over the pond. The sun dipped to the horizon.

MaryAnne stirred. She lifted her head from his chest to look at him. Resting on her elbow, she touched the hair of his chest, wound it around her fingers. She kissed him with the easy intimacy of a lover. "I hate to destroy this idyll, dear, but a mosquito just bit me on the butt. It's dusk and they're going to be swarming momentarily." She kissed him again, and stood. She threw back her hair, dove into the water, and swam to her clothes. He followed.

They pulled on their shoes and pants, and ran hand in hand through the twilight to the house. They vaulted onto the porch together and scattered the last hummingbirds of the day from the porch feeders. MaryAnne shut the screen door fast behind them, saving them from the imaginary horde of pursuing mosquitoes.

"Oh, dear," she said. "I seem to have lost my shirt and brassiere on the way to the pond."

"I noticed that."

"Would you be a good fellow and go find them for me while I start dinner?"

When Hunter returned with her clothes, she was building two drinks. "I assume you like gin and tonic? Boodles?"

"Boodles, huh? I guess I don't know it. I usually drink Tanqueray."

MaryAnne put on her bra and T-shirt while talking. "I used to drink Tanq—picked it up from David Brower when he spoke at Colorado State, and I helped him close down the bar afterwards. Then I read about Boodles in a Travis McGee mystery and tried it. I feel a little more racy drinking it."

"It's good. And you are racy."

"I'm glad you like it. Bartender's special for a special friend." She clicked his glass with hers. "Thank you for the compliment, too. I think that's the first you've ever given me. I expect more."

"You do, huh?"

"I do. I'm planning chicken Kiev tonight. I have a nice bottle of Pinot Gregio in the fridge chilling down to go with it."

"Doggonit, darlin'," Hunter said. "Is there anything you can't do?" He squeezed her up next to him.

She wrinkled her nose and eyebrows in thought.

"Well?"

"I'm thinking, I'm thinking. There must be something. But," she smiled in triumph, "I haven't tried everything yet, either." She kissed him lightly on the lips and shooed him away. "Make yourself at home in the living room. It won't take me long to get dinner going."

Hunter pulled off his wet boots and set them out to dry on the porch. His blue jeans were nearly dry after an hour of hanging from the tree limb in the air baked dry of humidity. He left them on. Drink in hand, he inspected MaryAnne's home. It was a classic turn-of-the-century adobe farmhouse: four identical square rooms set in an L, a pitched tin roof, a porch running along the inside of the L, two-foot-thick mud-brick walls plastered in white, and six-foot-tall windows set in every wall. The windows had traditional blue trim to keep away ghosts. A bathroom had been tacked onto the back side of the L at some later date; an old-fashioned bathtub with lion's feet sat in it. The kitchen had both a wood cookstove—unused in the summer—and a gas range that looked to be a leftover from Harry Truman's kitchen.

Her bedroom was the room at the end of the bottom of the L, her office was in the corner, and the living room and kitchen formed the upright. Cement block and board shelves stuffed with books and government reports lined the walls in the office and living room. A computer and laser printer were on a table in the office. There was even a fax and a copy machine. Reports, maps, and loose sheets of paper were scattered around the table. Two file cabinets flanked it.

An exercise machine sat in a corner of the bedroom. Hunter liked free weights. Testing the machine, though, he was impressed by the amount of weight she had on the cable. She couldn't weigh more than a hundred pounds—she was benching that. The bed was unmade but the sheets were clean, he noted. Her dresser drawers were pulled partly out, and clothes were piled in them and on top of the dresser. Outdoor gear was piled around the bedroom. She didn't keep house like June Cleaver.

"Would you do me a favor, sweetie?" she called from the kitchen.

"Sure." He would do anything she asked. Maybe even clean up her house.

She said, "Open up the windows so the evening breeze will flow in to help cool things down."

She joined him in the living room after the windows were opened, and lit candles scattered around the room. Jerry Jeff Walker saddled up on the stereo. She snuggled next to Hunter on the couch; they sipped their drinks and dreamed awhile. Armadillos flew from London to Amarillo with Gary P. Nunn.

"I have a confession to make," she said.

"What's that?"

"I planned to seduce you when you came to shoe Zeke if my daddy hadn't interrupted."

"You did?" he asked in phony surprise.

"Yep. While we were talking in the bar last week, I thought to myself, 'I'm going to love his ears off when he comes over to work on Zeke.' Of course, I've wanted to do that ever since way back when I was still in high school."

Hunter reached up and touched his ears. "Whew. For a minute there I thought they might be gone."

MaryAnne bit one. "You're lucky. They must be on awfully tight."

Hunter touched her nose and said, "Well, I may as well make a confession, too."

"What's that?"

"I was planning to seduce you, too. I was even practicing a poem. Wanna hear it?"

"How could I resist?" she smiled. "I'm a sucker for romantics."

"Good-night? ah! no; the hour is ill . . .," he whispered in her ear.

"Mmm," she purred when he was finished. "It's a good thing I never gave you a chance to ply me with that. I would have been putty in your hands. Instead of you being putty in my hands." She sipped her Boodles, and looked across the drink at him with lowered lashes. "Oops! Guess I ought to finish dinner." She jumped up from the snuggle. "The rice ought to be done. I'm starving. You wait there and rest for a few minutes. You get to work later."

Hunter leaned back with his drink and shut his eyes. Had he really gone crazy out there? A nagging voice in his head—or was it just Jerry Jeff's?—warned him of what he was getting into. He banished it. He wouldn't think about it—about the entanglements—at least for tonight.

"It's ready," she called from the kitchen.

Hunter ambled in. A candle was on the table. Stoneware plates and cloth napkins sat on matching place mats. The sizzling rolls of boneless chicken breast perched on beds of wild rice. Salad and steamed asparagus stood on the side. The wine chilled in an icy crock. She might not be a housekeeper, Hunter thought, but she set a fine table.

"Would you pour?" she asked as he sat down.

The "Kievs," as MaryAnne called them, worked as billed. Spiced butter flooded out over the rice with the first cut.

Hunter raved, and she thanked him for the compliments. Bare feet under the table stroked and pinched.

With his plate almost cleaned, Hunter asked, "So, MaryAnne, what kind of birth control do you use?"

"Oh, I don't use any."

A speared asparagus stopped midway to his mouth. "You don't?"

"No, I figure that as much as I run, my body fat's so low that I couldn't get pregnant if I wanted to."

Hunter chewed in silence. "Isn't that a little dangerous?" he finally asked.

"I haven't had any problems yet." When they finished their plates, she looked up at him. "But if you're worried, why don't you take the responsibility for it?" She held her glass out for wine service.

"I, uh . . ."

"Why should women always be the ones responsible for that?"

He poured. "I suppose you're right about that."

She swirled wine around in her glass. He filled his glass and sipped.

MaryAnne smiled and touched his hand. "I'm sorry to be mean, sweetie, but that's one of my pet peeves—that men always expect women to take care of contraception. Don't worry. I'm fixed."

"You're fixed?"

"Yep," she said. "My tubes are tied. Did it way back as an undergrad. When I had an accident, I went to this great abortion doctor in Boulder, who was also a wilderness activist and taught anthropology at the University of Colorado. Even though I was on the pill, I had gotten knocked up. The doctor suggested the operation since I was so vociferous about not wanting kids."

"You never want children?" Hunter asked.

"Nope. Can't stand the little ankle biters. I've never wanted to be a mom—not even as a little girl. I never played with dolls. Since I got fixed, sex has been a whole lot more fun. Though I'm not very randy. I can count all the lovers I've had on my hands. You're in rare company."

"I believe I am." She didn't want kids. That definitely racked up bonus points on Hunter's checklist. But, hey, it wasn't going to get that serious anyway.

"Well," she said. "Do you like the brown food group?"

"The what?"

"The brown food group. You know, chocolate. I have two goblets of bittersweet double chocolate mousse waiting in the fridge." She batted her eyes.

"Who do you want me to kill?"

After dinner, Hunter offered to wash the dishes.

"You get a gold star, sweetie," she said. "I didn't even have to ask. That was your work I mentioned earlier. Here's the apron. I'll await you on the couch."

After the dishes, he asked her where she kept the broom.

"Don't worry about that."

"Hey, sweeping the kitchen is part of cleaning up after dinner."

"Wow. Why don't you stick around? I could use a housekeeper."

"So I noticed," he said.

Just as he finished, she called from the living room. "Jack, sweetie, the wine seems to be all gone. Would you make us a couple more G and Ts?"

He brought the drinks and rejoined her on the couch.

MaryAnne put Beethoven's Ninth on the stereo. "A little ode to joy seems appropriate, don't you think?"

"I think," said he. Her head was on his chest. He stroked her hair.

"So, Jack, why is a person like you content to play horseshoer on the back side of the moon here in Rio Diablo?"

"I spent most of my savings wandering around the world the last few years, I bought the place down here from my mother after my father died, horseshoeing is about the only skill I have to parlay into money, and I like being on the back side of the moon."

"But with your master's degree and your experience in Washington, you could probably get a job teaching at Southwestern New Mexico College in Platoro. Why horseshoeing?"

"I don't want to think about politics, lobbying, or natural resource management. I got really burned out in Washington. About five years ago, I put my feet up on my desk and tried to figure out what I had really accomplished. Remember RARE Two—the Forest Service's second

Roadless Area Review and Evaluation in 1977 to '79? You know all the state-by-state RARE Two Wilderness bills that passed from 1980 to 1984? Like New Mexico's?"

"Yes. I helped daddy on the New Mexico bill in '80."

"I worked on all those in D.C. I bird-dogged 'em through the maze on Capitol Hill. And when it was all said and done, I looked back and realized that while we had designated seven and a half million acres of new Wilderness Areas, we had traded off nineteen million acres of roadless country to the timber beasts. What we protected was spectacular scenery, but a lot of it was rock and ice. The more important wildlife habitat lower down was released to the chain saws. It was hard to be enthusiastic about what I was doing after that. I stayed for a few more years, but my heart was out of it."

Hunter sat quietly with MaryAnne circled in his arm.

"Horseshoeing's not a bad trade, you know," he said. "Pick your own hours, be your own boss, don't have to take much shit from anyone—except horses, and when you're done, you're done. The only thing I've really got to think about is not to get myself kicked. Bill's daddy was a horseshoer, and Bill helped him after he was old enough. After our senior year in high school, he wanted Bill to go to the farrier science class at New Mexico State, and I decided to go, too. We were both stomps in those days. Rodeo and chew and hats and boots and all that. We worked part-time for his daddy while we were in college and he got us a job with an outfitter in Wyoming in the summers. . . ."

"Ah, where you encountered the famous Jumbo—the wellspring of your abundant humility."

Hunter put her head in a hammer lock. She nipped his chest. He let go.

"I kept up my farrier skills in D.C. because the ex had a horse. Even though we stabled it out in Virginia, I did the shoeing. I even tacked on a few shoes in Africa and Australia while I was traveling the last few years. When I was trying to figure out how to feed myself this spring, I talked to Bill, found out he was giving up his business, and he offered it to me. It really hasn't been that hard getting back into it, though I'm a little slow."

"Am I finally going to be allowed to give you a back rub?"

"You bet."

"You can spend the night if you'd like."

"I think I'd like." *Good* night.

9

When a mountain lion comes into heat, she and her consort may mate fifty to seventy times every twenty-four hours for seven or eight days. They can't be torn apart. Humans don't have estrus. But they do have pair bonding. New lovers of the two-legged kind can't hope to match how many times the big tan cats do it. But MaryAnne McClellan and Jack Hunter gave it their best shot. If they couldn't match cougars in quantity, they planned to beat them in quality. They rolled around in bed all the next day, until late in the afternoon when MaryAnne said she had to have her endorphin fix. She promised a short run—four, five miles max. No hill climb. She won him out of bed and into running shoes with further promises of skinny dipping. He spent the night, too.

Tuesday, they worked out together on her machine. He argued the superiority of free weights and dragged himself away to shoe horses. She let him go only if he would come back that evening and grill the famous pork chops he'd boasted about. After the barbecue, in the moonless night, they swam the pond with thousands of croaking frogs. They wallowed with the frogs on the muddy bank. They smeared each other with thick, black muck for mosquito protection and watched the stars.

"I gotta go to Platoro tomorrow, darlin'," Hunter said. "Bill set me up with the Hummingbird Guest Ranch to shoe all their horses. I'd rather stay right here in the mud with you and turn into an adobe brick, but I need the business."

"Oh, that's great, sweetie."

"You're that eager to get rid of me?"

"No, silly." She kissed his lips—about the only part of their bodies not caked in mud. "I'd like you to stay here in the mud with me forever, too. But I've got printing to be picked up in Platoro tomorrow. Would you be a sweetheart and get it for me? It'll save me a trip and let me get some work done. A certain man has kidnapped me from my wolf report the last few days."

"Sure, but you'll have to pay."

"Oh, how will I be able to reward you for that?" she cried. "I know! What you're picking up is two thousand copies of a flier asking for letters to Senator Reed and Congresswoman Montoya on the Diablo. I'll let you help me stick on labels tomorrow night!"

"Only if we can do it naked."

"That probably wouldn't be wise, sweetie. You see, I'm making a big pot of my killer spaghetti sauce, and Ralph Wittfogel is coming over to help us eat it and do the mailing."

Hunter started to protest, but she interrupted. "Besides, you'll like Ralph," she said. "He's even more misanthropic than you are. Wait until he gets going about Ebola Zaire. You'll be enthralled. He's pretty much of a recluse, but one of the real behind-the-scenes bulwarks of the Diablo Wilderness Committee. Has a really nice place up Zierenberg Creek—built and equipped like a fortress. Guns, several years' stockpile of food. Sort of a misanthropic survivalist, but a hard-core Wilderness supporter. He's a dealer in rare books and documents. And one hell of a hiker."

Despite himself, Hunter liked Wittfogel. The older man—Hunter figured Wittfogel was about ten years older than he was—was a fount of cheery information about emerging new diseases. He also knew poetry. He and Hunter entertained MaryAnne with misanthropic and cynical verse—Yeats, Swinburne, Stephen Crane, D. H. Lawrence, Robinson Jeffers. . . .

Hunter was glad when Wittfogel left, though. MaryAnne promptly shed her clothes and shot a post office rubber band at him.

So went the week.

On Saturday, he called and begged out from coming over, pleading exhaustion from shoeing. He said he wanted to get to bed early and catch up on his sleep. The real reason was that he had worked on the Clayton horses. Buck had been gone, and Jodi had had an itch that all the calamine lotion in the world couldn't fix, and Hunter couldn't figure an easy way out. Afterwards he had had an unfamiliar feeling of treachery. He hadn't liked it. Even the prying homunculus in his skull hadn't wanted to tease that rattlesnake.

Alone in his house, he hunkered down with gin and tonic. *Damnit, we aren't married or anything like that. I didn't do anything wrong. Why the hell do I feel like a creep?*

He called MaryAnne on Sunday morning and invited her over to his place later for dinner and bed and breakfast. Then he drove to Platoro for a second session with the horses at the Hummingbird, and to buy groceries. He was back by 5:00 P.M. and tidied up his house (something he had noticed she never did at her place before he visited).

The sunset was salmon and apricot set in a vast circle of Pinatubo pearl. The only clouds were a few wispy mare's tails in the west where the Rio Diablo boxed for its run into Arizona. Hunter and McClellan cuddled like kittens in a Caribbean rope hammock, strung between two willows near the irrigation ditch.

"Mighty fine stereo system you have here in your little love nest," said she.

"I only turn it on for special girls. Others have to make do with just the sound of ditch water," said he. "I reserve the frogs, owls, coyotes, and bugs for you."

Tonight was their one-week anniversary. She had ignored the warning label and had shot the cork from a bottle of Korbel Brut at him.

Despite their closeness, MaryAnne had brushed aside any talk about the wolves. Wait until we see the slides, she had said.

He had fixed dinner tonight: his specialty—tacos. Gourmet MaryAnne McClellan had lauded them, except for chiding Hunter that they needed more green chile. New Mexico, she had pontificated, is the land where chile is a vegetable. It is not a mere spice. He hadn't been sure if she had been serious. Damnit, his tacos were hot!

"Do you know we've never been in the wilderness together?" she asked.

"Pecos Wilderness additions. After RARE Two. Nineteen sev—"

She elbowed him in the ribs.

"Uhnn!"

"That doesn't count."

"You're right," Hunter said. "You were prepubescent then. . . . Ouch!"

"That was a day hike with a lot of other people. We've never been backpacking together."

"What are you doing tomorrow?" he asked.

"Oh, I . . ."

"I'd sort of like to get into the headwaters of the South Fork. Never been there before."

"Senator Reed's going to be at the Platoro airport on Monday, July fifth—a week from tomorrow. I've got to work on organizing the turnout for that."

"Two nights ought to do it. Be back Wednesday."

"You mean it?" asked MaryAnne.

"Sure. Why not? I don't have any horses to do for a few days. Now's the time to get high before the lightning starts sparking off the ridges. Anyway, I'd like to see you hump both our packs out of South Fork Canyon. . . . Ow!"

There was no question about who would lead on the trail. Hunter didn't mind. He liked the view ahead. MaryAnne had a natural rhythm to hiking—a hypnotic rhythm in the curvy legs beneath her gray backpack. It was a rhythm that lulled Hunter, that made him think of another pair of shapely hiking legs, legs longer than MaryAnne's, legs he had first watched many years ago.

Those legs belonged to a reporter for KOB-TV News in Albuquerque. He met her at a public hearing about the Wilderness proposal for the Sandia Mountains in 1977. She seemed to have a sincere interest in the issue, and they went to lunch to further discuss it. She asked about the Forest Service's claim that the Sandias would cheapen the Wilderness concept because they were on the doorstep of Albuquerque. The Cibola National Forest supervisor had proclaimed that from anywhere in the proposed Wilderness Area the urban sprawl of Albuquerque could be seen and the noise of the city could be heard. She wanted to know what the Sierra Club response was to that.

At the time Hunter was the assistant to the Southwest regional representative for the Sierra Club. New Mexico Wilderness was his bailiwick. He offered to take her hiking on the Piedra Liza Trail in what he promised was the wild north end of the Sandias where the city did not intrude. She accepted.

Suzanne was a beauty: a finely chiseled face, teeth as glittering bright as marquee lights, eyes as blue as the winter sky, a shimmering sunburst of champagne hair, and a long lean body that would fill the soaring fantasies of a state pen lifer. Despite her TV looks, she seemed real.

She liked the hike; Hunter liked her. In mid-afternoon, on the carpet of needles beneath a twisted old ponderosa pine, they took a break. Three thousand feet above them, the granite cliffs and spires of the Sandia escarpment leapt up to the snow-covered crest. On top, it was solemn white winter, but in the foothills spring was nudging gray with green. In between was a war-torn no-man's land where neither spring nor winter held sway. For a few days spring would have the upper hand, the air would grow balmy, birds would begin to sing, and flowers stir, but, then, like a cuckolded husband, winter would rush furiously back and spread a howling quiet upon the Earth.

It was spring as they lolled beneath the tree. Suzanne lay on her back on the pine needle bed and closed her eyes. Patches of sunlight cut through the tree's umbrella and toasted her in her sweater. She was suddenly surprised with a kiss.

Her eyes popped open with a start. "I wasn't expecting that!" Her smile belied the fib.

"Well, that's what's supposed to happen—kiss a sleeping beauty and she wakes up, or you turn into a frog."

She laughed. "You aren't green."

"Ribbit."

"What happens next?" The magnet of her Indian paintbrush lips pulled him down.

It was so easy. Every part of her seemed sculpted just for him; like pieces of a jigsaw puzzle, they fit. Her blue jeans wrapped around his, his hiking boots nuzzled hers, their sweaters caressed. Lips found lips and tongues found tongues. Eyes drifted shut in dreamy touching; fingers found buttons and zippers, then winter-pale flesh.

But the spring lovers were too soon interrupted by winter's return to the tree beneath the cold granite crags. Lost in each other, they failed to notice the graying of the sky, the fat white flakes in the air, the chill to the wind. They pulled windbreakers and caps from their packs and hurried back to his truck.

Three inches of snow erased the road when they got to her apartment in the rustic-artsy suburb of Corrales on the Rio Grande north of the city. Inside, she shut the door against winter.

"You realize, of course, that I can't let you go back out into this storm," she said with staged concern.

"You can't?" Hunter asked just as melodramatically.

"Of course not." She looked out the window. "I think we're already snowed in. You may have to spend the night."

Hunter remembered. Hot toddies, an outdoor hot tub in the snow—that night had been the beginning of something that moved very fast. When the last of winter's snow had run down from the mountains into the Rio Grande, they were married. She was eager to move to Washington, D.C., when the Sierra Club offered him a lobbyist job there that fall. A Colorado senator was a family friend, and she thought she could get a job with him as a media aide.

Because of their late start—MaryAnne had to make six phone calls and finish a few other chores on organizing the meeting with Senator Reed—they humped up the trail to make camp by dark. Hunter wore hiking boots with full leather uppers. They were heavy but not as heavy as his first pair of boots twenty-five years ago. Technology had improved some things, he granted. He had teased her at the trailhead about backpacking in running shoes.

"You're gonna wreck your ankles," he had said.

"Not a chance," she had smirked. "I have *great* ankles. Hiking in boots lets your ankles goof off and get soft. Then you sprain one. By hiking in running shoes, my ankles have to stay strong."

Hunter then had teased her about her clothes. "You look like a picture in the Patagonia catalog. Don't you buy any other clothes?"

"Listen, buster, not only are they the best, but Patagonia gives the Diablo Wilderness Committee grants. If it wasn't for them, we wouldn't be in business. I'm loyal. If you stick around long enough, you might find that out."

They plodded over the Apache Peaks and dropped down into Oso Park in the high rocky canyon of the South Fork. In the meadow—a dollop of softness in a rock-ribbed landscape—they grilled their elk steaks over an alder fire.

"Char-rare," ordered MaryAnne. Hunter was happy to oblige.

Last night she had turned up her nose when Hunter had described what he ate on backpacking trips. She had planned the menu—and had pulled the elk steaks out of her freezer. She had told him about her successful fall hunt with her father and Bill Crawford. "Maybe we'll let you go hunting with us this fall," she had said.

Hunter was no gourmet chef like MaryAnne, but he could grill meat. Down in the high desert of the Diablo Valley, mesquite would be the only wood he'd use. Up at 8,000 feet, Arizona alder—a small to medium tree that crowded the headwater streams—was the wood of choice. If it had been pork chops, ribs, salmon steaks, or chicken, he would have let the fire burn down to gyrating white coals. But because it was elk and because MaryAnne liked hers char-rare as did he, he cooked the meat low over a crackling fire. To char rare, the flames must lick the flesh and sear in the juices. The inside of a thick steak should be warmed only to the temperature of an overheated ungulate—overheated as it would be after being run down and speared.

The hot blood ran down their chins as they ripped meat from the bones with their teeth. MaryAnne wiped her face with her bandanna.

"Couldn't be this messy in Alaska," she said. "We'd be faxing every grizzer bear in the territory." She flung the bone into the darkness. "But it's nice to play Neanderthal. Someday, we'll have grizzlies back in the Diablo, too, and then our backcountry housekeeping will have to be impeccable."

Hunter thought about grizzlies in the Diablo, then the lobos pounced into his skull. It was a good thing he was having this torrid fling with MaryAnne, else his head would have been so full of wolves that he wouldn't have been able to think about anything else.

She eyed Hunter's picked-clean, shiny bone before he tossed it. "I've never had a better steak, dear, but I have a small complaint: Since you're without a beard or mustache, you're able to gnaw your bones as well as I can. With furry-faces like Daddy and Bill, I always get to clean up their bones."

"Sorry, darlin'. If these were po'k chops, I'd even eat the bones."

She snuggled close to him. "*Que hombre.* Mmm. I love to kiss a man with a hot greasy tongue."

She bounced up and rummaged in her pack. "Floss?" She tossed it to him after peeling off a bit. "Greasy tongues are one thing," said she, "but little wads of meat between the teeth are another."

After the campfire ritual of flossing, Hunter went through his cigar licking and clipping ritual. "Keeps mosquitoes away."

"In case you haven't noticed, it's already too cold for mosquitoes. Which means it's time for more clothes." She pulled a gray fleece jacket out of her pack.

"I knew it!" said Hunter, sending up smoke. "Patagonia. You're so chic, dear, a regular fashion plate. Since you're up, would you toss me my jacket from my pack?"

"See how sweet I am to you, even though you're mean to me?" she said, as she dug into his old Kelty. "Aha! Look what I found. Just like mine. Twinsies! This *really* proves we're meant for each other!" She threw a gray Patagonia fleece to Hunter.

MaryAnne had proclaimed it fate last night when she had discovered that they had sleeping bags with the zippers on opposite sides—thereby making it possible to zip them together.

"Bobbsey twins," she said and snuggled next to him.

He wrapped an arm around her and held his cigar in the other hand away from her.

"Is there anything better than a campfire to lie around at the end of the day?" He blew a line of smoke rings that rose like ravens on the fire's updraft.

"Wanna hear my theory about campfires?" she asked.

"Sure."

"Have you ever gone to someone's home to visit and they keep the television on while people sit in front of it and try to talk?"

"Yeah. That's really obnoxious."

"Have you ever wondered why television so easily and quickly became the centerpiece of the living room, how its flickering light became the navel of social intercourse?"

"Beats the hell out of me. 'Cause most people are boring and stupid?"

"Well," she said. "Look at how we're talking here in our living room. What are we looking at?"

"Uh . . ."

"The flickering light of a campfire! We, as a species—actually as a genus since our ancestor *Homo erectus* also had fire—we've been sitting around campfires in the evening for at least three hundred thousand years. It was around those campfires, those flickering lights, that human culture and society—religion, story telling, and so forth—developed. Television is an ersatz hearth. Its flickering light is a degenerate substitute for the campfire. . . ."

"Have you published your theory?"

"No . . ."

"You should. It's the best explanation I've ever heard for why television has the hypnotizing grip it does on most households."

"Then you love me for my mind as well as for my body?"

"I'm mad about all of you, darlin'."

The cigar was tossed into the embers. Zipped-together sleeping bags called. A waxing moon and a gadzillion stars roofed their bedroom. Light and shadow from the dying flames tattooed their flesh; night breezes explored their nakedness.

Hunter finally murmured, "Woof, woof."

MaryAnne asked, "Woof, woof?"

"Woof, woof," he said and zipped the bags closed. He plummeted into sleep. Usually he tossed for an hour or more, waiting for his mind to quiet enough for sleep to feel welcome. Tonight, just like every night this last week except for the one apart from her, he fell headlong into the delta zone.

But later, his mind slithered out of delta into REM. In that dream world, he journeyed back, back to Washington, back six years, back to a different woman.

Sleep would not come. He lay awake, arms crossed, teeth gritted. In his frustration, he thrashed like a beached whale. She slept tranquilly next to him, unaware of his discontent. Oh, she was beautiful all right—a golden piece of sculpture. The Arlington glow cascaded through the window and softly lit her sleeping form. He raised on one elbow to look at her. She may as well have been a statue for all the pleasure sleeping with her that night was bringing him. In her ethereal, ball-busting beauty, she was as cold, artificial, and airbrushed as a *Playboy* centerfold.

La belle dame sans merci.

Hunter rolled over and sat on the edge of the bed. The sedge had withered by the lake and the birds no longer sang. He wandered out of their bedroom and into the house office. He lifted the curtain. Shit fire, he didn't even have fresh air at night; Suzanne had to keep the goddamned air conditioner going all the time. He might as well be living underground or in a space colony. He shoved the window up, letting the breeze blow in the noise, the smell, the warmth, the humidity, and even the goddamned bugs of the Washington suburbs. At least it was real air, grimy and nasty though it might be. He watched a car go by. A dog patrolled the garbage sacks. Late at night like this, he sometimes saw raccoons and 'possums prowling the yards. He wasn't getting out into the wilderness enough. There was the pressure of work, yeah, but anymore Suzanne didn't seem to care that much about getting out.

How many times can a man be pushed away like a slobbering puppy dog? How long can he go on? How long can a man try to be romantic, try to retain that glory, that passion, that excitement—when his tries stir nothing in return?

Hell's bells. It's a hell of a thing when a thirty-four-year-old man married to a gorgeous woman has to find his sexual release the way he had when he was a fifteen-year-old kid. Alone and palely loitering.

Hunter's eyes opened wide. It was dark. He was unsure of where he was. It was quiet. Cold, fresh air flowed over his face. Far off, a poorwill called. This wasn't Washington. A woman was beside him. Who was she? MaryAnne. Lord, yes, MaryAnne McClellan. What a pistol this loving, lovely woman was. She stirred and, in her sleep, threw a leg and an arm over him, buried her warm breath in his neck.

He had chewed on it, he had fought it. For months he had hammered at it. He had tried to talk to her about it, discuss it, work it out. But there never seemed to be an opportunity, the time and place never seemed right. Finally, he realized there was no solution, that it never would be worked out. That it just had to be ended.

It had been the morning after another empty night.

She was inspecting herself in the mirror in preparation for putting on her power face.

He forced the issue. They argued. Unkind words were spoken. Somewhere, sometime, somehow, love had slipped out the back door like an unwanted child and ran away.

Hunter and MaryAnne stood shoulder-to-shoulder with their binoculars aimed. A red-faced warbler hustled down insects on an Engelmann spruce ten yards in front of them. Goldenpeas and penstemons nodded against their bare shins.

"I love these little guys," MaryAnne said. "They are so dazzling with their red face and breast and black and white head. I can't think of the high country without thinking about them." She bumped his rump with hers.

The warbler flew across the trail to a corkbark fir, then disappeared deeper into the forest. Chattering ahead drew their binoculars.

"Great!" said MaryAnne. "Red crossbills. Have you ever looked at those beaks?"

"Yeah, an amazing adaptation to get seeds out of conifer cones."

"Did you know that crossbills can be either right- or left-beaked—depending on which side the upper beak crosses over, like people being right- or left-handed?"

Hunter hadn't know that. His store of natural history was growing under her tutelage. She was one hell of a field biologist, this Dr. MaryAnne McClellan.

They moseyed down the high ridge trail. There was no hurry. The truck was only a couple of miles away. Light filtered through the quaking aspens. They walked together, holding hands. Hunter noticed that and grinned in spite of himself. But he didn't seem able to stay thoughtless, carefree, and childlike for long.

It wouldn't have been so bad breaking up with Suzanne if that was all. But it was only days later that she began having an affair with a lawyer for the Environmental Defense Fund, pretending that the affair had been going on for months, that it was her asking for the divorce.

Instead of two friends realizing that the time had come for a friendly splitting of the sheets, she put him through the wringer, tried to make him a cuckolded fool to make sure that no one would ever think that any man had dumped *her*. After their love, their friendship, their good times, their *intimate* times, how could she do that—try to hurt him?

Maybe that was what had triggered his dissatisfaction with Capitol Hill wheeling and dealing. More likely the two problems reinforced each other.

MaryAnne stood on a boulder above a talus slope. Hunter stood down the trail focusing his camera on his model. As he looked through the view finder, she pulled up her T-shirt and sports bra to flash a boob at him.

He had planned it differently. No more love. Casual sex—yeah, sure. A dozen, a hundred Jodi Claytons. But no MaryAnne McClellans. Falling in love hadn't been in the plans. Seeing a perfect flower fade in a lovers' fall. And then? Hurt. Inevitable hurt.

Back in Rio Diablo the next day, Hunter's worries were swept away. The United States Post Office was the most unfairly maligned institution in the country, he thought. His slides of the wolves were back from Kodak and were stuffed in little orange boxes in his post office box. Straightaway, he drove to MaryAnne's. After dark, his place, was the invitation.

Hunter was in a wolfy whirl. It had been two and a half weeks since he had watched the lobos. The thought of seeing them again—if only on a screen—made his hackles rise.

She watched the tray and a half of slides in silence. Hunter started with a blow by blow, but after seeing how the slides held her, he went silent. The slides were finished. Hunter turned on the lights.

MaryAnne stared at the blank screen, a finger over her smile. She looked at him with her green eyes. If she had a tail, it would be sticking straight up—no, straight back and wagging.

"Those are wolves, buckaroo. And those are fantastic slides. Would you run through them again for me, please?"

This time she questioned and commented. She was up from the couch looking closely at the screen. She explained behavior.

When the second showing was finished, Hunter said, "I still can't believe it. Wolves in the Diablo." He sighed, "Wow," and shook his head.

"You better believe it, cowboy," she said with a grin wide as the New Mexico sky, with fire flashing in her green eyes. "And they're the most important thing in the whole wide world."

She asked for custody of the slides and for permission to make duplicates. The originals would go into a safe deposit box in Albuquerque. She made him promise not to talk to anyone else about the wolves or to even hint at their existence. "Don't even mention them to me over the phone."

"Why the secrecy when the presence of a breeding pair of wolves in Mondt Park and Davis Prairie could be the strongest argument for Wilderness protection there?"

"Jack, what would Harry Jukes or Buck Clayton do if they thought there were wolves in the Diablo?"

"Yeah . . . you're right about that."

"We need to hold off on public knowledge until there are more wolves. Then we can use them if necessary to protect their range."

But there was more to it, thought Hunter. There was more.

10

The old adobe house in the middle of five hardscrabble acres had come into Jack Hunter's family in 1960. His father had thought to use it as a vacation getaway, but the law practice called more than did family, and he never fixed it up. Hunter bought it from his mother in the late 1970s after his father died of a heart attack.

His mother had hated the place; it reminded her of the dryland pinto bean farm in eastern New Mexico where she had been born and raised, where she had lived through the black blizzards of the Dust Bowl. Hunter's great-grandparents homesteaded in 1907. Their mule-drawn plows broke the virgin sod of the Staked Plains. Manifest Destiny had proclaimed that rain would follow the plow; ecological reality dictated that dust would follow the plow.

Hunter's mother preferred the modern home surrounded by green lawn in Albuquerque's North Valley. Despite her dislike of the farm, and her being married to a successful city man, she kept many of her country ways. When Hunter had begun to play cowboy in high school, he found a new fondness for her colorful expressions. He and Bill Crawford had vied over who could best "talk Texan." Jack Hunter had kept the habit in Washington. Like cowboy boots, it had been armor against yuppie sophistication, against Potomac fever. "Shit fire and save matches" and "hell's bells and little bitty pissants" had been his anchors to windward.

He and Suzanne had visited the Diablo shack only a few times while they were in Washington, but childhood memories of the run-down old place made it home for Hunter more than the fine house in Albuquerque's North Valley where he had grown up.

Hunter's adobe was of the same vintage as the old Delaney place where MaryAnne lived, but was even more spare. The mud walls formed a rectangle of three rooms: living room, kitchen, and bedroom. A covered board porch with a wooden railing ran along the front. A single outside door opened from the kitchen to the porch. A rusty tin roof kept the rain away.

There was no indoor plumbing; out back, the outhouse had been eaten by wind and snow, and had fallen into its pit. A shovel and the grove of Arizona white oaks in back did just fine. The kitchen sink drained directly through a pipe to half-a-dozen dead fruit trees. Hunter planned to replace them with new trees in the fall. He hauled his dishwater up from the irrigation ditch. Since taking up with MaryAnne, he had been getting his drinking water from her well; before, he had fetched it from a spring at road's end up Calkin Creek. Hunter had the money to drill a well stashed in a CD. The local well driller would get around to it sooner or later.

Hunter had a garden in the overgrown field below the concrete irrigation ditch. He had hoed out a patch in the cockleburs, careless weed, Johnson grass, and horehound when he had moved in two months ago. He wasn't much of a gardener, but the supermarkets of Platoro were far away, and Hunter liked vegetables.

He had weeded this morning. Now he sat, shirtless and dirty in the rocking chair on his swept porch, and oversaw the water at its job with the squash, corn, beans, onions, chiles, okra, carrots, tomatoes, cucumbers, bell peppers, and eight kinds of lettuce. No iceberg. Endive, green leaf, red leaf, escarole, romaine, butter, arugula, and raddichio. (MaryAnne loved the baby lettuce salads he brought her.) Hunter would have taken offense if anyone called him a yuppie, but, like skunk spray, urban sophistication lingers for a long time.

Hunter had scattered birdseed this morning on what passed for his front yard. A chain gang of feathered rototillers, drum major topknots bobbing, worked the gravel for it. These were Gambel's quail, but Hunter also got scaled quail.

He watched a pair of Bullock's orioles at their nest in the spreading Arizona walnut—*nogal*—above the ditch. Hunter corrected himself: They were *northern* orioles; the birding deans recently had lumped the Bullock's and Baltimore orioles into a single species. Tough luck for life listers. Hunter had had both on the list of birds he had seen. But there had been no net loss—he made up for the orioles because the American Ornithologists' Union at the same time split the yellow-bellied sapsucker into two species—the yellow-bellied and the red-naped sapsuckers. He had seen both of those races, now species.

The new love frenzy with MaryAnne had slowed down after two weeks. And a damn good thing, thought Hunter. He'd be dead if he had to keep up that pace any longer. What a firecracker. He'd never met anyone like her. That worried him. The thought of wolves in the Diablo and visions of her slugged it out for space in his head. There was room for little else.

It was time to clean up the yard and shed, and haul the hoarded trash and junk of decades to the landfill, but he was saved from starting that grimy task by the throaty purr of a motorcycle coming down the highway. The bike turned onto his road, and Hunter switched his binoculars from the Halloween-hued birds to it. Bill Crawford rode the motorcycle—or, as Bill would say, *motor-sickle.* Hunter went inside and returned to the porch with two cold beers and two cigars.

"How the hell you doin', outlaw?" Bill called as he shut down his bike in the front yard. The quail scattered with about as much noise as his oily Norton.

"Can't complain. What brings you out here?"

"Well, I felt like blowing the dust off the bike, and MaryAnne said you backed out at the last minute from coming to the airport to see Reed yesterday, so I thought I'd come out, give you some shit, and see if you were still alive."

"'Fraid so."

Bill dropped down onto the shaded porch. He leaned back against one of the roof support posts. The four by four creaked.

"Have a beer," said Hunter.

"Don't mind if I do." Bill took a long slow drink and blew out the heat of the highway. "Whew. Hey, man, we kicked butt yesterday!"

"Tell me about it."

"Heh, heh," Bill chuckled as a grin wrapped around his face. "I know this guy who raises pigs. So we borrowed one and painted a barrel around it and the words 'Not All Pigs Are For Federal Timber Pork.' We stashed the pig in a van at the airport parking lot. It was a good crowd for Platoro— about a hundred. Over half of 'em were prowilderness."

"Good, good," said Hunter.

"Hey," the big man said, "the best part of it was that we played it cool. Everyone pretended they were antiwilderness when Buck Clayton started shooting off his mouth when Senator Reed came out of his plane. Then MaryAnne and I hustled the pig out of the van and brought it up to Reed. *Hooee!* Ol' Buck was speechless! He didn't know what hit him! MaryAnne even got a Minicam from one of the Albuquerque TV stations to come—it was on their news last night. Then she handed Reed our petition with five hundred local signatures for adding Mondt Park to the Diablo Wilderness. And all our folks whipped out signs and started chanting 'Save the Diablo! Save the Diablo!' Heehaw. Ol' Buck looked like he coulda shit!"

"Damn good job," said Hunter. "That's the way to lobby Reed. You gave him the sense of local support for Wilderness that he needs. Excellent. Keep working on him." He thought of asking Bill about the wolves. Surely he knew about them. But, no, he had promised MaryAnne. No way was he going to court that wrath.

Bill clicked Hunter's beer bottle with his. "Hey, you seen Jodi Clayton lately?"

"Not for a week or so, but I've got another batch of her quarter horses to do. I better get over there tomorrow. Cigar?"

"I think I will. Thanks. Well, don't go over this afternoon. That's where I'm headed from here. I gave her a call and Buck's not around today. After the fracas at the airport yesterday, I don't think Buck would be happy to see me. Even less so if he knew what I was doing there!" Bill chuckled through his shit-eating grin. "Though I'm not sure he'd really care. I've always had my doubts about ol' Buck. Might not be as much of a real man as he pretends. He and Jodi do have separate bedrooms. I guess Buck's off overnight to Los Angeles to lick his wounds." He followed Hunter's lead and licked down his cigar. "Goddamn. Wouldn't it have been something to have had an older woman like Jodi get a hold of you when you were seventeen or something? What a pork chop!"

Hunter laughed. "It would've been something, all right." He clipped the end of his cigar, lit it, and offered the small guillotine and the matches to Bill.

Bill worked on clipping and lighting his cigar. Hunter blew a smoke ring.

"Hey," Bill said, eyes twinkling after he sent up a puff, "I understand you've been seeing another for sure pork chop. MaryAnne McClellan."

Hunter swallowed a mouthful of beer. "Yeah, some."

"Some, huh? Ain't it a little more'n that? I'm expecting wedding bells. Heh, heh. MaryAnne really turned into something else. Doctor McClellan. Hooee! What a darlin'."

"Yeah." Hunter was wistful and then added softly, "She *is* something else." The orioles chased an acorn woodpecker out of their walnut.

Bill puffed on his cigar and savored the smoke. "So, I heard you shod my mule."

"*Your* mule?"

"Yeah. Zeke. I've been boarding him up here at MaryAnne's."

Hunter blew a line of smoke rings to impress Bill. "I thought he was MaryAnne's mule."

"No, he's mine. I use him for packing in rafts for spring float trips and such. I was going to come up here and shoe him, but MaryAnne told me she had you do it. Said you did a good job."

"Thanks."

"Actually, MaryAnne could do it herself. I've taught her how to trim and shoe."

"Is that so?" Hunter blew another batch of rings. "Guess I better shut the gate on the ditch. Garden's gotten enough."

Bill Crawford followed him down to the ditch. "Damn, these are good cigars." He looked at the band still around his. "Partagas, huh?"

"It's nothing serious, though. Don't start getting ideas."

"Huh?"

"It's nothing serious—between me and MaryAnne. We're just friends. I'm not getting serious again—not with any woman."

"I don't know, Jack. You couldn't do any better than MaryAnne. Lord God A'mighty, I have to admit that I'd do back flips for the chance if she wasn't like my little sister."

"Yeah . . . but I'm not . . . I'm just not interested in getting involved. It's not worth it. I don't want any complications."

"Shit, complications are fun. Damn the torpedoes. Full speed ahead. See what happens."

"You never think about complications, huh?" Hunter asked as they plopped back down on the porch.

"Hell, no. You know that. My philosophy is to get on this ol' bronc and see where she takes me. Ride 'er to the end. Go for all the hooray, women, and wilderness I can get. That's what I'm after. That's what makes life worth living. The rapids. The grizzly bears. The jealous husbands. Ha!"

"Hell's bells, Bill," Hunter laughed and went inside for two more beers. "You get less rational every time I see you," he called from the kitchen.

After those beers and more embellishments about the coup at the airport, Bill Crawford took his leave. Buck Clayton's wife awaited him, and Bill Crawford hated to keep another man's wife waiting.

Despite the early afternoon beer bloat, Jack Hunter loaded up the back of his truck with junk and trash, and drove to the landfill. The little man upstairs searched around his penthouse for a smidgen of jealousy about Bill and Jodi, but didn't find it—instead he found relief sitting in its place. Hunter wouldn't feel like he was running out on her. . . .

Ravens overhead croaked at him to hurry it up. They eyed him like street hustlers checking out an easy mark.

"Sorry, *cuervos*, ain't nothing in here to eat. Check out my compost pile for the buffet." Hunter tossed the junk and trash into the smoldering trench. He looked up at the whaleback of the Apache Peaks. The most beautiful sanitary landfill in America. *Although*, thought Hunter, *the one in Moab, Utah, was pretty spectacular, too.*

He heard the phone ringing when he parked the truck back at his place. He caught it before the caller hung up. "Hello?" he puffed.

"And what have you been doing to be so out of breath?"

"Hauling trash to the dump, cupcake. Cleaning up 'Hillbilly Acres' as you so sweetly put it the other night."

"Well, I've decided to give you another chance," MaryAnne said. "I normally wouldn't ask a fellow out after he's turned me down once, but you're getting a unique opportunity to make up to me."

"How did I turn you down once?"

"I invited you on a date yesterday and you refused."

"Wrangling a pig in front of a United States senator isn't my idea of a date," said Hunter.

"Well, it was a date. And you stood me up. I'm shocked. Shocked. And hurt, too, I might add."

"It sounds like you're shocked and hurt."

"Anyway, I'm giving you a second opportunity. Would you like to go out with me, Jack, sweetie?"

"Where? What? When?"

"Jack! You don't look a gift girl in the mouth! Particularly when you're as homely as you are and I'm as pretty as I am."

"You are cuter than a pair of speckled sow's pups, MaryAnne."

"Why, thank you, darling. I think you do care for me even though you turned me down yesterday and broke my heart. So, it's a date for tomorrow?"

"What?" he demanded.

"A little drive. A picnic. Steamy passion under the stars."

"I've got to shoe horses tomorrow. I've got three clients promised."

"How about if we leave in the afternoon? I'll have you back home in a couple or three days. If you're sore tomorrow from shoeing, I'll even give you a back rub. How can you turn that down?"

"I guess I can't. I know I'm getting into something my better judgment would warn me against, but I'll just have to throw caution to the wind."

"That's the kind of talk I like to hear, lover. I'll have you trained in no time," she gloated.

"Before I completely commit, though, what are we doing? Will you at least tell me that, MaryAnne?"

"Oh, you want details! Well, last year a ranger on the Coronado National Forest in southeastern Arizona reported a wolf sighting. She believes she saw three wolves—one adult, two juveniles—run across a dirt road a few miles north of the Mexican border just west of the San Rafael Valley. That's oak savanna—classic Mexican wolf habitat. There's been a couple of follow-up sightings, but no positive confirmation. I'd like to go down and search for sign, do some howling and see if I get a response. Oh!" she said. "Remember me telling you about the job I might take running a field course on Mexican wolves? Next spring? For Round River Conservation Studies?"

"Yeah."

"Well, I'm going to do it. The Coronado National Forest might be the best place for the course. So I need to check study sites, too. I'd like some company. You did say once you'd like to go howling with me."

"Sounds like fun," Hunter admitted.

"Well, good, I'm glad you think so. We could also do a little birding. I hear that the elusive rose-breasted becard is building a nest near the rest area along Sonoita Creek. Thick-billed kingbirds and green kingfishers are also being seen."

"Great, I've never seen those in the states. South of the border, yeah, but not north of it."

"Then it's a date?"

"It's a date."

11

A sleepy Jodi Clayton met Hunter at her kitchen door the next morning.
"Oh, god, Jack, is it already nine o'clock?"

She ordered him off to the corral and told him to take his time—she
would be in the pool when he was done. Hunter's speed was picking up as
he did more shoeing, so when he finished, instead of going straight to the
pool, he found a cigar in the truck's glove box. He sat on the tailgate in the
shade and smoked it.

Cigars end, though. Hunter tossed the butt to a sizzling death in a
small puddle of horse piss. He headed up to the house. The temperature was
climbing into the nineties today, he reckoned. He wished Buck was home.

"I'm sorry, Jack. I must have looked a sight when you got here. I hope
I look a little better now."

She did. She was stretched out in the sun on a chaise longue beside
the pool, wearing her freckles and a bright red bikini. From the look of
her damp hair, she'd been for a swim but she was freshly made-up down
to her toenails.

Hunter stood in the shade of the sprawling weeping willow, which
lorded over the pool and patio, and wiped the sweat from his brow. "You
always look good, Jodi."

Bonaparte, the poodle, sniffed his boots. The dog hadn't been allowed out of the house or walled patio for a month. Barfed horseshit and hoof pairings on expensive rugs had sentenced him to life imprisonment. But on Hunter's boots and jeans were stories of the wilderness outside.

"It's so nice to know a man who lies properly. I'm having a Bloody Mary. Would you like one? Or a beer? I'll bet a beer." She pointed to the patio refrigerator. "Why don't you peel out of those dirty clothes and rinse the horses off in the pool?" She dove in.

Instead of a beer, Hunter plunked a couple of ice cubes in a glass and poured Jack Damage over them. 11:15 A.M. He drank it while watching Jodi in the pool, then climbed out of his boots and jeans. *So, asshole, now what?* asked the voice in his head.

After a few minutes of playing around in the pool, Jodi asked, "What's wrong, Jack? You seem far away."

If there was anything Hunter dreaded, it was having to discuss a relationship. Suzanne had seen to that. He weaseled. Jodi ferreted.

"You know, Jack, if you feel uncomfortable about us because of your little friend MaryAnne McClellan—yes, of course, I know about her, but I haven't told Buck, god, he'd have a stroke if he found out his horseshoer was carrying on with the wicked witch of the wilderness, that would be much worse than if he found out you were carrying on with me—that's fine. I'm paying you to shoe my horses, not to diddle me in the pool."

"I guess things are getting a little serious between me and MaryAnne, Jodi. I don't know. I didn't plan it that way, I . . ."

"Don't worry about it, dear boy. You aren't my only lover. Your big friend isn't as pretty as you are, but he doesn't suffer from existentialism either. You can still shoe my horses. Your check is on the table, under my Bloody Mary glass. I've got horses to exercise. Excuse me." She climbed out of the water and went into the house through the French doors.

Existentialism? He hadn't known she knew the word. Hunter looked at Bonaparte. He came up to the dog's withers. He pulled himself out of the pool and put on his boots and jeans.

Hunter drove into Rio Diablo from the Clayton Ranch. The Rio Diablo Cafe made a damn good chicken-fried steak. He gathered his mail next door at the post office. His favorite magazine, *Natural History*, was in his box.

In the cafe, he took a corner table as far from the smoking section as possible. His skull had had an unwelcome, unfamiliar visitor since Jodi had called the day before yesterday. A snake had slithered into the little man's penthouse and somewhere was lurking. It was a poisonous reptile previously unmet—guilt, a feeling of unfaithfulness. Hunter tried to track it down and chop off its head. *But why should I feel unfaithful?* he asked himself. He hadn't had sex with Jodi. Hadn't gotten out of it very elegantly, but he'd done it. He should be feeling good about himself. Proud. Even noble. He wasn't sleeping around on MaryAnne any more.

Yet the snake did not flush, nor did it chop easily.

Maybe you've misidentified this snake, said the little man. *Maybe it isn't guilt; maybe it's fear of the trail MaryAnne is leading you down. . . .*

Hunter stopped him. He was never sure which side the little creep would take.

The waitress brought him a glass of iced tea. He sucked down half of it and opened *Natural History.* If the snake couldn't be chased off, maybe it would go away on its own if it was ignored. Stephen Jay Gould's musty, fussy rummaging through the attic trunk of Darwinism went up against the snake. Next to David Quammen in *Outside,* Gould was Hunter's favorite columnist. Hunter had drifted out of his head and settled into Gould's, where leather chairs creaked and boxes of fossils and old volumes gathered dust, when he sensed someone beside his table.

"Howdy."

Hunter looked up.

Charley Rath was perhaps an inch shorter than six feet, but was sturdily built like the sawn trunk of an ancient alligator juniper in service as a corner post for a far-stretching barbed wire fence. And, thought Hunter, probably no smarter.

Charley put his hand out. Hunter took it with a big cat's wariness.

"I'm Charley Rath."

"Hi. Jack Hunter."

"No hard feelings?"

"No . . ."

"Man, no one never knocked me out before! Even that big Navajo from Magdalena that hit me in my last football game didn't knock me out. You knocked me out. That's something. It was cool." Charley's eyes twinkled. "Onis Luebner says you hit him harder than he ever been hit before. Thought you ruptured his gut. You're one for-sure-ass brawler, man. You took all three of us. I didn't think no one could do that."

Hunter allowed a small smile. "I didn't have much choice."

Charley giggled. "That's a good one! Well, no hard feelings?"

"No, no hard feelings."

"Want to arm-rassle?"

"Sorry, I've got a few more horses to shoe today."

"Oh, you're the new guy who's shoeing horses. That educated farrier, Mr. Clayton called you. No wonder you can hit so hard." Charley seemed as pleased with himself as if he'd just worked out the unified field theory.

Charley Rath stuck out his hand again. Hunter took it ready for the testing squeeze. Charley had a hell of a grip, but Hunter held his own without seeming to try. Nothing like arm-wrestling horses to build up your grip. Charley grinned an idiot's smile.

The plump waitress, old beyond her years, brought a platter of chicken-fried steak and mashed potatoes slathered in good white Elmer's gravy. A biscuit and canned peas were on the side.

Charley said, "Well, I like to fight. If you ever want to get it on again, let me know."

"I only fight when I have to."

"Well, good to meet ya!" He headed back to the regulars' table on the smoking side of the low room divider.

Hunter nodded after him. He was amused; modern styles seemed to have caught up even with the rednecks of Rio Diablo: Charley's chicken-soup-yellow hair was short and straight on top and long and crinkly in the back; he wore a sparse Fu Manchu mustache; and he had that peculiar but popular straight-across removal of the sideburns that made it look as if his ears had been cut off. Lord love a duck. What was next? An earring?

Hunter turned his attention to the chicken-fried steak. When the waitress returned to refill his iced tea, he glanced over to the regulars' table. The good ol' boys were leering like hounds watching a cat. Luebner was at the table. Jukes, too. Seeing that crowd, he appreciated the wisdom of MaryAnne's secrecy about the wolves. That thought gave him the shivers. He went back to the hammered, battered, fried, gravied meat.

But soon, his eyes slipped back to them. The cigarette culture, sniffed Hunter. Coors and instant coffee; Top Forty country and talk radio; television sports and tell-it-all talk shows; the sports page and supermarket checkout stand tabloids; white bread and Hungry Man frozen dinners; chain saws and bulldozers; mobile homes and real-man full-sized pick'em-up trucks; worm fishing and road hunting; quad runners and power boats; Rush Limbaugh and H. Ross Perot. The Real Americans.

In his smugness, Hunter had the words: The bumpkin proletariat. Poor white trash. Know-nothingism.

Cigarette smoking mirrored their attitude toward life, Hunter sneered. They didn't worry about the health hazards of smoking because they didn't understand cause and effect. Understanding the consequences of what they did was intellectually and philosophically beyond them. Just as they couldn't link smoking to lung cancer, they couldn't recognize that over-grazing caused erosion. That overcutting meant less forest and fewer logging jobs. That poaching meant fewer deer and elk.

Hunter's sense of intellectual and moral superiority was pissed on from a great height by the twit in his head.

It wasn't Hunter's cigars. Three cigars a week—not inhaled—were far from three packs a day of Camels or Marlboros (okay, okay, six or seven cigars a week).

But what about the consequences of your uninvolvement? Do you recognize them? Or do you pass over them like the bubbas pass over the consequences of smoking, grazing, logging, and poaching?

Hunter ground out the voice like a cigar butt under his heel.

Hunter shod one horse for a retired Park Service biologist and then trimmed a colt for Red Underwood. The colt was skittish, and Hunter caught a glancing kick in the thigh. He had been trying to identify the snake wrapped around his brain stem instead of watching the colt.

He had just enough time after getting home to soap off the horses in the irrigation ditch before MaryAnne arrived at six o'clock. Her Jeep was packed for several days of camping. He tossed in his sleeping bag and other gear. She was entirely too happy. The snake tightened its coil.

"I have a special picnic dinner and a special picnic place picked out for a special evening with a special friend," she said.

"What are we waiting for?" he said and kissed her.

Ten miles south on 666, she took a two-track dirt road three miles back from the highway and parked beside a giant alligator juniper.

"One of my favorite trees," she said, spreading out a red-checked table-cloth on the ground.

Hunter stroked its rough-checkered bark. "It's about as big an alligator as I've ever seen. Looks like a fifty-foot tall stalk of broccoli."

"I don't have any broccoli for our little picnic, but I do have some cold artichokes and asparagus, home-baked sourdough French bread, soft garlic cheese, some wonderful venison salami Daddy made, and a bottle of Châteauneuf du Pape."

Hunter pretended to faint dead away. Her kiss brought him back from his grave in the juniper-needle duff.

"You are a treasure, MaryAnne. And I am a lucky man," said the cowboy Lazarus.

"And don't you forget it," she said.

MaryAnne ate her asparagus in an obscene manner. Hunter trumped with the artichoke. They made goo-goo eyes at each other. She checked herself. "No. We need to make tracks. Let's pack up. We'll have more time later."

They loaded the Jeep in the sunset's brightness, and hit U.S. 666 for Platoro, Lordsburg, and southeastern Arizona.

MaryAnne said, "No monsoons yet, even though it's after the Fourth of July. Clear as a bell tonight; so we'll be able to just throw-down camp at this spot in the Peloncillos where I want to howl for wolves. It's almost a hundred miles east of the San Rafael Valley where the wolf sighting was, but the Peloncillos are prime habitat for lobos, too. I've been wanting to check them out."

South of Platoro, 666 wound through the oaken hills of the low Buckhorn Mountains and then dumped the travelers into the desert north of Lordsburg. The lower elevations between the Diablo Highlands and the isolated ranges—"Sky Islands"—of southeastern Arizona and extreme southwestern New Mexico were a western extension of the Chihuahuan Desert. Farther west, the Sonoran Desert was crowned with the saguaro—the giant columnar cactus that symbolized both the Southwestern United States and deserts around the world. In reality, saguaros grew only in southern Arizona, along the adjacent California side of the Colorado River, and in northwestern Mexico.

So much for pop geography, thought Hunter.

The Chihuahuan Desert, in contrast, was crowned by yuccas—shaggy trunks a dozen feet tall topped by corollas of bayonet leaves and tall slender spikes with fat white flowers. One hell of a lily.

Graceful little desert willow trees grew in the washes; mesquites and drab gray-green creosote bushes flecked the flats. Against the stars, isolated ranges rose above the curve of the Earth. Dry lake beds shimmered in the faint light. Warm air flowed at sixty miles an hour over the hand-holding lovers in the topless Jeep.

Hunter told MaryAnne about his lunchtime encounter with Charley Rath.

"He's sort of a sweet kid in some ways," she said. "Not too bright, rather violent, even predatory, but with a softness inside. This winter he came by my place with a raven he'd caught in one of his traps. He was genuinely upset. He said he'd heard that I knew a lot about animals and maybe I could fix up the raven. Poor thing. Its foot was nearly severed. I took it down to a woman with Plataro Audubon who does wildlife rehabilitation, but it didn't make it. Before Charley left he talked about critters. I think he really does care about nature. Of course, given the crowd he hangs out with, that caring will soon evaporate. It's sad." She shook her head. "Had he been born into a hunter-gatherer tribe, he'd be a fine person. But in this culture . . ."

Lordsburg was a stagecoach town turned railroad town turned interstate highway town. It had been the destination for John Wayne and Claire Trevor in *Stagecoach* as they fought the movie version of Apaches through Steins Pass.

MaryAnne drove a few miles west on I-10, took a cloverleaf exit in the middle of a big playa, and headed south on state highway 338 into the Bootheel, the southwestern corner of New Mexico, which looks on a map like the heel of a cowboy boot.

She said, "The cotton fields and chile farms end in forty miles. So does the twentieth century. In the southern Animas Valley, you almost expect to run into jaguars and renegade Apaches. Geronimo surrendered not far from where we're going to camp tonight."

The four-days-past-full moon rose over the spare hills to the east.

"So, darlin'," Hunter said, "you're a wolf biologist, you're nuts about big wilderness. Why'd you leave Alaska? It seems like Alaska would have been heaven on Earth for you."

MaryAnne drove a mile before answering. Then she pursed her lips and said, "It was, sweetie, it was. The Brooks Range, the Arctic Plain unfolding north to the sea . . . what a landscape. I've never felt a greater sense of wilderness than there. And then the caribou migration, packs of wolves attending them. Dall sheep like patches of snow on the mountain slopes, moose working the northernmost willows in the drainages of the north slope. Barren ground grizzlies where there is no cover, no place to hide, no tree to climb. Snowy owls and gyrfalcons. I've been to Africa once—a couple of months in Namibia on a research project—but I have never felt the presence of large mammals in a *wilderness* setting anywhere else like I have north of the Yukon River."

Hunter knew she was answering; he also knew that she took her own route and her own time. Open though she was in loving him, she kept secrets locked away in a pirate's chest in her head.

"There were several reasons I left Alaska, but the primary one was that it wasn't home. It *was* heaven, I'll go back—I hope many times. But this," MaryAnne gestured into the open darkness all around, "is home. The Southwest, and particularly southern New Mexico and Arizona, has my soul."

"I feel that way, too. But why? What's so special about this country?" Hunter asked.

"The diversity. This is the great zone of overlap in the Americas. Here is the mingling of the tropical and temperate regions of North America. There are lots of ways to describe a landscape scientifically. For example, geographers call this the Basin and Range Province—isolated mountain ranges rising out of basins. The Diablo is the Diablo Highlands Province.

"Botanists put their own overlay on the land. The Diablo, stretching from the Sierra Prieta northwest to the south rim of the Grand Canyon, is called the Upper Diablo Mountains Forest Province. As you know, the Diablo has vegetation similar to the Southern Rockies of northern New Mexico and Colorado. But it has a Mexican flavor, too. As the raven flies, right now we're sixty miles or so from the southernmost part of the Diablo. But down there," she pointed through the windshield, "is the Sierra Madre. Closer now than the Diablo. Much closer than the Rockies. So, the Diablo is where the Rockies and Sierra Madre begin to interdigitate. The Diablo has alligator juniper and silverleaf oak in the lower forest, Arizona sycamore along the streams. There are even a couple groves of Chihuahua pine and Arizona cypress. Magnificent hummingbird, red-faced warbler, javelina, coatimundi—all those are tropical. Even more a zone of overlap between the Rockies and the Sierra Madre are these mountains." She swept her hand again. "The Animas, Peloncillos, and over in Arizona, the Chiricahuas, Huachucas, Pinaleños, Catalinas, Santa Ritas, Pajaritos. The Sky Islands."

Hunter enjoyed the ecological lecture. When MaryAnne got warmed up, she was *Professor* McClellan.

"In their higher elevations, the Sky Islands have a strong Rocky Mountain forest influence—ponderosa pine, Douglas-fir, aspen. But true Rocky

Mountain spruce-fir forest ends in the Diablo. Mt. Graham—the Pinaleños—has a few thousand acres of Engelmann spruce and corkbark fir but no Colorado blue spruce. The Chiricahuas have Engelmann spruce, but no corkbark fir; the Catalinas have corkbark fir, but no Engelmann spruce. South of the Diablos, only Mt. Graham still has red squirrels—a species dependent in this region on spruce-fir. And that population is small and Endangered, especially so with the University of Arizona and the Vatican hacking out the site for a major astronomical observatory in the middle of the best forest."

She shook her head in anger, but quickly returned to her ecological description. "The Sky Islands are a classic example of island biogeography. During the cooler and more mesic climate of the Pleistocene, Rocky Mountain spruce-fir forest grew throughout this area. With the drying and warming after the end of the ice age about twelve thousand years ago, conifer forests could survive only on the Sky Islands and became isolated from one another. Species disappeared randomly—just as they would in an island archipelago cut off from the mainland and from one another by rising ocean levels. Ecologists call this *relaxation.*

"Though they've lost their Rocky Mountain spruce-fir forest, these ranges have Sierra Madrean trees that the Diablo doesn't have—Mexican piñon and Apache pine—and much more Chihuahua pine than the Diablo has. The mid-elevations have a well-developed Madrean oak woodland that peters out in the Diablo and doesn't exist in the Rockies. And the fauna. Lots more Mexican birds here than in the Diablo. And jaguar, ocelot, jaguarundi. Not to mention the herps—there are several tropical snakes and a few frogs."

Again, she stared out the windshield in silence. She smiled, pursed her lips, and said, "So, why is this home? Because in the Diablo, elk and javelinas graze and root cheek to jowl; in the Chiricahuas, northern goshawks knock thick-billed parrots out of the sky; and from the Diablo to the Sierra Madre, grizzlies and jaguars once hunted the same territory. This is where the Neotropics and the Nearctic—the two ecological realms of the Americas—overlap and mingle. I've seen green kingfishers on the San Pedro River in Arizona and on the Rio Macal in Belize. I've watched sandhill cranes on the Arctic Plain and on the Lordsburg Playa we just passed. And we can restore true wilderness to this landscape—lobo and griz and *el tigre.* . . ."

Hunter squeezed her knee. "I think I get it."

MaryAnne turned and looked at him. "Do you? Do you really, Jack? I hope so. It's very important to me that you do understand."

"I think I even understand better now why the Diablo seems so special to me."

"Yes," she mused, "as much as I love the Sky Island ranges of southeastern Arizona and the Bootheel, the Diablo is the center of my world. It's so big, so wild. We have to think about issues of scale in conservation biology. And the Diablo complex, including the Blue River country in Arizona, is the only regional-sized mountain wilderness in the Southwest. Small is beautiful in economics. But when it comes to wilderness, to biodiversity reserves, bigger is better."

They drove in silence through the night, toward the Peloncillo Mountains where ghosts of Apaches and wolves rose like invitations in the moonlight. The pavement ended.

MaryAnne was as bubbly as the bottle of Moet & Chandon White Star in the ice chest, thought Hunter, as they bumped down the gravel. He looked at her profile against the moonlight. Her enthusiasm was so damn attractive. It was also pretty damn contagious.

"Listen to this tape," she said and pushed it into the cassette player.

Hunter's hackles rose as the chesty bawl flooded his ears.

"This is what we're listening for." She tilted her head back and howled—a long, wavering, mournful call of the wild.

To Hunter's ear it was indistinguishable from the wolves on the tape.

MaryAnne said, "The turnoff for the Forest Service dirt road across the Peloncillos is just up here. When we get on it, I'll do some howling. It's a slim chance we'll get any answers, but let's see."

She stopped at the faint intersection. "The Geronimo Trail," she said. "I gotta go potty. Then we'll go over the methodology for wolf howling surveys." She slipped away into the moonlight.

The washboard road had pummeled Hunter's bladder, too. He stepped off the road to pee on the grass. He was thrilled about the chance of more Mexican wolves in the United States. Since hooking up with MaryAnne, he'd prowled through her library, reading the wolf books—Brown's *The Wolf in the Southwest*, Mech's *The Wolf*, and three or four others. Wolves had him by the throat and wouldn't let go.

"Isn't this great country?" she asked when she came back. "We've been driving through the Gray Ranch. The Animas Mountains over there to the east and this incredible valley between them and the Peloncillos are all owned by a rancher who's managing it for biodiversity. About five hundred square miles of some of the best wildlife habitat in the United States. There are more species of mammals on it than in any National Park or Wildlife Refuge in the United States."

"Yeah, even with just the moonlight, the grass in this valley looks incredible," Hunter said.

MaryAnne nodded. "Very productive, and in exceptional condition. Okay, we have seven or eight miles to drive before we reach the Coronado National Forest boundary. Then it's about a dozen miles across the Peloncillos to where we'll camp in Arizona tonight. Say, twenty miles in all." She spread a Forest Service map on the hood and used a small flashlight to show Hunter the route.

After her finger traced their path, she said, "I'll check the odometer. Every two miles we'll stop the Jeep. The procedure is this: At each stop, I'll howl four times in the space of twenty seconds. Two howls will have a break dropping to a lower register. The other two will be flat. Each howl will be in a different direction. We'll wait exactly two minutes for a response. You have your watch? Good. You keep time. Two minutes. Let me know, and I'll howl again—five times. Wait another two minutes for response. Here's a compass. If we get a response, we'll mark the direction line on the topo map. We'll drive half a mile and howl. If we get a response there, we'll put that azimuth on the map. The compass lines will intersect where the wolves should be. We'll go to that spot in the morning and look for tracks or scat. I'll make casts of any tracks. If we find possible wolf scats, we'll collect them. I know a geneticist at the University of California Santa Cruz who's developed a PCR-based DNA technique well enough to be able to distinguish wolf scat from other canid scat. I'll send her anything we find. Possible hair, too."

She pulled her briefcase out of the Jeep and rummaged through it. "Here are the log forms. We'll fill them out whether we get responses or not. Time, weather conditions, location. Also any kind of response—coyote, owl, dog, whatever. I have a set of topographic maps for the Peloncillos in this folder. Here's the one for the first part of the route. You be in charge of the maps. For a boy, you're pretty good with maps."

"Hmm."

"Mark each location where we stop and howl as accurately as possible on the topo map." She hushed and looked around. "This is great lobo country!"

Hunter couldn't help himself. He kissed her on the cheek and pulled her close.

"So, how do you like being the field assistant to a wolf biologist?" she grinned.

"I like it, pork chop. Out with you I see the country in a different way—a deeper way. This wolf survey is exciting. Even if we don't get answering howls, I'm psyched."

"So am I, sweetie."

Drive two miles, mark the map, howl four times, wait two minutes, howl five times, wait two minutes. Nothing. Drive two miles, mark the map, howl four times, wait two minutes, howl five times, wait two minutes. Nothing. Drive two miles, mark the map, howl four times. . . . Two hours of this and it didn't get boring. Twice, coyotes yipped in response.

"Scared the dickens out of those little buggers," MaryAnne cackled.

Hunter tried howling.

"Good," she said. "Make your voice as deep as possible. Low tones carry farther."

At the last site after no response, MaryAnne said, "Shucks. Oh, well. I was just hoping, not expecting. Let's camp here. In the morning I'll teach you how to distinguish a lobo from a coyote or a dog, and how to identify wolf tracks and scats. Not much sleep tonight. We need to roll out early tomorrow and get over to the Canelo Hills, San Rafael Valley, and Patagonia Mountains."

12

Before first light, MaryAnne rolled Hunter out of their zipped-together sleeping bags. They dressed, gobbled granola bars, and howled for wolves. She decided to look for tracks along the canyon bottom before driving on to the San Rafael Valley and the Patagonia Mountains.

"This country still says 'wolf' to me," she said. They slung on their day packs and grabbed their binoculars.

Hunter watched her in the growing light. They were moving quickly up the rocky canyon, yet MaryAnne's eyes took in everything; she stopped and listened every hundred yards. Birds in the sycamores and oaks drew only fleeting attention from her. She was on the scent of something rarer. She hunkered on her heels near a patch of damp sand in the now-and-then stream.

"Good-sized," she muttered to herself. "But these are coyote." The two college cowboys, Jack and Bill, had been bad influences on her when she was a little girl: She pronounced "coyote" like a Texan. *KAI-oat.* Not *co-YO-tay* like a Mexican, or *kai-O-tee* like other gringos. She pulled a plastic ruler out of her fanny pack.

"Now, you, of course, know," she said to Hunter who squatted beside her, "that canids and felids register four toes in their prints, while bears and mustelids register five. This front track is two and a half inches long, big for a Southwestern coyote. But a lobo's should be close to four inches or more. The biggest male Mexican wolves are ninety pounds. A small female will only go sixty. Mexican wolves are the smallest and most distinct of all the North American subspecies of gray wolves. But they are still much larger than coyotes. A large male coyote in the Southwest won't top thirty-five pounds."

She looked up from the track. Sun was hitting the rimrock at the top of the canyon. Oaks, yuccas, and grass climbed the low mountains. A stringer of Chihuahua pines, with their distinctive little black cones, shared the canyon bottom with massive sycamores. Smooth gray bark peeled back on the sycamore trunks and limbs to reveal even smoother white bark underneath. "They always seem to be in a state of undressing," MaryAnne confided to Hunter. Arizona sycamore limbs grow haphazardly as though they don't have to obey any rules. They twist and curve, often running parallel to the ground. More than any other tree, they gave a subtropical tang to the landscape south of the Diablo Rim.

She turned back to the print. "See how long and oval this coyote track is? A wolf track would be rounder."

They fanned out from each other as much as the twisting canyon allowed, so they could better cut for sign.

"MaryAnne!" His voice was a whisper but had an exclamation mark in it. Low voices were called for if you wanted to see critters. "How about this one? Four toes, rounder, and much larger."

"Dog," she said, squatting beside it.

"Dog? How can you tell?" Letdown huffed in Hunter's voice. After seeing the wolves in the Diablo, part of him was expecting to find them everywhere.

She laid the ruler on the print. "A big dog, like a German shepherd. Three and a half including the claw marks. See how the two middle claws splay out? A wolf would have them parallel. Note also that the hind print is here beside the front one. That's called a 'double register.' Wolves, when walking, put their hind foot in the track of their front foot. That's called 'single register.'"

She looked ahead. "Look at the next tracks. See how sloppy the line is? Wolf tracks would be in a straight line. And here," she pointed to the side. "a horseshoe print. I'd judge this was a dog accompanying someone on horseback."

Hunter nodded. "Okay. Almost four inches or more long. Middle claws parallel. Not a long oval like a coyote, but less splayed than a big dog. A straight, tidy trail."

"And generally single register when walking."

"Right," said Hunter as he rose.

MaryAnne stood. "Now a mountain lion will leave a track about the same size as a wolf. But it will be rounder. Sometimes wider than long. And asymmetrical."

"What do you mean?" he asked.

"In cat tracks the toes seem to point in a slightly different direction than does the heel pad. The heel pad will also be larger in proportion and differently shaped. It will be convex to the rear, instead of concave like in wolves or dogs. Cats, of course, usually do not show claw marks. But if they do, the claw marks will be directly joined to the toes. Wolf tracks will always have the claw marks separated from the toes."

She squatted again and pointed to the dog track. "See this? Well-formed canid tracks will show an 'X' because of the shape of the pad and position of the toes."

"Yeah," Hunter said, "that's really obvious. Why haven't I noticed it before?"

"Felid tracks will not have an 'X.' But a well-formed one will show a curved rim between the pad and toes. Look for the 'X.' It is very distinctive."

They turned back after half an hour. MaryAnne was itching to get over to where the forest ranger had seen the three possible wolves the previous year. It was another hundred miles west, half on dirt roads. Coming down the trail, she stooped beside a scat.

"Coyote," she said, picking it up with a biologist's lack of squeamishness. She sniffed it and held it up to Hunter's nose.

He drew back.

"Go ahead, smell it. It's not yucky like dog poop. Has a nice, mild, musky scent. If it stinks awful, it's dog."

"Okay," he said and sniffed. "I wouldn't call it 'nice,' but it's not dog shit."

She put it back on the ground and casually brushed her finger tips on her shorts as she reached for the ruler. "About seven-eighths of an inch wide. Toward the large end for Southwest coyotes. They average about three-quarters. If it's over one and a quarter wide, it's wolf, but in the zone

132

of overlap from just under an inch to about one and a quarter, you can't tell without lab analysis. Unless there's corroborating evidence like adjacent tracks or a sighting."

They stood up. "Oh, well," she sighed, "I didn't really expect to find wolf spoor. But with all the deer and javelina sign, this is obviously great lobo habitat. The Peloncillos are the key corridor to link wolf populations in the Diablo with those in the Sierra Madre in Mexico."

They had gone less than a hundred yards when MaryAnne stopped Hunter with her hand. "Shhh," she whispered.

A troop of outlandish creatures was crossing the stream bed from one hillside to the other. They had ski-jump noses and long tails that stuck straight up—if Bob Hope, a raccoon, and a baboon had been involved in a *ménage à trois* and had viable offspring, this was what they would look like.

"Coatimundis," whispered MaryAnne.

"There must be thirty of 'em."

"Look at the little ones. They're darling." The professional zoologist had been briefly elbowed aside.

Like a troop of baboons, the coatis moved across the canyon and up the other slope. Flipping rocks and delving into everything of interest (and many, many things are of interest to coatis), they were having a moving breakfast.

MaryAnne said, "There were few reports of coatis north of the Mexican border until after the turn of the century. Now they're all the way up into the lower elevations of the Diablo. The first ranchers to report them thought they were being invaded by monkeys. The Peloncillos, twisting from Mexico up to the Diablo, were a perfect corridor for their invasion. That's one reason why I think the Peloncillos are such a critical biological corridor to maintain a connection between lobos in the Diablo and lobos in the Sierra Madre. In fact, this might be the corridor the female lobo you saw took to get to the Diablo."

"Do you think that wolf and her mate are dispersers from Mexico, or has there always been a remnant population in the Diablos lying low since the last ones were supposedly killed back in the '30s?"

"Could be either; could be both." She looked after the disappearing *chulos*, and started down the canyon for the Jeep. "Whatever, the population of Mexican wolves in the wild is tiny, far from viable. The Diablo lobos are very vulnerable. Kingbird." She stopped and looked through her binoculars. "Big beak. Could it be a tropical?"

"No white terminal band on the tail," said Hunter as it flew up from the dead sycamore twig to hawk an insect. "It's not a Cassin's." It sortied out again after a bee. "And no white side stripes on the tail. Not a western."

"Yes, I think we have a tropical kingbird," said MaryAnne. "Wonderful." She lowered her binoculars and looked at him.

He turned to face her and she stretched up for a kiss.

"Birds and bees. . . ." he said.

"I'll bet we could find a nice little love nest over on the bank under that sycamore. I love the way sunlight looks filtering through sycamore leaves . . . wait. Look at that limb. About ten feet off the ground. See where it forks? Whaddya think?" She grinned whimsically. "I've always wanted to try it up in a tree. That is the perfect limb."

Hunter looked skeptical.

"Come on. You won't fall out of the tree." She grabbed his hand.

Back at the Jeep, MaryAnne grinned, "Arboreal delight like that, lover, slows me down. It's nice to finally learn how our far ancestors made whoopee, though."

"I have to admit something, MaryAnne."

"What's that?"

"I've always fantasized about making love in a tree like a monkey, but never thought I'd find anyone to do it with. You've made one of my dreams come true."

"You are so romantic. One of these days, I'm going to pin you down and find out what your intentions really are." She poked him in the chest with a finger. "However, you do make field work more fun. Distracting, but fun. Let's go find lobos!"

Less than five miles from the last night's camp, a coyote dashed across the road in front of the Jeep.

"Want another lesson?" MaryAnne asked, as she shifted the gears back up.

"Sure," Hunter, riding shotgun, said.

"A lobo would be at least twice as heavy. Much longer legs—you might even think it was a deer at first."

"Yeah," he nodded, "that was my first inclination when I saw them in the Diablo."

"A wolf would have a furry mane around the throat. A shorter, blockier muzzle. Shorter, more rounded ears—though Mexican wolves have longer, more pointed ears than other wolf subspecies. Now those distinctions between coyotes and wolves—long legs, ruff, blocky muzzle, rounded ears—also hold true to distinguish wolves from German shepherds, huskies, and similar dogs. A very important distinguishing mark is the tail. A wolf or coyote tail will never curl. It sticks straight out or hangs down. It *never* curls. Dog tails will show a curl. Coyotes are supposed to carry their tails down more than wolves, but both species will carry them down or straight back. Of course, with my experience with wolves, I can positively identify one with just a glimpse."

"Well, I'm not a complete amateur in the woods, my dear," Hunter said. "I did a pretty good job, I think, of determining that what I saw in the Diablo were wolves, not coyotes, even though I thought it impossible that wolves would be there."

She smiled. "You did indeed, horseshoer. Forgive me if I sometimes get into my piled higher and deeper mode. I'm in a tough profession for a woman."

"I can't imagine you ever having a tough time holding your own."

She looked at him with a twinkle. "Thank you, darling. I think that was meant as a compliment."

"It was." He pulled a pair of sunglasses out of his day pack.

"Sunglasses?" said she. "I thought real men didn't wear sunglasses."

"I may not be able to prevent destruction of the ozone layer, but I might as well keep from getting cataracts. You don't need to check them out; they're UV coated."

She smiled and patted his knee.

Dr. McClellan and her assistant stopped for gas in the artsy-fartsy old mining town of Bisbee five miles north of the Mexican border. Unfortunately, Hunter thought, gentrification couldn't do anything about the suppurating open-pit copper mine they skirted on their way west.

West of Bisbee, the highway dropped past limestone outcrops to the San Pedro Valley. The limestone was tacked down by a plant that looked like a dominatrix's whip collection at an S & M resort: ocotillo, little sister of the boojum tree from Baja.

The river is a long brown god.

Like the far-off howl of a wolf, that snippet of poetry crawled into Hunter's ear and curled up. His brain had grown rusty in the sixteen years since grad school. The rest of the poem would not pop above the surface of consciousness. Like a lazy, sounding whale, it stayed down. "But it is T. S. Eliot, isn't it?" he asked himself. "It's gotta be Eliot."

If it was Eliot, he must have known the Southwest, where the waters carried the silt of eroded landscapes. But rivers weren't the only long brown gods. This whole land is a broader long brown god, thought Hunter.

The Southwest is a lean, sere land, without much fat to make men rich. The white men who came to this land, with pickaxes and with cattle, to skim the fat off it, made the land even more lean, more sere. These men, heirs to pioneer culture and customs, were visitors on the land, transients unable to sink roots in it, able only to diminish it, to make it leaner, to make it harder, because they were unwilling to adapt themselves to the land, seeing it only as something to bend to their will. The American West is a culture that wears spurs.

Though they claim roots in the land, thought Hunter, and tout their homegrown culture, they are vagrants. Mining companies shut down mines as soon as they are no longer profitable—community stability and workers be damned. Timber companies do the same, closing lumber mills once they've exhausted all the nearby forests. Few of the ranchers in the West are any longer the legendary mom-and-pops with sweat-stained hats and scuffed boots. Most ranches now are owned by corporations or by big-city doctors and lawyers as tax write-offs. And many of those descendants of pioneer ranchers who remain on the land—like Buck Clayton—still see land as a commodity, as something on which to borrow bank money.

The real dwellers in the land are those like MaryAnne McClellan and Bill Crawford who, Hunter smiled at his friend's corny boast, "plant their spears" and defend their place.

But what about you, asked the disagreeable little man behind Hunter's sunglasses. *Aren't you a transient? Where's your commitment? The roots you'll defend? Aren't you like Huck Finn, always lighting out for the territory?* He picked at Hunter's guilt like a scab that couldn't be left alone.

Hunter found the question a bitter herb on which to chew. He was glad when MaryAnne interrupted him with her speculation on why more Mexican birds were being seen in the Southwest. On the western horizon, a blue mountain range rose to nine thousand feet.

"The Huachucas," MaryAnne said, "home to more species of hummingbirds—fourteen—than any other place in the United States."

They crossed the bridge over the trickling San Pedro River, and

MaryAnne told Hunter its ribbon of cottonwood and willow was one of the most important wildlife corridors from Mexico.

Soon after the San Pedro River, they turned off the state highway onto a Forest Service road. The sign read "Nogales 60 miles." Shortly, the blacktop turned to a washboard of gravel weaving through a woodland of fifteen-foot-tall oaks. Atop Montezuma Pass, she stopped the Jeep. They walked up the short trail to an overlook where she spread out a Coronado National Forest map, scale: half inch to the mile.

Immediately to the north, the Huachuca Mountains reared like a spooked horse. Mexico was a mile to the south. There, Sky Islands tumbled across the plain to a rendezvous with the Sierra Madre. West, a surf of oaks rolled down to a grassland sea: the San Rafael Valley. In the far beyond, oak woodland climbed the Patagonia Mountains. North of that range, the spire of Mt. Wrightson stabbed the sky.

MaryAnne swept hundreds of square miles through her binoculars. After several minutes of scanning the landscape, she put them down and grinned. "Somewhere out there, someone saw three lobos. Today is Thursday. If I can keep you out until Sunday afternoon, we have most of four days and all of three nights. I'll be back here for the spring semester with the Round River students and do an in-depth study of this area, so all we need to do now is a cursory survey." Her finger traced out the dirt roads she wanted to travel for howling. She suggested places to camp. "Let's go howl!"

For the rest of Thursday, Friday, and most of Saturday, they ran howling surveys on dirt roads in the Canelo Hills, San Rafael Valley, and Patagonia Mountains. Saturday afternoon, they came out to state highway 82, two miles southwest of the village of Patagonia.

"Time for a break from work," said MaryAnne. "Two miles southwest is the most famous roadside rest area in birdwatching lore. Wanna see if the rose-throated becards are still there?"

At the rest stop, Sonoita Creek was pinched between two buttresses of other-worldly red and white rock. Across the road and down to the creek went the birders. The rare (in Arizona) tropical flycatchers were at their pendulous nest in a sycamore along Sonoita Creek. A thick-billed kingbird shagged flies from the same tree. Both were U.S. records for Hunter, and he dutifully recorded date and location in his field guide.

Back on the road, MaryAnne turned east. Soon she jinked the Jeep off the highway and down a dirt road to a ford of Sonoita Creek. After fewer than five minutes of prowling the stream, Hunter started as a tiny, noisy flash of green blasted past them.

"Green kingfisher! Another first for the states!" He dragged out his field guide and pen.

"Now aren't I good for something?" MaryAnne asked. "Let's boogie. I want to get to camp north of here before dark."

Their camp was in the Santa Rita Mountains north of Patagonia and southeast of Tucson. MaryAnne picked a spot in the foothills with an eye-stretching view to the north, east, and south. Mt. Wrightson, the range's high point at 9,453 feet, was behind them to the west.

She sat on a boulder with a Bureau of Land Management map of Arizona in her lap. The map used different colors to show land owner-ship—National Forest, BLM, National Park, National Wildlife Refuge, Indian Reservation, military, state, and private. Drawn over the map was a web of red and green lines.

"The Santa Ritas are a perfect example of what's wrong with the way we've designated Wilderness Areas and National Parks," she said.

"How so?"

She took out the Coronado National Forest map. "Look at the bound-ary of the Mount Wrightson Wilderness Area. It looks like an amoeba. The boundaries were drawn to include only the higher elevations with hiking trails. Much of this lower Madrean oak woodland and oak savanna was excluded. It's a Wilderness boundary drawn for scenery and recre-ation, not for biodiversity."

Hunter nodded his head. The Mt. Wrightson Wilderness was one he had helped to designate. It had been part of the 1984 Arizona Wilderness Act. He had been the Sierra Club's Washington lobbyist for it.

MaryAnne continued her lecture. "Most of our Wilderness Areas and National Parks have been protected for scenery or because people liked to backpack in them. Wildlife habitat has been too often ignored. Moreover, we've set aside reserves like little islands in an ocean of human-dominated landscapes. An ecologist named Bill Newmark studied National Parks in the West during the '80s. He discovered that the smaller a Park was, the more mammal species it had lost. Even the largest National Parks, like Yellowstone, weren't big enough to maintain viable populations of griz-zlies and such.

"For even a minimally viable population of wolves you're talking a minimum of five thousand square miles needed as protected habitat. We don't have anything that size in the Southwest available as a reserve. Even the Diablo Wilderness after adding Mondt Park and other contiguous areas is less than two thousand square miles. And little areas like Mount Wrightson . . . what is it? Around twenty-five thousand acres?" She calculated in her head. "Forty square miles. It can't possibly stand on its own as habitat."

She took a thoughtful sip of her beer. "So you know what we gotta do?"

"What?"

"Protect metapopulations!"

"What the heck are metapopulations?"

"A metapopulation is a population of subpopulations. We protect or reestablish populations of wolves in the Diablo, in the Blue Range over the Arizona line, here where we sit, in the Chiricahuas, in the Galiuros north of here, in the Sierra Madre in Mexico, and we tie these core wildernesses together by wildlife movement corridors. As long as you get a few wolves moving between the different subpopulations every decade, you maintain necessary genetic vigor. And, if one subpopulation goes extinct for whatever reason, that area can be recolonized by individuals from another population in the metapopulation complex."

"So, that explains all the green lines connecting the areas outlined in red on this map?" Hunter asked.

"Right. Reed Noss and Larry Harris at the University of Florida developed this model about eight years ago. Core wildernesses surrounded by buffer zones connected by wildlife corridors. Focus on preserving viable populations and necessary habitat for large, wide-ranging predators like wolves, bears, and mountain lions, instead of isolated, island-like little Wilderness Areas and National Parks selected for scenery and backpacking trails. Voilà! A wilderness recovery network for the Southwest—no, for all North America—that will protect the whole range of native biological diversity and ecosystem functions!"

She was off. She was running. She was practicing her pitch for the Round River students. She pointed out the darkening mountain ranges and valleys visible from their perch and tied them to the areas of public land shown on the map and to the proposed web of wilderness cores and wildlife corridors she'd drawn. She explained the habitat values of the different places, the specifics of how to link them across Interstate 10 and other barriers.

The Round River students were damn fortunate, thought Hunter, as he lit a cigar. *Why didn't I have this while I was trying to push Wilderness bills through Congress?* He was mesmerized. At first. Then the doubts intruded. The hopelessness. He pushed them aside. Just for tonight, dream it can be done. Pretend there is hope for wilderness, for wolves, for MaryAnne McClellan. Even for Jack Hunter.

Late the next day, MaryAnne ended her howling survey. No wolves had howled back. No wolves had been seen through the binoculars. But she was intrigued by a single, faint pawprint Hunter had discovered earlier in the day near an abandoned mine shaft in the Santa Ritas. It was too faint for a plaster cast, and she didn't think Hunter's photographs would adequately show it.

"It's a possible, though, it's a real solid possible," she told her boyfriend. "It's corroboration—weak corroboration, I admit—of the ranger's sighting last year. There could be lobos using this region. If so, we ought to be able to confirm it next year with the Round River field course."

They loaded up the Jeep and headed for the highway.

"Well," said MaryAnne, "like Ade Murie said in Alaska, 'One need not see a wolf to benefit from his presence.'"

Because they wanted to get back to Rio Diablo that evening, they took Interstate 10, connecting with it twenty-five miles east of Tucson. She allowed him to drive her Jeep so she could work on her field notes. On the long grade out of the San Pedro Valley up to Texas Canyon, two semitrailer rigs blocked the road at thirty-five miles an hour.

MaryAnne glanced up from her notes. "Mormon roadblock."

"Assholes," Hunter snapped. "Why do they try to pass when they know they're going to drop down to a standstill?"

One of the eighteen-wheelers had a big sign on the back:
THIS TRUCK PAYS $4,318 IN ROAD-USE TAXES A YEAR.

"Right, asshole," said Hunter, "And does 16,893 dollars worth of damage." He rattled behind the trucks on the rutted, chuckholed interstate and stewed. But he did not stew silently.

"The business of America is the business of ripping off the commonwealth. Everybody pisses and moans about welfare, but the biggest welfare from the very beginning has been to those who already have wealth and who control the government."

MaryAnne put down her notes in the gloaming to listen to his rant with amusement.

The truck in the left lane finally pulled past the other and returned to the right lane. Hunter floored the Jeep and passed it.

"Yeah," he complained, "The business of America is getting the government off its back, but keeping its hand in Uncle Sugar's pocket. Welfare ranchers, welfare loggers, welfare miners, welfare farmers, welfare truckers. We've been a welfare state for the rich from the beginning!"

"You're such a wonderful curmudgeon, darling," she said and patted his knee.

"Curmudgeon?" He looked at her. "Am I old enough to be a curmudgeon? I'm only forty."

"I think you get your junior curmudgeon badge at forty."

"I thought you had to be older. I thought I was only an asshole. A cynic."

She laughed. "Well, you may be those, too, but I think you've earned your junior curmudgeon stripe. No wonder you hit it off so well with Ralph Wittfogel and have always gotten along with Daddy. Now, *there* are some curmudgeons. I think Ralph's fifty now. That's old enough for senior status."

"Yeah, Ralph's a character," Hunter said. "He and I were hiking last weekend, and he made an interesting comment about misanthropy: Misanthropes—who despair of humans in mass, who condemn the foibles of the human species—are generally fairly nice to individuals, while the great bleeding-heart lovers of all humankind—both right and left—generally don't like actual people."

"I've always felt that way," said MaryAnne. "I don't like our species, but I like individual members of it. People are always nicer in small groups or individually than in a mass. Or mob."

"You bet. Ralph knows his stuff. He's got more odd little facts of history and anthropology tucked away in his head than anyone I ever met. He sure is a loner, though."

"He's a loner? Jack, have you looked in the mirror lately? You claim to have resigned from the human race. I think I'm the only person you'd go out of your way to see, and I'm not even sure about that sometimes. You're so much of a loner that it's like pulling hen's teeth to get you to even help defend your home. Ralph is at least active in the Diablo Wilderness Committee, though I admit, he keeps a low profile."

"For chrissakes, MaryAnne, you all are just beating your heads against the wall. It's hopeless. How long did I work for the Sierra Club? I'm not even sure now. More than a decade. Wasn't that paying my dues? My rent for the Earth, as you put it the other night? But what did I really accomplish? The world's worse now than when I started. Yeah, I'm bitter, I'm cynical. Why shouldn't I be? Despite the best arguments of scientists like you, we go merrily on our way chewing up the world and spitting out the pieces. Yeah, I got a little burned out lobbying in Washington and failing to wake anyone up."

"I understand, Jack. I get frustrated, too. I haven't been in the conservation wars quite as long as you have, but nearly as long—we did first testify at the same Wilderness hearing, after all, even if I was only nine and you were nineteen. I understand burnout and cynicism. I get that way, too. But what I don't understand is how you can drop out when we're in the middle of the battle that's going to determine the future of what you call home, the battle that decides whether the Diablo stays wild and gets wilder, or whether its wilderness gets chewed up for two by fours. . . ."

"Did you ever think, MaryAnne, that maybe trying to solve problems just makes them worse and continues our estrangement from nature? That identifying problems and trying to solve them may be what got us into the mess that's destroying Earth today? Maybe the only way to make things better is to quit like I have. Only by withdrawing from activism, from fighting, can we change our own consciousness and that of others to a more respectful attitude toward Earth. But as long we continue to fight and struggle, we prolong the problem?"

"Where'd you come up with that? I can't believe you really believe a cockamamie notion like that." She shook her head.

"It was in some magazine I was glancing through at your house. Some magazine on Deep Ecology. Some philosophy professor was arguing against activism. Made sense to me." Hunter clenched his jaw.

MaryAnne waited half a mile before replying. "Such an elegant cop-out. Something only an ivory tower geek wanting to rationalize his own lack of courage could come up with. I know you don't believe that. Biologists used to argue something similar. 'Oh, we can't get involved. *We're* scientists. We only deal with facts. If we get involved politically to try to save the things we study, then our credibility will be compromised. We don't deal with values or judgments, only pure data. And we don't have enough data—we'll never have enough data—to be one hundred percent sure anyway.'"

She suddenly stabbed the air near him with her finger. Her voice rose to say, "But I tell you, Jack, biologists have woken up to realize that the world is in the middle of the sixth great extinction episode in Earth history, and that it's due to the activities of industrial humans! When we realized that, we started conservation biology. By god, we may not be able to save all biodiversity, but we're going to do our damnedest because—you know what?—we love it! We love all the salt and pepper of life, all the interactions of millions of species, the fecund joy that is at the heart of evolution, and we couldn't sleep nights if we weren't doing something to try to stop the destruction!"

Hunter shook his head in a condescending way. "MaryAnne, how can you hope to protect tigers in India, quetzals in Guatemala, rhinos in Kenya, lobos in Mexico, panthers in Florida when human population is doubling every thirty-five years?"

Back and forth, back and forth, they argued. Finally, tongues were no longer in cheek, grins were rubbed away. It got serious. Hunter pulled the Jeep into a rest area west of the New Mexico border and stomped off to pee. When he got back, MaryAnne was at the wheel.

"I'm sorry, Jack, to criticize you, but don't you think we have to keep trying?" The frost in her mouth belied the apology.

He felt like whipped dog. But real men don't show hurt—only anger. He hid the pain from her. At least he thought he did.

"It won't work, honey, it won't fucking work. I look at every reform piece of legislation we've passed. Know what? Every one was subverted, corrupted."

He took off on another rant. Just before Lordsburg, he ran out of steam and sighed like a big ponderosa pine falling to earth. "If you want to protect things, forget about trying to do it through Congress; just go out and do it. I don't know if even that will do any good, but it might."

"What do you mean?" she asked.

"I mean, just take it into your own hands. Pull up survey stakes, burn bulldozers, drive nails into trees to prevent them from being cut. Aren't there people out there still doing that? Like in *The Monkey Wrench Gang*?"

"Yes, I'm sure there are. I don't think it's time for that in the Diablo. If it is ever time for that sort of thing." She took the exit marked Platoro.

After two minutes, he continued, "And you know what? Even that won't slow it down. It's over, MaryAnne. It's hopeless. When I'm with you like the past few days, I forget reality, I forget all this. I have a wonderful time, I think we really can save the wolves. But it's a fantasy. I'm so damned fond of you, I wish you were right. I'm sorry to be such a wet blanket, but I don't see any hope."

Silence swept around them as they left the lights of Lordsburg and ran for the Buckhorn Mountains. The night became a screen for the movie in Hunter's head. Reggio and Glass were back. Scenes of destruction splatted across his eyes like bugs on the windshield. He spun downward into depression, into meanness.

In the oaks of the Buckhorns, he broke the silence with Yeats:

> Turning and turning in the widening gyre
> The falcon cannot hear the falconer;
> Things fall apart; the centre cannot hold;
> Mere anarchy is loosed upon the world,
> The blood-dimmed tide is loosed, and everywhere
> The ceremony of innocence is drowned.

He found another beer in the cooler and cracked it open. "Not only is a biological collapse occurring, a social collapse is also occurring. The blood-dimmed tide *is* loosed. In East L.A., in Bosnia, in Somalia, in the Caucasus, in Rwanda, in India, in Brazil, and in a hundred other places. The center doesn't hold anymore. The collapse of the Soviet Union was the beginning of the unraveling of industrial civilization. It is going to get very, very nasty before it gets better. And there's not a damn thing any of us can do about it."

"Jack, sweetheart, you recited *The Second Coming* that memorable evening you and Ralph were trying to top each other with cynical poems. You two were great entertainment for an innocent such as me. But aren't you forgetting Yeats's next lines?

> The best lack all conviction, while the worst
> are full of passionate intensity.

She paused, then continued, "Those are the words that stuck in my mind. Is the rough beast able to slouch to Bethlehem because *you* lack all conviction, while the greedy and ignorant like Buck Clayton and Bart Pugh are full of passionate intensity? Surrender if you will, I shall not!"

They passed the ghost-white mine tailings on the edge of Platoro.

She continued through clenched teeth. "I will not acquiesce to the destruction. I shall do my damnedest to preserve wolves and wilderness,

wilderness and wolves, whether I succeed or not. And, goddamn you, I *will* have a good time doing it! I will enjoy my life. I will not wallow in self-righteous, self-indulgent hopelessness!"

She saw through to his secret pain. But MaryAnne McClellan did not suffer fools—or weaklings—gently. She was tough—tough as a little girl whose mommy had been snatched away when she was only seven, tough as the last wolf, tough as life itself. There was no reason, no reason under the sun, why others shouldn't be as tough as she was.

"I've got news for you, buckaroo," she said. "Your angst, your alien-ation, your despair, your cowardice, all your private little devils—none of that matters. What matters are the wolves chasing down mule deer on Davis Prairie, the Rio Diablo in flood ripping through its canyon, the troop of coatis coursing through the Peloncillos, the rose-throated becards building their nest in the sycamore, the green kingfisher snatching little fish out of Sonoita Creek—the whole joyful, teeming, evolutionary dance of life. That is what is real. And it is far more important than our puny little lives. If you don't get that, then you deserve your hopelessness. The wilderness is real, my friend, not your existential angst."

So I'm an existentialist again, moaned Hunter to himself. *Where do I find these women?*

An hour later, silent except for the humming of tires on asphalt, MaryAnne drove up to Hunter's place. He gathered his gear.

Any other night, they wouldn't have discussed it. They would have spent the night together. This night they were going to sleep apart. Some-where on Interstate 10, a good-natured, wise-cracking romp had turned serious. Hunter planned to get very drunk tonight.

13

Jack Hunter was in a world of hurt.

Aldo Leopold had written that the penalty of an ecological education was to be aware that you lived in a world of wounds. Hunter was feeling the wounds of the world today. And his own. The sighting of the lobos had been a tonic and a bark that had lifted him into a healthy world. The three-week affair with MaryAnne McClellan had snookered him into almost believing that the wounding could be stopped, even that the wounds could be healed.

Is anything as optimistic and joyful as a fine champagne? MaryAnne was Dom Perignon. Getting high on her had greased his fall into today's pit of despair.

Hunter had declared war against horehound around his place, and was slaving like a hoplite against the Persians today. Horehound was a baneful weed around old homesteads in the mid-elevation Southwest. Hunter had heard that the old timers planted the nonnative plant as an herb for sore throats and coughs. That didn't mellow his outlook. The damn seed heads stuck to your socks and everything else. It formed a monoculture choking out native grasses and forbs. Birds didn't use it. His evil mood from last night's fight with the bitch gave his weeding an added ferocity. A hangover from Jack Damage added to his meanness with the hoe.

Hunter was thoroughly disgusted with himself. He was a manly man. Manly men do not show pain to others. They do not whine and whimper in public. Last night Hunter had shown weakness to someone. It was one thing to toy with Bill Crawford, to bait him with cynicism. But MaryAnne had broken down Hunter's cool, suave cynicism last night. He was not happy with himself this morning. He was ashamed.

The little man upstairs reminded him of Jodi Clayton. *Damn good-looking, great piece of ass, and not a handcuff anywhere in sight. You walked away from that to get beat up like you did last night?*

He turned a deaf ear to the telephone ringing inside, but the caller was stubborn. After the dozenth ring, he dropped his hoe and clomped up the board steps into the house. He hoped it wasn't his bitch-nemesis. He didn't want to talk to her today. He didn't want to see her. He didn't want to think about her.

"About time you answered. I was afraid you weren't home."

"Out chopping horehound, MaryAnne. Something you might think about doing around your place."

"Jack, would you come over? Now?"

"I'm busy. I'm in the middle of slaughtering nonnative vegetation."

"Please?"

It was a tone of voice Hunter hadn't heard before from MaryAnne. "Sure. I'll be right there."

That "please" kicked "bitch" from his vocabulary.

You are a sick bastard, said the homunculus, but Hunter strangled the little twit.

The gate was pulled across her road at the highway turnoff. That, too, was unusual.

She was sitting on the porch, her arms tightly folded. She stood when he walked up. "I'm really angry today, Jack, and I need a friend." She hugged him. Then she let go of him and walked inside. The screen door banged.

"What's wrong?" Surely she wasn't this upset from their scuffle last night. If she was, he'd read her wrong—real wrong. Besides, if that was what had made her mad, she wouldn't want to see him. Through the screen, he could see her wipe her nose with a wadded hankie.

He went inside. The shades were pulled; the house was dark.

"I need a lap," she said.

"Sure. What's wrong, MaryAnne? I've never seen you like this before."

"Later, okay? I just want to sit on your lap for a while."

Hunter sat where she pointed—in her big overstuffed chair. She plopped in his lap and put her head on his shoulder.

Damned if he knew what was eating her. She would tell him when she was good and ready. That much he'd figured out about their relationship. Relationship. What a goddamned unpleasant word. It was like "environment." Words the Greeks would have used. Abstractions. There was another one.

After ten minutes, she grumbled, "This goddamn place is getting to be just like Alaska."

"Hmm. I haven't noticed ice in the river lately," Hunter said.

"Not weather-type climate. Social climate. Political climate."

"Do you want to tell me what happened?"

She sat back and wiped her nose again. "Your fucking friend stepped on me today on his goddamned slouch to Bethlehem. Maybe my fucking innocence is drowning."

What was that supposed to mean? Whatever it meant, it was serious. MaryAnne was not a gutter mouth. When she cursed—which was rare—she cursed with deliberation, consciously dredging up the words and shaping them with her mouth for their intended effect.

Time crawled by like a tire-crippled tortoise before she spoke again. "I went by Underwood's today to get my pay for the last two weeks. Red told me that he didn't think they would need me to tend bar anymore. Said that their niece was coming back from Phoenix and would bartend."

"Surely, that's not what upset . . ."

"Hush, please. Do you want me to tell you or not?" She glared at him. "Okay."

She continued, "I could tell that he was standoffish, so I said, 'Red, I can tell that's not it. It's fine if you don't want me to tend bar for you anymore, but I think you should at least level with me about it.'"

Hunter nodded his head. He wasn't surprised; what was surprising was how long it had taken.

She jutted out her jaw and continued, "He got himself a Coors, poured it in a glass, and shook salt in it. God, how he can drink that, I don't know. He didn't offer me a beer. He was acting very cool toward me, like I wasn't a person anymore."

She glowered at the wall. "Finally he said, 'Okay, MaryAnne, I owe you that. When you started filling in here a year ago, you were very popular. Our business picked up. You're a pretty girl, really outgoing and friendly, uh, vivacious. Folks liked you a lot. I don't want to tell you that you have to keep your opinions to yourself or not wear wilderness T-shirts to work, but, doggonit, folks are not happy with you anymore. They feel you're pushing your wilderness ideas too hard. They're upset about you trying to bring back wolves. They don't want wolves back in the Diablo. Business at the bar has started to fall off. Some old friends have even told me that they aren't buying at the trading post anymore because you work here at the bar. Especially after the demonstration at the airport when Senator Reed came through.'"

Hunter marveled at the way she was able to recall—word for word—a conversation. But he knew she was accurate. She had done it before with conversations they'd had.

MaryAnne blew her nose. She looked at the crusted hankie. "Damnit, I hate getting stopped up. I need to go run about twenty miles and blow this snot out. Jack, I thought Red was my friend! I thought he might come around and support our Wilderness proposal for Mondt Park and Davis Prairie. I even thought he was open to the idea of wolf reintroduction. Why do people I trust have to fail me?!" She hit the arm of the chair with her fist.

She sat quietly in his lap. The tortoise limped along in Hunter's head.

She shifted in his lap and said, "Red was a key part of my strategy on Davis Prairie and Mondt Park. He likes that country, likes to hunt it. He told me once that he hoped roads wouldn't ever be built into it, that he didn't want it logged. Said that would ruin it. If he had publicly supported Wilderness designation for it . . . god, that would have helped. And now he caves in to the antiwilderness goons! Shit."

Hunter was smart enough now not to press her; he would let her tell it on her clock. She was fuming. He allowed himself the small private joke of hoping that his jeans wouldn't scorch from her sitting in his lap.

Suddenly she started in again. "Then he told me that I should be careful! He said the *New York Times* article on Fall County came out yesterday, and that it wasn't just 'horse puckey.' I guess Buck Clayton is quoted as saying he's surprised someone hasn't dry-gulched me. Red said it wasn't just Buck shooting off his mouth, but that people were mad enough about conservationists here that someone might actually do something!"

She stood up and threw her arms out. "Jack! This is my home. I live here. I own this place. I don't like feeling like a Jew in Nazi Germany here in the landscape I love the most. I don't take kindly to threats! None of the creeps around here are brave enough to do anything, but, if they try, I can sure as hell take care of myself! Goddamnit. Red Underwood treated me like he hardly knew me! Like he was washing his hands of me. What a chickenshit!" She folded her arms and paced the room.

Hunter wanted very much to tell her that he would protect her, that she could count on him. But he knew how much of a cliché that would be, that such expected machismo would not be welcomed, that it would only enrage her more. He knew that she was not scared, or even hurt, that is, in the traditional sense of a crying female. No, she was just very, very pissed off. Or was she? Maybe she was afraid. Maybe she *should* be afraid. Maybe she needed to hear him say he would be there for her. Maybe she would lambaste him for saying it, but needed to hear him say it anyway. Hunter exhaled. How long had he been holding his breath? Whether or not she was afraid, Hunter was. She was a ring-tailed roarer. If anyone tried anything, he would get a damn sight more than he had bargained for. But that didn't mean she was invulnerable. She was so goddamned precious to him. . . .

Suddenly, she sat back in his lap. He stroked her hair. Maybe it was best not to say it, just to let her feel it. She folded her arms and leaned against his shoulder. And sighed. Maybe she was a little bit scared. Maybe even this beautiful tough little bitch wanted someone to defend her. Hunter the lobbyist had been good at psychology. Figuring out motivations, reactions, weaknesses—he had been good at it, and had used his skill to coax members of Congress further than they had thought they would go. But he was lost here. This river channel was too murky to read.

He was getting riled, too. The more her story sunk in, the more steamed he got. Bunch of spineless, greedy, little people in Fall County. See if he bought another beer or cheeseburger in Underwood's. See if he touched another Clayton horse. Or filly? At least he'd cuckolded Buck. Better not share that smug little satisfaction with MaryAnne. Whew. It was getting really murky. The river had become a swamp. Time to head for higher ground.

"Why don't we drive into Platoro for dinner and go to the movie tonight?" he asked.

She turned on his lap and looked at him. "Are you finally asking me out on a real date?"

"We've been on dates before."

"Not a real date. Not with you asking me out. Not with us going to dinner and a movie. Not with you paying."

Hunter sighed as a token of defeat. "Okay. I'm asking you on a real date. Will you go to dinner and a movie with me tonight?"

She kissed him on the cheek. "Why, thank you, kind sir. Yes, I will go out with a dashing fellow such as yourself. Let me go brush my hair and put on a little makeup. I feel really homely right now."

"Pork chop, at your homeliest, you're prettier than any six other women that I know."

"Comments like that make me think that you aren't as dumb as you sometimes act. I'm sorry, that was nasty. I shouldn't take things out on you. I appreciate the compliment. I even need it. Thank you. My Galahad." She kissed his cheek again, hopped out of his lap, pulled up a couple of blinds, and went into her bedroom. She called from her mirror, "What's playing?"

"Oh, I think the Copper Queen has some rock-climbing movie."

"That one with Sylvester Stallone?" she asked warily. Or was she aghast?

"Yeah, but it's supposed to be pretty good. There're at least some scary climbing scenes. You ought to like it, an old rock jock like you. It's escape. Entertainment."

There was a skeptical grunt from the bedroom.

Hunter found himself a beer in the refrigerator. He stirred a swallow around in his mouth with his tongue while he thought about what Underwood had told MaryAnne. He hoped the blood-dimmed tide was not about to be loosed in Fall County. If it was, it would be loosed back the other way, too. "Count on that, assholes," he muttered.

She came out wearing high-heeled sandals and a bright summer dress with bare shoulders. She carried her fringed leather purse and a red and blue cotton Mexican shawl. Hunter was relieved that she was more like herself.

On the drive to Platoro, though, she became withdrawn again. She drummed her short fingernails on the outside of her door. When she was pissed, Hunter mused, she went off somewhere by herself and chewed on her tail. Before when they'd gone somewhere in his pickup, she had sat next to him, joking that they were a two-headed person like in all the other trucks.

"Where are you taking me to eat?" she finally asked.

"How about Mrs. Archuleta's?"

"Okay. I haven't ever been there."

"It's pretty good. The green chile enchiladas are hotter than El Tecolote's."

At dinner she admitted the chile was hot.

In his best John Wayne voice, Hunter said "Ya know, ya sure look purty when you're sweatin' from hot chile."

"I'm not sweating! I'm only glowing."

After dinner, she took his hand as they walked downtown's high sidewalks from the cafe to the theater.

"Don't you think you were expecting too much of Red?" he asked.

She dropped his hand. "I don't think I expect too much of anyone."

That was a hook Hunter wouldn't come near. He waited a minute and said, "Underwood is a nice guy, a good ol' boy, but he's a rock-ribbed right-winger. He might not be a rancher, he might even complain about them when you're around, but his family has been here for nearly a hundred years, and he believes in the resource-based economy, believes in the government keeping its nose out of local affairs, believes the county ought to run public lands. Sure he likes to hunt in the Wilderness Area, and he'd prefer them not to road and log Mondt Park, but he also supports the custom and culture bullshit."

"No, he doesn't!"

"MaryAnne, a week and a half ago I was in there for a cheeseburger at lunch, and heard him talking to the sheriff and a couple of ranchers. He's with them. Now he's no lyncher, he's no demagogue . . ."

"Okay, okay. You're right. I was fooling myself. I guess I'm just going to go through life being disappointed by men."

Another hook to shy away from.

MaryAnne escaped in the movie, Hunter was happy to see. She even tensed and gripped his hand a couple of times. The climbing scenes, unreal and corny though they were, scared Hunter, too—probably more than they scared her, he guessed. They took him back to days of sewing-machine leg on exposed granite spires in the Sandias. He did not miss the good old rock climbing days of college.

After the movie, she seemed to have slipped away from the surly bonds of melancholy. "Let's go have a drink!" she said.

"You call it," Hunter said.

She set off down the sidewalk. "Well, I know this place with a bar-tender who's even uglier than you."

"*You* would go to the Shady Lady?"

"Sure."

"I didn't think you approved of such places."

"I just better not catch you drooling over the dancers," MaryAnne warned.

"Not a chance. Unless you get up and dance." He smirked at her.

She stopped, put her hands on her hips, and raised her eyebrows. "Oh, really? I might just do that."

"Sure you will."

"Well, why not?" she said and began walking again. "I'm out of a bartending job. My grant for the wolf report isn't enough income. I'm going to have to figure out some way to bring in more money until my job starts with Round River Conservation Studies. I won't ask my daddy for more money. If I can't get some additional grants or consulting work, why not take my clothes off and dance? I have been told I have a not unattractive body."

"You do indeed."

"Besides, you'd probably like having a topless dancer for a girlfriend. It's the kind of seedy thing you'd like."

"I don't know." Hunter shook his head and smiled. "I'd have to sit beside the stage with a shotgun in my lap."

"Are you actually jealous?"

"I'm actually very fond of you." He took her hand.

"You're coming awfully close to saying you love me."

"Maybe I do."

"But you won't tell me if you do, will you?"

"Never."

"Hmph!" She dropped his hand and flounced away.

The Shady Lady had the most garish neon sign in Platoro despite being housed in an ancient tavern on a back street in the downtown section. Its neighborhood was the realm of alley cats, lowriders, and winos.

"Good golly, Miss Molly, look what the cat drug in!" said Bill Crawford from behind the bar.

The Shady Lady was smoky, shabby, and dark—except for the little stage lit by red and green and blue and yellow spotlights. MaryAnne and Hunter took stools at the bar. He found that he could watch the stage in the bar mirror without being too obvious.

"Do you have real drinks here, Bill?" asked MaryAnne.

"Anything I can make or that you can tell me how to make."

"How about a very dry martini? A double," she ordered.

"Okeydokey." Bill nodded and reached for a martini glass.

"Bombay Sapphire."

"Nope." He shook his head.

"Boodles."

"Nope."

"Tanqueray?"

"Nope."

"This isn't a very classy joint."

"If it was, do you think they'd have me bartending?"

"Good point." She raised up on her stool to look over him at the liquor selection. "Well, at least I see you have Beefeater. Why don't we make it a gin and tonic?"

"Okay."

"With a lime."

"I know to put a goddamned lime in a gin and tonic."

"Good."

"And the gentleman?" asked Bill.

"Pint o' Guinness. I'm driving," said Hunter.

MaryAnne took her drink and twirled around on her stool to look at the stage. "So, Bill, how much do you pay your poor exploited sex workers?"

"As little as possible, but the tips aren't bad."

"I might be looking for work. . . ."

Bill choked on the pint of Guinness he was nursing and sprayed brown foam on MaryAnne's bare shoulders. She turned around and whacked him over the head with her purse.

"Slob!"

"Ouch! Goddamnit, what do you have in that?"

"Only my . . ."

"Shit, MaryAnne," Bill whispered, "It's a felony to pack a piece in a bar."

"Oh, dear," she whispered and looked around furtively. "You won't turn me in, will you?"

"No, but try to behave. Turn around and I'll wipe off your back."

She handed her purse to Bill to hide behind the bar and presented her back to be cleaned, lifting each shoulder strap in turn. Hunter swallowed his chuckles with warm stout and checked out the reflection of the dancer on stage.

"So, Bill," said Hunter. "Where's your dancer girlfriend who's built like a sack of wildcats in heat?"

"A sack of wildcats in heat?" snorted MaryAnne. She turned back to the bar.

Bill shook his head and said, "Aw, Wendy moved on. These gals never stay in a podunk town like this. She decided to try one of the big show clubs in Phoenix. But what's this about you wanting a job, MaryAnne?"

"Well, I'm afraid my current boyfriend would object to my dancing, but I possibly could be persuaded to bartend now and then—if I could keep my shirt on. I notice you wear yours, after all." She told him about her conversation with Red Underwood.

Bill Crawford looked very earnest. "If any of those assholes up there try anything, let me know. I'll kill the motherfuckers. . . ."

"I might actually call on you for that, buckaroo, but I doubt that I really face any danger. I do appreciate your support, though, Bill." She took his hand in both of hers. "I hope I can also count on your no-account buddy here who seems to have taken a shine to me lately."

Hunter sighed. "Don't worry, dear. I'm there whenever you need me. But I agree, I don't think we'll be seeing any lynching parties. Clayton likes seeing himself quoted in the *New York Times* like a real Marlboro Man from Tombstone, but it's all talk. The yahoos in Fall County are cowards." Hunter hoped he was right. Also, he was miffed that Bill Crawford had gotten to shoot off his macho mouth without having been slapped down by the lady who needed no one to defend her. He had even gotten thanked.

Bill said, "You know, the politics suck in Cobre County, but they aren't mean and intolerant here like they are in Fall County. Lordy, there's no harassment here in Platoro, but you guys must feel like civil-rights workers in Alabama in '63."

"At least those of us who don't hide our true opinions," MaryAnne said.

"Some of us," groaned Hunter, "might just prefer not to rock the boat, and enjoy whatever we can while the world goes to hell."

"And some of us, sweetheart, are going to stand up for what we believe in, come hell or high water." She fixed him with her green eyes.

Oh, gawd, thought Hunter, let's not get back on this river again to-night.

Old friend Bill Crawford rescued them from that route. "I had hoped that Underwood might come around for us. I guess I won't put rafting customers up in his motel anymore. Sorry to hear that even a guy like him can be bullied by the local goose-steppers. Hey, I haven't told you all about the little adventure I had in Fall County yesterday."

"What's that?" asked MaryAnne.

"Somebody tried to kill me and my clients when we got back to the van at the trailhead."

"What?" MaryAnne was alarmed.

Hunter turned his attention from the reflection in the glass to Bill.

"Yep, one of my clients, a police detective from Chicago, said it was a definite murder attempt." Bill nodded his head authoritatively.

"One of your clients was a Chicago cop?" asked Hunter. "On a back-packing trip?"

"Hey, you wouldn't believe some of the people I get on trips. I have a very diverse clientele."

MaryAnne was impatient. "What about the murder attempt?"

Bill said, "Well, we got back to the Kezar Creek Divide trailhead early afternoon. As you both know, the road down from there is one tight switchback after another. You drop a couple thousand feet in just a few miles."

"Right, right," said MaryAnne.

"It's also a narrow, potholed son of a bitch. Worst road in the state, I think."

"So what happened, Bill?" she demanded.

"I'm getting to it. I had a blowout. Right front tire. Thank goodness it happened just after an elk ran across the road and we stopped to look at it. I was going about two miles an hour. At my normal speed on that road, a blowout would have put us over the edge. A real fast descent down about half the mountain. I got everyone out of the van and started changing the tire. I was really pissed because they were brand new steel-belted radials. Cost me a bundle. The tire blew out on the inside sidewall. While I was starting to put on the spare, this cop, Howie Wolchinsky, called me over to the other side of the van. He said, 'Look here at this tire.' I crawled under and looked on the inside of it where he was pointing and, sure enough, there was a slice on the inner sidewall. Almost, but not quite, through the tire. He showed me the same cut on the two rear tires. He said it was a deliberate attempt to kill everyone in the van."

"God, Bill, I'm glad you're okay." She took his hand back in hers.

Hunter sighed. "This is getting nasty." The worst *were* full of passionate intensity.

"What did you do?" MaryAnne asked.

"I hitched a ride with some Colorado backpackers down to Rio Diablo. I was going to leave my backpack pistol with Howie, but he had a nine millimeter in his pack. Man, I wish whoever did it had come back up and tried something. Howie would have given him the surprise of his short life. Both of you guys were away, but Ralph was home and loaned me his van to get everybody into Platoro. Then I had to buy a whole new set of tires for my van. Ralph and I got 'em on and here I am."

"You guys got to be careful," said Hunter. He excused himself to the men's room.

When he returned, MaryAnne and Bill were discussing the *Sunday New York Times* article from yesterday. Bill had a copy spread out on the bar.

"I knew I shouldn't have trusted that reporter, Don Samuels," she said. "He assured me it was going to be an article about the effort to protect the Diablo. Jeez, it ended up a puff piece on loggers and ranchers, making *us* look awful."

"I even gave the asshole a free float trip this spring," Bill growled.

"You all should have talked to me," said Hunter. "I would have told you that Samuels was no friend. He was doing antienvironment pieces for the *Times* back when I was in Washington. He's a cool, cynical jerk who specializes in hatchet jobs. He likes loggers and ranchers."

MaryAnne nailed him with her eyes and said, "If you will recall, lover boy, you've made it very clear to both Bill and me that you don't want to be bothered with our petty little conservation problems. Had we known of your willingness to be a media consultant, we would have called on you. May I assume that you are volunteering to help us in the future?"

Hunter kicked himself. He sure had bitten on that hook.

MaryAnne had a third gin and tonic (all doubles). She and Bill talked about the upcoming hearing. For the final time she gave him instructions for his road show. Bill was leaving for Las Cruces—the first gig—on Wednesday, in two days. Nine days later, he would finish with a big event in Platoro.

MaryAnne slipped back into silence on the hour-long drive home. Her head sagged against the back of the seat, her mouth fell open, and she snored. Hunter wished he had a tape recorder. She swore she never snored. He looked at her. It was the most uncomplimentary he'd ever seen her. He realized how very fond he was of her, how dear she was to him. *Are you saying you love the dame?* asked the skull box manikin. *Hoo boy,* thought Hunter. *I wasn't bargaining for this.* He was saved from further tickling of that rattlesnake when MaryAnne woke up and stared out the window.

Hunter took a chance. "What did you mean earlier by 'This is starting to feel like Alaska'?"

"Remember when I told you that I wouldn't radio-collar wolves again?"

"Yeah, when we were in the Patagonia Mountains."

"I had transmitters on a pack that used the south slope of the Brooks Range. I studied them for three years. I knew them." She stared out the window. "Some poachers got the radio frequency. I don't know how. I suspect a certain coward in the university. When my research was finished, they used the radio frequency to track my wolves down and shoot every last one of them. I know who did it."

"Damn," he whispered.

"A bigshot Republican state senator. Pilot. Businessman. Trophy hunter. Panderer to all the losers in Alaska who think they're pioneers and who depend on the Department of Fish and Game to raise moose for 'em. Those people hate wolves. Pitiful bunch of whiners."

The night air wrapped around her words. A mile, two miles slipped under the truck.

"I had a boyfriend at the time. A man I was living with. He worked for the Alaska Department of Fish and Game. He had a relatively important position. He had some clout. I wanted him to track down the men who murdered my wolves and have them prosecuted. He wouldn't do it. Said I didn't understand political reality. He will remain forever nameless. I hadn't slept with a man after that until you showed up a month ago."

Holy shit. Hunter didn't curse out loud this time, but he thought it with some terror. He stole a glance at her. She was staring out the window into the night, catching the road wind in her face.

"Do you understand now why I'm reluctant to tell people about my Diablo wolves?" she asked him and the night.

"Yeah."

When they arrived at her place, MaryAnne asked Hunter to spend the night. "I don't need a bodyguard, I just want a lover tonight. I missed you last night. I'm sorry about our disagreement. I was mean to you."

14

With morning's coffee came an announcement.

MaryAnne McClellan put her hand on Hunter's and said, "Jack, I'm going to miss you, but I've decided to go to Tucson for a couple of weeks. I have a significant amount of research and other work to do there on my Mexican wolf study. I've been putting it off because a very delightful man came into my life, and I haven't wanted to be away from him. But now is probably a good time to go. Away from Rio Diablo, maybe I can also sort out the new situation as it impacts our Diablo Wilderness proposal."

He squeezed her hand and said, "I can watch your place for you. Take care of Zeke."

"Thanks, sweetie, but that won't be necessary. I'm sure the place will be all right—though, on second thought, it probably would be wise for you to drop by and check on it every few days. However, Zeke won't be here anymore."

"Why not?"

"Oh, I guess you were in the potty last night when Bill and I talked about it. After the tire slashing, he's decided not to start his trips from the north side of the Diablo anymore. Too dangerous for his clients. Says he'll start going in from the south side in Cobre County. So he's going to stable

Zeke at the Hummingbird Guest Ranch. He'll be up today to get him. It will actually be more convenient for me, too. I won't feel guilty for not riding Zeke and showing him more attention."

"Do you have a place to stay in Tucson?" Hunter asked.

"Yes," she said, "a colleague who teaches biology at the University of Arizona is gone for the summer and I've got her house to use."

"I'll miss you," Hunter said. It wasn't quite the truth—her leaving was welcome. He needed a breather. The last few days had whipsawed him.

"I'll miss you, too, Jack." She drained her cup. "Before I pack, though, I need a very long, hard run. Wanna go do about twenty miles?"

"Do you want to kill me?"

"Not a chance. I'd like to have you around a while longer. How about if you come back here in four hours and join me for a good-bye swim?"

"I hear that you're a horseshoer," said the dusty voice on the telephone, "and built like a Tennessee jack."

"You've obviously seen my business card."

"I miss you, Jack. It's only been a week since you took advantage of me skinny-dipping and ravaged me in the mud, but I'm climbing the walls in Tucson without you. A nightly phone call isn't enough."

"I'll drink to that. When are you coming home?"

"Not for another week," sighed MaryAnne. "I'm getting lots done here, but I have more to do. I still need to get up to Phoenix to meet with the Mexican wolf folks at Arizona Game and Fish, and down to Buenos Aires National Wildlife Refuge to meet with the staff. I'm going to have to concentrate on the Diablo in August, so I need to do as much as possible now on my wolf report."

"Well, I miss you, too." This time it was true. While Hunter had welcomed the thought of solitude when MaryAnne had announced her trip to Tucson, now he realized how lonely he was for her. This troubled him. He wished he could decide what he wanted. This back-and-forth was killing him emotionally.

"I'm glad to hear that," she said. "How's business?"

"What? Horseshoeing?"

"Yes."

"Not great. I don't seem to be getting many new customers here, and I'm not getting repeat business from some of my previous customers. I'm trying to find more clients down in Platoro, but it's slow. If it wasn't for the Hummingbird Guest Ranch, I'd really be hurting. If it doesn't pick up, I don't know what I'm going to do. I might as well just go hike with Ralph Wittfogel and quit pretending to be a horseshoer." Hunter didn't tell MaryAnne that his biggest customer, Jodi Clayton, was one of the no-repeats.

"I hope you aren't losing customers because of your unpopular girl-friend."

"Well, if I am, fuck 'em. They can take their horses and shove 'em up their asses."

"Thank you, sweetheart. I'm touched."

"Buncha assholes here in Fall County. To hell with 'em." He didn't say that he was quietly boycotting both Underwood's and the Rio Diablo Cafe. This was no small sacrifice. Hunter liked their cheeseburgers, chicken-fried steaks, and enchiladas for lunch.

"Why don't you come over to Tucson for a visit? I need some loving." She blew a kiss through the fiber optics.

"So do I. But I'm broke."

"Would twenty-three horses sweeten the offer?"

"Twenty-three horses?" Hunter asked.

"Yep. A local conservation activist runs a riding stable near Saguaro National Monument West. She just fired her regular shoer—some old rummy. I told her I had just the fella for her."

"Great. Can't beat that with a stick."

"I'll even let you stay here. The dirty dishes are piling up. There's a family of four elf owls hanging out where I'm staying. Wonderful desert around, though it's been about a hundred and five all week. Also, there's an eared trogon down in Ramsey Canyon. I know exactly where it is. I'll take you to see it."

"You've sold me."

"Sometimes I think you love me just for the birds I find for your life list."

Hunter crossed the San Pedro at Benson. He checked his watch. Eleven o'clock. On schedule. The tardiness of the summer thunderstorms was taking its toll. The bursage was brown and withered, the waxy creosote drab, and the gaunt prickly pear looked like Auschwitz survivors.

But things were about to change. A thunderstorm had raked Rio Diablo last night. And today, even though it was not yet noon, the sky islands wore anvil clouds like Stetsons. Whatever happens in the atmosphere to bring rain to the Southwest was happening. The droughty high pressure system had moved off, and steam from subtropical seas was boiling into the sky and flowing up the Sierra Madre on rivers of air.

Jack Hunter had welcomed MaryAnne McClellan's trip to Tucson. He had been glad to get some space. She was demanding; she could be a bitch. He had thought it would be good to be single again for a while.

The first night had been good. The second night had been bearable. But the third night had been as lonely as a heart attack. *You're falling for the dame,* the voice in his head had said. *Screw you, twit,* Hunter had replied. Hunter had wondered if the voice was his conscience. Not a chance. A conscience wasn't supposed to be a jerk.

As he ran past the southern flank of the Rincon Mountains, his eagerness to see MaryAnne built like the thunderheads.

Dr. McClellan left the Coronado National Forest office in downtown Tucson at 11:30 A.M. Her boyfriend had an uncanny ability to be on time. ("I was never late for a meeting in Washington," he once had boasted.) She had given him directions to the world's greatest drive-in and they had agreed on 11:45 A.M. to beat the lunch rush. She didn't want to be late.

Down on Grande between St. Mary's and Speedway, a gunshot away from the interstate, down in the barrio, was Pat's Chili Dogs. Red and white tiles graced the front, "This is Wildcat Country" signs blended with the menu, and business was already hopping. MaryAnne pulled into an empty space under the sun roof. Years of crankcase drippings spread over each parking stall like little lava flows. 11:44. She had made it. A familiar pickup truck pulled in next to her. MaryAnne was pleased that the cowboy kissed her. He generally didn't like public displays of affection. Maybe she should leave him more often?

A young black man, built like a healthy black bear, took their order through the window.

MaryAnne said, "How about a family special—hot—and two extra-large iced teas?"

They grabbed one of the tables under the carport. A red and white sign above them read, "Keep a supply in your freezer. When the munchies get you, pop them in the oven!"

The four chili dogs (hot!) and mountain of french fries (greasy, made out of real potatoes) were as wonderful as MaryAnne had promised.

Lowriders and Beemers crowded under the parking shade. Bunched like feedlot cows on the narrow sidewalk under the overhang were rough cholos with tattoos, gorgeous thirteen-year-old girls ready to walk the aisle in Atlantic City, O'odham Indians built like rounds of lunch meat, dust-covered construction workers, the dignified older *gente*, downtown lawyers teetering on high heels or choked by neckties, and undercover cops (not covered up much) with beepers on their forty-inch belts. The gang inside laid out the buns, tossed in the dogs, slicked on the mustard, and spooned on the onions and chili.

"Well?" she asked.

"It's quite the symphony," Hunter mused. "Greatest drive-in in the world, just like you said."

"We'll need to run twenty miles to roto-rooter the cholesterol out of our arteries, though." She smiled and licked chili off her lips.

After gobbling down the chili dogs (Hunter: 3; MaryAnne: 1), he followed her north on Greasewood through the western outskirts of Tucson. The saguaros were so svelte they looked like Jane Fonda had been putting them through a workout. Over the mountains, the clouds pumped and flexed like bodybuilders on Muscle Beach. Hunter hit a patch of shade cast by one. He was glad for the clouds. Not only did the land need the rain, but they might keep the temperature down in the double digits for horseshoeing.

At the Saguaro Riding Stables, MaryAnne introduced him to the owner who introduced him to the horses. They divided up the horses for the next four or five days.

"Well, I'll leave you to your horses, Jack dear," MaryAnne said. "I'll be back about five to lead you to where I'm staying—just a couple of miles away." She bit her lip before giving him the bad news. "Bill and I are doing the Diablo road show here in Tucson tonight. I have to have dinner with Bill and our local organizers beforehand. You don't have to go if you don't want to . . ."

"No, I don't mind going—as long as we get to leave at some reasonable hour. I'd sort of like to . . ."

In a hot, empty horse stall, she kissed him. "So would I."

"I meant see Bill perform on stage. But this, too. Even more so."

Back at MaryAnne's Tucson digs after the post-show beers:

"What's this?"

"Sexy underwear. Don't you like it?"

"Sure I do. But you've never worn any before."

"I went out and bought some to celebrate us being back together."

Later she asked, "Well? Did it help?"

"What?"

"The sexy underwear. Did it help?"

"Sugarplum, you don't need any help. Bare-assed like a monkey up in a tree, or dolled up in lace, you're the sexiest thing that ever came down the pike."

"You are learning to say the things I like to hear. But—what's this? Again? Maybe the naughty underwear does help. . . ."

Much later she asked, "So, what did you think of our slide show tonight?"

"Very nice. One of the best I've seen."

"Thank you."

"How's your wolf study coming along?"

"Pretty good. But I'm worried that Fish and Wildlife is going to get beat up by the politicians in Arizona and New Mexico, not to mention the wise use/militia crowd, and they will go for a compromise."

"What kind of compromise?"

She sat up in bed. "Do you know how this wolf reintroduction game works? The U.S. Fish and Wildlife Service will want to designate any released wolves as an 'experimental nonessential population.' That weakens Endangered Species Act protection considerably for all wolves in the area of reintroduction. In this case, that area is all of New Mexico and Arizona between Interstate 40 and Interstate 10—a huge swath of the Southwest. Tucson to Flagstaff, El Paso to Albuquerque. Any wild wolves that happen to be in that area will also be classified as nonessential. The agencies brag that land use restrictions will be minimal with that classification. That doesn't help the wilderness or wolf recovery. It won't stop logging of Mondt Park or building a road in there. It also makes it easier for Fish and Wildlife—or for ranchers!—to kill or harass wolves that are suspected of preying on livestock."

She got out of bed and began pacing the room. "Now if we can prove that wild wolves are in the area and have bred and formed a pack, then they will come under full Endangered species protection—which can bring strong land use restrictions, including no new roads. Dispersing or lone wolves won't do it. They have to be breeding and have formed a pack. If we can prove that—and we can if the pups you saw survive as part of the pack until next spring—then even captive wolves released to supplement the natural population will be fully protected. Your slides are the perfect evidence because they show the location clearly."

She stopped and looked at Hunter with her green eyes. "But, if word gets out about wolves in the Diablo, the ranchers and loggers are going to be gunning for them. The yahoos will make sure the wolves are gone so they can't be used to prevent the experimental nonessential population crap. Do you follow me?"

"Yeah." Though dimly. Hunter had never before had to listen to a wildlife management lecture from a professor wearing a tiny bit of see-through black and red lace and silk. Especially one who looked as good in it as Dr. MaryAnne McClellan did. If there was a pop quiz afterward, he was dead.

She started pacing again. "I don't want to take any chance on my wolves getting killed until I know they made it through the winter, and I can take the Fish and Wildlife Service wolf folks there in late spring to prove that there is a breeding pack of wolves in the Diablo."

"What happens if some of the crackers in Fall County accidentally find out about the wolves?" Hunter asked.

"I've just got to cross my fingers that doesn't happen. The appeal I filed is certain to delay the Bearwallow Timber Sale. Without a road in there and without fellers dropping old growth, the rednecks won't get in there—they aren't going to walk. I just hope that the wolves stay in the roadless country and don't move out where they might encounter someone. There's such a good prey base—elk, deer, pronghorn, beaver—in there, I don't think they'll range out. Hunting season this fall will be the dangerous time."

Hunter cleared $800 from the horses at Saguaro Riding Stables. In six weeks, he would get to do it all over again. Between that and the Hummingbird Guest Ranch in Platoro, he could limp along. To hell with the horse-owning assholes in Fall County.

MaryAnne delivered as promised. On the way home to Rio Diablo, they swung south to The Nature Conservancy's Ramsey Canyon Preserve in the Huachuca Mountains. Sure enough, a couple of miles up the trail, five stream crossings after a trail junction, the eared trogon was *gronking* in a towering Douglas-fir.

Back in Rio Diablo, MaryAnne had little more than two weeks before the congressional field hearing in Platoro. She was bird-dogging the conservationist turnout; there would be no trouble getting a wide variety of folks from all over the Southwest to speak out forcefully against Pugh's bill to declassify the Diablo Wilderness. But she knew she had to get people talking about Mondt Park and Davis Prairie at the hearing to keep that country in the game.

Bill's road show to the major towns and cities in the Southwest was an organizing success. Considering that it was summer, with many conservationists gone for vacations and the ranks at the colleges thinned, the turnouts had been good, ranging from twenty-six in Los Alamos to over one hundred in both Albuquerque and Tucson. This wasn't due to luck. MaryAnne McClellan, Bill Crawford, and Phil McClellan had burned up phone lines the previous month to wheedle Sierra Club, Audubon, and New Mexico Wilderness Association leaders to organize meetings in their towns. The Diablo Wilderness brochure and a letter about the road show had been mailed to members of the Sierra Club, Audubon Society, Wilderness Society, New Mexico Wilderness Association, and half a dozen local groups in New Mexico, Arizona, and West Texas.

At least a car load in each community had pledged to attend the hearing. Over fifty organizations, not all specifically conservation groups, had come on board in support of the Joint Conservationists' Diablo Wilderness Area Additions Proposal. Endorsements were in the pipeline from the Santa Fe, Las Cruces, and Tucson city councils; state legislators from New Mexico, Texas, and Arizona would send in statements of support. Friendly newspaper stories and editorials favoring the conservationists' plan were popping up.

But something besides the hearing was gnawing at her bones.

By her reckoning, the wolves and their pups had left the den near Stowe Creek. Now was the time to get in there and document the hard evidence. Hunter couldn't wait to guide her to the wolfy nativity. She decided that she could be away from the phone for two days.

They went in from the north and, with hard trekking and no rest stops, made the den site an hour before sunset. To Hunter's surprise, MaryAnne dropped her pack and crawled down into the den. In two minutes, she and her headlamp reappeared.

"Okay, Jack, show me how to use your camera and strobe," she ordered, all business.

"Good lord, MaryAnne, is it safe to crawl down in there?"

"Believe me, this isn't the first wolf den I've crawled into. They're as comfy to me as my bedroom. I've crawled into a couple in Alaska that were occupied." She looked around. "By the way, be very careful around here. There might be prints still good enough for me to make plaster casts. Don't step on any."

After Hunter explained the strobe, MaryAnne grabbed it, a tape measure and notebook, and several zip-lock baggies, and slipped underground. Hunter settled in outside the den and fired up a cigar. He fancied himself daddy wolf with MaryAnne as mommy wolf in with the pups. He swelled up with fatherly pride. He scanned his domain. It was safe. He was the meanest sonofabitch in the prairie.

It was dusk when she emerged from the den.

"Lord, MaryAnne, what were you doing down there? I almost finished a cigar."

She was bubbling over like a four-wheeled champagne. "I was smelling it. I was soaking it in. I knew the wolves were here, I knew they were breeding after I saw your slides, but being here, seeing the evidence, is the *Yes!* I needed."

15

MaryAnne lay awake, jumpy as an aspen in a gale. She had sent Jack packing that morning so she could work. That evening she had made final calls to the car pool honchos in Albuquerque, Santa Fe, Las Cruces, El Paso, Tucson, Flagstaff, and Phoenix. All were still coming. Then she had edited her statement a final time and printed out copies. A glass—two—of wine out under the stars. Then bed. Sleep.

Poor Jack. Insomnia was awful. She was glad she rarely suffered from it. She shouldn't be fretting tonight. Everything was wired. Conservationists from all over the Southwest were coming. A dozen world-class biologists were mailing letters of support. All the groups were still on board for adding Mondt Park and Davis Prairie to the Diablo Wilderness Area. Everything had been done that could be done.

Lying awake was ridiculous. She calmed herself and willed sleep to come.

The congressional field hearing on the Diablo was held in the combination police station and fire house—the public safety building—of Platoro. It was to begin at 9:00 on Saturday morning, August 14, so, in Congressman Bart Pugh's words, "The working people of southwestern New Mexico can attend." By 8:30, a group of fresh-faced housewives and children, clean-cut students, and well-dressed men had gathered politely outside the building. They held placards and handed out flyers. A tall, dark, handsome man with a guitar played folk songs, and the crowd sang along on the choruses.

Upon arrival, Pugh beamed at them. As he marched forth with hand outstretched, though, his smile shattered when he read the words on the signs:

AMERICA NEEDS WILDERNESS

BALANCE THE BUDGET NO MORE WELFARE LOGGING

SAVE THE DIABLO WILDERNESS

WILDERNESS MADE AMERICA GREAT
LET'S KEEP SOME

SAVE MONDT PARK'S OLD GROWTH

He walked away wroth and befuddled. His people—the good, hardworking Americans with kids in Little League and Cub Scouts—were supposed to look like that. Not the wilderness freaks. The ecology pinkos were not supposed to look like they had just stepped out of the television from a Pat Robertson family special. They were supposed to look like the Manson Family or members of a rock band. Pugh was particularly upset by the men in hard hats carrying signs that read "Construction Workers for Wilderness." Pugh consistently voted against labor, but he pandered to the red-white-and-blue populism of blue-collar workers.

The congressman saw Buck Clayton's Lincoln pull into the parking lot. He waited outside the public safety building for him. The rancher, too, was vexed by the sign carriers.

"Now, I'd say that The Honorable Barf Puke is giving Squire Clayton a little heck for there not being a demonstration by Militia Thugs Against Wilderness," said Bill Crawford. He was standing outside the door to the public safety building. MaryAnne McClellan, Phil McClellan, and Ralph Wittfogel were in the group with him.

"It looks that way, doesn't it?" MaryAnne chortled. "Unless he's wanting to know why Clayton hasn't organized a goon squad to take care of them."

Bill nodded, a toothy grin slicing through his black beard. He flipped his clip-on sunglasses up on his dark-framed prescription glasses. "From the way ol' Barf went dancing up to them at first, I think he thought that they were his demonstrators, and that wilderness supporters would naturally be a bunch of dirty, flea-bitten hippies."

"It's so nice that Bill Oliver was able to fly in from Austin for this," said MaryAnne. "He's such a great performer. I hope we get a good turnout for his picnic concert tonight." She stood on tiptoes and popped the clip-ons off Bill's glasses. She tucked them in the breast pocket of his shirt under his sport coat. "Don't go into the hearing looking like a geek, Bill." She straightened out the collar on his corduroy western-style coat.

"Yeah, you're right. Thanks. Hey, it looks like the troops from Tucson have arrived, too." Bill pointed to the parking lot. He beamed like the full moon. "I guess my little road show did some good after all."

Phil McClellan smiled. "You did a fine job, Bill. By the way, how many businesses do you have signed on for your 'Businesses for the Diablo Wilderness' group?"

"One hundred and fourteen. Most from New Mexico and Arizona, but a few from elsewhere or national. And most of them don't have a direct connection to wilderness."

"Good, good," smiled Phil. "Combined with the poll results, that might make even Pugh sit back and take notice."

"We got the poll results?" asked Ralph.

"Last night," Bill said. "Monique Mueller with the League of Women Voters, who sponsored the poll, called me from Santa Fe."

"And?" Ralph asked.

Bill held the lapels of his sports coat and pushed his chest out. "In Fall and Cobre counties, fifty-two percent of those polled supported adding Mondt Park and Davis Prairie to the Diablo Wilderness."

"Excellent!" Ralph exclaimed. "And this will be in your statement?"

"You bet. That's not all. Only twenty-seven percent wanted the Diablo Wilderness declassified. The rest wanted the Wilderness to stay the same or had no opinion."

Phil stroked his beard. "I must admit that I'm surprised such a high percentage want the additions to the Wilderness. I thought we would do well, but not that well. I'm sure our opponents won't believe the figures."

"I wasn't surprised at all," Bill said. "There's a lot of support for Wilderness in the rural West. It's just that folks keep quiet when they disagree with the party line of rape and scrape."

Ralph nodded his head. "The most repressive places in the United States are rural counties and small towns."

"That's for sure," MaryAnne said. "We all have a little experience with that, don't we? Vandalism. Death threats. I know conservationists whose kids have been beat up in school. Some folks even lose their jobs." She smiled broadly. "Shall we find our seats?"

In the auditorium, Buck Clayton took a seat on the right side in the second row of chairs from the front. Jodi Clayton, wearing a Santa Fe–pricey denim dress with concho belt, squash blossom necklace, and designer cowgirl boots, sat beside him. Buck glared at MaryAnne McClellan and those with her when they sat opposite him.

Harry Jukes and six other stalwarts of Fall County's militia arrived and took seats behind the Claytons. There were low grumbles from them about the demonstration outside.

After they sat down, Phil McClellan said, "She came through for us. Look up at the dais. Monica Montoya is here. Between the demonstration outside and her presence, Pugh may actually remain civil."

Pugh was earnestly talking to a couple of plump suits near the back of the room. He slapped them on their backs and made his way to the front. Congressman Bart Pugh was one of those white-bread Texas Panhandle boys who look like a hog that's been shaved, bathed, perfumed, and dressed up in a suit and tie. Thirty years ago he had moved to Roswell in southeastern New Mexico, and had made—was still making—his fortune on federal oil and gas leases. He also owned a couple of big agribusiness spreads on both sides of the Texas–New Mexico line. He had cleared $88,000 in federal crop subsidies the last year.

Pugh's style with the hearing was that of a rich man playing it folksy—limousine populism. He smiled and drawled like he was hosting the State Fair Rodeo. "First of all, I would like to welcome the other members of this panel to the Second Congressional District of the Land of Enchantment. We are holding this field hearing in order to collect the views of the people of this state who must live with the laws we make in Washington. I recognize many good friends in the audience today and I am sure we will hear strong and thoughtful opinions from the people of New Mexico. I have, as all of you know, based my career on my concern for the impact on the working people of New Mexico of the laws we sometimes make in our isolation in Washington, and, more particularly, with the impact of bureaucratic regulations by the executive branch of government on private property rights. Of course, I am even more concerned now with the recent change in administrations and the willingness of the current administration to once again interfere in the economic lives of our citizens."

His mien had become sober, even weighty. He cleared his throat. "We will be discussing today the management of our natural resources—resources that must be managed to provide for the jobs, community stability, public safety, and recreation of our families. The people of southwestern New Mexico have suffered long enough from the Wilderness Area experiment imposed upon them by faraway bureaucrats in Washington, D.C., and have asked me for relief. My bill, HR 2273 will repeal the designation of the Diablo Wilderness Area and open up that vast area to environmentally sound multiple use of logging, grazing, mining, water development, and developed recreation that is imperative if the businesses, homes, and ranches of southwestern New Mexico are to be protected and if the area is to grow." He droned on in a similar style for another five minutes. Even Clayton grew restless. Finally he finished.

The Chairman of the Fall County Commission, a rancher from the Homestead area, read a resolution full of "whereases" and "therefores" supporting the Pugh bill, and invoking the triple mantra of jobs, private property, and local custom and culture.

The representative of the Platoro Chamber of Commerce, in a tight suit spun out of dead dinosaurs, had the build of an overripe avocado—perfect for making guacamole, thought MaryAnne. He supported the Pugh bill.

Buck Clayton was called. All his life he had wanted to be "charismatic," though no one had ever called him that. "I'm going to knock them dead. I'll put these wilderness Goths in their place today," he boasted to his bored wife, whose eyes touched Bill Crawford's across the room.

Before speaking, Clayton took a rhetorical pause to make eye contact with the members of Congress and their staffs on the dais. In an airline magazine, he had read that was a good thing to do with your audience. Pugh was the only one who looked back at him. The others were thumbing through paper. No matter. Clayton went to his written statement.

"Since Jamestown and Plymouth, three hundred and seventy years ago, our charge has been to civilize this continent. For nearly four hundred years, we have been beating back the savage wilderness, reclaiming this land for a prosperous, family-based society. It is now popular to praise wilderness, but this, quite frankly, is a heresy in direct conflict with the course of Western Civilization. The wilderness zealots of today are modern pagans. They are the barbarian hordes who want to turn their backs on all of the benefits science, economics, technology, and civilization have brought us. They are inherently against the order and stability of civilized society. Wilderness is fundamentally chaos and anarchy. The supporters of wilderness are the most dangerous terrorists in the modern world. Their goal is not limited to the goals of the murderers backed by Libya, Iran, and Cuba; they want to overthrow all of civilization, and to throw out the rationalism of the Greeks, the values of Christianity, and the order of the United States, the heir to the British and Roman empires."

Despite the flourishes, Clayton's delivery was wooden, no, it was particle board—that old charisma problem.

"Buck is showing his Deerfield and Harvard education today," Ralph Wittfogel muttered.

"But dig his hairdo," MaryAnne whispered. "He must have half of Prudhoe Bay locked up in that pompadour. I'll bet he hasn't changed it or his sideburns since he first saw Elvis Presley on the Ed Sullivan Show when he was in prep school."

Clayton had forgotten about making eye contact with the congressional panel. He concentrated on reading his statement. "Wilderness is the howling demon that has continued to menace Man ever since we struggled out of the Stone Age to domesticate cattle and plant crops, to build cities and empires, to write books and to bring the power of our intelligence to overcome the raw forces and tyranny of nature in order to create wealth and health for modern Man. Make no mistake about it, wilderness is only the first step. Next they will want to bring back the grizzly bear and the wolf—beasts, predators, Nazis of the mountains—that my great-grandfather paid Ben Lilly to exterminate; they will demand that all logging be stopped on the Diablo National Forest because it might endanger some damned onion or owl. These modern-day witches and druids will not rest until they destroy American Civilization just as the Ostrogoths destroyed Rome. That is their true agenda. They are not Christians, they are not Americans. They are pagans and anarchists who want to force all of us to go back to the Stone Age, to wear animal skins and pick berries and gather roots. They worship irrationality. They are a greater menace to America than the Russian Communists ever were. Their ultimate goal is the utter destruction of civilization and the end of the dominion of Man over this Earth."

"I'll drink to that," said Bill Crawford.

"Now, now, Bill. Take the bone out of your nose before you testify," MaryAnne said.

But it was she who was next called.

MaryAnne stood easily at the lectern and made a wry smile. "I apologize for disappointing Mr. Clayton. I will not be able to conform to his picture of a conservationist. I am not a witch, though I would not be surprised if in his view all women are witches; rather, I am a scientist. I have a Ph.D. in wildlife ecology from the University of Alaska, although I am a New Mexico native living on land I own in Rio Diablo. I plan to continue to make my home in Rio Diablo, Fall County, New Mexico." She turned her head to look directly back at Clayton.

Harry Jukes leaned forward and whispered, "That's the worst witch of them all, Mr. Clayton."

"You don't have to tell me that, Harry. I know, I know."

Jodi Clayton very slowly turned her head to look at them.

Dr. MaryAnne McClellan turned back to the panel and continued. "We face a question today much larger than the fate of more than a million acres of the finest mountain and forest wilderness remaining in the Southwest. The fate of the Diablo is only one part of the central question facing humans at this hour: the destruction of the diversity of life. In the nearly four billion years life has been on Earth, it has never faced a crisis like that being caused today by human overpopulation and destruction of habitat. The extinction rate today is ten thousand times the background rate of extinction throughout the fossil record. This extinction rate is accelerating so fast that leading scientists, like Dr. Michael Soulé, founder of the Society for Conservation Biology, and Harvard's famed E. O. Wilson, warn us that within forty years one-third of all species on Earth could become extinct. They and other leading ecologists tell us that soon after the turn of the century, the only large mammals left on Earth will be those we consciously choose to allow to exist." She paused briefly to let that sink in.

"My prepared statement goes into detail about the biodiversity crisis and how the Diablo Wilderness fits in to the solution. Let me summarize it by dealing with a common misconception of what wilderness is. Wilderness is too often thought of only as a recreational area—a yuppie backpacking park or outdoor exercise yard, if you will. But wilderness is really the crucible for the evolutionary process, the arena for future evolution, the reservoir for biological diversity. Backpacking, horse packing, river running, hiking, fishing, hunting, viewing scenery—all these are compatible uses of Wilderness Areas, but they are not the reasons for protection of Wilderness Areas. We must consciously, rationally, scientifically design Wilderness Areas and National Parks in order to provide habitat for all native species and to include samples of all ecosystems. In the Diablo, it is vital that an area of unsurpassed biotic significance be protected as part of this large area. It is the old-growth ponderosa pine forest of Mondt Park and the high-elevation grassland of Davis Prairie that form the most pristine forest and montane grassland ecosystem in the Southwest. The highest value of these areas is as a nature reserve. They must be part of any Diablo Wilderness Area."

"When is someone going to shut that bitch's mouth for good?" Clayton asked quietly. Jodi Clayton looked at her husband the way Phyllis Schlafly might look at a bum choking his chicken in public.

MaryAnne McClellan finished her statement by saying, "If life in all its fecund, blooming, buzzing, beautiful diversity is to survive, we humans must find within ourselves the generosity of spirit and the greatness of heart to make room for the full flowering of other species and natural life processes. It is from that basis that the Diablo Wilderness Committee and many other groups have developed our proposal to add Mondt Park and other important areas for a 1,118,000-acre unified Diablo Wilderness Area."

Other speakers from conservation groups followed, each taking a different angle. Some spoke of their experiences in the Diablo, making emotional pleas for its preservation, others focused on the economics of below-cost timber sales and road construction by the Forest Service.

Everyone in the room came wide awake when Bill Crawford recited the results of the public opinion poll.

"Bullshit," said Buck Clayton in a stage whisper.

Before calling the next person, Congressman Pugh said, "I wonder what planet that poll was taken on?"

"Not this one!" hollered one of the Fall County militiamen.

Representatives of mining companies, timber companies, labor unions, regional banks, and the local chamber of commerce testified that opening up the vast Diablo Wilderness Area would allow for greater production of red meat, timber, minerals, and jobs for a growing America.

Big, shambling Jim Eaton of Rocky Mountain Empire Timber Company testified that he would like to cut the timber now locked up in the Diablo Wilderness Area and that he might be able to construct a new mill in Platoro if Congressman Pugh's bill was approved. He proclaimed, "There are trees in this Wilderness—trees that could build more homes for America. Locking up these trees in a Wilderness is like taking Miss America with a luscious big bust and a solid flank and making her a nun. It is a goddamn waste of talent."

The first speaker after lunch was an ill-favored, fat woman. Her husband was a tree feller in Homestead, and she called the Wilderness supporters thieves. "I look on all of those wasted trees in that Wilderness and you know what I see? I see that new washing machine I need. I see that big-screen color TV and satellite dish I can't have." She wagged her finger at the members of Congress. "You people in Congress had better wake up because there's going to be another American Revolution!" She left the hearing room after speaking.

Bill Crawford looked around. "Most of the antiwilderness types have left. Guess they get bored pretty easy." He snorted. "Even some of Buck's serfs have split."

Late in the day, Frank Mayer, Sheriff of Fall County, was called to the podium by Pugh.

"Ahh, I didn't know our defender of law and order and the American Way of Life was going to speak," said Ralph Wittfogel. "If he can speak. I don't think I've ever heard him speak. Just glower."

Frank Mayer was a short man built like a fireplug. The skin was wrapped too tightly about his skull—like wet rawhide left to dry overlong in the sun.

He gripped the sides of the lectern as though it would shoot off into orbit if he didn't.

"He's so tight," said Bill Crawford, "I bet he shits once a week. Dried-up little rabbit pellets."

After a quick summation of the county supremacy doctrine, Sheriff Mayer said, "There's going be violence in these parts if the environmental extremists don't back off on spotted owls and ghost hawks."

"Was that a threat? Was that a threat?" Wittfogel asked. "These storm troopers are going to kill someone, mark my words."

The hearing wound down through the afternoon as only out-of-town conservationists were left to testify. Shortly after five, Pugh closed the hearing.

MaryAnne ticked off her list of those testifying. "Pretty good. Seventy-eight for wilderness, twenty-nine anti, and two too confused to call." She looked around the emptying room. "And the audience of three hundred was overwhelmingly in favor of wilderness. We did great. You did great, Bill, with your road show."

"Ol' Barf looks like he's really steaming," Bill said.

"I think we impressed Monica Montoya, however," said Dr. Phillip McClellan. He turned to his daughter. "Let's get up there now and talk to her."

Bill Crawford and Ralph Wittfogel loitered in the parking lot while MaryAnne and Phil talked to Montoya.

Buck Clayton came storming out of the public safety building after talking to Pugh. Jodi followed him. The big man stopped, looked at Bill Crawford, and stomped over. He was a little taller than Bill and about the same weight—though not quite as well packed.

"Well, Crawford," he snarled, "I never picked you for one of these goddamned commie environmentalists when I was paying you to shoe my horses."

Bill laughed. It was not a jovial laugh. "Well, heck, Buck, I guess I'm just smarter than you are. 'Cause I always knew you were the most pompous asshole in New Mexico."

Clayton glared. "What are you doing now that you aren't shoeing horses?" He jabbed his forefinger into Bill's chest. "You on welfare? Like that little bitch who's in charge of you all? Doesn't she get government grants for her subversive work? That's welfare. All you people are on welfare that I have to pay for . . ."

Bill Crawford smiled and poked him back—hard. "Now, Buck, if you want to talk about welfare, maybe you're the one we should talk about. You rugged individualist public lands ranchers are the biggest welfare bums in the country. Why you make some welfare queen with a dozen kids in East Saint Louis look like a piker. You good ol' boy welfare chiselers get less-than-market value grazing fees, you get subsidies on import duties for foreign beef, the Forest Service lets you overgraze my public lands without considering the damage you do to my wildlife, range, or soil. If it wasn't for the welfare you get from the government, ain't no way in hell you could stay in business. Shit, you're nothin' but a leech, a tick, a sow's pup hanging onto the government tit."

An audience had gathered in the parking lot as Crawford and Clayton faced off like Godzilla and King Kong in a Japanese horror flick.

Buck Clayton rose to his height of eloquence. "Why don't all you goddamned commie Jew ecologist queers just go back to New York City where you came from?" He stabbed Crawford's chest with his finger again.

Bill smiled an eager grin. "Let me tell you a story, Buck. A grizzly bear was taking a shit in a meadow, and he looks down and sees a squirrel taking a shit, too. The griz says, 'Hey, squirrel! Do you have trouble with shit sticking to your fur?' The squirrel says, 'No, not really.' And the grizzly says, 'Great!' and reaches down and grabs the squirrel."

Here Bill squatted and demonstrated a bear wiping its ass with a squirrel. He straightened up and grinned again. "Know what, Buck? Unless you back off right now, you're going to find out what that squirrel experienced."

"You can't talk to me like that!" Clayton shoved Crawford in the chest with both hands. "Remember who I am!"

Bill Crawford spread his arms wide to the side and opened his palms. "Take your best shot, Buck. Take your best shot." He grinned with a mouth full of hungry teeth. "Then I'm going to clean up the parking lot with you."

Through clenched teeth, Clayton said, "Watch your ass in Fall County, communist. We're forming a militia to handle your kind and any forest rangers who go against our custom and culture. Next time you see me, watch out!" He turned on his heel and stalked to his Lincoln. Jodi followed, shaking her head in . . . amusement? Disgust? Sympathy?

Bill Crawford called, "How much does Marlboro pay you to keep the cowboy myth alive, Buck?"

Hoots and hollers from the crowd trailed after.

16

Jack Hunter got to the Hummingbird Guest Ranch a little after 7:00 P.M. Chickens were being barbecued; kegs were being tapped. Bill Crawford was telling his story of facing down Buck Clayton for the third or fourth time. MaryAnne was sparkling like all the stars in a high-country, moonless night.

After the conservationists had fed, Texas troubadour Bill Oliver unlimbered his guitar and entertained them with his conservation ballads and sing-alongs. Hunter had had his doubts about a conservation minstrel, but, he had to admit, the man from Austin was good. MaryAnne danced with all the men and drank too much. She deserved it. Hunter drove the sleeping champion of the Wilderness to a motel. It wasn't much of night, but it was a great morning.

Back home in Platoro, MaryAnne was as busy as a hummingbird before nightfall in the high country. Hunter was impressed. He had thought she would take a break after the hearing, but she only hunkered down to turn out more letters against Pugh's bill, and in favor of adding Mondt Park to the Diablo Wilderness Area. She was a real professional, he thought. He admired that. It was a good summertime stretch of days. He even wrote letters to Representative Montoya and

Senator Reed—hey, why not, MaryAnne deserved it, and it might actually do some good.

Late one morning ten days after the hearing, Hunter hung from the chin-up bar on his front porch, slowly raising his legs straight out to a ninety-degree angle. It was a hellish torture, but he had to do it. Yesterday, MaryAnne had shamed him by doing more of them than he could do. He was training for a rematch.

The telephone rang. He let it ring as he wrung out two more of the damned leg raises. Abdominal muscles cramping, he dashed in to the phone.

Yesterday she had called with a voice full of champagne bubbles. She had won her appeal of the Bearwallow Timber Sale in Mondt Park. Diablo National Forest Supervisor Bob Cooter had withdrawn the timber sale until a full environmental impact statement could review it. There would be a party tomorrow to celebrate. But MaryAnne had wanted to party immediately. Brut was on ice. Would Jack come over?

He had. It had been a starry lover's night.

Today her voice was as flat as the Lordsburg Playa. "Dennis Wilson screwed us."

"What do you mean?" Hunter asked.

"The new Forest Service proposal for additions to the Diablo?" MaryAnne's voice carried the venom of a Gila monster.

"Yeah?"

"It leaves out most of Mondt Park and Davis Prairie."

"No. When was it released?"

MaryAnne sighed—not a sigh of resignation, but a sigh of disgust, of disappointment. Can a sigh smolder with rage? This one did. "It hasn't been released yet. Daddy found out about the boundaries through an old Forest Service friend in Washington. The appeal victory will be temporary. Wilderness designation is the only permanent protection we can count on." She paused. Then fury flooded into her voice. "Just as we have a couple of successes with Pugh's kangaroo hearing and the withdrawal of Bearwallow, the assistant secretary of agriculture screws us! I knew the Forest Service wouldn't recommend much, but we've been putting a lot of pressure on Wilson—and on the White House. The Sierra Club lobbyist in Washington thought we were having an impact. But no, a gutless political appointee in the Department of Agriculture just gave us the shaft. We are going to come out swinging, Jack. I know that Wilson is supposed to be a conservation friend, but the word is that it was him who didn't enlarge the Forest Service proposal. We'll attack him with a press release. . . ."

"Whoa, whoa, whoa. That might not be the best way to influence things."

"He did it, Jack. Dennis Wilson screwed us. He misled us. He is the enemy as much as the Forest Service. . . ."

Hunter exhaled loudly. He made his voice as calm, as soothing as he could make it. "There's no disputing that he failed us, but think before you . . ."

"Don't you screw me, too, Jack Hunter. Whose side are you on?"

The conversation got only a little better from Hunter's standpoint. He was able to convince her that the best strategy would be to try to head off the weak administration proposal before it went public. She agreed to organize a fax and phone blitz to Wilson, who, as assistant secretary of agriculture, oversaw the Forest Service and was the official responsible for the proposal. The summer of organizing for the hearing had given her a meaty list of Diablo supporters. She planned to use them.

Hunter cussed himself as he worked on Ed Winslow's horse and replayed the conversation with MaryAnne. It was too goddamned hot to be shoeing horses this afternoon. Winslow was a retired National Park Service biologist. He had been a great conservationist in his time: a man responsible for many of the National Parks in Alaska. When he and his wife had retired to Rio Diablo, local conservationists had been overjoyed. He could help. But, no, he was retired. He had done his part. Now he wanted a peaceful retirement without controversy. He wanted to get along with his new neighbors.

He stayed out of the fray. He watched the five species of hummingbirds at his feeders. He fed the raccoons. He planted cottonwoods and willows along the Rio Diablo through his property.

Hunter cussed himself. Why can't Jack Hunter drop out, too?

Hunter cussed MaryAnne. She was the reason he was being dragged back into the fight. Damn her. Ever since he had gotten involved with her, his life had gotten complicated.

Harry Jukes had come home drunk last night. He had slapped his bawling three-year-old son so hard he had knocked out one of the kid's teeth.

When his wife Candy had tried to stop him from hitting her little boy again, he had turned his hand against her. He had beaten her and the boy before, but knocking a tooth out of a three-year-old had been too much. So what if he was out of a job running a bulldozer on the new logging road project because the preservationists had stopped the timber sale? That was no excuse to beat his wife and little boy. When he had passed out drunk on the couch, black-eyed Candy had quickly packed two suitcases and had driven her ratty old Buick Le Sabre to Mesa, Arizona, where her parents lived.

Harry Jukes was doubly pissed when he woke with a hangover and no wife to fix coffee. He was triply pissed after showing up for coffee at the Rio Diablo Cafe, where Candy worked as a waitress, and finding the note that she was "gone for good!"

Jukes slapped two quarters on the table and stormed out. The screen door banged. He gunned his Dodge pickup, slammed it into reverse, and peeled out of the parking lot. He fired a finger at the honking Winnebago.

Two miles west of town, he braked and downshifted. The pickup whipped off the highway onto the gravel road to the sanitary landfill. He braked hard beside the smoldering pile of garbage.

A pair of ravens lifted off as he drove up. He yanked the mini-14 out of the gun rack. Barely pausing to aim, he emptied the magazine. Not amused by the game, the ravens soared away.

Later in the day, Harry Jukes was loitering outside the post office with the other layabouts in the daily ritual of waiting for the mail to go up in the boxes—not that any of them received urgent mail. His spleen over the Bearwallow Timber Sale being yanked was boiling like cowboy coffee.

He told his friends, "That McClellan cunt and her wilderness bunch have gone too far this time. She just cost me my job. A couple of you boys coulda been hired on the crew, too. Somebody needs to teach her a lesson. A serious lesson."

Jukes went silent when he turned around and saw that Jack Hunter had walked up to the post office door. His friends had been trying to shush him—they had seen Hunter before he had.

Hunter sidestepped Jukes the way he would have sidestepped a fresh dog turd on the sidewalk.

Jukes was so wroth that he had lost his good sense. He was without fear. "You, too, horseshoer. You're a preservationist, too, aren't ya? That cunt's your girlfriend, isn't she?"

Hunter stopped, turned, and took one step back to look down on Harry Jukes. "What makes you think that, tough guy? Maybe I just don't like punks who try to hit women. Why don't you try to teach me a lesson?" Hunter looked into Jukes's face and waited for a reply. When none came, he shook his head and said, "I thought so." If Jukes was the rough beast hereabouts, he wasn't very daunting.

Loyalty was a passing fancy among the good ol' boys of Fall County. Jukes's friends were happy to josh him after Hunter faced him down.

But as Hunter walked away with his mail, he felt no better than Harry Jukes. He should have proclaimed publicly that yes, indeed, he was a conservationist. But he hadn't. Like Ed Winslow, he wanted to get along with his new neighbors, even if he considered none of them to be friends. And: You're damn right MaryAnne McClellan is my girlfriend and if you or anybody else even thinks about touching her, you're going to have holy hell in the name of Jack Hunter to deal with.

But he hadn't. He had denied her. He had betrayed her. Like Simon Peter and . . .

You are a chickenshit, said the voice in his head.

The planned victory party for withdrawal of the Bearwallow Timber Sale became a war council for the Diablo Wilderness Committee.

Phil McClellan drove down from Albuquerque. He had a faxed map from Washington showing the boundaries of the draft Wilderness additions proposal. Half-a-dozen conservationists drove up from Platoro. Bill Crawford, Ralph Wittfogel, and Jack Hunter were already at MaryAnne's place. Hunter listened quietly as they kicked the problem around like Hutus playing soccer with a Tutsi head.

The wolves, of course, were the key. But they were not discussed. Hunter didn't know who in the group knew about them and who didn't. As he listened to the blustering over the administration's stab-in-the-back, he made his decision.

"You've been silent, Jack," said Phil McClellan. "What are your thoughts? You know Washington better than any of us. Is it still possible, in your opinion, to change what Wilson has recommended? Can we prevent a bad proposal from the administration?"

Hunter moaned. He couldn't see any way out of his own dilemma— the way out. A fortunate few invent their own lives. The rest, as Thoreau knew, live lives of quiet desperation. But sometimes events and circumstances force choices on us that we would not have picked, that make us into persons we do not wish to be. Hunter was trying to invent his own life, but he felt like he was living one of quiet desperation. Now, damn it all to hell, circumstances intruded.

He rubbed his eyes and leaned back. "When I was in Washington with the Sierra Club, Dennis Wilson was staff counsel for the House Public Lands Subcommittee. He and I were friends."

Hunter didn't say that when he and Suzanne had broken up, Wilson had put him up until he had found his own apartment. He didn't talk about the fly-fishing trips.

He did say: "We worked on a lot of legislation together. I think I have some influence with him still. And—let's face it—in D.C., connections are what count."

Hunter reached for the bottle of red wine and refilled his glass. "I still have my suit and a couple of ties. I can't pick up the plane fare myself because the horseshoeing business isn't as good as it could be, but if the Diablo Wilderness Committee can raise some expense money, I'll fly back to Washington as soon as I can get an appointment, and talk to Dennis about the boundary. I'll spend every favor owed me and all the goodwill Dennis has for me, and see if we can save Mondt Park and Davis Prairie."

MaryAnne beamed and touched his hand. "Jack . . ."

"But, and this is a big but, I've got to be free to tell—and show—Dennis why our area is so important. Friendship is only worth so much when it goes up against political reality."

MaryAnne withdrew her hand. She leaned back and folded her arms.

Hunter looked around at the others. He was damned if he knew who knew about the wolves. He spoke directly to her. "I don't know any other way to change this thing at this late date."

"Okay." MaryAnne's voice was small. Reality had slapped her as well. The time had come to let someone else know about the wolves. It might be their only hope. "Sure. That's reasonable. I trust your judgment, Jack. Daddy?"

"I think it may be time to break out the champagne—to finally toast your victory on the Bearwallow appeal, MaryAnne. And to toast the new lobbyist for the Diablo Wilderness Committee."

It was four years ago that Jack Hunter had lit out of the District of Columbia. The East Coast was so different from the Southwest that memories of the capital had seemed a dream, a black and white movie shot in the 1940s. Nonetheless, seeing the layout of the city through the drizzle as the airliner made its approach over the Potomac, it all seemed real again as though he had never left. The Southwest now faded into the dream world. At least it was in Technicolor. He did not want to make this trip, so he was shocked when the view teased out a feeling of home from him.

Below in the river were the Three Sisters, now the Washington Canoe Club on the D.C. bank, Key Bridge, Georgetown, the glass towers of Rosslyn in Virginia, Roosevelt Island, the Capitol dome in the distance, Washington Monument, the Reflecting Pool, Kennedy Center, the marshy flats and runway of National Airport.

Despite his position of power as assistant secretary of agriculture, Dennis Wilson still looked like Dennis the Menace, thought Jack Hunter. Same Dutch boy haircut, same open friendly grin, same goofy wooden clogs.

When Hunter was ushered into his office, Dennis Wilson came out from behind his desk to hug him. "Damn you, Jack, where have you been the last couple of years? You sent me some postcards from Africa and such places, and then disappeared. The rumor mill says you're a *horseshoer* in New Mexico. That can't be true, can it?"

Hunter put on his best aw-shucks grin. "'Fraid so, old friend. I wasn't planning to put this suit back on."

"Well, it's wonderful to see you. Though I'm sorry I don't have much time. I've got to fly to Portland this evening. I'm in one hell of a tar baby on the Northwest ancient forest issue. I hope that's not what you're here for."

"No, I promise I won't say a word about that. I really do appreciate you seeing me on such short notice, Dennis, particularly after my bad manners the last few years. I'll be quick."

If I have to be in Washington, I deserve it, thought Hunter, as he savored the first glass of Bordeaux at Chez Debbie. So what if I blow out my budget? I've been too long away from my favorite restaurants.

He hadn't wasted Dennis Wilson's time. Hunter had brought his own slide projector. Slides of wolves had gone up on Dennis's wall. Slides of the landscape around the wolves had gone up on the wall. Then had come a slide of the Diablo National Forest map with the conflicting boundaries for additions to the Diablo Wilderness.

"This," had said Hunter, "is where, two months ago, I photographed these wild Mexican wolves naturally recolonizing and denning in the Diablo National Forest. This is the proposed Wilderness boundary of the Diablo Wilderness Committee. This is the draft boundary in your proposal. This is the route of proposed logging roads. These are the proposed timber sales."

He had switched to a slide of mama wolf and pups at the den, had left it projected on the wall, and had spread out a Diablo National Forest map with all the boundaries, proposed roads and timber sales, and the wolf den penned in.

Now, Hunter sipped the dusty-dry red wine and slurped up oysters Rockefeller. Not a bad approach, ol' buddy, he toasted himself.

Of course, Dennis had been floored by the wolves.

Of course, Dennis had seen them as a pressing argument for including Mondt Park and Davis Prairie in the Diablo Wilderness.

Of course, Dennis had fumed that he hadn't received this information earlier.

Of course, Dennis had said the administration had been under political pressure from the Democratic governor of New Mexico to limit the size of proposed additions to the Diablo Wilderness.

Of course.

Jack Hunter had explained the reasoning for the secrecy about the wolves. Wolf expert Dr. MaryAnne McClellan would take U.S. Fish and Wildlife Service biologists into the area next spring. A formal petition was being prepared for critical habitat designation. Sponsors were being sought for the conservationists' Wilderness bill.

Dennis had agreed to put the administration's proposal on ice. Thanks to Dr. McClellan's timber sale appeal, the area in question would be safe for the time being. He would see to it that there would be no reoffering of the timber sale and no environmental impact statement on road construction, for at least a year. He had pointed to the stack of faxes and phone messages opposing the administration's draft proposal. They would be a handy excuse for holding off. In return, conservationists would pressure the governor to back off. Perhaps the administration proposal could be modified to include most of Mondt Park and Davis Prairie early next year.

"But, remember, Jack," Dennis Wilson had said, "you guys have to be the barbarians at the gate. You've got to force us to enlarge our proposal."

As good as could be hoped for, thought Hunter, as he tucked into his rack of lamb. Tomorrow he would make the rounds of the conservation groups to solidify their support for the Diablo Wilderness Committee's proposal. Tomorrow night he would fly back to Albuquerque.

Admit it. You like playing Shane. The white knight. Riding in to rescue the damsel in distress. Whether she's wolves, wilderness, or MaryAnne McClellan.

"You bet."

The chocolate mousse arrived.

Back in Albuquerque, Jack met with MaryAnne and Phil, and staffers and volunteer leaders of the different conservation groups. He reported on his meeting with Wilson—without mentioning the wolves, except to the McClellans. A strategy was cobbled together for a legislative campaign to add Mondt Park to the Wilderness. MaryAnne, Phil, Bill Crawford, and a couple of others volunteered to go to Washington to find cosponsors for Monica Montoya's Mondt Park bill if she introduced it. Tasks were assigned; people got to work.

After the meeting, Jack, MaryAnne, and Phil drove to the McClellan home in the foothills of the Sandias.

MaryAnne led Hunter to her bedroom.

He was nervous. "Your dad won't mind?"

"No, silly. It's not like he didn't have a few girlfriends over here when I was in high school. It's not like I'm a little girl. I'm an adult, in case you haven't noticed. You might even be considered an adult."

Her bedroom was still a 1970s high school girl's bedroom. But the posters weren't rock stars. They were gymnasts and wild animals—wolves, bears, and cats.

Before they drifted off to sleep, she asked, "You sure you don't want to go to Washington with us? Show me around?"

"I'm sure," he grunted. "I've been there. You guys don't need me. You'll do fine." He faked sleep. He had done his part. He would do no more.

17

It was the time of the night before full darkness. A faint glow of blue tarried on the western sky-border. Brighter stars hung in the west; dimmer ones hid unseen. The valley trees and mountains beyond faded into shades of gray. The moon wouldn't rise for another three hours.

Jack Hunter sat alone on his porch. He leaned back in the rocking chair and crossed his feet on the blue-painted wooden railing. A beer was in his hand, a cigar in his teeth. It should have been the close of a good day—a great day. He had hiked seventeen miles, alone, in the high country. He had watched a bear for fifteen minutes. Crossbills and red-faced warblers had hunted the spruce and fir. He had gotten a good view of a northern goshawk. It had been a day like a day when the world was young, before there were wise apes. Before Lord Man spoiled it. There was a pleasant, painless tiredness in Hunter's legs from the hike.

Something was missing.

The thought crawled into his head like an unwelcome alley cat. *All you need,* it purred, *is a woman. MaryAnne. There's an emptiness only she can fill.*

Hunter's finger picked at the paper label on the Pacifico bottle. Faraway down the valley a dog barked. Up on the mesa coyotes yipped their jeers. A family of javelinas rooted through the compost pile. A bat fluttered by. A last nighthawk. The night was warm. Still. The only sound was the river, the river moving, always moving, moving to the sea, to the Gulf of California. Somewhere safe to sea.

MaryAnne's there. Just up the valley. You could be there in twenty minutes on foot, five in the truck, mewed the unwelcome tomcat. *She's yours for the asking. She loves you. You love her. It would be good to have a woman—that woman. That best of women.*

Hunter wished the little man in his head would chase away the alley cat.

A kitten of a breeze tip-toed down the valley like Robert Frost's fog. It, too, purred and rubbed against his bare shins. He got up and walked to the edge of the porch. He leaned against the corner post. His feet were crossed, one flat on the boards, the other bent at the toes. One hand rested with its thumb thrust in a belt loop; the other held the beer. He caught the breeze in his face, on his bare chest. He listened to the river, and looked east to where MaryAnne lived.

He could try to make it work, make it last, but it wouldn't. It couldn't. Sure, there was romance and excitement and passion now with MaryAnne. But the passion never lasts. There had been romance and excitement with Suzanne at first. Where had it gone? It can't last. Togetherness makes it fade. That's the curse of it, the bitter irony. You hunger for excited romance, for true, heart-shaking love. But in finding it, in gaining it, you destroy it. Even with MaryAnne.

Hunter sat down again. He drained the beer. Hell's bells and little bitty pissants. When you take love, it disappears. Besides, if he stayed hooked up with MaryAnne, he would be dragged back into the political quag. Before he knew it, he would be in the middle of the fight for the Diablo. And that was hopeless. It would only depress him more. Hunter knew that if he was to keep a toehold on sanity, he had to steer clear of the hopelessness that came from tilting at windmills.

He remembered Blake:

> But he who kisses the Joy as it flies
> Lives in Eternity's sunrise.

Wrong, Billy Boy, wrong. I've kissed joy as she flies. And now I live in eternity's sunset.

He heaved the empty beer bottle into the yard with his disgust. It shattered against the propane tank. The noise startled him. He went inside for something stronger.

The night before, MaryAnne and Jack had sat in lawn chairs down by her pond and watched the evening light show. Just above the horizon, the sunset was the color of a properly cooked salmon steak. The cloud over the Diablos to the east looked like a pinkish-white punk Afro, though this hairdo belonged to the bride of Frankenstein because sparks were shooting through it.

"Jack, snookums," she said.

"Mmhmm?"

"The last couple of months have been heaven. I've never felt so good with a man as I feel with you. I've been thinking about us."

Hunter's butt puckered. This could be a dangerous trail.

"You know, we spend a lot of time together. More often than not, we eat dinner together and spend the night together, either at my place or yours."

It *was* a dangerous trail.

"Maybe it would make sense for us to just move in together."

Jack Hunter had been coasting, enjoying the good life. Now, down the trail came a grizzly named commitment.

"Cat got your tongue?"

Hunter drew a deep breath. "Well, this summer has been wonderful for me, too. You know how I feel about you." He bit his lip. "But are we rushing things a little? Would we risk spoiling what we have if we lived together?"

A chill settled over the pond. MaryAnne sat more stiffly. "So you're saying you don't want to live with me?"

"No, no. I'm just concerned about things going too fast. Maybe our separate homes help our . . . our relationship." There was that dipshit abstract word he hated.

She was silent for half a minute. "If you don't want to live with me, Jack Hunter, just say so. But don't beat around the bush. Don't lie to me. Be straight. If you don't want to make any kind of commitment, okay. But be honest about it. Don't worm your way out of it."

He was quiet. She stood up.

"Maybe I've just been wasting my time," she said. "Maybe I've been deluding myself. Maybe all you've ever wanted from me was an easy piece of ass—like with Jodi Clayton."

Jesus, how's she know about that?

"Maybe we *are* rushing things. Maybe we ought to just cool it for awhile. *Really* cool it for awhile." She stalked off toward her house.

Hunter stood. "Sweetheart . . ."

She stopped and turned. "Don't 'sweetheart' me, Jack Hunter. Not if you don't mean it. Not if you don't care enough to make a commitment— or to at least to be honest with me. Think about it, cowboy. Think about us. Then give me a call when I get back from Washington. But don't bother me until then. I need a break from your chickenshit bullshit." She disappeared into the night.

"Jesus, where'd all that come from?" he muttered. He stood up and kicked over his lawn chair. "Shit." He stomped off to his truck. Halfway there, he snarled, "*Keer*ist, what a bitch! Well, I'm out of that. It wasn't fun, but, goddamnit it all to hell, at least it's over! I'm free of that bitch and her goddamned high and mighty ways. I can get back to my own fucking life!"

Ahh, and what a grand life it is, said the treasonous little man in the skull.

Hunter stood on the porch with his gin and tonic. The taste of last night was not good. What a stupid little fight, he thought. How did something that picayune break us up? But, damnit, let her be the one to apologize. She's the one who made it a big deal. Hell's bells, I was just sitting there.

The breeze picked up and he turned his face into it.

Well, she's going to be gone to D.C. in another day. If I want to make up, I better get my butt over there. No, let's just wait it out. See what she does. Maybe she'll mellow out a little after her trip to Washington.

Aw, hell. Maybe it's a sign that this thing isn't going to work. Lord knows I wasn't looking for something serious. But what a pistol she is. What a woman . . . what a pain in the ass.

Homestead was forty miles north of Rio Diablo and sat at about 6,000 feet elevation. Scattered ponderosa pines grew in the wide valley and on north-facing slopes. On drier south-facing slopes, junipers reigned. The homes were a mixture of old adobes and log cabins, 1950s-era suburban-style ranch homes, and—of course!—mobile homes up on concrete blocks. Satellite receivers sprouted like sci-fi sculptures. The Baptist church had a white steeple; the Catholic, Jehovah's Witness, and Church of Christ buildings were more modest. A bank, a phone company office, two grocery stores, and five bars made up the business district. About a thousand people—almost half of Fall County's population—lived in the county seat.

Frank Mayer, Sheriff of Fall County, had his office in the ugly two-story, orange brick county courthouse in the middle of Homestead. MaryAnne McClellan was surprised at herself for stopping and filing the complaint.

Walking to the door, she growled to herself, "Too bad I don't have a boyfriend I can depend on. Ex-boyfriend! Darn it, I have been as easy as I could be. Getting him to help on the Diablo has been a pain in the butt. If the wimp won't commit to me, he's not worth it. I can't believe he was such a coward when I suggested living together. How stupid could I have been. . . ."

The sheriff's dispatcher-receptionist-secretary-file clerk was a lumbering dreadnought, built out of Rainbo bread and lunch meat, a granddaughter of the female aurochs described by H. L. Mencken in his dispatch from the Scopes Monkey Trial. She had a row of chins like a long line of pelican bill-pouches strung down her throat. Her hair was a frizzy bleached-yellow helmet. Marlene Dietrich's eyebrows were painted on her forehead. MaryAnne recognized her from the hearing. She had been the woman late in the day whining about a new washing machine. She buzzed the sheriff. MaryAnne's name came out of her long fat pharynx like a phlegm ball.

Sheriff Mayer came out and stood on the other side of the counter from MaryAnne. He said nothing, didn't ask her what she needed. He simply looked.

"I want to report a death threat," said MaryAnne.

There was no reaction from the sheriff, no comment. He continued to look, without blinking. He had a prissy mouth with tight muscular little lips, lips made for slurping up bottom scum.

MaryAnne almost turned and left, but decided this pig was not going to intimidate her. She pulled out a manila folder from her briefcase. She opened it on the counter and indicated one sheet of paper. A photocopied newspaper photo of her face was on it. Cross hairs were drawn across her face. NOT WANTED IN FALL COUNTY was printed in heavy letters above her picture.

"I found this pinned to my front door yesterday morning."

He still said nothing. MaryAnne forced herself to remain civil.

"This," she pointed to an envelope, "was in my mail this morning."

He made no move to pick it up or to take out the contents.

MaryAnne pulled the folded letter out of its envelope and spread it on the counter. A heavy scrawl read, "DON'T COME BACK TO FALL COUNTY BITCH OR YOU DIE."

The sheriff put the two sheets of paper and the envelope in the manila folder, turned, and walked away with it.

"What are you going to do?"

He turned and smiled. "If you turn up dead, I suppose I'll have to appear to investigate."

"If you aren't going to do anything, then give me those threats back!"

"Sorry. This is now formal evidence. We'll keep it here." He closed the door to his private office.

MaryAnne stood at the counter with her fists clenched. She was furious with herself for even coming in, more so for letting Sheriff Frank Mayer make off with the papers. She hadn't even made copies. She should have taken them straight to the New Mexico Attorney General's office, she should have . . .

Damnit! She cursed herself. *How could I be so stupid? That sonofabitch Jack Hunter has gotten me so messed up that I can't even think straight. Rotten sheriff! He probably sent them himself—or knows who did.* Biting her tongue, she turned on her heel, and marched to the door.

"You know, MaryAnne," came the smug voice of the dispatcher, "you brought this all on yourself."

MaryAnne spun around.

The fat woman leaned back. The chair creaked. She dragged on her cigarette and blew twin plumes out her nostrils. "We get along in Fall County. We take care of each other. We don't like outsiders coming in and trying to destroy our jobs, our homes, our customs and culture—our way of life. We welcome newcomers. But not those who are un-American. That's what you environmentalists are. Un-American. My husband calls your kind 'watermelons'—green on the outside, red on the inside. You don't care about the environment. You're trying to destroy the American system—or, if you're sincere, you're being duped by the Rockefellers and the Jewish socialists running the rich environmental groups in Washington. The House of Windsor is behind it all. The New World Order. We know all about it. You're young, so maybe you don't know any better. Those of us in Fall County are the real environmentalists—ranchers, loggers, miners. We take care of the land because we depend on it for our living."

She looked closely at MaryAnne. "You be careful, young lady. You've made some people in this county very, very angry. It's not safe for you here. There are real patriots in Fall County who will defend our way of life. We aren't going to let any agents for the United Nations betray us."

MaryAnne obeyed the speed limit for one hundred miles until she was out of Fall County. Jack Hunter was crazy if he thought she would ever ask him another thing. He was history!

18

Jodi Clayton lit a cigarette and propped herself up on the big pillows of her California king-sized bed. The hired help was banished from the manor this afternoon. Except for one.

Hunter was back. Shoeing her horses. Servicing her.

Trying to forget MaryAnne. Trying to convince himself that the path of noncommitment was the path he wanted. With Jodi, Hunter didn't have to show his scars, and she didn't have to show hers. But a nagging voice kept asking him if, once again, he was taking every wrong direction. *Isn't that an old Kris Kristofferson song?* he asked himself. *Quit living a country oldies life, asshole.*

"You know a lot about the animals around here, don't you, Jack?"

"Yeah. A fair bit."

"And you go into the wilderness a lot, don't you?"

"I know it pretty good."

"Well, maybe you can tell me: Are there wolves here?"

The question shocked like a finger in a light socket.

"I don't mean like coyotes," Jodi said. "I mean wolves. Real wolves."

Hunter quickly replied, "Wolves were exterminated here by the 1930s. I think the last authenticated one around here was killed in 1936."

"So you don't think there are any left?"

"No."

"You don't think they could have come back? Like from Mexico?"

"Not that I know of. I sure haven't seen any sign of wolves. And I've seen wolves in Alaska and other places. I know what a wolf looks like. If anybody is claiming to have seen wolves, it's probably just a big coyote. There aren't any wolves here. Haven't been for sixty years." Hunter was worried by Jodi's interest in wolves. They'd never had this kind of conversation before. What was she getting at? He wanted to brush away any rumors of wolves, but knew he needed to be careful not to protest too much.

"Well, then, tell me what this is." She stubbed out her cigarette in the night stand ashtray and wrapped a gauzy robe around herself. She headed for the bedroom door.

Bonaparte, the poodle, trotted after her.

Hunter followed, first pulling on his jeans.

She led him to Buck's den.

"Buck claims this is a wolf."

Around Hunter the darkness dropped.

The mounted animal was a wolf. It wasn't just any wolf. Hunter at once knew it as the female wolf he had seen at the den—the wolf in the slides that he'd shown to Dennis Wilson and MaryAnne McClellan.

He tried to mask the horror he felt.

"So, is this a wolf?" Jodi asked.

Hunter hoped his voice wouldn't crack. "It's a wolf, all right."

The poodle stood in the doorway looking at the wolf. Shivers ran up and down its body as Jerry Lee Lewis's fingers would over a burning piano.

Jodi Clayton said, "Onis Luebner told Buck he trapped it over on our other ranch. The one next to the Wilderness Area, around—what's the name of the place? Mount Mesa? Something like that."

Hunter's mouth had gone dry. "Hmm. I wonder if that's where he trapped it, or if it's from somewhere else. Maybe Luebner's trying to pull a fast one on Buck. Maybe he's trying to get him to pay for a wolf from somewhere else." It was too late, but Hunter grasped at anything to throw them off the trail.

"Mr. Luebner doesn't appear to be that clever, in my opinion."

"Yeah . . ."

"He told Buck that he thinks there are *more* wolves over there. Buck told him to get the rest of them. He said that if the wildlife service finds out about them, they'll make them an endangered species like the spotted owl, and shut down our grazing, and stop the logging road contract Buck is trying to get for our construction company."

Hunter couldn't take his eyes off the trophy wolf. His worst fears had come true. The bastards had found the wolves. And they were killing them.

"But you aren't going to do anything, are you?" said Jodi. The question wasn't a plea or even a request. It was a statement of fact.

The movie of the she-wolf at the den with her cubs played on the screen in Hunter's head. No, it wasn't a movie. Hunter's skull box had become a cave lit by a smoky torch. The little man was painting the wolf on the wall with red ochre. The green fire that had been in her eyes was replaced with a cold, glassy stare. *Lobo! Lobo! burning bright . . .*There was no fire now. No fire burned bright in Hunter, either. Just the horror.

"No," he mumbled. What could he do? The bell had tolled, it had tolled for wolves, it had tolled for wilderness. It had tolled for Jack Hunter.

"I thought so. We're very much alike, Jack, dear boy. We've both surrendered."

No wonder Hunter had no need to show his scars to Jodi. She knew them all too well.

Jodi shut the door to Buck Clayton's den. The poodle began to bark—a high-pitched, savage wail.

Hunter drove across the cattle guard much in need of a drink. *Welcome to the world of hollow men,* taunted the voice in Hunter's head. The black brooding belly of a monsoon cloud swelled out from the mountains toward the valley.

Hunter sat on the porch with a bottle of tequila. The thunderstorm died after sunset, and he shuffled to a lawn chair in the yard. After the bottle slipped from his hand to join the cigar butts on the ground, the clouds gathered back, rain turned to hail, and thunder shrieked like great trees crashing to earth. Like dying wolves.

In the briny deep of alcohol-poisoned sleep, Hunter rode the stout sea swells with Swinburne. The waves foamed and broke and dashed them against shore-rocks in spumes of spray. Hunter clawed his way out of the death trap. He lurched to his feet; the hail hammered at him like machine gun fire. Thunder echoed from valley ridge to valley ridge. Lightning turned the night into a strobed horror show. He made the porch and collapsed.

Swinburne's last words in the surf ripped through his ears like thunderbolts:

> We thank with brief thanksgiving
> Whatever gods may be
> That no man lives forever
> That dead men rise up never
> That even the weariest river
> Winds somewhere safe to sea.

Hunter's tequila sunrise came at about 9:00 A.M. The world looked a little different this morning. It had been many years since Jack Hunter had felt as bad as he felt today. Whatever had been in his stomach had long since been puked out. Even the bitter bile, the bile so bitter it had tasted like his heart, was gone. But it had not been good.

His head was a bullroarer—one of those contraptions Australian Aborigines spin around to make noises of the otherworld. He whimpered to the universe. The words stumbled out of his mouth like sailors leaving a Filipino whorehouse at dawn.

"I feel like I've been et by a coyote and shit off a cliff. Like . . ."

Hunter lost voice as the dry heaves snatched him up and shook him as Thoreau had wanted to devour the woodchuck.

Swinburne was puked out. Into the void in Hunter's brain came a barked order from Ezra Pound: *Pull down thy vanity.*

Hunter put his fist through his reflection in the kitchen window.

Jack Hunter sat on the porch with a headache like split cord wood and a stomach whipped like Huck at the hands of Pap. As he bandaged his bleeding hand, he brooded. He was sitting out the Diablo fight like Achilles sitting out the siege of Troy. But he didn't have the excuse of an Agamemnon taking his Briseis to justify his pout. No, this dumb shit of an Achilles had run Briseis off all by himself. Was she Briseis? Maybe she was really Patrocles. Or was she a combination of Briseis and Patrocles? Now, Hunter was not only disgusted with himself, he had doubled his headache with his deep literature theorizing.

Hunter sipped at the hair-of-the-dog noon beer. Whit-*wheet.* Whit-*wheet!*

"*Et tu,* Crazy Bill?" he asked the curve-billed thrasher eating ants in the yard. "Even you laugh at me?"

The bird regarded him with a mad yellow eye.

Is it finally time to stop whining, old friend?

You bet.

It was time for Hamlet to become Henry. It was time to leave Elsinore for Agincourt.

Hunter knew he couldn't run any more. It was time to stick his spear in the ground and fight for home. He saw the grand cottonwoods and bouncy stream of Stowe Creek Meadow. He saw the tall ancient pines of Mondt Park. He saw the wolves on Davis Prairie. That was what was real. That was what was important. That was what made his life worth living. By god, he would fight for it now. No matter what the cost.

An engineered all-weather gravel road suitable for passenger cars cut east-west across the central part of the Diablo National Forest. Wooden signs marked it as Forest Road 20. Fifteen miles south of it was the boundary of the Diablo Wilderness Area where roads and cars were banned. Between U.S. Forest Service System Road 20 and the Wilderness Area boundary was a wild expanse of country without protection. Yellow-belly ponderosa pines grew there; some were five feet in diameter and five hundred years old. South of the main road, a one-lane dirt track (Forest Service Road 914b) pointed like a dagger at the heart of the wilderness. It ended after four miles; a rocky, rutted, four-wheel-drive trail sputtered along for another three or four miles before becoming a pack trail impassable to vehicles.

Onis Luebner parked his two-and-a-half ton Chevy flatbed where 914b stopped. He pulled out the ramp and drove his motorized tricycle down it. He strapped on a leather holster holding a .22 magnum. With trapped coyotes, he simply stood on their chests to crush their lungs and heart. He wasn't about to do that with a wolf. The .22 magnum would kill with trivial damage to the pelt.

Onis Luebner knew how to trap wolves. He had learned his skill as a boy at the knee of a hoary old fart who had worked for the federal government's Predatory Animal and Rodent Control agency in the glory years of wolf extermination.

Luebner's trap line was scented with a godawful witch's brew the old man had taught him: coyote entrails, glands, tongue, windpipe, lungs, eyeballs, brains, spinal column, and feet pads ground up with coyote gall. For four days, it had been left to stew in the sun in a corked five gallon jug with three gallons of water. A half pint of what resulted had been mixed with twenty-five drops of spirits of asafetida, two drops of anise oil, two drops of tonquin musk, and twenty drops of Canton musk. This had been placed in a gallon jug that had been filled with dog urine. Luebner's hounds hadn't taken to peeing in the pans he had set out, so he had fitted them with crude catheters, secured by radiator hose clamps, connected to jugs. They had been short-chained in the sun with un-limited water to drink. He had gotten his gallon of dog piss, by god. But the dogs were determined never again to reveal their penises to the master.

If the traps along the ATV route didn't get all the lobos, Luebner would go into the wilderness on horseback. There, he would find their tracks, figure out their "runway" (wolves have a regular hunting circuit they may take two weeks to cover), and place his traps at bottlenecks where they couldn't easily avoid them. If that didn't work, he would shoot two or three deer and lace their carcasses with strychnine.

After loading the trapping tools onto the ATV, he puttered off to run his trap line. Mr. Clayton had paid big money for the wolf. He had prom-ised much more to get them all.

On the rimrock to the west, something watched.

Luebner stopped at each trap on the line paralleling the trail. The location of each was marked by a bit of engineer's flagging tied to a branch beside the trail.

The first ten traps held nothing. Luebner was full of hope when he stopped at the next trap. Eleven was his lucky number. But as he walked down from the rutted trail to the dry creek bed where the trap was bur-ied, he cried out in pain as steel jaws snapped around his ankle.

Cursing, he struggled to take off the trap. What the fuck? He hadn't put a trap here. Was someone putting their traps along his trap line? He started as he heard the motor of his three-wheeler.

"Hey!" he yelled and limped-ran back to the road.

Onis Luebner stood where his motorized steed had been parked. Dust rose in the morning air to mark its passage back to the main road. The revolver in his hand was useless.

It was two miles back to the flatbed. Onis Luebner was fuming. That was a long hike for a man of his weight (two-forty) and age (forty-seven). Particularly for one with a bruised ankle from a trap. Even through his boots, it hurt like hell.

After the first mile, Luebner had to rest. He sat on a log by the side of the road and sucked wind. He lit a Camel Wide, crumpled the empty pack, and tossed it. Fear struck him. Was that the last cigarette? He checked his pockets. It was the last cigarette. The spare pack had been on the ATV. He glanced down the road. There was a carton in the truck. "I'd walk a mile for a Camel," jingled into his mind. The song did not please him. His heart was working overtime. It had taken him thirty minutes to get this far. His ankle was throbbing. If he found out who had trapped him and stole his ATV, he would . . .

Black petrochemical smoke billowed up a mile north on the road.

No, no, no!

Onis Luebner stumbled down the trail as fast as he could, fearing—knowing—what he would find at his parked truck.

Twenty minutes later, lungs gasping, heart pounding, the best trapper in Fall County saw what was left of his truck. The ATV was parked on the flatbed. Both were burned hulks. Nothing was salvageable.

Fritz Firebase—the nearest place with people—was twenty miles away. Luebner sat in the dust of the road. Twenty miles was too far. He hoped that he would meet someone on the main road. But, sweet Jesus, that was four more miles. Now he was really without a Camel.

Onis Luebner was a close-mouthed man. He had never been one for chit-chat. The hippie backpackers from California who picked him up on the road and drove him to Rio Diablo weren't able to even pry a name out of him. He told them where he wanted to go, asked if they had cigarettes, and then sulked. Damn hippies. Shoulda known they wouldn't have cigarettes—at least ones with tobacco. He waited to unload his story until he saw Mr. Clayton.

Buck Clayton listened carefully and asked questions. It was clear to him that the assault on Onis Luebner was retaliation by someone who knew about the wolf. If the arson of Luebner's truck and ATV was reported, the investigation could ultimately lead to Fish and Wildlife agents discovering the trapped wolf. Had to be careful here. After deliberation, he decided it was best not to report the arson. He told Luebner he would pay for his truck and ATV. Had to keep this thing quiet for awhile. Luebner took his leave with a generous check.

In the dusk, Buck Clayton sat alone by the pool with The Glenlivet. The Mexican cook worked on dinner inside. Jodi was in her room reading a book—or whatever she did. The mounted wolf would be moved tomorrow for storage in Los Angeles.

Things were under control in the walled-in patio of the Clayton compound. Over the wall, beyond the Lombardy poplars and the weeping willow, the Diablo Mountains rose. Wilderness up there. Wolves up there. Again. With the breakdown of society, with the corruption of the American Empire, wilderness was reasserting itself. Wolves were returning. He feared another Dark Age. He looked at the stars.

He stood up. The night air had taken on a chill. He walked to the big wrought iron gate and looked at the wilderness.

What kind of person would defend wolves?

They were different, more frightening than the wolf itself. They weren't demons of the night—like wild beasts or Iraqis. They were people in Clayton's own community, people he might pass on the highway. Thus they straddled the line between night and day. They were the twilight-spoilers.

A chill like a skulking wolf crept up Clayton's spine as he chewed on that horror.

Jack Hunter sat on a rimrock deep in the Wilderness Area. The stars spangled out across the sky. He had walked many miles today, not stopping until it had been too dark to go farther. There were twenty-three more miles to do tomorrow. His truck was parked at a trailhead on the southern edge of the Diablo Wilderness Area, just north of Platoro—a long way from Mondt Park. He chewed the end of his cigar and smiled at what he was—terror for fat burghers on far plains below. Graves would have approved.

Hunter blew a smoke ring. When it widened in the still air, he blew a smaller one through it.

Compromise.

Cowardice.

Surrender.

No more.

Let me fight!

If this be folly, then make the most of it.

19

The five-day stubble on Jack Hunter's face invited a caress about as much as would a thicket of teddybear cholla cactus. It could have been that, or it could have been the sour misanthropy sweated out of his pores that made the Shady Lady dancers less flirtatious than usual tonight. Or it could have just been night moths in his skull. No matter. Hunter knew the woman he wanted. And she wasn't here. The pint of Guinness and the dance-hall darlin's couldn't make him forget her tonight.

Hunter sat back when Bill Crawford sauntered in. He was a big bear back to reclaim his salmon stream. A kiss was blown to him from the stage, and the two dancers between sets slipped beside him for hugs at the bar. He regaled them with stories of Washington, D.C., and dropped the names of all the big shots he had seen, whether he had talked to them or not.

Hunter waited his turn. His big buddy would notice him in the dark corner sooner or later. No reason to horn in on his time in the spotlight.

Hunter ordered another Guinness.

That rarity drew Bill's eye. "Jack, ol' buddy!" he roared. "I didn't see you over here." He brought his pint to Hunter's booth.

Hunter stood for the *abrazo*. "Couldn't help but notice you, amigo. The conquering hero, huh?"

Bill leaned back in the booth and spread his arms out on the top of the backrest. "Well, not quite. It coulda been better. Had a couple of close calls. But we stopped Puke's bills for now. And Montoya introduced our bill. We got about a dozen cosponsors—including two Republicans that I nailed down. It looks like more will sign on. Guess these things take time."

Hunter slapped Bill on the shoulder. "Good job, hoss. You're going to turn into a lobbyist yet."

"Right," Bill snorted and took a long pull on his pint. He did seem pleased with himself, though. "Boy howdy, Puke was steamed when Montoya introduced our bill, and the others signed on. But he ain't too popular in Congress, except with the other goonybird right-wingers." He unloaded his new war stories on Hunter.

Hunter didn't tell Bill about the trapped wolf. Or about the payback. Luebner and Clayton seemed to have gotten the message. He had seen no further efforts to trap the wolves, and no sign of poison. He would tell Bill about the wolf later. Hunter didn't look forward to that. Much less to telling MaryAnne, even if through Bill Crawford. Hunter also didn't tell Bill that he was in the game for Mondt Park now; that could wait as well.

It was time for another round. Bill bought. He clicked Hunter's glass with his. "By the way, you helped a lot, my friend. By putting Dennis Wilson on track, you made a hell of a difference."

"Good."

"I hope you're planning to make up with MaryAnne."

Hunter looked at his friend. Never any subtlety with Bill Crawford. "Is she back?"

"Yeah. We flew back from D.C. together yesterday. I think she was going to drive down to Rio Diablo from Albuquerque today. You're a damn fool if you don't try to make up with her. . . ."

"I'm not sure she wants. . . ."

"Don't be an idiot. She won't admit it, but she's still hung up on you. Why is beyond me."

That was enough for Hunter. He left thirteen ounces of stout in his glass. Bill dutifully finished it. Wasting Guinness was a sin.

Hunter coasted to a stop in a pull-off by the side of the road. The stout flowed out. The air had a hint of fall. October was tomorrow. The asphalt strip beside him was deserted—he had met only two cars in the twenty miles since Platoro. The mountains glowed in dim pastels with the rising of the moon.

He looked overhead to the faint stars. There they were: heroes and heroines, gods and goddesses. Perseus, Heracles, Andromeda, Orion. . . . Arthur and Beowulf should be up there, too. Along with Hamlet, Lear, and that crowd. Where they belonged. In their place. In cold, stony, starry eternity. *There* was the place for grandeur, for greatness, for glory, for fame. For hubris. In the stars. In myth. Time was too short for that on Earth. Mortal life was too brief for romantic tragedy. Time was too precious to waste on the stuff of gods and demigods. Time only to live, to enjoy, to experience, to fight . . . to love. No time for noble suffering. For tragic greatness. For existential angst. For despair and surrender.

All his life, Hunter had been up there. In the stars with Perseus and the rest. A man of destiny. A man born to greatness, to achievement, to fate. Through Boy Scouts, high school, college, Washington, he had been the chosen one, the bronze-muscled Perseus—a hero, not merely a man. At least in his own mind. Even now as a hard-drinking, sullen horseshoer in a backwater nowhere—a myth, a legend, a tragedy. Consequence tossed aside. A noble heart ripped asunder by a golden beauty. Denial of an Earthly love freely offered. A marble statue broken on the lone and level sands. . . .

No more. It was time to step out of the stars, out of cold stone, out of cracked parchment, and into life. It was time to cast off the demands of the ages, to return to flesh and blood. To just be a man.

Hunter finally understood that it was time to pull down his vanity so what he loved would not be torn from him.

Moonlight wrapped around him with the taste of mortal freedom.

"I love you, MaryAnne McClellan."

His reverie was broken by the high-rpm roar of an engine. Hunter buttoned up his jeans and turned toward the road as lights sped around the corner and illuminated him. It was the Rio Diablo ambulance flying to Platoro. No doubt some car wreck victim or a retiree with a heart attack.

A minute after the ambulance, another set of headlights fixed Hunter in their beam.

Jesuschrist, this bat out of hell was Ralph Wittfogel, Hunter realized as the vehicle squealed around the corner. Ralph never drove like that, he was an old woman behind the wheel. Fifty feet past Hunter's parked truck, the van's brake lights flashed on. Tires screamed on the highway. Wittfogel's van zoomed backward through the stench of burned rubber. Brakes again howled like tortured cats as he came even with Hunter.

"Ralph! What's going on?"

Wittfogel thrust his head out the driver's window. He was ashen-faced. "It's MaryAnne. She's been beaten. Woody's getting her to the hospital. He says it's bad."

Hunter ran to his truck, peeled out of the gravel pullout into a U-turn, and took off after Ralph's vanishing taillights. Immediately he knew something was wrong. The telltale thrump, thrump, thrump of a flat tire made him curse. He barked two knuckles rushing to change it and heaved the flat into the back. He took the road as fast as it would permit.

The Platoro hospital was as quiet as a ghost with the Rio Diablo ambulance beside the emergency entrance. Hunter sprinted across the parking lot.

Inside the emergency waiting room, Ralph Wittfogel was Stravinsky's "Rite of Spring" on a 45 rpm LP being played at 78 rpm. His rage barely allowed him to cough out words to Hunter's questions.

MaryAnne had gotten back to Rio Diablo from Washington and Albuquerque around 3:00 P.M. Ralph had gone over that evening to get the scoop. He had found her half-naked on the kitchen linoleum, her head in a pool of blood, semen puddling between her akimbo legs. A bloody butcher knife had been on the floor beside her, but it had not caused the head wound. Blood and hair on the sharp corner of the kitchen table showed she had hit her head there.

Ralph mumbled to the floor, "She came to, briefly."

Hunter forced himself to speak. "Could she talk? Did she say anything?"

"Yeah."

Hunter waited for more. It didn't come. He asked, "Well, what did she say?"

"Just gibberish. It didn't make sense."

"What did she say?" Hunter's tone demanded an answer.

"She said 'Jew.'"

"Jew? Is that all?"

"That was it. Then she passed out again." Ralph continued to stare at the floor. "Why did she just say 'Jew' to me?"

They were interrupted when Woody Sizemore came into the waiting room. Hunter had met him at the celebration after the Diablo hearing.

He and his wife, Nancy, were freelance biological consultants and the volunteer EMT-ambulance drivers for Rio Diablo. He was boiling.

"That motherfucking sheriff. I just called him. He said he would *try* to get a deputy down to Rio Diablo tomorrow to look for evidence *if* she dies. There's going to be thunderstorms tonight. Any evidence will be long gone. Motherfucker."

Hunter buried his face in his hands. He could think of a dozen suspects. Faces of the local goons flashed across his mind's screen. The slow waltz of depression quickened to the rage of gangsta rap. One face came back again and again.

Jukes.

Jew. *Jukes!* MaryAnne hadn't been calling Ralph a Jew like he thought, she had been trying to say "Jukes."

Woody again: "I can't believe this happened. I can't believe we could lose MaryAnne. She's just too full of life to, to . . ." He couldn't say the word. "Nancy's in there working with Silverman and the ER nurse. We got there within minutes of Ralph calling. Her blood pressure was dropping. I've never driven so fast."

He was on the same turntable as Ralph.

"Nancy started IV fluid resuscitation in the ambulance. She stopped breathing. Nancy bagged her. I radioed Silverman and relayed the symptoms Nancy gave me. Silverman said he was calling the helicopter from UMC in Tucson. MaryAnne probably has a hemorrhage inside the skull. He intubated her as soon we got here. Started a Mannitol IV. Dopamine, too. Gotta increase that blood pressure but without fluids that'll increase the pressure inside the skull. Where's that fucking chopper?"

Hunter wanted to run from Woody's staccato rap. It was like flashing ambulance lights to Hunter's ears. It stopped only when Dr. Bob Silverman walked into the waiting room. The three men stood.

Only Woody was able to ask, "What are her chances?"

"It's bad," came Silverman's choked reply. Emergency room doctors have to steel themselves against emotional involvement. In this case it was impossible. Silverman was a pillar of the Diablo Wilderness Committee. MaryAnne was his friend, his leader. Hunter knew him. He had been at the barbecue after the hearing.

Silence settled like a shroud.

"Fast as you got her here, we missed the golden hour," he finally said. "With a major head injury like this, immediate care makes the difference.

She could have a subarachnoid hemorrhage. She needs a CAT scan. Pressure monitor. Brain surgery. We can't do it here. Tucson can do it. If she gets there soon enough. It's a toss-up."

Hunter wanted to ask more but his vocal cords wouldn't work. They were dry as sand.

"Chopper," said Silverman before anyone else heard. Woody rushed back into the ER with him.

Hunter and Ralph followed the flock-flock-flock of the helicopter's blades outside. It was impossible to see MaryAnne's face as she was loaded. Ralph turned to speak, but Hunter had vanished.

Jack Hunter forced himself to stay within the speed limit. He couldn't chance a stop by police. Fall County's white trash danced like Mexican Day of the Dead puppets in the high beam along the lonely road. Hunter went round and round with every memory that might help him figure out who did it. That roulette wheel always stopped in the slot named Harry Jukes. Jukes. That had to be what MaryAnne had been trying to say. If he hadn't done it, he would know who had.

Hunter realized he was nearly to Jukes's place. Jukes lived a hundred yards off the highway about four miles before the village of Rio Diablo. Three old trucks and a broken-down small bulldozer littered the dirt yard around his ratty mobile home. A cracker castle. Hunter switched off his headlights. He used the parking brake to avoid brake lights and coasted to a stop down a spur dirt road on the other side of the highway.

Before opening the truck door, he removed the bulb from the dome light. He dug out a pair of old running shoes from behind the seat and put them on in place of his cowboy boots. Leather gloves went on. There was a roll of duct tape in the truckbox in back. He checked the .357 magnum for ammo. Five. Empty chamber under the hammer.

Outside, he checked the visibility of his truck. A grove of sycamores masked it from the highway.

Using the shadows, Hunter did his best copycat of a jaguar stalk to Jukes's trailer—he snapped only one branch over the two hundred yards. Jukes should be alone. Hunter had heard no rumors of his wife and son coming back to him.

First, Hunter checked out the battered old Dodge pickup in front. It was packed for a long trip. A bit of confirmation.

A stealthy inspection through the windows revealed that Jukes was not alone. Onis Luebner lay on the couch. His bloody shirt was on the floor, his shoulder was swaddled. Jukes was trying to pour whiskey down him. That explained the bloody knife Ralph had found. MaryAnne had gotten her licks in. Bet they hadn't been expecting that kind of fight. The injured Luebner was further confirmation of Hunter's suspicion.

Ratfuckers. They're gonna pay, goddamnit, they're gonna pay, MaryAnne. I promise you that. I promise you that, darlin'.

And then, the mouthed silent words: *Please don't die. I love you, MaryAnne McClellan. I'll never leave you again. I love you, girl.*

Jukes took his own belt from the bottle of Old Granddad. He disappeared down the hall. He reappeared with an Okie's suitcase.

Hunter slipped into the shadows of the porch when Jukes came out. Jukes set the suitcase down and stood on the edge of the porch to piss into the bed of dead flowers his wife had left.

Hunter quietly approached from the rear. His hard forearm snaked around Jukes's neck. The barrel of the revolver crunched into the back of his head. It was an easy maneuver when you were six inches taller than the other guy.

"Uhnhh . . ." Jukes peed down his leg.

"This is a three-five-seven. You try anything and your brains'll be in Arizona."

Jukes was frozen. He did not reply. Harry Jukes was one of those guys who could do anything with a lit cigarette in his mouth. This time, though, the cigarette fell from his lip. It burned Hunter's arm briefly before dropping into the flower bed.

Hunter grabbed him by his skinny neck and slammed him facedown into the plank floor of the porch. He pressed his knee hard into Jukes's back. Then he grabbed Jukes's stringy, greasy black hair and pulled his head back against the barrel of the revolver.

"Spread your arms out to the side and leave 'em there."

Jukes quickly obeyed.

"Okay, you sonofabitch. You did it. You did it."

"Whaa . . . ?"

"Don't deny it. Don't lie to me. You know what. Now, ratfucker, you have one chance, just one chance, to live past tonight. If you tell me who else helped you, I'll turn you over to the sheriff. If you lie to me, I'll kill you so slow you'll think you're a Korean dog. Got it?"

Jukes remained dumb.

"Got it?" Hunter bounced Jukes's face into the redwood lumber of the porch. His glasses fell off. Hunter pulled Jukes's head back against the gun barrel again. He cocked the hammer. "Got it?"

"Y-y-ye-yeah . . ."

"Talk, then. Tell me who helped you hurt MaryAnne McClellan."

"Onis. Onis Luebner."

"Who else?"

"Charley Rath."

So much for loyalty, thought Hunter. He hadn't expected Jukes to rat so readily. The smell of fresh human shit wafted up to Hunter's nostrils.

"Where's Charley?"

"His place."

"Where's that?"

"He's living in the old Stutz place. Down past the 666 junction." Jukes's words were the whimpers of a beaten dog.

Hunter knew where it was.

"Who else?"

"No one."

Hunter pressed the gun.

"No one! That's all!"

"Devil help you if you're lying."

Hunter let down the hammer with his thumb—New Mexico gun control—and brought the barrel of the pistol across the back of Jukes's head in a glancing blow. He hoped it wouldn't kill Jukes but only put him out. He picked up Juke's glasses and slipped them into the breast pocket of Jukes's shirt. A dirty handkerchief was in Jukes's pocket. Hunter stuffed it in Jukes's mouth, then wrapped his mouth and the rest of his face, including his eyes, with duct tape, leaving only enough space around his nostrils for him to breathe. Hunter then duct-taped Jukes's wrists and ankles securely. He found a throw rug in the trailer, rolled Jukes in it, and tied it tight with rope.

Ain't no way he's going to get out of that, Hunter thought.

Onis Luebner slept fitfully on the couch. His face was pasty. The new dressing on his shoulder—a white T-shirt—was already soaked through with blood.

Jack Hunter straddled him and clutched his throat. He shoved the gun into his face.

"No trouble, Luebner, or I'll blow your brains clear through the floor to hell."

Luebner's eyes briefly flickered.

"Who did it? Who hurt MaryAnne?"

Death rattled against Hunter's gloved hand.

Hunter sat back. He looked and listened for signs of life. Uh-uh. Luebner was dead. Died with Hunter's hand around his throat. Died with Hunter straddling his belly. Bled to death.

Hunter hadn't seen any green fire in his eyes. But there had been green fire in the eyes of the wolf—the old she-wolf that Luebner killed. And there sure as hell had been—was—green fire in MaryAnne's eyes.

"You reap what you sow, asshole," he told Luebner.

Hunter jogged back to his truck. One vehicle passed on the highway and Hunter hid behind a tree. He listened for the sound of any approaching cars. Nothing. Without turning on the headlights, he backed out, cursed when the reverse lights came on, and drove down the lane to the trailer.

At the trailer, Hunter wrapped Luebner in towels and sheets to keep his blood from getting all over everything. The big dead guy went in the back of the truck. So did Jukes. Hunter picked up a .22 pistol lying on the coffee table and stuffed it under the truck seat. The truck crept out to the road and back into the sycamore grove. He pulled out the bodies—one dead, one alive—and hid them under branches and left.

Hunter shook off Luebner's death. He was still on the hunt. And the biggest game was yet to come.

Charley Rath was a different animal than Jukes or Luebner. Jukes was a chickenshit little coward. He was mean and wiry, but not a formidable foe. Luebner was—had been—a big guy, tough and mean. But gone to soft. Besides, MaryAnne had already taken him out. It had been easy playing Clint Eastwood with those two.

But Charley.

Ah, yes, Charley Rath. Likes to fight. Healthy. Strong as a young Hereford bull.

Hunter had heard the stories: high school bully, terror on the football field, troublemaker around town. His father had thrown him out when he couldn't whip the boy any longer. Tough kid.

Of all the riffraff in town, Charley had been the one with whom Hunter most wanted to avoid trouble. There was no choice now. Hunter soothed his jitters by reminding himself that he had a couple of inches and fifteen pounds on the boy.

And he had knocked him out in their first fight. That gave Hunter a psychological advantage. That was, if Charley Rath had enough brains to have a psychology.

The old Stutz place was four or five miles south of the junction on 666. Almost fifteen miles away. *Better get him quick. Now.*

But what are you going to do with him when you get him?

Fuck it. Sheriff Frank Mayer of Fall County, New Mexico, United States of America, wouldn't do anything to bring Jukes and Rath to the bar of justice. If they were charged and tried, a Fall County jury would never convict them. Society had abdicated its responsibility here. The law hadn't protected MaryAnne McClellan. If Hunter had been there it wouldn't have happened.

But you weren't there, were you, asshole?

Words were remembered. Words Hunter had spoken to MaryAnne two months ago at the Shady Lady: "I'm there whenever you need me." *Right, asshole, right.*

The guilt was fully undressed. Hunter had abdicated responsibility, too. His fear of a commitment had led to . . . to this.

Hunter climbed five hundred feet on 666 out of the Rio Diablo Valley. In the moonlight, the Diablos hung heavy to the northeast, little hills scampered off to the southwest. A broad, flat plain sprawled between.

The light was on in the old Stutz place. It was more a shack than a house—weathered board and batten with a rusty tin roof. It sat a quarter mile off the highway in an overgrazed cow pasture of snakeweed and sand. A thick mesquite bosque flanked the cow-cut arroyo behind the house. Distant lightning played beyond the horizon to the west.

Charley Rath sat in the living room drinking beer, watching Penthouse videos on the VCR. A dozen Coors cans littered the floor around his chair. No one else was there. After his scout, Hunter walked in and leveled the .357 magnum. He couldn't tell if Charley was surprised or not.

"Who helped you tonight, Charley?"

The words poured out. "Harry Jukes. Onis Luebner. I just went along for the ride. I just thought we going to scare her a little bit. It was Harry's idea. He's the one who hit her and made her hit her head on the table."

"But you were there. You raped her, too. Didn't you?"

Charley Rath's lips formed a "no," but no sound crawled out of the hole. His face was scratched; he had a black eye. His big fist gripped the beer can and it crunched.

"Let's go, Charley."

Charley let the crumpled can fall. Beer ran out. He stood and walked toward the door. Suddenly he lunged to the side and knocked Hunter down. He ran.

"Goddamnit!" Hunter cussed himself. He scrambled after Charley.

In the moonlight, he saw Charley running to his four by four.

"Charley!" The blast of the revolver emphasized his words. The slug splatted the ground hard between Charley and his rig. Dust rose in the moonlight.

Charley broke to the side and faded into the blackness of the mesquite thicket.

Hunter followed. In the stone age rush, he could taste the dread. One question tried to elbow in: *Now who's hunter and who's hunted?*

Jack Hunter shut it off.

He moved carefully through the mesquite, alert for any flicker. His eyes strained to sluice out Charley from the shadows, from the trees, from the low-growing snakeweed. Hunter's ears reached for a sound made by man, a sound to cull from wind or night voices. His internal radar was at high pitch.

There. Behind that mesquite. Charley. Hiding.

Pretending not to notice him, Hunter went suddenly into a crouch and aim. Shit. Not Charley. Just moonlight and shadow. Still in a crouch, Hunter heard a rush behind him and spun around, both hands on the revolver, thumb cocking the hammer. A jack rabbit barely escaped with its life.

This was maddening. Not only did he have to guard against an attack, but he had to make sure that Charley did not slip out of the brush and back to his place—to his truck or to a gun of his own.

The silence was like water around Hunter—still, deep water. It was a curious combination of sensations—or lack thereof. It was a sensory deprivation chamber; he was floating in nothingness. Then again, he was shaved down to raw nerve endings. . . .

Charley Rath hit with the power of a big drop wave. Hunter felt carried away by the force as if he had flipped a whitewater raft. The two men went down. The magnum scudded away in the dust. The still water had quickened.

Charley scrambled over Hunter to get the revolver. Hunter grabbed him by his belt and dragged him back. Both men clambered to their feet. Charley charged into Hunter.

Charley Rath had the force of an immense wave Hunter well remembered. Twenty years ago. Yampa River. Warm Springs Rapid. It had flipped Hunter's raft as if it had been a flapjack. Hunter remembered the force of that water, and now tasted the blood in his nose, in his mouth.

Mesquite tore at them as they thrashed between tree-shadow and moonlight. Hunter saw Charley's face full of blood, saw his fist smash into it. They went down, and dark swallowed them.

Fighting each other and the mesquite, they struggled back to their feet. The revolver shone in the moonlight. Charley landed a blow that knocked Hunter back. Charley bolted for the gun. Hunter ripped himself out of the thorns and dove after Charley.

They danced in the moonlight, in the scrub, in the dust: a deadly *pas de deux*. The gun was high overhead, four bloody hands fought for control. Hunter slammed his knee into Charley's crotch. The young man's finger jerked, and a bullet hurtled to the moon.

Hunter twisted their arms down and slammed the back of Charley's hand into a thick mesquite branch. He felt Charley's grip weaken, and he tried to pound Charley's hand against the branch again. But Charley twisted—and the four hands and the gun were between their bodies. Hunter's stomach muscles cringed for the gut-ripping piece of lead.

Instead, the slug was swallowed by the night.

Two rounds left.

Hunter wrenched their arms and the gun overhead again. The Devil's minuet resumed. Charley pushed against Hunter. Hunter pushed again Charley.

Suddenly, Hunter yielded. Charley pushed Hunter back, and Hunter went with the flow.

Then Hunter dug in and spun. Charley was twisted around. His inertia carried him backward. Now Hunter became the big curling breaker and drove Charley back.

They smashed into the trunk of a big mesquite. The overhead pistol fell from Charley's grasp. Hunter scooped it out of the dust and stepped back.

Charley stood against the mesquite trunk. He grinned. "You are one for-sure . . ."

Hunter watched the gnarling of his face, lit now by the moon.

It took all his strength, but Charley pulled himself away from the mesquite. He stood briefly on his two legs. He grinned again. Then he crumpled to the ground.

A mesquite branch half as thick as Hunter's wrist, broken off by a cow into a deadly dagger. The moon was so bright, Hunter could see the red of Charley's blood on it.

Blood gushed from a hole in Charley's back—below and inside of his left shoulder blade. The mesquite had speared him through the heart.

Owls hooted back on the ridge. But for them, Hunter realized, he was alone.

He stood over the body. Gawd. The die was cast. It wasn't philosophy any more. He had killed a man. It was real.

The moon glow on Charley's face hardened into a death mask—a death mask that would hang forever inside Hunter's skull.

The short, happy life of Charles Rath.

Or had it been the short, unhappy life of Charles Rath?

Who knew?

Had Charley known?

"I'm sorry it came to this, Charley. I really am."

He looked so young lying dead on the ground.

There is nothing so pitiful, so expendable as an adolescent male mammal.

Hunter trotted back to his truck and drove it up to Charley's house. He found a tarp in the bottom of the big locking truck box. Back in the mesquite, he wrapped Charley in it, manhandled his one hundred and eighty-five pound corpse onto his shoulders, and carried him to the truck. He stuffed him into the truck box.

A couple of cool beers swam in melted ice in the little cooler. Hunter pounded one down and tried to catch his breath. Then he remembered the TV playing porno flicks. Better turn it off and check the place for evidence.

On the drive back to Rio Diablo, he was on the roadblock before he realized it. Flashing blue and red lights. Official vehicles. But—thanks for small favors—it was not the highway patrol or the sheriff. Border Patrol. Wetback spot check.

Hunter stopped, relieved. Then it hit him. A dead man was in the back of his pickup. A man he had just killed. The confrontation with society, with authority, loomed.

The man in uniform approached. "Hello. Border Patrol. American citizen?"

"Yeah."

"No one else with you?"

"Nope."

The officer shone his flashlight in the back of the truck. He played the light over the horseshoes, the anvil, and the wooden box of nippers, rasps, and curved shoeing knives. The flat tire.

Hunter was sure he had put everything bloody away in the truck box. He was sure.

The border patrol agent knocked on the metal truck box.

Jesus, thought Hunter. *What do I do if he wants to look inside? Run? Drive away? Shit. What? No. Refuse. Isn't a locked truck box constitutionally protected from a casual roadblock search?*

Ohjesusmotherfuckingchrist. No wonder he's suspicious. Probable cause. My torn clothes, bloody dirty face . . .

Hunter's heart was a frog trying to leap clear of his ribs. Sweat soaked his palms. He wiped them on his dirty jeans.

"What's in the box?"

"Just horseshoes and stuff."

"You a horseshoer?"

"Yeah." Hunter pointed to the sign on the door.

The flashlight illuminated it.

The agent shone the light in the back again.

The frog in Hunter's chest became the celebrated jumping frog of Calaveras County.

Another voice. "Hello, Jack. I thought that might be you." A second uniformed man approached from the Border Patrol paddy wagon.

"Hey, Howard. How's it going?" Hunter hoped his voice sounded calm. It did.

"Fine, fine. Boy, the horse is doing much better with that fancy shoe you put on it. The limp is nearly gone."

"Good. Those trailers will do that. I should stop by next week and check on it. One more corrective trim and shoe, and I think your horse will be ready for riding."

"That'll be great. My kids will be really happy to be able to ride old Brownie again."

"Good . . ."

"Good lord, Jack, what happened to you? You look like you've been in a fight."

Finally Hunter's brain worked. The flat was good for something. "Naw. I had a flat tire. The spare rolled down into an arroyo. I fell down the slope and got scratched up in the mesquite and gravel trying to get it. One of those fucking days when nothing goes right."

"Yeah, I know days like that. We'll see you next week, then."

"See you, Howard. Say 'hi' to Ethel and the kids for me."

"Will do."

The lights of the roadblock disappeared behind a hill in the rearview mirror. Hunter whipped the truck off the road. He pawed around the back of the truck for the ice chest. Thank god: another beer. He popped the top and drained half of it.

He leaned against the truck.

"You sonofabitch. You motherfucking sonofabitch."

These were not the silent words of the little man in his skull. Hunter was talking out loud to himself.

"You chickenshit bastard. This night of goddamned hell wouldn't be happening if you hadn't run from commitment. MaryAnne wouldn't be . . . you wouldn't have just killed someone. All you had to do was stand up for what you loved."

Yeats echoed inside the walls of his skull:

> The best lack all conviction, while the worst
> Are full of passionate intensity.

Hunter stood in silence.

Calm settled her wings over him. He took the rest of the beer into the cab and drove very deliberately to Jukes's place.

He made one reconnaissance pass. There was no stir around Jukes's. Again switching off the headlights and using the parking brake, he pulled into the sycamores on his next pass. Jukes and Luebner were still there. They hadn't gone anywhere. Into the truck they went.

Hunter had two mental lists tallied by the time he got to his place. Things to do. Things to take.

He peeled out of his running shoes and torn, bloody clothes and stuffed them in a paper sack for later disposal. There was only time for a quick bath in the irrigation ditch, but it washed away most of the dirt and blood.

He loaded the little cooler with beer and ice from the refrigerator. Better have one (or more) for the road. Now the truck was loaded. Everything on the two lists was done. It was time to go to Tucson—after one little detour—and . . . and . . . Hunter didn't want to think about what he might learn at University Medical Center in Tucson.

There are things—ultimate things—which change you irrevocably. Killing is one of them.

It is a door through which you pass. And the You beyond it is a different You than the one before it. You cannot return through that door. You are a different person. There is no going back.

Hunter was not sure, after meeting his new self, whether he liked this one any better than the old one. He hadn't much cared for the old one.

He was startled out of French philosophy by headlights bumping down his road and across his ford. *Not again!* Hunter pulled the dusty .357 and headed for the darkness.

The vehicle stopped at his gate. Voices.

But they were voices Hunter recognized: Bill Crawford and Ralph Wittfogel.

"You here, Jack?" came the holler.

"Yeah, but keep your voice down, Bill," Hunter whispered as he stepped from shadow into moonlight.

Now what? He wanted to do it alone. There was a slight hitch in his plans, though, a hitch with which his friends could help. He had Jukes and the two stiffs, but Jukes's pickup was still sitting packed outside his place. If it were to vanish, it would make their disappearance look better. It would take the heat off a local search for them. Maybe it was time to trust someone.

Before Bill or Ralph could speak, Hunter said, "I need some help."

"Well, we're here to track down the . . ."

"Keep your voice down, Bill, or I'm going to lay this three-fifty-seven along the side of your stupid head."

"Yeah, Jesus. I'm just so fucking . . ."

"Yeah, buddy, I know, I know." They wrapped arms around each other.

Bill sniffed. "The law here ain't gonna do nothin'. We gotta track the fuckers down ourselves, man."

"It's done."

"Done?" asked Ralph.

"Done." Hunter led them to his truck. He pointed to the lumps under the tarp in the back. "Done."

"Holy fuck," Bill whispered.

"You guys want to help? Here are the keys to Harry Jukes's Dodge pickup. It's still at his trailer. Be real cautious picking it up. Throw away any shoes that leave prints at Jukes's. Don't drive off the pavement in your van there. Wear gloves. Take Juke's rig to the *zona roja* in Agua Prieta and leave it. Leave the keys in the ignition. Leave three wallets in it. Get the fuck out."

"Jukes," Ralph whispered.

Hunter turned to look at him. "MaryAnne wasn't calling you a Jew, Ralph. She was trying to tell you who did it."

"Jukes. The bastard. We'll leave immediately," Ralph said.

"You bet," said Bill.

They would do it. And Hunter knew the secret would be as safe with them as it would be with Harry Jukes, Onis Luebner, and Charley Rath.

"We'll see you at the hospital in Tucson?" Ralph asked.

"Yeah." *If I make it,* thought Hunter to himself.

"None of this ever happened."

"None of it."

There is a mine shaft. It is east of Mt. Wrightson in the foothills of the Santa Rita Mountains. A jeep trail comes within two hundred yards of it, but the shaft is forgotten, hidden, and overgrown in the Sierra Madrean oak woodland that cloaks the skirts of that range. It is the mine shaft beside which Dr. MaryAnne McClellan and her field assistant, one Jack Hunter, had found the pawprint of a Mexican wolf two months earlier.

It is a deep, straight, vertical mine shaft. Dr. McClellan's field assistant had dropped a rock down it. They never heard it hit bottom. A boulder teeters on the edge of the shaft.

Jack Hunter had a perfect mental picture of that mine shaft and of the way to get to it. It was four hours from where he now was. Sunrise was over five hours away. There would be a predawn burial today. Three clients lay in wait for the Lobo Outback Funeral Home, J. Hunter, proprietor. The deceaseds' belongings were being otherwise disposed of.

Tonight, Hunter did not speed. Two beers between Rio Diablo and Lordsburg had calmed him down. Now, in the middle of the night, and with 131 miles of limited access, divided interstate highway ahead, his adrenaline needed the kick of caffeine. The twenty-four-hour McDonald's in Lordsburg was good for something. Two large coffees to go. Why not? Throw in two Big Macs. And a large order of fries, please. The cheeseburgers and fries were awful. No Lotaburger. No Pat's Chili Dog's fries. But they were fuel, and Hunter felt like he was running on empty.

Against the underbellies of the storm clouds, he could see the glow of Tucson when he turned off the interstate onto Arizona State Highway 83. It had started raining soon after he had left Rio Diablo, but had stopped before Lordsburg. The sky here was ragged, and the clouds could cut loose before dawn.

The disc jockey on COOL, the Tucson oldies station, played Creedence Clearwater's "Bad Moon on the Rise," and afterward gave his own warning that "we're in for nasty weather": the U.S. Weather Service had issued a violent thunderstorm and flash flood warning for the rest of the night and early morning in southeastern Arizona.

The unseasonable weather was good news to Hunter. Let the storm wash away tonight's story.

Twenty-five miles south of the interstate, Hunter turned onto a dirt road in the Coronado National Forest. It wound through a dwarf forest of juniper and oak, along canyon bottoms and flat ridges. The clouds broke, and the full moon brought out the details of the landscape. A rough two-track road snaked off to the right. Hunter doused his headlights and followed the track by moonlight for two miles. He stopped with the parking brake. There probably wasn't another human for ten miles, but that was no excuse to be careless.

He switched to an old pair of heavy hiking boots. Couldn't take a chance on a sprain.

Hunter heaved Luebner's body up onto his shoulders. The sonofabitch must weigh three hundred pounds, he groaned. Thank Lady Luck for the moon. It would have been impossible to tote this fat stiff and use a flashlight. Thank also a remarkable ability to remember country. Hunter walked—or staggered—right to the shaft.

Onis Luebner went down without ceremony. Hunter was on his way back to the truck before the wolf trapper found bottom.

Charley was next. He was lighter than Luebner, but Hunter was dragging now. Luebner had plumb tuckered him out. One hundred yards from the shaft, Hunter slipped and skinned his knee. Charley's body rolled twenty feet down a slope.

"*Fuuuck* me," Hunter whined.

Getting him back up on the shoulders was harder than carrying him. By the time he dropped his burden down the shaft, Hunter was puffing. He sat on a rock beside the shaft, sucking wind, listening to the once-upon-a-time Charley Rath ricochet off the sides, dislodging rocks as he went. Hunter was glad the shaft was unstable. The more earth on top of these guys, the better.

At least the last one could walk. Too bad he was the lightest of the lot. Hunter tucked the .22 in his jeans behind the name "Jack" on his wide leather belt; he laced the hiking boots more tightly.

Jack Hunter cut Jukes out of his mummy wrap and gave no heed to his hair when he ripped off the duct tape. He even cut the tape from around his wrists. For long hours Jukes had bounced around the back of the pickup truck, scarcely able to breathe, terror-stricken at his fate, wrapped up in his own shit. He revealed the horror when he could speak.

"Where the fuck are we? What're you going to do?" Harry Jukes wailed out the words like a Hereford circled up by a pack of wolves.

"Welcome to Hell," said Hunter.

"You promised to hand me over to the sheriff. . . ."

"I lied. So sue me."

Hunter pushed the piece of human flotsam down the ridge. Pants caked with feces and urine stank to high heaven. Hunter had utter contempt for Jukes.

Hunter was also dog-tired. Tail-dragging tired. He had been up for nearly twenty-four hours. He had done some heavy lifting tonight. He'd had one hell of a fight. Emotionally, he was frayed to tatters—like a bandanna left on a mesquite thorn to blow in the wind and sun and rain for a couple of years. He still had hours to go before he could sleep and might well face the most painful moment of his life . . . he didn't want to think about MaryAnne's chances now, though. Now, he just wanted to be done with Jukes and the other assholes. He wanted this *done*.

Clouds clumped around the peak of Wrightson; fog-banners streamed out across the sky. The wind picked up. The smell of rain was on the air. The landscape went dark as a cloud moved across the moon.

Harry Jukes was on the ground at Hunter's feet. Whimpering. Gutless asshole. What mercy had he shown. . . .

"Please, oh God, don't kill me, please, please," he bellered and bawled like a castrated calf.

Hunter stood over the groveling thing in the dark of cloud; disgust was so thick in his mouth, he could taste it. This was not a human being, it wasn't any kind of living creature. It was a sack of garbage, a pile of stinking, rotten offal. Hunter wanted only to dispose of it and be gone.

"Chickenshit asshole," Hunter snarled as he reached down to jerk Jukes to his feet.

Jukes was as fast as a striking rattlesnake.

Hunter ducked and parried the blow, but the palmed hammer-stone hit him hard on the crown of his head.

Hunter dropped like a chain-sawed ponderosa and sprawled out on his back. His rattled brain shorted out.

Dimly, Jack Hunter imagined himself down a mine shaft. Consciousness at the surface was so far away. He could barely see it glowing above. He was tired. So tired. Just a little nap . . .

Wake up!

The voice was not the snooty Truman Capote-like bray of the little man in his skull. It was a woman's husky voice—a voice of old cabernet and trail dust.

Hunter opened his eyes. Harry Jukes straddled him. His two hands overhead gripped a rock about the size of Mt. Wrightson—a rock about to be smashed down on Hunter's skull. Behind Jukes and the rock, the moon sailed out from behind the clouds.

Somewhere, Travis McGee had said that if you wanted to hit something really hard, aim your fist past it.

Hunter aimed his fist at the moon. Jukes and his big rock tumbled ass over teakettle.

Hunter realized that he couldn't see out his left eye, there was so much blood from the wound to the top of his head. Or was it blinded from the blow? He was going to have one hell of a headache. The right eye was enough, though, as he lurched to his feet and kicked Jukes in the ribs.

Jukes lay in a fetal position, refusing to get up.

More careful this time, Hunter jerked him to his feet, and slapped him once, twice. Hard. Hunter was slapping himself as well. *Stupid fool. Don't get lulled again.*

Hunter got Jukes to the mine shaft. He pulled the .22 from the back of his belt. Around them the wind turned wild.

"Okay, tough guy. Take a look at your grave."

"You can't just shoot me in cold blood. . . ."

"My blood's pretty hot right now, ratfucker. But—this is your lucky night."

Hunter stepped back five paces from Jukes.

"The best woman in the world may be dead tonight. She's only thirty goddamn years old, you bastard. But there are two men responsible for what happened to her. Only one of them is going to walk away from here tonight. The other one is going to die to pay for it."

Jukes licked his terrier lips. Something unexpected was going on here. He might have another chance.

"Yeah, asshole, I blame myself as much as I blame you. I deserve to pay for it as much as you do. If I'd been there like I should've been, we would've spitted the three of you Fall County militiamen like chickens at a barbecue. But I wasn't. So it's my fault, too."

Hunter laid Jukes's revolver on the ground between them and took five steps back from it.

"Go ahead, it's as close to . . ."

Jukes dove for the gun as fast as a Juarez dog for a dropped tortilla.

Hunter knew he couldn't match the speed of the smaller man. But there was another reason for the hiking boots he wore. Almost a quarter of a century ago, Jack Hunter had played his last football game. It had been his senior year at Valley High. The score had been tied. It had been the end of the game. Quarterback and Captain of the Team Jack Hunter had kicked for the final field goal that would win it. The ancient steps came back easily and, even with just one eye, Hunter kicked the ball held by his buddy, Bill Crawford.

Jukes's head didn't feel like a football. It felt like a rotten watermelon.

EPILOGUE

It took Hunter a good fifteen minutes to find the .22 revolver. When he kicked Jukes, the gun flew into the night and the oaks. After finding it, he stuffed the pistol in his belt for later burial. Then he trudged back to the truck for a shovel and the hydraulic jack. When he returned to the shaft, he sent Jukes to sleep with the bats. With the flashlight, he found the patches of bloody earth and shoveled the soil into the mine. The rug and rope and duct tape used to truss Jukes also went down the hole. Hunter broke a juniper branch from a tree and brushed away the footprints and signs of struggle. As light rain began to fall in the early dawn, he wedged the jack behind the big rock and tumbled it down the shaft.

The clouds gathered and the rain came down, and Jack Hunter drove the truck out to the highway. There, he cleaned himself up as well as he could with canteen water. His straw cowboy hat would cover the bloody wound on his head. He had much to do before going to University Medical Center in Tucson; it was all on a memorized mental list:

1. Clean fingerprints off both pistols and bury them separately at least twenty miles from the shaft;

2. Check into a motel in the border town of Nogales and bathe;

3. Clean and bandage wounds;

4. Change into clean clothes and different boots;

5. Buy a new set of tires and have them installed;

6. Gather up the clothes, boots, gloves, and anything else worn or used during the night; leave them and the old tires in the well-picked dump across the Sonoran border; and

7. Use a self-service car wash to clean all blood, mud, dust, and fibers from the bed and underside of the truck and from the truck box.

Shortly after noon, stomach roiled by coffee and *huevos con chorizo*, muscles and joints bruised and frazzled, Hunter found the hospital near the corner of Speedway and Campbell north of the University of Arizona. He was sent to the intensive care waiting room on the sixth floor. Phil McClellan, Bill Crawford, and Ralph Wittfogel were already there. Phil had flown in on the earliest flight from Albuquerque to Tucson; Bill and Ralph had ditched Jukes's pickup in Agua Prieta without incident and had camped out in the waiting room since five that morning.

After two more hours, the operation was over. Phil McClellan talked to his daughter's surgeons; she was critically injured, but she was strong and the operation went well. The degree of recovery was uncertain.

After a week, she was well enough to go home to her father's house in Albuquerque. Hunter followed and set up an office for the Diablo Wilderness Committee in one of the spare bedrooms. He made two trips to Washington. By the time she demanded to go home to Rio Diablo, there were twenty-one cosponsors of Monica Montoya's bill to add Mondt Park to the Diablo Wilderness. Senator Karl Reed introduced a similar bill in the Senate.

Red Underwood condemned the attack on MaryAnne McClellan and called for "cooler heads to prevail" in the debate over the interests of Fall County. He was ousted as chairman of the county Republican Party at the next meeting of the central committee. Jodi Clayton filed for divorce and moved to Santa Fe. It was rumored she was involved with a rising young Tesuque Pueblo painter.

Sheriff Frank Mayer, Buck Clayton, and Congressman Bart Pugh said the "accident" had nothing to do with natural resource issues or county sovereignty and most likely was the result of a lover's quarrel. The sheriff said he would question the associates of Dr. McClellan. He never did. The disappearance of Harry Jukes, Onis Luebner, and Charley Rath was officially ignored.

Dave Foreman has worked as a wilderness conservationist since 1971. From 1973 to 1980, he worked for The Wilderness Society as Southwest Regional Representative in New Mexico and as Director of Wilderness Affairs in Washington, D.C. He was a member of the board of trustees for the New Mexico Chapter of The Nature Conservancy from 1976 to 1980. From 1982 to 1988, he was editor of the *Earth First! Journal*. Foreman is a founder of The Wildlands Project and was its chairman from 1991–2003, and executive editor or publisher of *Wild Earth* from 1991–2003. He is now the Director and Senior Fellow of The Rewilding Institute, a conservation "think tank" advancing ideas of continental conservation. He was a member of the national Board of Directors of the Sierra Club from 1995 to 1997 and is currently a member of the Board of Directors of the New Mexico Wilderness Alliance. He speaks widely on conservation issues and is author of *The Lobo Outback Funeral Home* (a novel), *Confessions of an Eco-Warrior*, and *The Big Outside* (with Howie Wolke). Foreman is the lead author and network designer of the *Sky Islands Wildlands Network Conservation Plan* and the *New Mexico Highlands Wildlands Network Vision* from the Wildlands Project. He received the 1996 Paul Petzoldt Award for Excellence in Wilderness Education and was named by *Audubon Magazine* in 1998 as one of the 100 Champions of Conservation of the 20th Century. Foreman is a backpacker, river runner, canoeist, fly-fisher, hunter, wilderness photographer, and bird-watcher. He lives in his hometown of Albuquerque, New Mexico.